THE GIRL FROM VICHY

France, 1942. As the war in Europe rages on, Adèle Ambeh dreams of a France that is free from the clutches of the new regime. The date of her marriage to a ruthless man is drawing closer, and she only has one choice — she must run.

With the help of her mother, Adèle flees to Lyon, seeking refuge at the Sisters of Notre Dame de la Compassion. The sisters are secretly aiding the French Résistance, hiding and supplying the fighters with weapons.

Adèle quickly finds herself part of the Résistance. But her new role means she must return to Vichy, and those she left behind, no matter the cost.

Each day is filled with a different danger and as she begins to fall for another man, Adèle's entire world could come crashing down around her.

ANDIE NEWTON

———◆———

THE GIRL FROM VICHY

Complete and Unabridged

MAGNA
Leicester

First published in Great Britain in 2020
by Aria
an imprint of Head of Zeus Ltd
London

First Ulverscroft Edition
published 2021
by arrangement with
Head of Zeus Ltd
London

This is a work of fiction. All characters,
organisations, and events portrayed in this novel
are either products of the author's imagination or
are used fictitiously.

*A catalogue record for this book is available
from the British Library.*

ISBN 978–0–7505–4881–6

Published by
Ulverscroft Limited
Anstey, Leicestershire

Printed and bound in Great Britain by
TJ Books Ltd., Padstow, Cornwall

This book is printed on acid-free paper

To Matt, Zane, and Drew

Historical Note

On a warm June day in 1940, inside a train car deep in the Compiègne forest, France signed an armistice with the Third Reich—something no other invaded country had asked for. Under the armistice's terms, France was split in half, one part occupied militarily by the Germans, the other free, where France's leader, Philippe Pétain, and his newly formed Vichy regime had unfettered control. To the French people, Pétain promised a separate state of peace, but to Germany he promised collaboration.

1942

1942

1

Vichy, France

I stopped running just under the large clock that hung above Gare de Vichy's stone archway, my heels skidding on the cobblestone ground. I had seen the clock hundreds, maybe even thousands of times before, having lived near Vichy my entire life, but this was the first time I heard it ticking and saw its pointed, metal hands actually moving. Across the street behind a kerbside flower cart was my sister, Charlotte, watering a blooming fuchsia hanging from a hook outside her maternity boutique. A feeling hand swept over her pregnant belly, and I tugged my beret down low.

Squeezing my pocketbook, I could all but feel the letter inside addressed to the Sisters of Notre Dame de la Compassion, asking them to take me in. They'd never know Mama was the one who wrote the note, forging it in Papa's best handwriting just moments ago in her kitchen.

'I want what you want,' Mama said as she slipped the note in my hand. A smile twitched on her lips, and I pretended not to notice.

'And for the almsgiving? I'll need a donation.'

Mama opened a drawer underneath the woodblock she used for cutting meat. Inside, bundles of francs tied with string. She counted them one by one, '*Un, deux, trois . . .* ' until she had completely emptied the drawer.

3

'Give it all to the sisters to ensure a long stay.' Mama stuffed the money into my pocketbook along with some of her cigarettes and the cloisonné lighter from her pocket. 'Take only what you need for travel.'

I took a deep breath. My wedding to Gérard Baudoin, a gendarme in the Vichy police, was the following morning. An icy shiver waved over my body. *Marry a collaborator.*

The police had become goats to our new government under Philippe Pétain, the leader of the Free Zone. Papa believed, like many in Vichy, that it was best to support Pétain and his regime. He was our nation's hero, and we should trust him. But I believed what Mama said, that heroes don't send their soldiers to a *stammlager* — a German prison — or take orders from the Reich on how to run the Free Zone.

I pulled my wedding dress off its padded hanger and held it at eye level, yards of Mechlin lace hand-stitched into the bodice scrunching in my fists. A train of white satin pooled onto Mama's parquet floor. Papa arranged the marriage himself. *He will be angry, I thought, and hurt when he finds out I had left.*

Mama nudged the dress box on the floor, scooting it closer to me with her toe. 'Don't waste your time thinking about that collaborator.'

'Gérard?' I said. 'I'm not thinking about *him*.'

There was a moment of silence shared between us. Running away from a marriage I didn't want was one thing. Disappointing Papa was another.

'Stick to your plan,' she said. 'Hide out at the convent and let me take care of your father. He

4

brought this upon himself, Adèle — cosying up to the regime as he has. Charlotte too, encouraging this marriage. Your life should be your own.'

I breathed in her words. '*Ma vie.*'

Mama plunged her hands into her apron pockets. 'You choose your destiny.'

I dropped the dress into its box. Heaps of lace and crème fabric mushroomed from every corner, the smell of lily wafting from the sachets inside snuffed out like candles.

'Even if it means living with the nuns in Lyon?'

My words came out as a question, but I merely wanted to make sure Mama knew the stakes. Mama grew up Protestant, often saying that gold, crystal, and decoration inside the sanctuary were idols for the hypocrites.

'We do what we have to, Adèle.' Mama kicked the dress box, sending it sliding across her kitchen floor. 'When we have to.'

The box hit the back door and stopped next to the rubbish bin.

2

The seats in premiere class felt velvety and plush; it should have been easy for me to relax, especially as the train rolled out of the station. Yet my thoughts were dizzying, one rolling into the other as we steamed down the track. Was Mama going to wait until the wedding ceremony to break the news, or was she doing it right now? I patted my face and felt my throbbing head. I already knew Gérard would be furious and Papa would be hurt, but Charlotte — she'd be crushed — she was excited for me to be married like her.

I folded my hands in my lap only to unfold them, trying to breathe slower, deeper, but nothing seemed to work. Teacups clinked from the buffet car and old women chatted over their cigarettes. I slipped off my shoes and rested my feet on the vacant seat in front of me, eyes closing, thinking that would help calm my nerves, only to be barked at seconds later by a woman standing over me in the aisle.

'*Excusez-moi*!' she said.

I shot up in my seat, trying to piece together the last fading moments before putting my feet up.

'My seat!' She pointed. 'Your feet are on my seat.'

'Oh . . .' I gave her some room, swiftly putting my shoes back on as she sat down in a huff. 'Pardon me,' I said, as she fit her bottom into the seat cushion, getting comfortable, smoothing her beige skirt over her lap. 'The seat was empty when we left Vichy.'

She glared, setting a book she'd brought with her on her lap. 'It's taken now.' Her gaze turned out the window, looking at the lavender fields as we travelled through the country, a light smile meant only for herself replacing the scowl. I found it incredibly hard not to stare. A businessman in a suit bumped my elbow on his way back from the lavatory, apologizing with a flick of his newspaper, and I sat up a little straighter, but still watching her.

Her voice had seemed deeper than a woman's ought to be, and her nails were natural, not a fleck of paint anywhere on them. And her jewellery — she didn't wear a necklace, a bracelet, or a ring. In fact, aside from her long hair and the dreadfully plain dress she had on, there wasn't anything feminine about her.

She must have felt my gaze rolling over her body because she flashed me a condescending smile. 'Is there something else?' She traced an invisible circle on top of her book, over and over again, on her lap.

'*No*,' I said, fluttering my fingers into a wave. 'Nothing else. Sorry for bothering you.' I reached for a cigarette, digging around in my pocketbook looking for my case, mumbling to myself about how I didn't know the seat was taken. I sat back in my seat when I found it, and then sank down low when I felt Mama's cloisonné lighter. She'd never shared her lighter with me before, keeping it in her apron pocket for as long as I could remember, but I was glad she had. The silver was dull — a

7

nice patina from years in Mama's hand.

I struck the flint wheel and the woman immediately gasped, squeezing the spine of her book,
getting as close to the window as she could as I
puffed my cigarette to life. A throaty cough followed her shifting eyes.

'Are you all right?' I finally asked.

She flicked a finger at the ashtray. 'I have an
affliction to cigarettes, if you must know,' she said.
'It's the smoke.'

It was then that I noticed a blotchy rash bubbling up her neck. As painful as it looked, it was
the colour that concerned me — pink as a fresh
slap on white skin. I sat straight up. 'Sorry,' I said,
immediately smashing what was left of my cigarette into a pile of ashes.

Two old ladies across the aisle had just lit up
and blew plumes of smoke from their mouths. It
wasn't hard to notice they were smoking Nation-
ales, much thicker and cheaper than the slim I
used; much more smoke spewed from those cigarettes than from mine. 'Maybe you'd be more
comfortable in third class, where you can open a
window.'

'No seats available,' she said, closing her eyes
briefly. 'Now, if you please, I want to be left alone.
You've caused me enough problems today.'

'I was only trying to help.'

She opened her book, and I turned away.

I tried to relax again, putting the woman out of
my head long enough to think about the convent,
but then someone yelled that the train was making an emergency stop. The train shimmied with
a loud squeal, metal on metal, slowing to a crawl,

8

and people popped out of their seats to move into the aisle. The woman gripped her book tightly, eyes strained, and then oddly relaxed like a lumpy blanket just as the French police burst through the doors at the end of the train car.

I bolted to a stand, clutching my chest, first from the sound and then from the looks on their faces as they ran down the aisle toward the other end, boots thumping with rifles slung over their shoulders.

'What's going on?' I said into the air.

A burly gendarme with grit in his teeth pushed one of the old ladies back into her seat, but she stumbled, throwing a weak little hand against the window to catch herself, which made many of us gasp. More police rushed in and ran down the aisle, only this time the diplomats who'd been reading their papers trailed behind them like dogs on a tether.

The doors closed suddenly on both ends of the train car. A piercing quietness followed. Few people moved, aside from their eyes. Heat waving up from the tracks into our still compartment roasted us like chickens. A baby's cry from somewhere buoyed the restless uncertainty ballooning among us all, then a whisper of sabotagers swept through the car almost faster than the heat, louder and louder until someone finally said, 'Résistance.'

Résistance? I stood on my toes, trying to see into the other train car, when a man caught my eyes through the body gaps. 'They're invisible,' he whispered, eyes tormented and grey. 'Phantoms in the night and in the day.'

I gripped my pocketbook, suddenly feeling

nervous, watching police run along the outer edge of the car, looking under the train as if there was something or someone to find. Seconds passed, holding our breaths, mouths as wide as our eyes, waiting for a shootout, arrest or both. Then the police stopped running, lit cigarettes and appeared to be chatting.

The whole train exhaled at once.

Some looked relieved nothing serious had happened; others chuckled as if watching the French police run around with nowhere to go was amusing and worth the trouble. The doors opened, sending a burst of fresh air into the train car. The woman across from me who'd seemed unnerved by the gendarmes rushing around was now in a tizzy, bolting from her seat and pushing herself into the crowded aisle. 'If you please,' she said, the heel of her clunky shoe smashing the top of my foot. 'Out of the way!'

I yelped, though it did nothing but startle the old ladies next to me as she elbowed her way through the train car and past women and children as if she were the only passenger who mattered. I followed the pack, shuffling toward the exit, armpits near my face with hands pushing me on the back.

People walked around outside in a daze, unsure where to go or what to do. A young mother balancing a toddler on her hip told passengers the train would continue on, all we had to do was wait, but the blaze of the afternoon sun made the thought of waiting seem unbearable.

A lone train conductor ran a hand through his dishevelled hair next to the loading steps.

'When will we be off?' I said, slinging my

pocketbook over my shoulder.

The conductor stopped fiddling with his hair and put his cap back on, fitting it tightly onto his head. 'Secure a ride,' he said. 'Before they're all gone. The regime is searching the train. Bomb, probably.'

'Bomb?' I threw a hand to my chest. 'Secure a ride?'

'Look around.' He waved a finger at the swelling crowd; some were unloading their own freight. 'These are the general passengers we had on the train. The other passengers are from the regime, filled up most of the compartments. If you don't catch a ride now, you think the government will give you one of theirs?' He pointed. 'Look.'

Two Armistice Army soldiers stepped off the train, and my stomach twisted into a knot. I turned away, shaking my head. One moment I was safe on the train, and now I wasn't sure if I'd even get to Lyon at all. I walked around asking — begging some would say — for a ride from the cars that had seen the train stop and had enough sense to drive over from the village. 'All full,' I was told.

An old man in a wheelchair smacked his cane against the side of the train. 'They're Germans dressed like the French!' he cried as I ran by. 'Get away! Get away!' The porters tried shushing him, ducking and dodging the old man's stick as he whirled it in the air. A squadron of Vichy fighters droned overhead. 'Traitors!' The old man pointed his cane at the planes, and I looked up, covering my ears.

I heard Gérard's voice in my head instead of the planes, yelling for me. *Adèle! I'm going to find you!*

11

Just imagining his voice sent a shudder through my body, and then to my utter shock, a lorry pulled up in the dirt and three police jumped out, but not the local police. *Vichy police.*

'Oh Christ,' I breathed.

One of them talked to a woman and when he showed her a photo, I felt my heart beating — really beating right out of my chest.

I turned left then right in a panic, but there was nowhere to go without being seen. 'Excuse me!' I said, pushing my way through the crowd. 'Sorry, sorry . . .' And I jumped the couplings between two railcars, pulling my dress up to my thighs to clear it, and to my surprise, on a country road without any people, I saw a bald man tying a wooden crate to the rear bumper of a beat-up Renault Vivastella.

I ran over, trying not to alert others still looking for a ride, smoothing my hair and catching my panicked breath. The planes had flown off, and I tried to act calm though my neck was sweating.

'Hallo?' I adjusted my beret. 'Monsieur? Hallo.' A burning cigar protruded from his mouth and oily stains decorated his simple white shirt. His wife — I assumed she was his wife — stood next to him, watching him mess with the rope, trying her best to fold her arms over her bulging, flabby breasts. In the back seat, the shadowy outline of their only passenger sat with the door held wide open by the heel of their shoe. *Must be who the crate belongs to*, I thought.

'Do you have room for one more?' Grey and black exhaust spewed from the tailpipe between us. 'I'm going to Lyon.' I pulled several francs from my pocketbook and flipped through the notes.

He used his knee to hold the crate in place while tying his knots. 'No room.'

I shook the francs in front of him to take. '*Notre Dame de la Compassion*.' I thought that if he knew I was going to the convent he'd think I was worthy of becoming a nun, and that might change his mind if the francs didn't. I smiled big.

He dropped his foot from the rear bumper, tightening the rope with one swift pull. A bead of sweat dribbled from his brow to his cheek as he plucked the cigar from his mouth.

'Convent?'

I nodded, fanning the francs out with a licked finger. 'I won't take up much room.' I peeked into the back of the car, catching a glimpse of their passenger fanning themselves with their hand. 'What's one more passenger?'

He took a hard look at his wife, her face changing from pink to red, arms compressing around her chest, pushing her breasts into her fatty neck. Neither of them said a word — their eyes fighting it out. When she moved her hands to her hips, he shouted at the both of us.

'Fine!'

The wife gently pulled the francs from my hands. 'Get in before he changes his mind.'

I flung open the door and hopped inside, getting comfortable on the cracked leather seat. *Victory*, I thought. Then I saw the other passenger: that woman who'd taken the vacant seat on the train. She had been looking at her book and was unaware I had just negotiated a ride with the driver.

'You?' I said.

'You!' she said back.

Her eyebrows rose into her forehead, and I could tell she was more shocked than upset by my sudden appearance in the seat next to her. She defiantly swiped her hand over the seat to separate our dresses so they wouldn't touch.

The driver got into the car, followed by his wife, who'd rolled up the francs and pushed them deep into the slit between her breasts. They'd barely closed their doors before the woman reminded them that she had paid for a private transport. 'Looks like you know each other,' the wife said.

We answered at the same time, stopped to allow the other to finish, and then talked over each other again, saying the same words.

'No — '

'We met on the train — '

'Well,' I said. 'We didn't exactly *meet*.'

'You're right,' she said. 'I don't know you.'

We sat in silence, the warm air inside the cramped car rising like a blazing furnace, sweat trickling down my back. Then the engine revved from a heavy foot lying on the accelerator, and we lurched into a sudden drive with rocks spitting out from the tyres. Once the dust had settled both of them rolled down their windows and hot air raged into the back seat.

I held my hand out. 'Adèle.' Strands of hair blew across my face, tickling my nose as I waited for her to take my hand and shake it.

She offered me three limp fingers. 'Marguerite.'

'Nice to — '

She'd pulled her hand away before I could finish, and we raced down the lone country road,

14

the back tyres fishtailing over the loose gravel. My knee kept knocking hers from being crammed in the back seat together. She'd huff, shifting this way and that, but then our hips or our forearms would touch. Until finally — after many minutes searching for a space of her own — she somehow managed to create a gap between our bodies.

'There,' she breathed. 'Finally.' She smoothed her hair to one side before gazing back out the window, looking as lifeless as a statue.

* * *

We drove north through the Beaujolais country-side and into the Saône Valley where the region's Gamay grapes hung from thick green vines. Gusts of fermented oak and the earthy smell of dark top-soil filtered in through the windows.

I breathed it in.

As children, Charlotte and I would run bare-foot through Papa's vineyard in the Vichy hills of Creuzier-le-Vieux, until the evening chill had numbed our sun-soaked arms and our feet had turned black as tar from the volcanic soil that made Papa's pinot taste so rich — but never in the Gamay vineyards. Papa forbade us from running through our neighbour's farm, said the grapes made *vin de merde*. Shit wine. And that we'd come back smelling like it, worse, transplant that grape's unique aromas into our vineyard and create something new and awful.

We were close to the convent; I could feel it in the valley air, and for the first time since leaving Vichy, I thought about what life would be like living with the sisters. Papa had me take communion as a child, but I hadn't memorized any scripture and wondered if I'd be expected to. I'd have to remember how to hold a rosary.

'How much longer till the convent?' I said.

Marguerite jerked in her seat — suddenly very much alive. 'Convent?' She grabbed the wife from behind and pulled on her shoulder. 'You're not taking her to the train station?'

The wife looked to her husband, mouth in an open gasp, but all he did was grip his steering wheel tighter. There was an awkward long pause as Marguerite dug her fingertips into the woman's fleshy shoulder.

'Of course you're going to the convent!' Marguerite let go, but not without giving the wife a nasty little shove.

It didn't occur to me until that moment that Marguerite might be headed to the convent also. Her makeup-less face, her drab clothes, and those odd silent stares out the window started to add up. I reached for the book on her lap, that same book she'd been clutching the entire two hours I'd known her, and flipped its cover back: *The Holy Bible*.

'You're going to be a nun,' I said, 'aren't you?'

Marguerite snatched her Bible back. 'This was supposed to be a special day for me, and you've all but ruined it with your intrusions.'

I sat still, hands recoiling into my lap, not sure what to say or where to look — a postulant's arrival at her convent was indeed special; even I knew that — I felt bad, trying not to look at the rash still puffing on her neck.

16

The car skidded to a screaming stop. 'We're here,' the driver said. 'Now get out.' He flung open his door. The wife folded her hands together and muttered something that sounded like a prayer while he went around the back and untied Marguerite's crate from the bumper.

I got out of the car and, to my surprise, the convent was a medieval-looking castle perched on a hill. A massive stone wall enclosed the grounds and seemed to go in both directions for kilometres on end. A long drive led up from an opened iron gate to the front door, which I could barely see at such a far distance. Willow trees lined the path, weeping, swaying subtly from a breeze sweeping through the valley.

Marguerite walked slowly past me with one hand on her hip, the other on her forehead, looking somewhat disappointed.

'It's so beautiful —'

'Shh,' Marguerite said, throwing her hand in the air. A garden of yellow wildflowers cascading down the hill toward the city of Lyon seemed to only add to her disappointment.

Moments passed. The couple slammed their doors closed without so much as a goodbye and sped away. Pebbles shooting out from underneath spinning tyres hit Marguerite's legs as she stood stoically still, her eyes set on the convent's massive stone turrets peeking through the willow trees, her straight brown hair matching her lanky body and her long arms.

I couldn't help but think how different we were. Brown, thick leather shoes and wide heels, scuffed ankles that grew into legs — I wondered if she'd ever tried to look pretty, or desired it. These were the type of women I'd be living with, ones with a devotion to Christ I couldn't fathom, although admired, but also a strict aversion to fashion — and bad language. I had to watch my language. *God, if it wasn't for Mama's mouth!* Be sensitive.

I will help her, I thought, and the tension that had followed us from the train would disappear. I cleared my throat.

'I'm sorry, Marguerite. Your journey didn't go as planned. Neither did mine, but we're here now. That's what matters.' I picked up one end of the crate, trying not to grimace from the overwhelming weight of the load inside, but it was too heavy to manage by myself. 'Ugh! What's in here?' I dropped the crate, only that's when she decided to pick her end up, its contents clinking and clanging against each other from the abrupt shift.

'Marguerite?'

She made no mention of my apology, but rather ploughed down the path toward the convent with the crate dragging behind her, spooking a covey of quail that left pulls of breast feathers wafting in the air. I hurried after her, picking the crate up by its dragging end, and walked the rest of the way with her.

A Sister of the Order flew out of the castle's wooden front door as we approached, her arms in a welcoming stretch. I dropped the crate, working to straighten my beret and smooth my hair.

'*Bienvenue!*' Her habit ruffled around her ankles as she made her way through the courtyard. 'Welcome to our convent. I'm Sister Mary-Francis.'

She threw her arms around Marguerite, whose walnut-shaped eyes peeped over the sister's shoulders.

'Thank you for the welcome, Sister,' Marguerite said with a small curtsy.

The sister turned to me, her eyes rolling from my gravel-scuffed pumps all the way to the top of my head. 'And who's this? You brought someone with you?' She noticed my pocketbook and seemed more curious about it than Marguerite's wooden crate.

'I don't know who she is,' Marguerite piped up.

My jaw dropped, momentarily lost for words as the sister studied me. I realized Marguerite and I had just met a few hours ago, but she made it sound like we'd never spoken, which I didn't appreciate. I'd apologized, and as it were, just helped her carry that monstrosity of a crate up the gravel path.

'Actually, we met on the train,' I said. 'I'm Adèle Ambeh.'

The sister offered me her hand to shake. 'Very nice.'

'I come from Vichy, seeking refuge.' I pulled the francs Mama had given me from my pocketbook and piled the bundles into her hands. 'Is this enough alms to let me stay?'

The sister struggled with the growing stack, dropping some to the ground. 'Seeking refuge, you say?'

'My father wrote a letter.' I unfolded the note Mama had written and held it in front of her eyes since her hands were full of francs.

She read it aloud at first, but then mumbled her

19

way through the last half. 'Oh, I see.' She smiled and nodded — Mama had written there would be more money the longer I stayed. 'Well, Adèle,' she said. 'We do need help with the girls.'

'Girls?' I said.

Marguerite took a step back and watched us with folded arms.

'Yes . . . rehabilitation. Girls displaced by the war . . .' Marguerite huffed from her nose, and the sister suddenly seemed torn between the two of us. 'Oh . . . umm . . .' She motioned for me to make my way to the front doors while trying to manage the francs in her hands. 'I'll get you acquainted inside, Adèle, if you wouldn't mind.' I made a move toward the front door, but then she yelped. 'Wait — what skills do you have?'

I winced instantly, standing with my back to her. I suppose I should've thought about these things on the train, but how could I with all that commotion? Truth was, I went through trades quickly, and I hadn't done much at all since I quit setting hair, but the sister didn't know that. I could clean a floor if I had to — the thought of Gérard waiting for me back at the altar was enough for me to say anything if it meant she'd allow me to stay.

I cleared my throat before turning around. 'I can — '

Another bundle of francs slipped from the sister's hands. 'It doesn't matter,' she said, picking it up. 'Go ahead inside.' She pointed at the convent with her eyes. 'Wait in the foyer.' She shouted for someone to come outside and the door opened again.

A girl, someone who was not a nun, with a slick

of mousy bangs pressed to her forehead and a blue smock hanging from her small frame. She clasped her hands behind her back and looked at the ground, waiting for the sister's instructions.

Her eyes shifted once toward Marguerite, but just briefly.

'This is Adèle,' the sister said. 'We've found our new mistress — she'll join you with the girls. See that she gets settled.'

The girl clicked her heels and asked me to follow her, which I did, gladly. Halfway through the courtyard, I stopped and held my hand out to shake — I wasn't going to make the same mistake I did with Marguerite; it was important for me to start off on the right foot. 'Nice to meet you . . .'

'Mavis,' she said, just above a whisper.

Birds chirped in the trees, but even so, her voice was very soft. 'Pardon — Mavis was it?'

She led me by the elbow toward the convent, nodding as we walked. 'Yes,' she said. 'I'm a postulant.'

'Oh!' I said. 'Just like . . .' I turned around, pointing to Marguerite, only her and the sister were gone.

3

Rehabilitation, as Sister Mary-Francis had called it, was a place for the delinquents of France — girls between the ages of twelve and seventeen whose families thought they had strayed in God's eyes. Just a few had been destitute from the war and placed with the convent out of desperation, until their families could reimburse the sisters monetarily or through service.

As their mistress, I escorted the girls to the sewing centre once a week in the city, inside a seventeenth-century building the sisters once used as their convent. The girls didn't complain about the sewing. They knew the conditions at the convent were better than most. The summer heat was another matter entirely, and often on the mornings when the clouds were scarce and the sun beat down like a blister in the sky, they'd voice their displeasure in subtle ways. On these days, finding shade and staying in it was a necessity.

The bells in the tower clanged and clanged, and the girls scooted from the pews, hurrying out the side doors of the cool sanctuary into the warm outside. I clapped twice for them to make a line against the wall, but as soon as they felt the sun on their faces, they slumped against the convent as if trying to suck the last bit of morning dew from the castle's weathered stones.

One girl picked at the crumbling mortar. 'I'm sweating already,' she said, pushing herself away from the wall to fan herself with her hand.

I snapped lavender sprigs off a nearby bush and handed each girl a piece big enough to rub under their armpits. 'Pretend it's your mother's Chanel.' They moaned.

Just as we were about to leave, Sister Mary-Francis burst through the door, out of breath and panting with her arms in the air. 'Adèle!' The rosary pinched between her fingers flung around her wrist. 'Thank goodness! I thought I'd missed you. We got word there's a special visitor in Lyon today and Mother Superior — '

I touched her gently, worried she was working herself into a state. 'Sister, are you all right?'

'Yes, yes . . . ' She glanced up at the convent behind me, taking a deep breath. 'Mother Superior requests that you take the girls to the square — *Place des Terreaux* — to represent the rehabilitation centre.' She took another deep breath, but this time exhaled very slowly.

The sisters counted on the money we made on orders. I couldn't imagine who'd be important enough to interrupt our scheduled day of sewing. '*Visiteur spéciale?*'

She nodded. 'Our beloved Pétain. He's giving a speech — veterans for Pétain parade is to follow.'

'Oh,' I said with a gulp. 'I see.' Even I heard the snarl of disinterest in my voice.

'The Vichy regime put God back in the schools, Adèle.' Her face pruned, and I instantly regretted my tone. 'We owe a debt of gratitude to Pétain.'

'I understand, certainly, Sister — ' the girls lifted their eyes, pulling their collars from their necks ' — I meant no disrespect. I'm merely

23

concerned about the heat. The old convent feels like a wine cellar; it's cool, and on a day like this . . .'

Her face loosened, though not completely. 'It's Mother's wishes. In the main square in one hour — ' the girls groaned '— after the speech you are to come right back and take reflection on the convent grounds, in the cloister. No sewing at all today.'

No doubt there would be police in the square. Some may know Gérard, might even recognize me. I sighed — there was no way I could get out of it without coming across as insubordinate.

'You'll be there?' she asked, though they were orders. 'In one hour?'

'Yes, Sister.'

'Good.' Her eyes flicked again to something behind me, and I swear I saw her nod. This time I turned, but looked right into the sun. She touched my shoulder and I looked away. 'We will see you there.'

I nodded once.

As soon as she left, the girls whined and slumped against the wall as if they had just finished draining the last bit of coolness from the stones and had completely wilted from the heat.

'Pétain,' I said to myself. 'A speech.'

Mavis licked her palm, running it repeatedly over her mouse-brown bangs until they were smooth and damp. 'This must be terribly important to Mother if she's interrupting a sister's private prayer.' Her voice squeaked when she talked fast. 'Shall we leave?' She played nervously with her fingers.

'Leave?' The realization of what I was about to do kept my feet from moving — I felt no glamour in supporting Pétain, standing in a crowd waving and smiling. Mavis's concerned, little brown eyes stared up at me, waiting for an answer as I took a hard look down the path that led away from the convent, fingernails in my teeth.

'*We do what we have to,*' Mama had said before I left. '*When we have to.*'

'Girls,' I said using my head to point the way. 'Looks like we have a speech to attend.'

Some of them seemed excited to do something other than sew, while others lumbered down the path, rubbing their armpits with the lavender sprigs. The last sprig went to Mavis.

'Sorry,' I said, realizing I'd given her the smallest one. 'I picked the bush clean. There might be more down the way.'

She smiled, taking the sprig. Then something caught both our eyes. A shady presence set high up in the castle wall, in a narrow window with its shutters pushed wide open, right above where the sister and I were talking. A leafy vine of ivy that hung over its opening fluttered from having been moved, but there wasn't a breeze.

'Mavis.' I elbowed her. 'Did you notice anyone in that window earlier? Seemed like Sister Mary-Francis was distracted by something.'

'I saw Marguerite.'

'In the window?' I looked at her once. 'Watching me?'

She nodded. 'I think so.'

A hand reached out from the dark middle and closed the shutters. I stood for a moment,

25

wondering why Marguerite would do such a thing, when Mavis spoke up.

'She asked me about you.'

'What did she ask?' I said, but Mavis shrugged as if she didn't know.

The girls travelled farther and farther down the path, and now I could only hear them.

'Come on,' I said, 'or we'll miss the autobus into the city.' And we hurried on after the girls.

* * *

People poured into the square from all directions waving Vichy flags to stand and wait in front of the Hotel de Ville, under the building's gold-dipped heralds where a long and narrow stage had been set up, shuffling in, dragging their children by their shirt sleeves. People wearing sandwich boards with posters of Pétain pasted to each side, begged for coins and talked about unity. The sun's reflection shining off the glass set inside all three storeys of the Hotel de Ville's barrel-arched windows cooked us all. And for the first time since I had arrived at the convent, I was thankful for the peasant dress the girls and I had to wear, which was made from the thinnest of fabric.

We weren't the only congregation in the square. The nuns from the neighbouring Saint-Pierre convent had gathered on a one-step bleacher, each of them squinting in the face of the sun under their wing-tipped headpieces. I looked over the crowd for Mother.

A squadron of Vichy fighter planes droned overhead, and eyes went to the sky. Mavis covered her

26

ears. I copied. Then the other girls did the same.

'Where's Mother?' Mavis said, under the rumbling engines, but I only saw her mouth move.

I shrugged. 'I don't know.'

The planes had flown off, and I directed the girls to line up next to the Saint Pierre nuns, mainly because I wasn't sure where else to go, and inspected them — backs straight and feet together — reminding them that we were leaving as soon as the speech was over, which I thought would keep their whining down. Mavis bobbed on her feet as if she'd forgotten to wear shoes and had just realized the ground was hot. She put a hand to her forehead, as if searching.

I fanned my neck, waiting. The Saint Pierre Mother Superior stood next to her congregation, arms folded like the rest of them, in front of their bodies, with their hands tucked into their long and heavy sleeves. I turned to Mavis. 'Mother doesn't expect us to represent our entire convent, does she?'

A finger poked my shoulder and I turned around. Claire, a seventeen-year-old girl under my care looked up at me. 'What are we to do now?' Her face had flattened, and her eyes looked as tawny as the square's cobblestones in the morning sunlight.

Claire was sweet, and I felt sorry for her in a big sister kind of way. Her father was in a German prison, captured on the Maginot Line, and her mother couldn't afford to keep her around, unmarried. The convent, she had told me, was her only option.

I shook my head, looking into the crowd once

27

more for Mother Superior or anyone from the convent. 'Stand here, I suppose. Sister Mary-Francis said all we need to do is make an appearance.'

Claire pulled a lock of hair away from her bun and twisted it around her finger. 'But we're with *those* nuns from Saint Pierre.'

Two sisters turned to Claire, who shrank under their gaze, her eyes growing to the size of saucers under the cast of their shadows.

The Saint-Pierre nuns were known for their vows of silence. Most hadn't spoken a word in over a decade, which was intimidating to some of the delinquent girls, whose idea of commitment reset with each new day. I smiled politely at the sisters, apologizing for Claire's rude remark, and they turned back around, facing the growing crowd.

Claire sighed with relief. 'Thank you, mademoiselle,' she said, giving up her hair to rub her shoulder. 'Hmm.' She looked at me as she rubbed. 'Something isn't right.'

'What do you mean?' I said.

'My shoulder hurts,' she said. 'It's a sign.'

'A sign of what?'

Claire pressed her thumb heavily into her joint. 'I don't know,' she said, mouth drawn up, 'but something.'

A laugh puffed from my lips, a laugh I couldn't control after watching Claire mess with her shoulder as if it were a cable from the sisters. She dropped her hand and stood board straight.

'Mother Superior must be waiting for us at the sewing centre,' Claire said. 'It would explain why she's not here. I'll run down to the old convent

28

and make sure.' She turned to leave and Mavis shook her head, but it was me who spoke up.

'She wants us down here, Claire. In the square. Besides, Pétain's speech will start any moment.'

Mavis nodded with what I'd said, licking her palm and wiping it over her hair for the second time since we'd arrived. Time dragged on — every minute that passed felt like five in the hot square. Soon enough, people wondered out loud where Pétain was, and why he was late. The crowd swelled, and we found ourselves squishing up against each other shoulder to shoulder with supporters waving hand flags to keep cool. I could barely see the podium that had been set up in the middle of the stage.

A few thin Armistice Army soldiers walked out with giant Vichy flags on poles and stood on each side of the stage, which made me think the speech was going to start any second, but still we waited. Sweat beads slid down my neck under my dress, soaking my undergarments.

'What time did we get here?' I asked Mavis.

'Oh ... ah ... ' Mavis squinted at the clock set in the tower.

'We got here twenty-three minutes ago,' Claire said. 'On the dot.'

I pinched the front of my peasant dress, peeling it from my dampened skin, trying to get some air between the fabric and my body. I couldn't remember a day as hot as this. At least in Vichy we had the river and the spas to keep us cool. I used my hand as a fan, still looking for Mother Superior, when the French police walked out onto the stage.

The police! I gasped, looking to the ground.

I'd thought about all the ways Mama ended up breaking the news I'd left. Each one ended with Gérard vowing to find me, drag me back to his headquarters and punish me for the humiliation I'm sure I'd caused him. Thinking about the police at the convent felt different from seeing them close-up, with their guns. My guttural instinct was to run.

I slowly glanced up, feet stepping on toes, watching the police as they looked into the crowd, heads and eyes shifting, scanning us like pigs in a pen. *It's all right*, I told myself. If they stay on the —

My heart sank.

Gendarmes walked off the platform into the crowd, taking positions among the flag-waving people, strategically arranging themselves like pegs on a board. There was nowhere to hide. One of them could easily recognize me at this close distance and report back to Gérard where I'd run off to.

'I'm . . . I'm going down to the old convent!' I said to Mavis, who shook her head vigorously.

'I'll go,' Claire said, and I looked at her, only a gendarme was now walking toward us, moving girls out of his way, getting closer, close enough to see the dimples in my cheeks.

'No —'

I bolted before Mavis had a chance to say anything, skirting between supporters and their flags, disappearing into the alley where just a smattering of people were still making their way to the square. I looked back once; glad I had gotten safely away from the police.

I walked on to the convent, only it was a short walk, shorter than I thought, shorter than I hoped. I turned the final corner, and the buildings looked abandoned with drawn window shades.

And the streets were quiet.

Strangely quiet, except for the light din of the busy square lofting above the rooftops.

I reached for the doorknob, but then reconsidered — not one other soul walked the normally busy street, and the sisters were obviously not here since the door wasn't propped open. I shivered in the sun, suddenly thinking I shouldn't have come, and that I should hurry back to the square before anyone noticed that I'd disobeyed a sister's direct orders. But then I heard a loud thump come from inside the building; then another, followed by something big and heavy being dragged intermittently across the floor. The murmur of voices wisped through a crack in the door.

Men's voices.

I looked over both my shoulders — still nobody was in the street. I stepped up on some wood pallets I found nearby to reach the one window that hadn't been blacked out, and peeked inside, my eyes rising above the stone ledge.

Men dressed in field trousers dragged rolled-up carpets across the floor, in between our bulky stitching machines and down the stairs into the dark crypt. A woman with flowing blonde hair walked into the middle of the room. The men moved out of her way. She had a rifle slung over her shoulder and a revolver gripped in her hand. She motioned to one of the rugs, and guns, loads

31

of them, spilled out onto the floor.

'Mother of Christ,' I said, immediately clamping a hand over my mouth. *Résistance*. I should have left — I should have run — but my knees had locked up and so had my arms.

A woman rushed out of the crypt and motioned for them to hurry up, roll the carpets back up. A shout came from inside — someone noticed me — and the woman turned around, one wide eye focusing on me through a clean spot in the glass. Walking closer, closer, and then running toward me.

I gasped — letting go of the ledge and falling backward to the ground with a thud and the crash of clanking wood pallets caving around me.

I lay for a moment, stunned, whimpering, with my back flat against the cobblestones, but then scrambled to get to my feet, only a hand grabbed hold of my arm. 'Ach!' I threw my hands over my head, my body curling up on the pavement with my eyes clenched tight as fists. 'I didn't mean to —'

'There you are!' My eyes popped open when I heard Claire's voice, and I lowered my hands, taking stock of the situation I'd found myself in, while Claire rambled on about how I shouldn't have left.

'Marguerite's real mad at you.' She paused, her face scrunched up with questions, glancing at the pallets and then to me. 'What were you doing?'

'Trying to see inside,' I scoffed, doing my best to act normal and unshaken, but my heart beat from my chest and blood glugged in my ears from the fall and what I'd seen.

'Come on, we should hurry,' I said.

Claire was still looking at the pallets and trying to figure everything out when I grabbed her hand and took off toward the square. 'Slow down,' she said, but my legs moved at an alarming rate, in between a run and a walk. 'Why so fast?'

'I have to find a toilet, all right?' I said, and I don't know where that came from but somehow it fit and she stopped putting up a fuss.

I rejoined the girls only to find Marguerite standing piously next to Mavis with her chin jutting into the air. She straightened the bodice of her blue postulant's dress, seemingly unaware I had come back and was standing in line, but then turned her head and looked me up and down with the coldest of cold stares.

'Are you all right?' Claire said.

I opened my mouth but no words came out, looking at Claire and then to Marguerite. A man walked out onto the platform and a cheer erupted from the crowd, rescuing me from Marguerite's horrid look and from answering Claire.

'It's him!' Claire shouted. 'Pétain!'

He stepped up to the podium and paused briefly before tipping his French kepi. Then he shocked everyone with an announcement.

'My fellow Frenchmen.' He cleared his throat before continuing, and supporters waved their hand flags. 'I am Marcel Moreau, a friend of our beloved leader, Marshal Philippe Pétain.' The excitement building in the crowd fizzled when they realized Pétain had sent his lookalike. 'He regrets to inform you that he is unable to speak to you fine people today.' He carefully unfolded a piece of paper and then squinted, tilting the page into the sunlight as if he had trouble reading the words. An aide rushed onto the stage and handed him a pair of wire-framed spectacles. Dogs barked behind the podium. Chatter wondering where Pétain had gone to swept through the crowd, and he seemed nervous, wiping sweat from his forehead, face and neck. 'That is all.' He turned on his heel and walked swiftly off the stage.

The Saint-Pierre nuns stood like statues, looking quite confused. Others lingered as if not sure what to do after all that waiting. A delayed applause crept up from the back of the crowd, but faded away once it reached the front where people had already started making their way to the parade. The gendarmes had left, but to where I didn't know.

Mavis tugged on my sleeve, shrugging her shoulders like a little girl. She started to talk, her dove mouth opening and closing, but I couldn't hear anything that came out of her. When she spoke again, I only caught a few of her words. 'Quick . . . speech.'

A haggard old woman pointed her finger at the empty stage. 'Coward!' she shouted. 'Pétain tucked his tail and ran — the Résistance breathing down his neck.' A wry, crackled laugh burst from her lips before she started wheezing and holding her chest with her free hand.

I didn't want to be caught looking, and turned my back to gather up the girls who had started to wander like cats, but bumped right into Marguerite. She had a scowl on her face that turned so cold I felt a chill brush against my skin.

'Where were you earlier?' She crossed her arms. 'I saw you leave when the gendarmes arrived.'

I looked at her blankly. 'When the gendarmes arrived?'

'You're repeating my words.' She squinted. 'You defied a sister's direct orders. You could have ruined things for the convent, leaving the girls unsupervised.'

'I was only gone for a second.'

'You have a habit of ruining things.'

I looked into her beady eyes, suddenly realizing she was still angry with me for what happened on her arrival day. The girls swarmed around us, asking when we were leaving, dividing my attention between Marguerite's pointed stare and their whining cries.

'Marguerite . . . I . . .'

Without further comment, Marguerite turned on her heel and walked away, leaving me with a handful of complaining girls in a near-deserted square.

4

As instructed, we didn't go to the sewing centre
after the speech, but took reflection in the cloister
with our devotional journals near the convent's
nave. I sat on the ground, my journal unopened,
staring off in the distance at a stone wall, thinking about what I saw in the crypt, and wondering
if they knew who'd seen them. Of all the places
I could have picked, a convent with ties to the
Résistance? My fingers shook a little from the
excitement, remembering the dragging sound of
the rugs moving across the floor.

Mavis touched my shoulder, and I jumped,
clutching my chest.

'Oh my,' she said, sitting on the ground in front
of me. 'Thinking about something important?'

It took a moment for me to recover. 'I didn't
hear you walk up,' I finally said. 'That's all.'

Mavis's face looked smooth as porcelain, white
and matte, and she smelled of menthol. Had I not
known the nuns washed only on Sundays, I would
have thought she'd just taken a bath. She adjusted
her skirt, tucking it under her folded legs. She had
a Bible in her hands, which was bound in leather,
tiny pieces of paper she used to mark her thoughts
dangling from nearly every page. She smiled
politely before opening it up, scanning the words
with a loosely pointed finger, her eyes wondrously
searching for something new and exciting.

'Mavis,' I said, looking at her curiously. 'When

did you know you wanted to be a nun?'

Her voice was quiet-soft. 'Oh, I don't know . . . maybe twelve or so.' She smiled. 'I'm twenty-two now.'

I was surprised to hear she'd decided at such a young age, and I was sure she could see it on my face. 'Twelve? You knew . . . at only twelve? But at that age you — ' I paused, hoping I wasn't going to sound too disrespectful, but there wasn't a delicate way to say it. 'You've never been in love. You won't know what it feels like. Ever.' I felt sorry for her instantly, but she only laughed.

'Jesus is all I ever needed, or wanted.'

'Certainly, but the touch of a man, a brush of his finger on your bare shoulder, the smell of his cologne on a warm day — '

'My, Adèle!' Mavis blushed from my words. 'Sounds like you're well versed in these things. Have you been in love?'

I shrugged. With Gérard I only felt shivers. 'My sister said being in love first feels like a butterfly's wings fluttering deep inside, that it pulls from within making you feel wonderful yet vulnerable and fragile as a hollow egg.'

'I feel that with Jesus, Adèle . . . ' She had sat up and talked about the first time she knew she wanted to be a nun, how she could hear bees buzzing even from kilometres away and that everything seemed crisp and clear as a freshly washed glass. Her voice didn't squeak like it had earlier, and for the first time since knowing Mavis these past long weeks, I admired her for knowing what she wanted to do with her life, since I was still searching. 'I knew my love for him before I arrived here. A postulant

37

has to be sure. Temptation for another would get me dismissed, and I'd be ashamed.'

Mavis held her Bible close to her chest, pausing. 'What about you? When did you realize you wanted to help the sisters? Something must have inspired you.'

'Me?' I put my hand to my chest.

I didn't want to think about the day I decided to leave Vichy, mostly because of how I left things with Charlotte. There were no bees or epiphanies about the world that got me on the train like Mavis, but something rather unexpected and serendipitous.

Charlotte sat in a cushioned chair with her feet propped up, wrapping a wide yellow ribbon around a bouquet of peonies, talking about how happy she was I had decided to put down some roots.

'Just one more day,' Charlotte said. 'Then you'll be married like me!' She smiled, tightening the ribbon around the stems. 'You'll look lovely with this bouquet in your hands tomorrow.'

'At my funeral,' I said, but she paid no attention to me as I sat in the windowsill of her boutique, looking out into the street.

'I'm not the only one excited about your union. Henri is very pleased as well.' She smiled, but then again, she smiled every time she mentioned her husband's name. 'He'll be there, you know, for your wedding.'

Henri was always working, either in Paris or in the south for the regime. I know his absences pained Charlotte, but she never mentioned it.

'Oh, that's nice,' I said, and she looked up.

'You know how hard it is for him to get away,' she said.

'Yes,' I said. 'I know.'

'I heard Gérard got a case of expensive champagne for after the ceremony, and you'll dance and you'll be in love, and . . . ' Charlotte kept talking about my wedding and then stopped abruptly and patted her pregnant belly. 'And who knows, maybe in no time we'll be mothers at the same time too!'

'Mmm.'

A mother with her young daughter walked into the boutique. Charlotte instantly lit up. 'Adèle!' She waved for me to bring her a few extra flowers, and then gave them to the little girl. I watched Charlotte as she talked to her, brushing a golden lock of hair from the child's eyes as if she was already a mother herself with babies all around.

'You are the sweetest thing,' Charlotte said to the girl. 'If it's all right with your mama, I have some sweets in the back if you'd like . . . '

I'd gone back to the window, listening to Charlotte talk to the little girl. Two nuns dressed in heavy black and white habits stood outside the train station, about to walk inside. There was a small convent in Vichy, but an even bigger one in Lyon, which was several kilometres away, I thought.

Nobody would find me in Lyon — at a convent.

I bolted out of Charlotte's shop. I heard her calling for me, 'Adèle . . . Adèle . . . your bouquet . . . ' But I had gotten into Papa's car anyway and drove off.

'Mavis, I don't . . . ' I looked at her helplessly, trying to think up something to tell her that wasn't the truth when Claire plopped down next to me, her knees jittering as if she had drunk too much coffee. 'Are you all right, Claire?'

'This is yours,' she said, holding a journal out

39

for me to take. 'They must have gotten switched when we mopped the floor earlier.' Mavis had gone back to her Bible, which I was glad about; I didn't want to answer any more of her questions.

I flipped through the pages of the journal I had in my lap, expecting to see the notes I'd been making about how Catholics behaved, but Claire was right; our journals had been switched, and we exchanged.

'You're quite the drawer,' she said, pointing to a diagram I had drawn on how to hold a rosary.

I folded my arms around my journal, pushing it into my chest. 'Thanks,' I said, closing my eyes so she wouldn't say anything else about my drawings and notes. I rested my head against the stone column, trying to send her a message to leave me alone, but she piped up again.

'Could you believe that old woman in the square?' she said. 'And what about Marguerite?'

'Marguerite?' I sat up. 'What do you mean?'

'Her electric eyes. Hideous . . . just hideous!'

'Shh,' I said, patting Claire on the knee. 'That isn't nice.' As much as I agreed with her, I shuddered to think about the reprimand I'd receive if I was caught talking badly about a postulant.

Mavis studied her Bible, either pretending not to have heard Claire say mean things about Marguerite or completely ignoring it.

'I think she wants to put you on a stake and set you on fire.'

My mouth gaped open. Claire was seventeen — I didn't expect her to act as old as me, certainly, but she did talk with a sort of unfiltered naïveté that made me wonder about her upbringing. Mavis

40

heard Claire this time, pulling her eyes away from her Bible.

'She hates you!' Claire said.

Mavis shook her head. 'No, Claire. That's not true.'

'Did you see the look she gave Adèle?' Claire said to Mavis, but then turned to me. 'We all saw it. You have to tell us . . . all of us are wondering.' She smiled deviously. 'What did you do?'

Mavis looked lost and worried, the way her eyebrows bent in the middle like broken arrows and her pupils dilated like an owl's. I couldn't have her thinking I wasn't a good fit for the convent. I had to protect myself and squash any kind of rumours the girls might have already been discussing. I sat up tall.

'We got stuck on a hot train together, and it had an emergency stop. Résistance, you know. They made our journey here a nightmare. I think she might blame me a little for her discomfort because I had a cigarette and she's sensitive to the smoke.'

Mavis listened with a drawn mouth, and then sighed in relief as if she *had* wondered what I had done to Marguerite and was glad to hear it wasn't too serious.

Claire's eyes narrowed and I had the distinct feeling she believed I was holding back. Last thing I needed was for Marguerite to cause me trouble, get me sent back to Vichy — she'd already noticed I had hid from the police. I couldn't let that happen. Not now, especially not after what I saw in the crypt. I should have answered her in the square and then apologized again just to get her off my back. Now I was afraid I'd made things worse.

41

'A postulant's arrival to the convent — any convent — is a momentous occasion,' I said. 'I'm sure with some time Marguerite will soften. I owe her a proper apology.' *Perhaps from my knees.* 'I'll talk to her.'

Mavis looked relieved. 'Maybe when we do our crafts this afternoon?'

Crafts. Craft time was always so busy. I certainly didn't want to apologize with so many people around, but when else was I supposed to do it? The postulants were expected to participate.

The bell tower chimed, announcing midday, and we all stood up. 'Yes,' I said, but two whole days passed and I still hadn't seen Marguerite, and I started to feel a little anxious with the passing time. She was like a spectre in the night and in the corridors, her voice always loud and echoing, though never seen. I worried I'd bump into her again unexpectedly like I did at the parade, and I was constantly looking for her, fearing I'd have to apologize while in a rush.

Mavis must have asked me ten times if I had made amends with her since talking in the cloister, which didn't help. On the second day I knew that if I didn't see Marguerite during craft time, I would have to set out to find her.

I stood at the craft table. We had a choice to either make ashtrays out of clay or paint on canvases outside. Neither sounded enjoyable. I decided to paint, since the conservatory was too hot, and I picked through the brushes.

Mavis walked up, whispering. 'Today?'

'Today,' I said, glancing around the room as the girls gathered their painting supplies, listening for Marguerite's husky voice, and looking for her plain face. 'If she doesn't show up, I'll personally go find her.' *I must find her.*

Mavis patted my shoulder so lightly I barely felt it. 'Good,' she said.

I held the door open as the girls shuffled outside with their canvases and brushes. Claire stopped in the doorway, canvas under her arm, not giving a second thought to those behind her. 'Mademoiselle,' she said. 'I — '

'Move on,' a girl said from behind, which I think Claire would have been happy to ignore, but when she saw it was Victoria, the girl with the ginger hair and freckly face, she stood her ground.

'I'm talking,' Claire said, glaring, but by now she'd backed up the line four girls deep, all trying to balance their painting supplies in their arms.

'We can talk outside,' I said to Claire, and she huffed, giving Victoria another glare before finally walking over to where Sister Mary-Francis told them to set up their easels.

'I don't like her,' Claire said.

'Who?' I said, setting up my canvas.

'That one,' she said, pointing with her head. 'With the red hair.'

'You were holding up the door,' I said.

'It's not just that,' Claire said.

Mavis brought out chairs for everyone and we got settled on the eastern slope of the convent grounds, in a field of swaying grass that popped with white wildflowers, partially shaded by the willow trees. Claire painted on with zest, first with a glop of green paint and then smearing it all over the canvas, spreading it from edge to edge, talking

43

to me about everything and anything. 'And who likes chicory coffee?' she said, which came out of nowhere.

I looked around for Marguerite, over my canvas, and behind my back, but she was nowhere in sight. I dabbed my brush into some paint. 'I don't like chicory,' I said, starting my painting, thinking about Marguerite, her snarling face, that beige skirt she wore on the train to go with her beige face, and all the trouble she could cause me if I didn't find her.

'We're in the Free Zone,' Claire said. 'You'd think we'd have better — '

'Claire!' Sister Mary-Francis yelped, and Claire dropped her brush in the grass. She ran over, almost tripping on her long, black habit. Her mouth gaped open, staring at Claire's painting. 'We . . . We . . . ' She scolded her immediately, pointing to the canvas and then to Claire's palette where she'd swirled her brush through every colour, making a mess. 'We can't sell this!'

'Sorry, sister,' Claire said, shrinking. 'I got carried away.' She ran a cloth over the canvas, taking off some of the paint. 'I'll fix it. You'll see.' She smiled.

Sister Mary-Francis looked briefly toward the sky, folding her arms, but then noticed my canvas. 'And what's this?' She was pleased this time, smiling.

Claire whipped her head around.

'Oh,' I said, pulling my brush away. 'It's nothing . . . '

'No, Adèle,' Sister Mary-Francis said, 'this isn't nothing. This is — ' Her raised face took on

44

a questioning expression. 'You never painted like this before.'

Girls set down their brushes and ran over to see what the commotion was all about.

'I . . . I have a sister who paints,' I said as if that was an explanation. 'She taught me,' I said, which was a complete lie. I'd never had a lesson in my life. In fact, Charlotte hated me using her paints. The only time I got to use them was when I stole them out from under her, and that was when I was just a girl.

I got off my chair and stood back with the others. It wasn't the kind of painting my sister would have liked; it was more modern, with boxes for faces, and colours that didn't make sense.

Sister Mary-Francis carried my canvas away. 'Now this,' she said. 'This is how you paint, girls.'

'Is that a Picasso?' someone said, and I burst out laughing, but after a second or two I realized I was the *only* one laughing. I thought it was ugly as sin and looked more like my thoughts, which were solely on Marguerite. Only Mavis thought it was as ugly as I did.

'Get back to work, girls,' I said, and they went back to their own canvases.

'Adèle . . . ' Mavis whispered, pointing her brush to something over my shoulder, and when I turned around, I saw a few nuns not that far away, flashes of black as they walked the perimeter of the castle grounds, and one postulant. *Marguerite.* Mavis patted my shoulder, but this time I felt it.

I handed her my brushes. 'I'll be right back,' I said, and I ran off through the field. Claire called after me, but Mavis must have gotten to her.

45

I followed them around a stone turret, trying to think of who the other nuns were with Marguerite. I didn't recognize them, but they also had their headpieces on and it honestly could have been any one of the sisters at the convent. I practised how I'd say sorry.

'Marguerite,' I called out, just quietly enough for me to hear. 'Do you have a moment?' I thought that would be a good start and when she'd look at me with her dagger eyes, I'd offer her all the apologies I could muster. Maybe with the other sisters there it would break the tension. *Maybe she won't be so nasty.* I hadn't thought of that before, and skipped off a little faster, turning my head just once to see the girls behind me on the far hill painting, and then around the corner.

Only nobody was there.

I stood in the dirt, staring at an empty courtyard. 'Where'd they go?' I said out loud, and then threw my hands up. A deep breath followed. Getting all worked up and then having nowhere to go only made things worse. My stomach ached, and not the kind of ache I'd get from eating the sisters' dinner soups. It was a nervous ache; one I couldn't control no matter what I put in my mouth.

My head felt light from running, and I sat down on a wood bench next to a statue of a saint whose name I didn't know, and lit a cigarette, where yellow flowers grew willy-nilly in between the cobblestones.

The clouds hid the sun in patches and cast handfuls of shady spots on the ground, a welcome relief from the heat that had roared through earlier in the week. After a few puffs, and suddenly having a few quiet moments to myself, it was easy to drift off and think about home, back at the chateau, in the Vichy hills of Creuzier-le-Vieux.

I thought about Charlotte and all those times we'd lain in the meadow behind Papa's vineyard, gazing at the clouds with our hands tucked behind our heads like pillows. Papa's wavy hair had started to grey, looking like flecks of salt and pepper. Wavy, where Charlotte's was curly. And Mama, and her summer salads with herbs from the garden. If she were here, she'd tell me to stop looking at the clouds and start thinking about what I needed to do to make up with Marguerite.

Gérard.

I wanted to cry. If I didn't find a way to reconcile with Marguerite, get her to stop watching me and forgive me, I'd find myself back on a train before I knew it. *Lyon isn't far enough away*, I thought. I should have gone the other direction and all the way to Spain.

'Adèle?' a voice said.

I shot up — Mother Superior! I instantly snubbed out my cigarette, only to stop and hold the smashed little thing unwelcomely in my palm. I had broken one of the convent's rules. There was no hiding that now. I closed my eyes, taking a deep breath. 'Sorry, Mother.' I hung my head down, slinking back onto the bench.

She picked up my lighter, which had fallen on the ground. 'It's all right, Adèle,' she said, holding it out for me to take, 'but do try to remember.' I reached for the lighter, but she pulled it back after taking a second look. 'This lighter . . . '

'It's my mother's.'

47

'It's a cloisonné. The enamel . . . the inlay . . . '
Mother talked as if she knew a thing or two about
expensive lighters, which surprised me. 'And this
one looks — '

'She's had it since her nursing days in the Red
Cross.'

She gasped through her open mouth, glancing at me just briefly, but then many minutes
passed with her still holding the lighter, rubbing
her thumb over the smooth sides, smiling at times
and then frowning. I reached for it again, but she
ignored me so I put my hand down after tossing my spent cigarette over my shoulder into the
bushes.

'Do you know much about her time there? And
your father? What of him?'

Thinking about Mama and Papa fighting made
my head hurt, and I had enough on my mind with
Marguerite. 'My father . . . he's . . . they are . . . '

'I'm sorry.' She looked up, smiling oddly while
examining my face. 'Too many questions?'

'Perhaps just a few.'

Mother hesitated, and I wondered if she
expected me to explain. Then she motioned at
the empty space next to me. 'Do you mind some
company?'

Before I could answer she had already made
use of the space next to me, her habit laid out like
a blanket, covering every limb. Her white wimple
and black veil rubbed up against each other, and it
sounded incredibly uncomfortable as we sat, not
talking. I caught myself leaning forward to catch a
glimpse of her natural hair while she adjusted her
veil. She looked at me, pausing, with fingers on

her headpiece, and my eyes went to the air.

'Now, Adèle.'

'Yes!' I sat board straight.

'I heard there is an issue between you and Marguerite.'

'What?' I gulped. 'You know?' *Mavis*.

Mother batted her eyes slowly, majestically, and they were beautiful, sea green eyes set wide on her face, which made it hard for me to gauge her feelings. 'We are human, after all,' she said, giving my knee a pat. 'Find a way, a path of compassion. Make amends with her. About her arrival. It's what God wants.'

'Amends?' My voice peaked.

She got up from the bench and picked one of the flowers growing between the cobblestones. 'An unexpected flower in an unexpected place.' She handed me the lighter, and the metal felt very warm from having been in her hand for so long. '*Au revoir*, Adèle.' She walked away twirling the flower under her nose.

My whole body collapsed onto the bench, nearly lying down, searching my pocket for a cigarette, but then decided I better not and took a moment to just breathe.

And breathe I did.

A workman's lorry in need of a new muffler rumbled past me on the dirt road and then stopped abruptly in front of the loading platform the sisters used for laundry drop-offs. I watched the driver as he unlatched the lorry's double doors. He looked strong and attractive from what I could tell, which caught my eye through the cracks of the bench.

Sister Mary-Francis rushed out of the laundry

in a quiet panic. He waved to shush her, and she covered her mouth, nodding. Together they rolled several laundry carts from the back of his lorry into the laundry room. Some of the carts looked empty, while others overflowed with soiled bed linens from hotels that couldn't afford, or find, soap to do their own laundry — something the sisters no doubt prepared for, having gone through a war once already.

I sat up slightly to get a better look, enthralled by the mundane acts of convent life. But then Marguerite came out of the laundry and I ducked. She stood next to the lorry's double doors, her hands resting impatiently on both hips, tapping her foot as if to hurry them and periodically glancing up into the sky, until Sister Mary-Francis rolled the last cart into the convent and shut the doors behind her.

And then there was Marguerite, practically alone, standing prim in her blue postulant's smock.

I bolted up, heart racing. *Now's the time.* I took a breath through my nose. 'Let this work,' I said, exhaling. 'Let this be it and done with.'

I started the short walk over, back straightening, but then stopped cold right next to the loading platform. Something wasn't right. Marguerite and the driver had hidden behind the lorry. There were no voices, no words of any kind.

All was quiet.

Moans and romantic gasps followed a thump against the lorry's passenger side door, and my heart practically stopped, watching Marguerite and the driver kissing each other passionately through the window on the other side. He cradled her face, her veil slipping from the pull of his hands as he worked his way from her mouth to her neck.

'Mother of Christ,' I said. 'You're in love with a man!'

They froze. Not a sound in the world could be heard. He peeped through the window, blurry-eyed with slobbery lips, and caught sight of me before they both raced to straighten themselves. He hopped back into his lorry and peeled off down the road, leaving me and Marguerite staring at each other through the dusty air.

5

The wave of relief I felt was indescribable — I wasn't going anywhere. A postulant in love with a man — grounds for dismissal Mavis had said. I popped a fresh cigarette into my mouth — my eyes set on Marguerite — and took several drawn-out pulls as I lit it.

'Nice day,' I said, closing the lighter with a click, and I imagined a thousand thoughts raced through her mind as I stood there, staring at her, a smouldering cigarette tight between my fingers. 'Isn't it, Marguerite?'

Her mouth pinched up like a drawstring bag, and I thought she was about to come after me, but then suddenly Claire came trooping around the corner with a handful of delinquents and interrupted us both.

'Afternoon crafts are over,' Claire announced, as the girls fell in line behind her. 'Mavis wants us to gather for Bible study.'

I took a breath — I hadn't even noticed I was holding it — and thought about how Marguerite treated me the first day we met, the way she looked at me in the square and that damn Bible of hers she brought with her on the train, pretending to be a saint. I pointed to Marguerite with my cigarette, and she snatched a switch from the ground.

Claire stumbled back, using a stiff arm to keep the other girls out of the way as Marguerite walked toward me. 'What's going on?' Claire said.

Wpssh! Marguerite whipped my knuckles with one very powerful swat. I bent over, cupping my hand as the cigarette slipped through my shaking fingers onto the ground. The little gasp that had come from my mouth turned into a breathless smile — the day I went back to Vichy would be because I decided to, not because of Marguerite.

Marguerite stormed back into the laundry room, kicking dirt up behind her with her shoes. The girls' mouths hung open, not sure what to make of Marguerite's devilish behaviour and then my smirking face.

Claire was the only one who had the nerve to ask. 'Mademoiselle?'

I lifted my head up, trying to appear serious. 'Don't smoke at the convent, girls.'

* * *

I skipped dinner service, stood in the corridor and listened to the nuns slurp watery noodle soup from wide spoons. Every now and then I'd catch a glimpse of the delinquents clearing trays or carrying soup tureens to and from the kitchen for the sisters. All I could think about was Marguerite. And that man. The way he touched her, with his mouth on her neck. I took a breath just thinking about it, loosening my collar. I'd never seen kissing like that before.

The more I thought about Marguerite, the more I thought she was a spy — a German mole, probably sent here to take notes on the sisters, maybe even turn them in. *I should have known she was German with those thick ankles and pointed eyes.*

53

Several times I took a step toward the dining room, but each time a restless simmer in my gut held me back. I needed to do something . . . but what? If I could sneak into Marguerite's chamber and go through her things, I bet I'd find something — something tangible to use against her. Evidence.

Mavis had been watching me through the gap in the door. I held my stomach, grimacing as if I had an ache, and she went back to eating. Claire had had enough of me standing in the corridor and used a tipped-over a tray as an excuse to leave the room for cleaning supplies and come talk to me.

'What's going on?' She stood a breath away from my face, eyes dilating.

'Nothing,' I said.

I wanted to blow her off, but started to think that perhaps I needed some help. She kept staring at me, her eyes shifting from one eye to the other. 'It's Marguerite. I know it.' Claire poked her head into the dining room. A row of black-veiled heads bobbed up and down from their soup bowls while the delinquents walked around and picked up their trays. She turned back toward me, satisfied nobody could hear us. 'It's more than the whipping — all the girls are talking about it. But they're a bunch of adolescents. Think you did something. I think it's the other way around.' Claire's brow furrowed as she cupped her shoulder with her hand. 'It's a feeling I have.'

'Christ, Claire. Again, with your shoulder?'

Her face scrunched when I said Christ's name, but I didn't apologize. I had a lot on my mind.

'You're saying there's nothing going on?'

I looked at her, thinking about what she'd say if I asked her to help me with Marguerite. I couldn't ask Mavis, nor would I want to. The other girls were too young. Claire was the oldest delinquent at the convent, and I had the distinct impression she craved a little excitement.

'All right, listen,' I said, pulling her in close. 'I need some help. I'm not sure how much time I have.'

She nibbled her fingernails. 'To do what?'

'I need access to Marguerite's chamber. At a time when I know she'll be occupied.'

'You want to get her back for whipping you?'

I wasn't about to tell Claire I thought Marguerite might be a spy. If I did, I'd have to confess what I'd seen in the crypt and she'd tell every one of the delinquents before breakfast.

'That's right. The whipping,' I said. 'I need to think of a good time. In the morning, during prayer?' Just as I said the words, I knew morning prayer wouldn't work because everyone would notice I wasn't there.

'What about vespers?' Claire said.

Vespers was an after-dinner prayer service only the nuns and postulants attended. They locked themselves in the nave, all very secretive, and chanted in Latin. It was perfect.

'I'll need a lookout.'

Claire nodded, excitement glinting like a firework in her eye.

★ ★ ★

55

The sisters' private chambers were in an area off-limits to the rest of us, through a set of thick wood doors and up a flight of steep stone stairs. The postulants were on the ground level, behind the staircase, in what I heard were much smaller rooms.

Claire and I watched Marguerite and the rest of the nuns file into the nave and shut the door behind them. I flicked my chin. 'This way.' Claire nodded, and we snuck down to the private entrance, tiptoeing past freshly lit candles hanging from wrought-iron sconces bolted into the wall. The sisters' chants spiralled hauntingly down the castle's stone corridors.

'*In adiutorium meum intende . . .*'

'This way,' I said, turning my head for one second, when Sister Mary-Francis and someone new passed by us, someone whose habit looked pieced together and a size too big.

'Adèle,' Sister Mary-Francis said, but then sounded much more suspicious. 'What are you doing out here?'

'Oh, uh . . . '

'We're going to the infirmary, Sister,' Claire piped up, and I looked at her. 'Mademoiselle has a stomach ache. I offered to walk her.' She smiled, and I looked at Sister Mary-Francis, slowly moving my arms to my waist.

'Oh?' the sister said. 'Are you sick? I noticed you weren't at dinner.'

'Uh, yes,' I said, holding my stomach. 'I'll be fine though.'

I tried not to stare, but I wanted to get a look at the new nun's eyes, see if she was the same woman

56

I saw in the old convent with the guns. My heart sped up, leaning in, and her eyes slowly lifted from the floor, but then more doors slammed shut down the way and the chants turned even more muffled. 'We better hurry!' Sister Mary-Francis said, and the pair rushed off down the corridor to vespers.

I watched them leave as Claire pushed me to move on. 'Come on,' Claire whispered, and once they were out of sight, I moved.

'What was that about?' Claire said.

'What?'

'You were staring,' she said, almost laughing. 'Like you had never seen a nun before.' She waved her hand around. 'Look where we are.'

'It was nothing,' I said, thinking about how it was even more imperative that I get to the bottom of Marguerite's story. 'Come on.' I grabbed her by the arm and walked to the end of the corridor where it opened into the foyer. 'Shush,' I said, and we listened for what was up ahead before blindly walking around the corner. All seemed quiet. Nothing out of the ordinary.

She pushed me with her knee. 'Let's go,' she said. 'They're all in vespers — '

'Shush!' I said, and I peeked around the corner, thinking Claire had to be right — we heard the drone of vespers, there was no mistaking that — but to our surprise not all the sisters had made it.

Sister Mary-Gertrude, a nun who was too old to do anything other than sit in a rocking chair, sat just in front of the main entrance to the private chambers. As upsetting as that was, it was seeing

Mavis pacing around with her hands on her head that surprised me.

'What's Mavis still doing here?' Claire whispered. 'That old nun would fall asleep in that chair if she'd leave.'

'I don't know . . .'

Mavis would only miss vespers if she was ill, as devout as she was, and not just for a little stomach ache — she'd have to be vomiting. Besides, she didn't have a chamber with the other postulants. Mavis slept in the delinquent corridor with us, in the basement under the convent's bell tower.

'Maybe she's on guard duty,' Claire said.

'Guard?' I looked at her. 'What is there to guard?'

'Their crucifixes,' Claire said.

'Gertrude is older than this castle. The sisters prop her up in the chair because they don't know what else to do with her.' Minutes passed, but still Mavis stayed put. 'This changes everything.'

Mavis licked her palms, getting ready to smooth them over her limp hair and Claire scowled. 'She's disgusting.'

'Shh.' I patted her hand, rethinking my plan. I had to get into Marguerite's room. But how? Mavis bent to one knee, meeting Gertrude at eye level, looking very absorbed. *Damn it. What will I do now?* I turned to leave but Claire tugged on my arm.

'Marguerite's room is on the ground floor,' she said, leaning into my ear. 'You can climb through the window.'

'The window?' I was shocked at first, thinking of her suggestion, climbing through the window like a child-thief. But did it matter how I got into her room if the results were the same? It was my only chance.

'Let's go.'

* * *

The sun had set behind the lush green hills that surrounded the convent. The delinquents' giddy laughs on the other side of the meadow settled over the convent's grounds as they picked wild flowers for breakfast service the next morning. The scent of lilac soap bubbled through the laundry doors.

Marguerite's chamber was the last window at the end of a very long stone wall shaded by a leafy tree. Instead of lead-lined glass panes like the rest of the nun's windows, Marguerite's window had glass planks that slid into moveable wood brackets, the kind I normally saw in the toilets.

I looked at Claire. 'Are you sure you want to help me?'

She nodded.

I carefully slid the planks out of the brackets and handed them to Claire. She bundled them in her arms before setting them on the ground, careful not to make any clinking noises. My heart raced once all the planks were removed and I could see into her room. I had to find something to expose Marguerite with and get her kicked out of the convent.

'What are you going to do in there?' Claire said. 'Smoke? You'll make her break out.' She laughed nervously thinking that was what I had planned.

59

'Yes! That's it.' I took a cigarette from my case and lit it quickly with my lighter. 'You know she's sensitive.' I hadn't planned to smoke, but it was a plausible revenge. I pointed to the window. 'Help me up.' She laced her fingers together, and with a little grunt and a moan, pushed me over the window ledge, sending me tumbling onto Marguerite's wood floor on the other side. I didn't expect such strength coming from her little arms, and lay on my back, wondering if the thud from landing on the floor was as loud as I thought it had been, before slowly moving to my feet.

Marguerite's room looked simple: a bed, mute coverings and a tiny crucifix hanging on the wall above her headboard. A modest chest of drawers made from bleached oak sat in the corner, an oval mirror centred on the top. Nothing looked out of the ordinary. In fact, aside from her pillow, which had the slightest impression of a head set into it, I would have thought the room was vacant.

'What are you looking for?' Claire asked, peeping over the window ledge.

I puffed hastily on my cigarette, eyes rolling over Marguerite's bare walls. 'Nothing.'

'What?' she said over the ledge.

'I don't know!'

Claire turned her back to the window while I examined Marguerite's chest of drawers. It was about the same size as that damn crate she lugged with her from the train. The knobs were shiny and made from some kind of ornamental metal. Odd, I thought, since nuns didn't like fancy things, but hardly the evidence I was looking for.

Inside she had a dozen or so neatly folded

60

postulant aprons and skirts separated into stacks. I ran my hands between the cottony layers and along the interior edges of the wood drawers. Nothing but a dried-up vanilla sachet that had lost its scent.

'Hurry up,' Claire said in a shouted whisper. She looked worried, shooting sharp looks over her shoulder. 'The sun's setting.' A shady darkness fell into the room as the sun completely disappeared behind the hills. 'She'll be coming back!'

I puffed more and more on my cigarette, frantically moving about Marguerite's room, thinking about how I was running out of time. Ash flew from my cigarette when I pulled back her bed quilt, yanking the sheets from the mattress like a mad dog. Nothing. Frustrated, I kicked the bed, and a piece of paper slipped through the metal bed frame and landed upright on the floor — a list, a long list.

I paused in shock, and then reached for it. The names of nearly every sister and delinquent at the convent written in ink and in sequential order. Beside each one was a star or a check-mark. Around my name was a dark circle that had been traced over so many times the paper had torn.

My mouth drew open, cigarette sticking to my lip, surprised by the amount of ink and the darkness of it around my name.

'Someone's coming,' Claire whispered through the window in a frantic, breathy shout.

The duelling clip of footsteps echoed down the corridor — *clip, clop, clip, clop . . .*

I gasped, looking at Marguerite's closed door, heart pounding.

'Hurry!' Claire said, and I heaved the mattress back onto its frame and spread the quilt into place faster than I had taken it off. I lunged for the window, but then realized I still had Marguerite's list in my hand. A key slipped into the door lock. I shoved the list back under the bedframe and dove head first out the window with my cigarette pinched between my lips. Just as my legs slipped over the ledge, Marguerite's door unlocked.

The door creaked open, and we heard the whisperings of two women in the corridor, chatting as if they were in no rush to come inside. We hurried to slide the planks back into the window brackets, their voices quieting just as we slid the last one into place. We froze, then the door swung wide open, and the room lit up with candlelight.

Claire and I dropped to the ground.

Footsteps trudged to the window, the end of my cigarette burning closer and closer to my lips, a ribbon of smoke teasing the hairs in my nose. With a flick of my tongue, I flipped the burning cigarette over into my mouth and clenched it in between my teeth. Then I prayed.

Please, God. Please . . .

Seconds passed as Claire and I crouched quietly in the dark space below the window, the ominous feeling of Marguerite's eyes hovering above us. An eerie pause followed as I felt her presence standing dangerously close to the window, followed by the clink of a hand touching the planks.

Claire squeezed my hand, harder and harder and harder until I thought it might split in two.

'Achoo!' Marguerite sneezed, and I closed my eyes, stuffing down a smoky cough.

Please . . . God . . .

Marguerite's fingers slipped from the planks, and she walked away from the window. Seconds felt like minutes, the ember burning ever so close to my tongue, until finally I heard the soft click of a shut door.

I spat the cigarette from my mouth, gasping for clean air. 'You can open your eyes now, Claire,' I said, coughing into my shoulder. 'She's gone.'

Claire whined like a caught little mouse.

'Claire?' I said, but she'd let go of my hand and run back into the convent.

6

I slept soundly, as soundly as one could in the dank, grey basement under the convent's bell tower, when I heard Marguerite's heavy, almost manly voice bark my name. 'Adèle!' She loomed over my cot, the shadowy outline of her postulant's veil hiding her face. Her breath seemed forced, laboured, as if it was hard for her to breathe. She tapped the soft part of my hand, in between my knuckles, where it was still tender from the lashing she gave me the day prior.

I propped myself up by the elbows and focused on her face, but all I could see was the collar of her white tunic and her pocketed blue skirt against the slate basement walls. She leaned into a shaft of sunlight that had just broken through the paned window-well. '*Regardez-moi!* Look at me!'

I sat bolt upright.

Marguerite's right cheek swelled like a balloon and her eyes shined pink like a rabbit's. Raised, red splotches trailed down her neck and then vanished underneath her collar. She swallowed, wincing as if her throat hurt as much as her face.

She threw a cigarette butt on my blanket. 'You left this outside my window.' After a brief pause, she smoothed her veil to her head, taking a breath. Her eyes fluttered vigorously, as if she had prayed for patience but it hadn't arrived. Seconds passed. Only a few seesawed squeaks could be heard from other girls' cots as they woke from the commotion.

Marguerite exhaled, and her nose tooted like a smashed trumpet, swelling faster than her cheek. Her face turned redder.

'Mother Superior wants you.' She yanked the wool blanket from my bed and threw it on the ground before walking out of the basement.

I fell backward onto my cot, bed linens twisted around my body, and thought about the severity of Marguerite's face. Some girls lay still under their covers, hiding. Others sat on the edge of their cots and bounced questions at me faster than I could answer them.

Claire put her hands to her forehead, mumbling to herself. Then she winced and massaged the bony part of her shoulder. 'My shoulder . . . it's aching.' There was a slight tremble in her voice.

'Again, with the shoulder?'

'It's a sign, mademoiselle.'

'A sign of what?'

'Expulsion,' she whispered.

Mavis sat up in her bed, a hand to her mouth, the sound of the word 'expulsion' filtering through the gaps of her fingers. She scrambled to her feet and took off for the sanctuary with her Bible, still dressed in her sleeping gown.

Claire stopped rubbing her shoulder to wrap both arms around her waist. 'What were we thinking?' She groaned as if she was getting sick, looking directly into my eyes. 'Her face, from the smoke. Don't you feel terrible?'

The room turned stone-cold quiet. Girls sat up, slouched, and then pulled their bed covers up to their necks. Others waited for me to say something, anything, with their mouths drawn open. I

65

thought about Marguerite's tryst with the deliveryman — sinner that she was — and the note I found under her bed — my name circled over and over again, a list of women she no doubt had it in for.

'No,' I said. 'Marguerite deserved what she got.'

Claire bit at her fingernails, chewing them like a dog. The convent was her only option, which I should have remembered before I asked her to get involved.

'Don't worry, Claire. I'm not going to mention your name.'

She looked relieved. I had manipulated Claire into helping me spy on Marguerite, and if I felt bad about anything, it was that I involved her in something she couldn't understand at her age.

'This is between me and Marguerite.'

★ ★ ★

Mother Superior's office was at the top of Chancery Tower, up a wide spiral staircase in the keep of the oldest part of the castle. The murmur of whispering voices rolled downward; lies, no doubt, Marguerite was spilling into Mother's ear. I collected myself on the landing, smoothing my hair into a messy bun, before setting my eyes upon Mother's office through the cracked doorway. A large mahogany desk covered in loose papers sat in the middle of the room, and full bookcases of various sizes lined every wall; which seemed incredibly cramped, not what I had expected in such a large castle with so many rooms to choose from.

Mother Superior gazed out an open window, her hands bracing the stones on each side. 'Take a seat, Adèle.' She spoke without turning around.

I walked inside, taking the chair next to Marguerite, smiling, expecting her to snarl, but her eyes were glued to a letter she had gripped in her hands. I thought up how I was going to tell Mother about Marguerite, how I saw her kissing the deliveryman, passionately, making love with her lips, when Mother turned away from the window.

'I know your secret.'

'Secret?' My hands flew to my chest. '*My* secret?'

She moved toward me, put her hand under my chin and looked into my eyes. 'I know about the man you had in the Vichy police. I know about Gérard.'

She let go of my chin, and my mouth dropped.

'There's a reason for everything,' she said, unpinning her black veil, 'and there's a reason God sent you here to us.' She'd placed her veil on the desk and pulled her white wimple over the top of her head, sending waves of blonde hair falling over her shoulders and down the back of her neck. 'It was me you were spying on in the crypt, and an associate of mine from the Résistance.'

'No — Mother!' I glanced at Marguerite, worried she had said and shown too much already in front of the imposter, jumping from my seat. 'There's something you must know.' I pointed a shaking finger at Marguerite. 'She's not who you think!'

'Sit now, Adèle,' Mother said. 'I know all about Marguerite, and she's well aware of what's happening in the crypt.'

67

Marguerite folded the letter up and put it on Mother's desk, and I slowly withdrew my pointed finger. 'You know about the deliveryman?' I asked Mother, and after she nodded, I sat down as asked. 'Is that why I'm here?' I swallowed. 'You think I was spying?'

'I know you weren't now,' Mother said. 'I realized that when I saw your cloisonné lighter yesterday.'

'My lighter?' They stared at me curiously while I felt blindly around for it in my pocket. 'It was Mama's.'

Mother smiled. 'I know.' She pulled a tiny box from her pocket and unwrapped it carefully, unfolding the layers of tissue paper until I saw what was inside. 'You see. I have one too.' A cloisonné lighter that looked just like mine only shiny; definitely never used.

'I don't understand.'

'The inscription,' she said, 'on the back.'

Mother squared her lighter with mine. The silver on Mama's lighter had dulled along with the enamel, but the engraving was a dead match: Women of the 1914 War. An inscription I had never seen before, now so visible. 'I was a nurse with your mother in Ypres during the war. The lighters were given to a select few by a special friend, now dead. After the war I joined the church and we lost touch. But we have a bond, which is why she wrote back so quickly.'

'You wrote to Mama? When?'

Mother rewrapped her lighter before tucking it back into her pocket. 'Last night. We passed messages through a courier.' She pointed to the letter Marguerite had been reading. 'Sister Mary-Gertrude left for Vichy just after vespers.'

I reached for the letter. 'She did?' I remembered Sister Gertrude sitting in her chair outside the nuns' private entrance. But I had to wonder how she made it to Vichy, much less out of that chair as old as she was.

Mother laughed. 'I know what you must think, but all the more reason to send her. Nobody suspects a woman of that age doing anything of importance, now do they?'

I read the letter feverishly. Mama addressed Mother Superior by her given name, Elizabeth, and there was an underlining familiarity in her tone. She told Mother Superior about Gérard and of our politics. *We are Gaullists*, she wrote, the words written in ink with a steady hand.

It was the first time Mama referred to us outright as supporters of Charles de Gaulle, Pétain's rival and leader of the Free French.

'I'm glad she gave you the lighter, Adèle. It means a great deal and says quite a lot about your character. Your mother wouldn't have given it to you if she thought you weren't worthy. The inscription, its meaning, far outweighs the lighter's function.'

Mama didn't talk much about her time as a nurse or the 1914 war. Papa even less, but it wasn't uncommon for veterans to keep their memories to themselves. She certainly never mentioned the lighter's significance when she gave it to me. 'She handed it to me as I rushed out the door. An afterthought.'

Mother shook her head. 'Even after all these

years, I know nothing with Pauline is ever an after-thought. And if you're honest with yourself you'd realize it too. What you did was very brave, Adèle. Leaving a man like Gérard. Leaving Vichy. She wrote about your father and sister — you were in a very difficult position.'

Marguerite had stood from her chair and rested her backside against Mother's desk. Her eyes skirted over me while Mother talked, which made my back straighten. The white had returned to her skin, and her cheek seemed less puffy, one hand patting it down like a pillow.

'I've been at this convent for over ten years,' Mother said. 'I'm devoted to Christ first and foremost. Secondly, I'm devoted to France and the sanctity of life. This government knows nothing about these things. With the decrees against the Jews, the laws in Germany becoming part of French policy, dictated by our very own Marshal — it's revolting.' Mother clasped her hands together and looked up at the ceiling, talking directly to God, before crossing her chest with the sign of the divinity. 'You know about the statutes on the Jews, don't you, Adèle? In Vichy, Lyon . . . arresting foreign-born Jews inside our borders, the ones who escaped here to receive France's protection are now being sent back and straight to a camp — some never to return.'

'I know about the laws. Gérard — he has arrested many. That's one of the reasons I wouldn't marry him.'

Mother nodded, looking at us both. 'Now, let's address what's going on between you two.' Mother glanced at Marguerite and then back to me. 'First impressions can be fooling. Can't they, ladies?'

Marguerite pinched the bodice of her postulant dress. 'I'm not a postulant. I'm a résistant, a member of many groups, most recently with the *Francs-Tireurs*,' she said, and air blew from my mouth.

The Francs-Tireurs.

She waited for a reaction, and rightfully so — the Francs-Tireurs were known to be as brutal as the Nazis when protecting France, sharpshooters who not only knew how to find guns — steal guns — but also how to use them. All I could do was nod, watching her blot the corner of her watering eye. I suddenly felt very lucky she had only got me with a switch. 'Sorry about your face.'

Marguerite raised her eyebrows, nodding slightly. 'Yes well, that is over. Now — ' she looked at Mother and then to me ' — we must know, will you help us? Join the French Résistance?'

My heart skipped. 'Me — the Résistance?' They watched me as I got up from my chair and stood for a second. 'I didn't expect this.' I put my hands on the window stones; much like Mother had done earlier, and looked out through the trees.

'Help us get France back,' Mother said. 'The life you had before.' She moved closer, about to touch my shoulder, but then thought better of it.

'Give her a moment,' Marguerite said, and Mother withdrew her hand.

'Before,' I breathed, and I was thrown into a forgotten memory, remembering Mama walking through the garden with Papa, pointing to the herbs she'd grown near her laundry lines, and Charlotte and me pan-frying leeks in vanilla oil.

71

Field hands rotated barrels in the barrel cellar with the nutty air of summer breezing in the air. Mama held on to Papa's arm, calling to us from outside. 'Is lunch ready?' They went back to talking, pointing to the herbs.

'Just a moment, Mama,' Charlotte answered, but then whispered to me. 'Have some more wine first.' She topped off my glass with a forgotten bottle of Papa's pinot.

I giggled. 'Stop there,' I said, but gladly drank what she'd poured me, stirring the leeks, browning them just so, popping in the pan.

Charlotte cut that day's bread into tiny rounds and arranged them on a painted plate with crudités and sliced lemons. 'And the tomatoes,' she said, looking over the counter, and I pointed to the ones I'd picked that morning with the vines still attached. 'Let's go,' she said, and we clinked glasses, downing what was left.

I scooped the leeks out of the frying pan and set them in a dish, drizzling them with oil. 'Anything we're missing?' I said, wiping my hands on my apron 'Oh, wait,' I said, and I drank what was left in the bottle. One last sip, and laughed when I caught Charlotte watching me with a strange face.

'Stop giggling, Adèle, I swear you're going to be the death of us,' Charlotte said. 'They'll know we've been drinking.'

'They'll know,' I said, and I motioned to the window as Papa smelled the rosemary in Mama's hand. 'Look at our parents, Charlotte.' I sighed.

We watched them kiss. 'Girls?' Mama said, and we ducked.

'Coming!' we both answered back, followed by more giggling.

72

We walked outside, to the long oak table where Mama and Papa had already sat down, and ate lunch together in a pleasant shade.

'Adèle?'

I turned around, only to see them both staring at me, the last memory of my family together, fading.

'What do I have to do?'

Mother smiled, looking relieved and happy at the same time. 'You'll be Marguerite's partner for now. Here at the convent.' A commotion outside in the courtyard stole Mother's attention: people talking, some shouting, coupled with the purr of a car. She quickly smoothed her hair behind her ears and then slipped her wimple back over her head.

'Mother,' I said, and she glanced up. 'Who was the other woman . . . the one I saw in the crypt with you?'

'She's the leader — goes by the name Hedgehog.'

'Hedgehog?'

She smiled. 'In the beginning we used numbers, but the Germans started to figure those out so we changed our call signs to the names of animals.'

Sister Mary-Francis burst through the door just as she pinned her veil into place. 'They're here, Mother,' she said, panicky. 'They just pulled up!'

The bell tower chimed, announcing morning prayer.

'I'll be right down.' Mother put a hand on Marguerite's shoulder. 'Adèle isn't the mole, but someone is. We've got to find out who she is before it's too late.'

73

'So, there is a spy?' I asked.

'Someone living among us. Our situation is dire.' Mother looked at us both. 'I suggest you get to know each other. You may need one another someday, when you least expect it.' Mother reached for the Bible she normally carried with her during her walks. 'Now, I must go. Remember, I have a convent to run too.'

'Wait,' I said, thinking we must have a name, just like all the famous Résistance groups. 'You said group. Do we have a name?'

Mother stopped in the doorframe, her heavy black habit covering every bit of her body, and looked over her shoulder. 'The Reich has named us Noah's Ark, but we call ourselves the Alliance.'

★ ★ ★

Marguerite burned the letter Mama wrote, dropping it into a golden urn and loosely closing the lid. The Marguerite I thought I knew was gone, and in her place was someone different. It felt odd, to say the least. 'Perhaps we should start over.' I held my hand out for a shake. 'As if we just met.'

She took my hand, but instead of shaking it she pulled me in close. 'Wait for my word. Stay quiet. The less others know about you the better. Make up a lie about where you're from if you must. If someone finds out you're a résistant they will go to where you live and kill your family just to get to you.' Marguerite took a long pause before continuing, listening to Mother's voice lifting from the ground below as she greeted her guests outside. 'Is that going to be a problem? There's no place

74

for weaklings in the Résistance, Adèle.'

'I understand,' I said, and she let go of my hand. 'And I can make up some lies.' Then I wondered with all the guns around, if she'd give me one. 'Will I have to carry a gun?'

She laughed. 'I'm not giving you a gun.' She paused. 'Do you know how to shoot one?'

'No,' I said, and she shook her head.

'I'm not giving you a gun unless you already know how to shoot,' she said. 'Besides, we need you for surveillance. Not to shoot people.'

She fingered a mix of fresh and wilted flowers on Mother's desk. 'I will sift out this mole,' she said as petals fell through her fingers. 'If it's the last thing I do.'

'Do you have an idea of who it is?' I thought about the list I'd found under her bed. My name was the only one with a circle around it. 'Now that you know it isn't me.'

Marguerite stopped fiddling with the flowers. 'It could be anyone. Even one of the girls.'

'The girls?' I shouted though I didn't mean to.

'Shh.' Marguerite put a finger to her mouth and a hand over mine. 'Be quiet!'

'But they're so young,' I whispered.

'Before I came here, I helped a twelve-year-old strap dynamite to her chest. This war knows no age.' Marguerite walked over to the window. The party Mother had been talking to had gotten back into their cars and sped down the road that led away from the convent. Marguerite watched them until they disappeared.

I paced in a circle, wondering who at the convent had the balls, as Mama would say, to spy on the sisters. Someone who didn't want to stand out, perhaps. There were a pair of cousins who looked rather devious, and then there was . . .

'Watch the girls carefully,' Marguerite said. 'We'll meet in private and compare notes. I'll make arrangements. As for now, they'll have to believe our relationship is still contentious.' Marguerite ran a finger along her jawline where she still had a few pink bumps. 'There's no escaping that fact.'

'Right,' I said. 'The girls think I came up here to get expelled from the convent.'

'Do they know you broke into my chamber?'

'Some do, but they think I was retaliating for the whipping you gave me. Truth was, I was afraid you'd cause trouble for me, get me kicked out. My goal was to find something in your room to use against you, when the time came. Something . . . to go along with what I saw near the laundry.'

I blushed the moment I thought about her and that man's kisses. I wasn't going to ask her who he was outright, but I wanted to, and I could tell by the look on her face she knew I was curious. I had never seen so much passion before.

'I see.' She looked away. 'Well, you can't leave here without a proper punishment. If you do the girls will wonder why.' Her eyes skirted over the things in Mother's office, over the bookcases and along the walls as she picked some things up and then set them back down.

As much as I hated to admit it, she was right about the punishment. 'What are you thinking?' I expected her to say I'd have to do lavatory duty for the week.

76

Marguerite walked to Mother's coat closet and grabbed a shiny brass hanger that wasn't being used. She turned on her heel, slapping the hanger into the palm of her hand as if she was about to whack something good — a book, a chair — I didn't know what.

Then she looked at me.

7

My hands curled up in to my chest, wearing them like a vest. 'No!' I said, but Marguerite shook her head and walked slowly toward me.

'The girls will have a tough time believing you didn't get expelled as it is. At the very least they'll expect some whipped knuckles.' She slapped that damn hanger into her palm.

I took a deep breath, wondering what Papa would think if he knew what I had become: a résistant, about to let a woman whip my hand with a hanger. Mama would wonder why I let her do it when I had a perfectly good arm to do it myself, especially after Marguerite had already swatted me with a switch.

I snatched the hanger away from Marguerite. 'I'll do it.'

Marguerite folded her arms, watching me as I drew the hanger high into the air. I winced, pausing, before whacking my hand once. '*Ouch!*' I cried, doing a little hop, and Marguerite held in a laugh.

She found a bandage in one of Mother's desk drawers. 'Here,' Marguerite said, hiding a smile. 'Now, you better get back to the girls.'

She saw me to the bottom of the stairs, but then disappeared down a dark corridor without saying goodbye. I walked back to the basement. A buzzing silence swept through the room. Claire kept her head down, turning slowly away from me as

78

I shuffled to my cot. Others made quick glances at my bandaged hand before making busy work, tucking in bed linens and gathering up laundry. I hissed in pain for effect.

My bed had been made, the wool blanket Marguerite had thrown on the floor tucked tight under the cot's thin mattress.

Mavis sat on her bed with her Bible placed squarely in her lap.

'Can you look after the girls today?' I said.

She took a hard look at my bandaged hand before nodding.

I fell asleep after Mavis gathered up the girls and left. Thunder rolling over the meadow behind the castle woke me in the afternoon, and rain, lots of it, some spitting through an open window. I started to worry about the delinquents out in such a storm when a handful of them rushed into the room giggling, chatting about the rain, their feet sloshing around in their wet summer shoes.

Mavis herded them from behind, her voice barely able to rise above theirs, telling them to gather their journals and reflect on the messages God had given them throughout the day. Claire knelt next to my cot and whispered softly.

'How are you?'

'Good,' I said. 'Why?'

She looked at my hand, eyebrows raised. 'Because of what happened with *Marguerite*.'

'I'm fine,' I said, though it did hurt. 'May take a few days to heal.'

'You didn't get expelled. I'm glad.' Claire smiled.

'Just punished,' I said.

79

'I was worried sick, wondering what was going on in Mother's office. Then when you came back . . . well . . . I'm just going to say it. I'm sorry for being aloof. I thought I was next.'

'I told you before, Claire. This is between me and Marguerite. You're safe.'

Claire sighed, lowering her head. 'I can't go back home. My father's in prison somewhere, and my mother — '

'I know,' I said. 'Don't worry. It's over.'

With that, Claire popped up with a smile and sat next to me. 'It sure was fun, though. Breaking into her chamber. I haven't felt that kind of excitement in a long time.'

'I thought you were scared?'

'I was!' she said. 'That's what made it so thrilling.' She bounced on the edge of my cot. 'Let's play a game!' She smoothed her wet hair over one shoulder and played with the drippy ends. 'It's raining out — what else can we do? I mean, other than *pray*.'

'No game,' I said. 'I'm not in the mood.'

Claire patted my shoulder, her lips slimmed into a thin, apologetic smile. 'I understand.' Then she rushed to the opposite side of the room and joined two other girls gathered around a table dealing cards to each other.

Mavis sat on her cot, her hair strung across her face in wet strands, ringing out her wet postulant's veil. She seemed out of breath, and her eyes had lost their glow. I asked her if she was all right, and she fell backward onto her cot and lay there like a slug. 'These girls are a handful.'

I smiled, watching and listening to them. 'I

80

suppose they're better than children. Toddlers, that sort of thing.'

Mavis used her elbows to prop herself up, looking very confused. 'Do you have children?'

I laughed. 'What would make you think that?'

'I'm not sure. You've talked about men before . . . ' Her eyes rolled to the back of her head, and she collapsed onto her cot again. 'I must have misunderstood you.' The rain had picked up and sounded like a million tree frogs jumping on the cobblestones outside. 'Children are a blessing,' she breathed from her pillow.

Charlotte. I sighed. She must be close to having her baby, if she hadn't delivered already. I wondered what she'd say if she knew I had joined the Résistance — she wouldn't like it, supporting Pétain as much as Papa, but still, I had to wonder what she'd think about me being part of a group who did powerful things.

Mavis sat up again, giving me a very strange look.

'What?'

'I heard you sigh.'

'Oh, that,' I said. 'I'm just thinking about my sister,' I said, but then caught myself from elaborating further. I smiled.

'Mmm,' Mavis said, lips pressed.

The girls danced around in circles with locked arms, giggling, slapping their wet braids on each other as if they were towels from the bath. Sister Mary-Francis brought in a tray of kettles filled to the brim with steaming hot consommé, which warmed the room with humidity. Mavis and I moved in close, joining a handful of girls who had

81

poured the soup into chipped porcelain mugs that looked more like bowls. Claire, seeing us gathered in a circle sipping something hot, put down her cards mid-hand and joined us.

Mavis's slurp sounded like her voice, and I kept glancing at her to see if she was talking until finally, she did. 'We never see rain like this in Aix.'

'Is that where you're from?' I said.

She nodded, licking her lips. 'Where are you from, Adèle?'

'Yes, where are you from?' Claire said, followed by another girl, and when I paused, several more girls joined in. 'Tell us! Tell us!'

I gulped a mouthful of consommé. Our conversation happened so quickly, so easily, and I wasn't prepared to answer such details. Marguerite had warned me not to say too much about where I was from, who I was, and I had already talked about having a sister. I slurped more consommé to buy some time, but spilled some on my dress from a sudden shake of my hands.

I shot up. 'Damn!'

Mavis laughed softly. 'That doesn't sound like a good place.'

The girls giggled when Mavis joked. I sighed, setting my mug down, hoping that would be the end of Mavis's questions, but she pressed on.

'Are you from Lyon, Adèle?'

I patted my dress dry. 'Paris,' I blurted, and as soon as I said where my story fell into place — Mama spent her summers on a farm just north of Paris when she was a girl; that place was as good as any. 'A village on the outskirts. I could tell you the name, but you wouldn't know it. Lots

82

of cows . . . dairy farms.'

Mavis blew into her mug. 'Paris,' she said to herself. 'Dairy.'

'Well, where is everyone else from?' I wanted to get the attention off me, and pointed to each girl with my eyes, but nobody seemed interested enough to answer, except Victoria, the girl with the chicken legs and ginger hair, who sat up just slightly and moved the mug away from her mouth.

'I'm from Colmar.'

All conversation stopped. Victoria looked around. Claire stood up. Girls who had been sipping consommé set down their mugs; others sat still, everyone suddenly very interested. Colmar was a French border city in the Occupied Zone with a long history of having more Germans in it than French. And although we didn't talk about it, nobody wanted to be friends with a German, even a mixed one.

'What's wrong?' Victoria said.

'Are you German?' Claire asked.

'Claire!' I shouted.

Victoria squinted. 'How dare you!' she said to Claire.

'You're from Colmar,' Claire said. 'What else am I to think?'

An eerie stillness hung in the room. Rain ticked the ground outside and against the windowpane. Our eyes swung like pendulums between Claire and Victoria, watching them as they stared at each other in utter silence.

'You. Think. Nothing.' Victoria's lips thinned.

'Girls,' Mavis said in her squeaky little voice. 'We're all in this together. God's work, in God's

83

house.' She smiled, and a twinkle set deep in her eyes lit up the dark, dank room as if they were lanterns, but none of the girls were paying attention to notice.

'Listen to Mavis, girls,' I said. 'Let's not talk about the war, the Germans. The convent is too nice and good to bring up such terrible things.'

Nods and a few noises came from the girls, but Victoria and Claire remained locked on each other in a blink-less stare. Victoria's hands curled into balls, and then in one quick motion she jumped from her seat and lunged at Claire. Girls shrieked, hands to their cheeks, scattering in every direction while I held Victoria back, keeping her from hitting Claire with one of her white-hot fists. Mugs rolled around on the ground, clinking and clanking against each other, spilling the girls' consommé on the floor. Claire lay on her back, her hands and feet searching the ground for leverage, her face stretching like dough.

'Victoria!' I yelled, and she froze, her breath rumbling through her nose and throat like a muffler on a banged-up car. 'This is not the answer.' I couldn't remember why Victoria had come to rehabilitation, but I guessed it had something to do with crime and penitence by the look in her eye and the strength in her lean, muscly arms.

Sister Mary-Francis stood near the stairwell against the stone wall watching the scene unfold, her black habit camouflaging her body against the dark stones. I tried not to look at her and kept my eyes on the girls, as distracting as her willingness to do nothing seemed.

'We've all suffered in this war. And those

sufferings most likely played a part in what brought you here.' I slowly pulled my stiff arm away from Victoria's chest, just to see if she'd back off from Claire on her own. 'Bashing Claire's face in isn't a remedy to heal old wounds.'

Victoria's shoulders relaxed and her breathing calmed. Then she burst into tears. I patted her on the back, and she latched on to me much like a young child would. Claire sat down on someone else's cot, the terror in her face giving way to relief, before curling up into a ball and wrapping herself up in blankets.

'We're all here for different reasons,' I announced, 'and from different places.'

'Why are you here?' Victoria asked between sobs. 'You're not taking vows like the postulants.'

Mavis bobbed up from the floor, sopping up spilt consommé with linens from the closet, as if trying to listen to what I'd say. I felt a shiver; suddenly everyone in the convent looked and sounded suspicious, even the girls who'd retired to writing in their journals.

'Adèle?' Sister Mary-Francis stepped into the light. 'Would you help me?'

Victoria got up to brush her wet hair out with a wooden comb while I piled dirty mugs and kettles onto the sister's tray. 'Thank you, Adèle,' she said, and I followed her up the narrow stairwell to the kitchen, carrying the tray.

'You handled that argument beautifully,' she said.

'Argument? Victoria had her fists clenched, Sister.'

She stopped under one of the wrought-iron

85

sconces bolted into the stone wall, its drippy, low-burning candle flickering yellowed light onto our faces. 'Fight, I should say. At any rate, you handled the situation. You're very good with them, Adèle.'

'Thank you, Sister.'

'I can take things from here.' She slipped a piece of paper into my hand as she took the tray.

'Sister?' I said, but she had turned and charged up the stairs.

The candle on the wall crackled. A message. I unfolded it quickly in the passageway. *Meet at lights out, south stairs.* Before I could think, I heard a noise down below — a scuffling of shoes against the cold stone steps.

'Hallo?' A moment passed in complete silence before I heard the panicked traipse of footsteps retreating down the stairs. 'Who's there?' The door closed below. 'Hallo?'

8

I dunked the note into a pool of hot candle wax and ran downstairs. I fixed my hair moments before opening the door, tucking loose strands back into the bun at the base of my head. Victoria was still gazing at her freckly face in the mirror, humming a strange tune and shaking water from her comb. Her eyes shifted to mine when I paused in the doorway.

I flashed a quick smile. Mavis sat on her cot reading her Bible and Claire was still curled up on her bed. 'Was that you I heard on the stairs?' I said to Victoria, but she had gone back to combing her hair. 'Victoria?' I said, and she looked at me. 'Was it you?'

'What's that, mademoiselle?'

Hearing Victoria's voice, Mavis had looked up and so had Claire. Then another girl from across the room stood up.

'Nothing,' I said, my voice catching. 'Never mind.'

After dinner, I ordered the girls to bed early if only because I was nervous about the late-night meeting. 'Lights out,' I said, clapping at them.

Victoria watched Claire from her cot, eating tree nuts she'd gathered from the garden the day before. Mavis watched Claire, and Claire looked at me, the crack and snap of nuts grinding between Victoria's teeth.

'Lights out means no eating,' I said to her, and

she stuffed her nuts away and flopped onto her pillow.

'Finally!' Claire said, and Victoria shot up, popping a nut in her mouth and chomping much louder than anyone ever should.

'Enough!' I said, 'Mother will have both of you on toilet duty as it is. You want there to be more? Look at my hand, girls!' I said, and that seemed to end it.

My mind was a flurry, lying in bed waiting for the girls to fall asleep, wondering what secret kind of meeting Marguerite had planned. Then somewhere in between the fantastical thoughts of Marguerite giving me a gun, and thinking about Mother's gorgeous long, blonde hair, I fell asleep.

Marguerite pounced on me in the dark covering my mouth, and my heart leapt from my chest. 'You fell asleep,' she hissed. 'Get up!'

I rolled out of bed, and we snuck down the corridors through the empty, dark convent, and all the way to the south stairs. She stopped at a door I thought was a closet. 'What are we doing?' I whispered, and she opened the door. Though instead of opening to a closet, the door opened to another staircase, one that went down and down and down. Flickering light shone at the bottom. Marguerite pointed, and I did what she asked.

The room was small and damp and smelled like the sewer. More like a prison nobody used, or had forgotten about, with two spindly chairs, a table with some metal instruments on it, and candles. Lots and lots of candles.

Marguerite followed me downstairs after locking the door behind her.

'Smells awful in here,' I said, plugging my nose. 'Worse than the toilets.'

'You failed,' Marguerite said. She walked to the table and picked through the metal instruments. 'I asked you to meet me at lights out, yet you didn't show up.'

'I didn't mean to,' I said.

'Tell that to someone when it counts.'

The longer she stood at the table, picking through the instruments, the more I realized she had something serious planned, something other than seeing if I'd make the rendezvous on time. I held my hand, tightening the bandage. 'What are you going to do to me?'

She looked over her shoulder, smiling. 'Nothing.'

I laughed in jest. 'I don't believe you.'

I noticed black tally marks on the stone wall, flickering under some candlelight. 'What are those for?' I said, pointing to the wall.

'What do you think they're for?' she said, and I walked closer.

'I don't know,' I said, shrugging. 'Numbers.'

'Hmm.' She went back to the metal instruments, but then picked up two pieces of paper and a pencil.

'You're not going to tell me?' I said, and she shook her head. There was a bottle of liquor on the table too, which I hoped to God wasn't for sterilizing. 'What about the scotch?'

'That's for after,' she said. 'You'll want a drink when this is over.'

I exhaled, very much relieved and she laughed.

'Did you think — ' She smiled. 'I'm not going

to do anything permanent,' she said, and my brow furrowed. 'Adèle, this is your training. A series of tests. You failed the first one. Don't let that happen again.' She pointed to the chair. 'Now, let's get started.'

She handed me a paper with three letter groupings strung out like sentences, but they were just letters. No words. I looked up from the paper. 'This is what you woke me up for?'

'You're good as dead if you don't learn some skills, fast,' Marguerite said. 'Be glad I'm taking the time. I never had training.' She pointed at the paper. 'These are the codes we're going to use. Each grouping stands for a commonly used word. You need to memorize them. Meet, leave, drop, hide, help . . . '

I counted the groupings as she talked. 'There must be fifty,' I said, looking up.

'Be glad it's not a hundred.' Marguerite turned back around and picked through the metal instruments when I laughed.

'All of them . . . Tonight?' I said, and she looked over her shoulder at me.

'Tonight.' Marguerite handed me the key, the other piece of paper in her hand.

I sighed heavily. 'Give me the pencil,' I said, and I got to work memorizing the codes, writing them down, only to erase what I'd wrote and start over, flipping the paper front to back, over and over. After an hour or two she thought I was ready, and we practised writing messages to each other.

She pushed the metal instruments aside and slid a piece of paper to me on the table, message side down. 'No cheating,' she said.

I flipped the paper over and read the message. By now, I knew these codes. At least I thought I did. My heart raced the longer Marguerite stared at me, waiting for me to figure out her message. 'You're taking too long,' she said, and I groaned.

'Give me a second.' The candles flickered very low to the melted wax and my eyes felt strained, and tired. Oh, so tired. 'Meet at noon,' I said, and she snatched the paper from my hand.

'Wrong,' she said, and I threw my head to the table. 'Dammit, Adèle, you have to learn these. We've been down here for hours.'

'I do know them,' I said. 'I do. I'm tired. All right? That's all. When it counts, I'll get it right.' My eyes closed and then my body jerked from having a nod.

'Get up!' she said, and she lifted me by the arm-pits.

'Stop it,' I said, swatting at her. 'I can stand by myself.'

'Well then do it,' she said, and she walked me through some sensory techniques to stay awake, which I had to admit worked. 'Your ears,' she said. 'Feel that?'

I rubbed my ears, and was surprised to feel a little more awake. 'Strange,' I said. 'I never knew. Are you going to tell me what those instruments are for now?' I said, pointing with my eyes.

'They're to scare you,' she said.

'What?' I said, and she laughed.

'Like I said, I'm not going to do anything permanent.'

I picked through them myself, three pointy ones, sharp enough to be knives, or at least take

91

the place of one. Marguerite moved the chairs together and we sat in them side-by-side. 'If you're ever interrogated, they might sit you next to someone, someone moaning or crying, someone who will get you to talk. Either out of pity or fright. Never look at them. Whatever you do, don't look. It's what they want. And your mind can't erase what you've seen. It will make you weaker.'

'All right,' I said, looking at her, and she yelled at me.

'Adèle!'

I looked away, wincing. 'Sorry.'

She got up in a huff. 'It was a simple request. Don't look.'

'Have you been interrogated before?' I said, and Marguerite stared at the wall, looking very distant, and my stomach sank thinking she'd been questioned by the police or a German. My hands twisted in my lap, watching her. 'Have you?'

She turned around sharply. 'Some résistants will never get interrogated,' she said. 'It's best to prepare. My work is different than what we're asking you to do.'

I felt better. Best to prepare. 'What's that wood barrel for?' I said, but she only glanced fleetingly at the floor. 'Can you at least tell me what time it is?'

Marguerite picked up one of the metal instruments, waving it in the air, pointy side up. 'Are you afraid of this?'

'Well, no, you've already told me — '

She lunged at me, pointing it at my eyes.

'Ack!' I threw my hands up and she stopped a mere breath away from my face. 'Christ,

Marguerite. What the hell are you doing?' My heart thrummed, pulse thumping in my ears. I clutched my chest.

'Were you afraid that time?' she said, and I nodded. 'Heart beating rapidly? Talk backward from ten to one and think of the sun and lying in long grass,' she said, but I was too busy clutching my chest and breathing like a dog.

'Do it!' she snapped, and I closed my eyes, counting backward and thinking about the grass. 'Is it working?'

I shook my head.

'Think about where you're from. The long grasses in the field, in the vineyard when the sun's out. Maybe you've run through them when the sun rises or lain in them when it sets . . .'

I thought about Charlotte and me running down the hill behind the chateau, me chasing her with the sun on our calves and her dress kicking up behind her legs. Both of us giggling.

'Did it work?' she said, and I opened my eyes, feeling my bare skin under my sleeping gown.

'I don't know . . .'

'Use the counting technique when you feel your heart rate jump,' she said. 'When you're scared and you need to be in control. Germans are notorious for knowing when a person's nervous. The more you practise relaxing the better you'll get at it. You won't be able to close your eyes all the time. And don't forget to breathe. I taught myself that trick. I wish I'd known it when it counted.'

'Did something happen?' I said, but Marguerite turned away to pull a barrel out from behind the table. I was surprised to see it was full of water.

She flicked some on my face.

'It's cold!' I said, cowering.

She laughed. 'Step in.'

'What?' I said. 'In there?'

She motioned with her eyes for me to get in, and I took off my socks. 'Damn you, Marguerite,' I mumbled. 'This isn't training. You're just being mean,' I said, and she shook her head.

I got in one foot at a time. And it wasn't just cold. It was damn cold. Ice cold. 'How long,' I said, shivering, 'do I have to stay in here?'

'Ten minutes.' She looked at her watch, and I stared at the wall.

'Did you have to do this?' I said, and she shook her head, looking at her watch.

'I told you I never received any training,' she said.

'Then why do I — ' I groaned.

'Almost done.' She smiled like she was enjoying my suffering. 'Look at the wall. Focus on it,' she said, and my lips pinched up, staring at the wall, but still talking to her.

'Is it time for that drink?' I said.

'Time's up!' she said, and I jumped from the barrel only to fall on the floor with numb feet.

She laughed, grabbing the bottle. 'Come on.'

She gave me a blanket for my feet, and we sat down on the stone floor with our backs against the wall because the last thing I wanted to do was sit in that chair one more second. The liquor was warm and strong and burned my throat. 'Scotch,' I said, feeling the bite of it on my tongue. 'Where'd you get scotch?'

'You ask a lot of questions,' she said. 'Just enjoy

it.'

'Did someone give it to you?' I said.

'Mother Superior,' she said, and my mouth gaped open for the second time that night.

'No,' I breathed, but she nodded, and we shared it, taking swigs straight from the bottle.

'You know what this needs?' I said, as she took a drink. 'Something sweet. Crumbling cinnamon bread or I know —'

'Candied almonds,' we both said, and then laughed.

'Yes,' I said, and she handed me the bottle. 'Sugary and sweet, a touch of cinnamon. The market in Vichy has the best ones. Up from the south, in Marseille.'

'I haven't eaten those in so long,' Marguerite said. 'And the soup here is absolutely revolting,' she said, and I burst out laughing. 'I told them it was fine, but it's one step above terrible. The almonds though. I do miss those. They're my fiancé's favourite too.'

A quiet moment passed between us after she mentioned a fiancé. I could only imagine he was the man I saw her kissing near the laundry.

'He's handsome,' I said, and she looked at me. 'The man you were kissing . . .'

She blushed, and I never thought I'd ever see Marguerite blush. 'His name's Philip.' She reached down the front of her postulant smock and pulled out a silver locket. 'He's a patriot,' she said, opening it so I could see the photos stuck inside the two halves. One of her and one of him. 'It's by luck I get to see him so often.'

'Lucky to see him, yes,' I said, 'but also because

95

you found love.'

'Yes,' she said. 'Love in the Résistance.' She gazed at the photos, smiling. 'He is handsome, isn't he?'

I was the one who blushed this time, thinking about them kissing, and she slid the locket back under her collar, passing me the bottle. I took another swig, pointing at the wall as the candlelight flickered. 'Are you going to tell me what those are?'

'The tally marks?' she said, and I nodded. 'I have no idea.' She patted my leg. 'Now, time to get back to work. It's near morning, and we have another day to live.'

She held out her hand to help me up, and I took it.

* * *

I stumbled back into delinquent corridor and fell face first onto my cot in the dark. I woke to Mavis poking me in the back of the head. And when I looked up, a handful of girls circled around, watching me struggle to open my eyes. 'What?'

'It's morning, Adèle,' Mavis squeaked, but I'd nodded off. 'Adèle?' she said, and my head lifted again.

'What?' I said, eyes still closed.

'Morning,' she whispered.

'She can't hear you,' Claire said, moving closer. 'It's morning,' she yelled very near my ear and I bolted up.

'Christ!' I said. 'Why'd you do that?'

Several girls covered their mouths, while I shook

96

my head awake, replaying the night in my mind. *Marguerite. Codes. Scotch.* I rubbed my ears, and my eyes widened just a hair.

'She cursed,' someone said, followed by many whispers. 'She slept through the morning bells.'

'Sorry girls,' I said. 'I'll pay for that later at Confession.' My eyes closed briefly, and I rubbed my ears a little more, which got me to stand.

'You've already missed morning prayer,' Mavis said. 'You don't want to miss crafts too. The sisters sold your last painting for five kilograms of winter coal.'

I yawned. 'They did?' I rubbed my ears. 'That's nice. Such an ugly painting too.'

The girls had gathered by the door, waiting to be led outside where we'd make our way to the conservatory. 'Are you going to lead the girls?' Mavis said.

I yawned again, this time closing my eyes. 'I'll be there. Go ahead without me.' I waved for her to leave. 'I'll follow you in a second.'

I heard Mavis scoot off while my eyes were closed and then the door shutting, followed by a quiet room. My head hit my pillow, and I was off to sleep again. Painting, coal, scotch, ears, were my last thoughts and then I was out, only to wake moments later to Marguerite's grabbing hands.

'Get up!' Marguerite huffed, and she yanked me up by the armpits to a standing position. She rubbed my ears, and I swatted at her.

'I'm up! Chri — '

My eyes bugged open. Mother Superior was standing right next to her.

'Crafts,' was all Mother said before turning on

her heel and leaving in a swoosh of black.

Marguerite folded her arms. 'Crafts.'

I blew air from my mouth. *Crafts.*

★ ★ ★

I slipped on a clean dress and pulled my hair back the best I could without a brush and found my way out to the conservatory, in the incredibly bright sunlight. The sisters had set up a table of yarn, if we wanted to knit, or a pottery station for ashtrays.

I saw Mavis before I heard her, standing in the grass. 'I have your canvas,' she said, and I squinted, still trying to adjust to the sun and the morning. 'Adèle?' She held the canvas out for me to take.

I took it, but not before letting out a little groan. 'It feels so early.' I looked around, one eye still squinting, over the grassy field and to the few girls who were now setting up their easels. 'Where is everyone?' I asked, but then changed the subject. 'What time is it?'

Mavis stepped closer, sniffing the air, and it was then I realized she probably smelled the alcohol on me from last night. I backed up. 'Never mind,' I said, and then pointed to the other painters. 'I'll go set up.'

'Are you in charge again?' Mavis asked. Her eyes flicked to mine before looking at the ground. 'The girls don't listen to me like they do you.' Her words hung in the air, and what I really heard was her asking what was wrong with me, and why I was so tired.

I yawned, one eye open, but it was a yawn of

convenience. 'I was sick last night,' I lied. 'In the toilet,' I whispered, and she looked confused as to why I'd tell her the particulars, but I wanted to wash away all her doubt. 'I'm all right now. Not to worry.'

I patted her shoulder and she went into the conservatory even though we were all outside.

'Yes, have a rest,' I said as she walked away. 'I'll take care of everything this morning.'

I made my way over to the grassy hill, where so many of the girls had already started to paint. Sister Mary-Francis inspected the artwork, hands folded behind her back.

'Mother wants you to paint more of the same today,' she said. 'We need more coal. And your painting fetched us a mint.'

I didn't understand what the fuss was about, why someone would trade a fortune in coal for that glob of paint I slapped on the canvas the other day. Art was subjective, Charlotte had told me once. I suppose it isn't up to me to understand. I smiled. 'Yes, Sister.'

I set up my palette and chair, listening to the girls fight over the last tube of blue paint when I noticed the sister staring off toward the front of the convent. I got off my chair and walked over when I felt something wasn't right. 'Something wrong?'

She shook her head slowly from side to side, still looking at the front of the convent, and to a car that had just rolled up. Vichy police, and not one, two or three of them, but four gendarmes got out of the car and walked the courtyard, lingering, kicking up dirt and fingering their batons. Mother

Superior walked out to talk to them. Voices were raised.

The bell tower chimed, clinging and clanging with so much force even the girls turned around. 'What time is it?' they asked. 'Why are the bells ringing?'

Sister Mary-Francis walked off without so much as a word, disappearing into the laundry.

'Where's Marguerite?' I said to anyone who'd answer, eyes still on the gendarmes, but only a few looked up from their canvases. 'Girls!' I said, and they all looked at me this time. 'Where's Marguerite?'

The bells had stopped ringing, but the hum still echoed in my ears and over the convent grounds. Vibrating. One of the gendarmes noticed me, but then his fleeting glance turned into a stare. He pointed for another gendarme to look, and then Mother. My stomach sank.

I ducked behind a canvas. He'd found me. I don't know how, but he'd found me.

'Girls,' I said, trying to sound calm but my heart was racing. There was no time for counting and to think about lying in the grass. 'I'll be right back.' I winced hard. 'Don't move.'

'Where are you going?' one asked.

The cloister wasn't that far away, and the sanctuary would still have sisters kneeling in the pews, which would provide a little cover. Then I could make it to the south stairs, and down into the secret room where I had my training. They wouldn't find me there.

I used my canvas as a cover. 'I need a new canvas,' I announced, and I made a dash for it, making haste to the bell tower, looking for a place to stash the canvas, but then decided to ditch it for the doors.

The sanctuary was empty. Not one sister. Prayer candles flickered.

The chapel doors flew open and Sister Mary-Francis walked in swiftly, down the aisle and past all the pews to the altar where she crossed her chest with the sign of the divinity.

'Sister — '

'Shh!' She bolted toward me, her habit swishing around her feet, but then whispered as she passed. 'Out the back, far meadow. Hurry!'

9

I ran through the far meadow and found cover under a big willow tree, hiding in its spindly branches, where I waited, but for what I didn't know. I felt like a turkey in the wild waiting to be shot, breathing heavily, then standing nervously, biting at my fingernails.

A crackling behind me nearly scared me into the branches, but then my stomach hit the ground in relief when I saw it was Marguerite. 'Christ, it's you — '

She rushed up, hands out, clamping them over my loud mouth. Her lips felt dry in my ear. 'Shh . . . ' She peeled her palm away from my face and we looked at each other. 'The police got a tip about the guns.'

I covered my own mouth. 'The mole?'

'Who else?' she said.

'Did they arrest Mother?' I said, and she shook her head.

'They only asked questions, and how many sisters and delinquents we had. She gave them a tour of the grounds, of our chambers and the sanctuary. We knew what they were really there for.'

'What now?'

'We make a rendezvous.' She checked her watch. 'And hope our funds are secure, and pray the mole didn't know about the big transfer today. We'll have to walk.'

She pointed into the reedy birch forest off the

convent grounds, a place I'd never been before, and we walked the bank of a curvy stream that ran through it into the country. 'Wait.' She stopped me with a stiff arm, and she searched the sky, listening. Her face went pale. 'Hear that?' she said, and as soon as she said it, I heard an engine sputtering.

We crept up the way just a bit more and found a road.

Marguerite gasped, sucking a mouthful of air through her teeth when she saw a truck with its driver's side door flung open. She bolted a few steps, but stopped abruptly when we heard a woman's voice telling the driver to be quiet and die over the scrape of his boots digging at the floorboards.

Marguerite pulled a revolver from her pocket. 'Hands!' She aimed the gun. 'Let me see your hands!' Her face instantly perspired.

The woman backed slowly away, two white legs behind the open door and the lavender hem of a delinquent's peasant dress.

My heart stopped. 'Claire?'

A pink welt puffed on her cheek and her hair had been pulled from its bun and lay unkempt in a tousled mess. 'Help,' she said, voice shaking unlike anything I'd ever heard before. 'This man needs help!'

'I'm on to you, Claire,' Marguerite said, cocking the trigger.

'Please,' Claire said. 'I — '

'*Arrêtez*!' Marguerite blasted.

Claire backed up further, this time with bloody hands in the air. 'I don't understand. I found him while on a walk. I'm trying to help.' Her voice was weepy, and she looked to me for help. 'Mademoiselle?'

'What's going on?' I cried, but she kept walking backward until her heels met the pebbly edge of the stream, where water rushed over large boulders and white foam pooled in the eddies. 'Claire?' Tears welled in her eyes and then spilled over her cheeks, her gaze rolling over the both of us and the man who lay dying, drowning in his own blood.

'I . . . I . . .' Claire's voice was garbled and nearly inaudible next to the rushing stream behind her.

I reached out for her even though I was many feet away.

'Claire's the spy,' Marguerite said, and I pulled my hand back.

'What?' I said, looking at Marguerite and then to Claire. 'No, she can't be . . .'

Marguerite closed one eye, the other locked on Claire, looking straight down the barrel of her gun.

Claire bent to her knees, weeping. Then her face went white as a sheet, and the tears streaming down her face evaporated right from her skin. '*Ihr seid beide verrückt!*' she said in perfect German. 'I'm the one that got away!'

In the blink of an eye, Claire threw a dagger she had hidden in a sheath under her arm, but Marguerite's bullet hit her first and square in the chest. *Pop!* The knife cut through the air, missing Marguerite by a hair and me by a foot, landing somewhere behind us.

Claire fell effortlessly backward, her face frozen in a waxy expression, her lips half smiling with

104

a bullet-hole spot of blood soaking into the thin fabric of her peasant dress. The rolling rapids took her away, her torso riding bubbling whitecaps.

'She's gone!' I clutched my chest, frantically searching the whirling water for signs of life as she floated away, but all that was left of her were the imprints of her knees pressed into the pebbly embankment of the stream.

Marguerite stepped back, shuffling at first and then scrambling to see about the man in the truck. She looked at him with arms long at her sides, the gun shaking in her hand against her thigh.

I stumbled toward her with legs of jelly, peering into the cab of the truck. His head had flopped back and a knife stuck straight out of his chest like a blunt stick. She turned him toward her by the chin and then burst into tears when she saw his face, crying his name. 'Philip . . . Philip . . .'

I gasped. 'Your fiancé!' I said, only now he was dead.

She brushed a tuft of dark hair from his eyes, which were blue and glassy, her fingers trembling from one last touch of his cheek.

'Marguerite . . . I . . . I . . .' I'd only seen dead people at funerals, in their coffins. Not in a truck with a knife sticking out of their chest. 'I don't know what to say . . .'

She shook her head for me to stop talking, moaning with her head down, her hands on his body. And I stood there for a minute or two, not sure what to do, watching his blood drip off the floorboards and into the dirt. I touched her arm, and she broke away in a panic, wiping her face of tears.

'We need to get him out of here.' She sniffed. 'Clean it up.'

'Don't you want more time with him?' I said.

'We don't have time.'

She moved away, and I caught a whiff of warm blood wafting from his body. I was reminded of meat Mama sometimes left on the counter on a hot day. My belly roiled and I felt faint, grabbing the side of the truck to hold myself. 'I think I'm ... I'm ...' Mucus coated my throat like off-milk and then vomit spurted from my mouth and all over the truck's back tyre.

Marguerite waited for me to finish heaving, crying into her sleeve, when I looked up at her, wiping the remains of last night's soup from my lips.

'Welcome to the Résistance, Adèle.' The sun had crested over the foothills and beamed a shiny white light onto the water that glistened behind her like fallen snow.

She wiped her red eyes. 'Now, get up.'

★ ★ ★

We hid Philip under a blanket and pushed him up against the door, putting his arm over his head as if he was sleeping. 'If the police stop us, tell them he's drunk and that he's passed out,' she said, and then commanded me to drive the truck out of the birch forest and down a dirt road dotted with covered gypsy wagons and laundry hanging from trees.

She had found a tan duffle bag stuffed as fat as a pig in the truck's bed and had been rummaging

106

through it since we left the stream. 'Keep driving until I tell you to stop,' she said through the back window, which had been busted out.

'Why would we get stopped?' The wheel spun loose in my hands, and my arms ached from trying to keep the truck steady. I lifted my eyes from the road just long enough to glance over my right shoulder.

Marguerite's head bobbed up from the back of the truck. 'Because you're driving like a juvenile!'

I stepped on the accelerator.

We stopped at a cottage at the edge of a wheat field that hadn't been ploughed in years. 'Don't say much,' she said, reaching for the duffle bag to carry inside. 'They get paid to help us.'

I nodded.

I got out of the truck and followed Marguerite up to the door. She went to knock, but the door opened before her knuckles hit the wood.

'*Zut alors*!' The same bald man who drove us to the convent stood in the doorway, which surprised me, though I wasn't sure why, not after seeing Claire get shot in the chest or riding in a truck with a dead man.

He threw his hands to his head, and yelled for his wife.

The wife scolded us with her eyes, but me more so, probably wondering what I was doing with Marguerite. They drove the truck around the back of the cottage where weeds and tangle grass grew up like flowers. We watched them from the screen door in the kitchen with the duffle bag at our feet.

'What are they going to do?' I said.

They lifted the body out of the truck. Marguerite

turned away when she saw them take him by his limbs, each grabbing a foot and a hand. 'What do you think they're going to do?'

She paced the room, holding her stomach, looking visibly ill, but then dropped to her knees and prayed, murmuring prayers I'd heard at the convent. I put my hand on her shoulder when she sobbed into her hands. The sound was gut-wrenching.

Marguerite stood up after crossing her chest, and wiped her eyes, moving to the duffle bag.

'Are you going to be all right?' I said, though I wondered how she could be.

'We knew this might happen,' she said, sniffing. 'He died doing what he believed in. There's some comfort knowing this.' She paused, giving her eyes one last wipe. 'And that I killed the German bitch who did it to him.'

I pointed outside where the couple was preparing the body. 'But . . . But . . . '

Marguerite looked at me from the ground as she opened the duffle bag. 'I have to carry on because that's what Philip would want. We must honour the dead's wishes.' Marguerite unzipped the duffle bag and sat on her knees, spilling thousands of loose francs out onto the floor.

I watched the couple outside prepare for the burial as Marguerite counted the francs on the floor. The bald man pointed a finger around his property after they laid the body on the ground. The wife nodded, hands planted on her hips, her lungs huffing and puffing from having lifted something heavy.

I closed my eyes, thinking about Claire. Her

body would wash ashore eventually, waterlogged and bleached from the sun. Maybe someone would bury her, maybe not. I'd never know. At least this man would get a burial.

Marguerite had pulled an envelope from the bag and paced around the room in quick bursts, feverishly reading the note inside, still wiping her tears. I got worried.

'What does it say?' Marguerite ignored me, and I asked again. 'What does it say . . . Marguerite!' But still she wouldn't answer, and I could tell it was something serious. I reached for the paper. 'What does it — '

We stood staring at each other, tugging on the piece of paper between us. 'Sometimes it's better to be kept in the dark,' she said, and then snatched the letter away with a quick jerk, only the part I'd grabbed tore between my fingers.

Marguerite struck a long match she snagged from the fireplace mantel and set it to the paper. Just before the flame reached her fingers, she threw it into the cold ash of last winter's fire. 'You'll have to trust me.'

A young girl riding a bicycle rode up from the field. Marguerite went out to talk to her, alternating a pointed finger at me through the screen door and the couple by the tree before bringing her inside.

'She's going to the convent to get some things. Do you have any possessions you want her to bring back for you?'

'You mean . . . we're not going back?'

'Is there anything you want?'

I opened my mouth, but I couldn't form any

words. I had to think. Did I have anything? 'My pocketbook. It's under my cot.'

The girl set out on her bicycle and rode away, disappearing behind the derelict wheat field.

'What do you mean we're not going back?' I tried to hide my disappointment; I was good with the delinquents. Sister Mary-Francis told me so.

'I am,' she said. 'You're not.'

'You're leaving me here? Alone?' My head pained instantly, thinking about spending my days on the farm with the bald man and his wife. I reached into my pocket for a cigarette, but then threw the case across the room out of frustration. 'You can't leave me.'

Marguerite took a deep breath. 'The nuns can't know what happened to Claire. Killing her wasn't part of the plan they agreed to. Now we must cover it up. The delinquents will ask questions. So will the nuns.' Marguerite glanced outside where the couple was burying the body, but then quickly turned her face away. 'I need your help somewhere else.'

'But I was good there,' I said. 'At the convent. With the girls.'

'Are you a keeper of delinquents, or a member of the Résistance?'

'Why can't I be both?'

There was a long pause. Marguerite stared at me, her lips dry and cracking, and I could tell she was struggling with what to say. 'You want to know what was in that letter?'

'The one you just burned?'

Marguerite held her breath as if she was about to deliver something big before exhaling with

110

a groan. 'Claire thought you were the leader, understand? Someone who gave guns to the Free French — the mastermind behind the guns in the crypt.'

'She thought I was involved?'

'She didn't believe you were just involved. Claire believed you were the Chameleon — that's my codename.' Marguerite pointed a finger at her own chest. 'She thought you were me.'

'Why does that matter?' I said, shaking my head.

'It means the convent's not safe for you. We don't know exactly what she's told her superiors. It's all very uncertain.' She paused. 'But one thing I know for sure. Claire was a professional and probably has killed before. If she had pinned me with that knife, she would have pulled it out and stuck you with it too.'

I shook my head, though I knew she was telling the truth. Claire was the one who wanted to go to the crypt that day of the speech, and then showed up without permission. She had taken my journal, and now that I thought of it, Claire was the one who brought up the idea to jump through Marguerite's window after I wanted to give up. She had used me to gather information about the guns in the crypt. The thought made me feel small, and in a flash the sadness I felt for Claire's unburied body drifting among the cattails vanished from my heart and my mind.

'Now do you understand why you can't go back?'

'I understand.'

I watched the couple from the screen door as they argued over Philip's body. The bald man traced the outline of a coffin in the dirt while the wife wiped sweat from her chest with a hanky she pulled from her cleavage. She shook her head from shoulder to shoulder and he threw his hands in the air. He laid down in the dirt next to the body, scooting close to it, ravens circling over both as the wife compared their sizes with a squinted eye.

'Are they almost done?' Marguerite said.

'I think so.'

Marguerite walked a few steps away, her eyes welling with tears. Turning away seemed to help, and after a few moments of deep breathing, her face got straight again, though I could tell she wanted to weep, and weep good, but by the grace of God was somehow able to hold it in.

'I'll tell you when it's done,' I said, and she nodded.

The wife struggled to bend the man's legs, which looked like they had started to stiffen. She grabbed him by the foot and made chopping motions with her hand. The bald man nodded and then disappeared into a shed.

Oh, Christ.

'Adèle,' she said, from the other side of the room. 'There's something else.'

I walked away from the screen door when the bald man reappeared from the shed with a hatchet in his hands, and went to zip up the duffle bag on the floor — something to keep my mind off what was going on outside. I swallowed hard.

'What is it?' I said.

'Remember when Mother said there was a reason God had sent you to us?' she said. 'We need you somewhere else. Somewhere other than Lyon, this farm.'

I felt some relief — no farm. I thought maybe she'd say Paris or Calais, or maybe someplace very far away like Carcassonne. 'Where?'

'You're going back to Vichy,' she said, and I looked up.

'What?'

'And back to Gérard.'

I bolted to a stand. 'You're mad!'

Marguerite squeezed both my shoulders. 'You must!'

'I came to the convent to escape from Gérard,' I huffed. 'Now, I'm supposed to go straight back to him? Absolutely not. I thought the police came to the convent to drag me back.'

'Be realistic, Adèle. You have the contacts. We need the connections.'

'Contacts?' I scoffed. 'I have contacts in the hair business, if you can call them that. Other than that, I'm not sure what you mean.'

'You don't know . . .'

'Know what?'

'Gérard. He's working for the regime at the Hotel du Parc.'

'I already know he's a collaborator. That's one of the reasons why I didn't marry him.'

'He's more than a collaborator, Adèle. We have word that he's behind the recent overhaul of the regime's witch-hunt on the Résistance. In some cases, he's the one making decisions for the Vichy police.'

My shoulders had gotten tense when she put her hands on them and then got tenser when she told me of Gérard's escapades. 'You're forgetting one thing, Marguerite. Gérard hates me. He must. I left him the day before our wedding to join a convent. Humiliation isn't something Gérard takes lightly.'

A bird flew in from the wheat field and landed on the windowsill. He pecked at some crumbs that had flaked off an apple tart the wife had put there earlier to cool. Had the bird been any smarter he would have gone for the whole tart, which sat just inches away with no tea towel to cover it.

Marguerite used a delicate finger to scoot the tart closer to the window. 'That's your first test,' she said, as the bird moved toward it. 'Get him to trust you.'

I scoffed. 'And forgive.'

'Adèle, you must have a way about you that's attractive to him. He won't be able to resist you if you're yourself.' She looked at me just as the bird dug into the tart. 'From what I heard, he's a man who doesn't like to lose, especially not to a woman. He'll forgive you because he wants to win.'

Be myself. 'You make it sound so simple,' I said.

I thought about Gérard's bulging muscles, his condescending voice and feeling hands. He had a taste for women, and if I'd learned anything from my time with him, it was that he definitely didn't like to lose. As much as I hated to admit it, Marguerite was right. I was in a unique situation — a situation that could benefit the French Résistance — if I allowed myself to be put back in it. But I'd be taking a chance, a big chance, which hinged on Gérard's feelings toward me, which I had no way of knowing unless I went back.

'I can't marry him, Marguerite.' I gulped.

'Think of a way to postpone,' she said. 'You already ran away. It would be normal for you to ask to take things slow.'

I closed my eyes briefly. *Gérard take things slow.* 'What then?'

'Inside his office is a cigar box. Underneath is a set of numbers — a combination. Memorize them.'

I had worried Marguerite was going to get me sent back to Vichy, but in the end, it wasn't her I needed to worry about. It was me. I nodded.

She exhaled after holding her breath. 'Thank you, thank you, Adèle.' She held my hand. 'There's a flower cart in front of the Hotel du Parc that only sells flowers out of tins, never baskets. Ask for a single daisy. Then leave a coded message with the old woman that you're ready to meet, and I'll be in touch.'

'When will I leave?'

'Tonight. After the girl comes back.'

Out the window, I saw the couple drag Philip's body over to a hole they'd dug and push him in — Marguerite had no idea the pair had just sawed his legs off at the knees. I closed my eyes briefly, praying for Philip, the man who died doing what he believed in. 'Tonight it is.'

The wife took hold of a rusty shovel, scooped up some dirt and tossed it into the hole.

10

I waited inside the cottage as the sun set, watching Marguerite kneel under the oak tree next to the mound of dirt piled on top of Philip's grave. She blew kisses from her fingers at the ground. A mournful cry followed, and she clutched her stomach before collapsing onto the ground. It was in that moment, when I saw Marguerite crying in the dirt, that I wanted to get the numbers for her and not just for the Résistance.

She would've had a few moments to grieve alone if it weren't for the bald man, who came up behind her shouting. It was hard to tell who was angrier, both cursing at each other, pointing to the grave and then to me in the cottage. Marguerite shoved money into his hands, which he immediately started counting. He stopped her when she tried to come back inside, and then she drove away in the truck the wife had cleaned.

The couple drove me back to Vichy that night in the same dusty black car I had ridden to the convent in. We drove with our headlamps off, the full moon casting a soft glow over the rolling hills, which looked black and grey in the distance. When I left Vichy, my pocketbook was stuffed with money to bribe the sisters, now it was stuffed with money Marguerite had given me for a dress — something to help with Gérard, something sexy.

I wasn't sure where I'd begin once I got back

home, but I knew with whom I had to begin. *Papa*. I'd have to trick him as much as I had to trick Gérard. The thought made my throat turn dry. I reached for my cigarette case, but then remembered I left it at the cottage. 'Christ!'

The bald man slammed on his brakes. My body jerked forward before slamming back into the seat. I thought he was mad at me for cursing Christ's name, but then he yelled Marguerite's name and sneered.

'Get out.'

'What?' He had stopped in a valley between two jet-black hills that hid the moon. 'You can't stop here. I don't know where I am.'

He turned around in his seat, striking a flame from his lighter so I could see his pitted old face. 'You don't expect me to drive to the Hotel du Parc, do you?'

'Well . . . well . . . ' I stuttered. 'No.'

He kicked open his door and mumbled to himself about getting rid of me. Then he opened my door, wide, as if I was as big as his wife and needed the space. 'Get out!'

'But what direction am I to go?'

He reached through the open window and turned the headlamps on. 'Walk that way,' he said, pointing down the dirt road where the hills split into two. 'Creuzier-le-Vieux is over there. Vichy is after.'

It was late. I didn't have a watch, but I assumed it was sometime around midnight. I pulled a few francs from my pocketbook. 'Perhaps some money.'

'Yes!' the wife yelped. She stuck her arm out

117

the window and motioned with her hand for the money.

He yelled at her and then turned to me. 'Keep your money. And this.' He shoved a crinkled note into my hand and got back into the car, slamming his door. I tried the handle but he pushed the lock down.

'Wait!' I cried, with pounding fists as he rolled the window up. 'Don't leave me here!'

He jammed the car into gear without even turning his head and then bolted down the road. His wife's hands flailed in the air, smacking him on the shoulder as their red tail lights faded under whirling dust.

Everything was quiet.

A RAF balloon drifted over my head, dipping and plunging in the air, spilling propaganda leaflets from the sky. And I walked; down narrow dirt roads that turned into wider ones until I saw black, twisted grape vines growing on the hills in the distance — Creuzier-le-Vieux, Papa's vineyard and the chateau.

Some of the winemakers in Creuzier-le-Vieux made wine only for themselves, planting grapes in their gardens so they'd have wine at their supper tables. Others, like Papa, made a good living off their vintages, owning acres upon acres of ancient Vichy vines. The wrath of grapes rolling over the darkened hills, dotting plots of country land here and there, was a stark contrast to the abruptness of the city only a few kilometres away, and the dull glow of city life.

The sun crested the horizon and I'd finally made it back home. I was exhausted, choosing to sit down on the grassy slope behind the chateau before going inside, rubbing my blistered, bloodied feet, banged up from walking all night in the wrong shoes. I pulled the note the bald man had given me from my pocket, and read Marguerite's coded message. Three days, it said.

The chateau looked the same as I remembered with its eighteenth-century stone façade and blue shutters. The clay pots where Mama grew her favourite herbs were still on the patio: mint, basil, and fennel by the bushels. Wrought-iron arbour arches in the garden overgrown with light pink roses buzzed with swarming bees.

I fell back into the grass without meaning to, feeling the blades in between my fingers. A budding French catchfly had broken through the volcanic soil and fluttered in a twist of morning light, its distinguishing, prickly stem too new to poke back. Then I thought about it, the day I realized I couldn't — I wouldn't — marry Gérard.

He stopped by the chateau one afternoon in early June, as he had been doing for the last few weeks to talk to Papa, often asking me to take rides in his sidecar or go wine tasting in the valley.

'We need each other, Adèle.' Gérard swept a lock of hair from his eyes, which looked yellowy-brown. 'Your country needs you.' He spread a blanket onto the tall grass and told me to sit on it, smiling back at the chateau to Papa who was watching from the window.

'My country?' I folded my arms. 'Who are you to tell me what my country needs?'

'I'm a gendarme in the Vichy police,' he said, pushing me down. 'Don't you know what that means? What woman would turn down such an opportunity:

a prominent place in this nation?'

'I have a place.'

He laughed, uncorking the bottle of wine Papa had given him. 'And where is that? Your sister told me you've done nothing since you quit setting hair at that salon.'

I held up my glass. 'Just give me some wine. Papa is watching. I know how much you like to put on a show.'

He poured me a glass, and I drank it down before he had a chance to pour his own. Then I played with the grass, running my fingers through it, wondering how long I'd have to listen to him talk about my place in this country.

'I asked your father for your hand. We are to be wed in a week.'

I sprung up. 'You can't be serious.'

'He arranged our meetings. Surely you know what's happening when a man visits your home for two weeks straight.'

'Papa said I needed to be nice to you. I thought it had something to do with his wine, a big purchase for your parents' spa . . .'

'Your family needs a marriage to a man like me, Adèle. You may not survive the war if you don't make the right connections. The Germans run the Occupied Zone. If they join with the Free Zone outright and you're not on the winning side, what will become of you?'

'Papa can't tell me who to marry.'

'You go ahead and tell yourself that. But there will be a wedding.'

'But why me?' I said, and he laughed deeply from his throat, looking at my bare toes and running his eyes up my body.

'You don't know?' he said, and I scooted back.

Gérard popped his head up above the grass, and after realizing we were hidden from Papa's peeping eyes, he pushed me down low until I was completely flat and his body was on top of mine, his muscly build like a truck compressing on my chest.

'Get off!' He kissed me, nearly biting my tongue as he dug his way into my mouth. I kicked my legs out from under his, struggling to break free, when the back door swung open and closed with a squealing crack. He sat up and wiped his lips with the back of his hand, laughing. Mama stood on the patio, glaring at us, which made me think Papa had just told her the news.

'Relax, Adèle. I'll save the rest of that for next week.' He looked at his watch. 'I have to go, as it turns out. A big arrest. Nicholas Fenoir.'

I stood up in a daze, stepping away from him. 'The cripple?'

'I suppose we did cripple him last time. I'm an aggressive interrogator, what can I say? He won't have to worry about being a cripple where he's going.'

'But he has a family and small children.'

'Yes, and I knew him growing up.' He smiled, his teeth taking up most of his face. 'Doesn't matter. He's a résistant, Adèle. Anyone who fights the regime is an outlaw. Punishable by death. The Reich wants it this way. I have informants hidden here and there, you see? And we all know how the Reich feels about the Jews.'

Gérard dumped his glass in the grass and then wadded up the blanket and lobbed it at my feet. 'See you at the wedding,' he said, recorking the half-drunk bottle of wine and sticking it under his arm. He went to kiss

121

my cheek, and I jerked away.

'So, it is true.'

'What?'

'The Vichy police . . . they are . . . you are — '

'Don't hurt yourself, Adèle,' he said. 'Maybe you should think before you talk.'

Collaborators. Just like Pétain's regime.

'What happened to you, Gérard?' I said, remembering the boy who used to buy wine from my father, the one who said please and thank you and treated women kindly.

He glared at first, and then straightened. 'What's happened to all of us, Adèle?'

He walked down the grassy slope to his motorcycle. I wanted to be mad at Papa, tricking me as he did. But by the look on Mama's face, I figured he'd get it from her better than from me.

Gérard tossed the wine bottle into his sidecar and then put on his helmet. 'One week!' he shouted just before he drove away.

Mama stormed back into the kitchen, the screen door clacking against the doorframe. I dropped to my knees with the realization of what had just happened, wishing the ground would crack open so I could disappear.

I heard a yell and my hands slipped from the grass with my thoughts jolting to the present. Birds spooked by the sudden noise flew out of the chateau's eaves, their wings flapping with great haste over my head toward the vineyard. I stood when I realized it was Papa's voice. The morning sunlight beamed through Mama's kitchen windows, and I saw her leaning over the sink, her arms bracing its porcelain edge. Papa stood behind her dressed in Sunday clothes, a black valise clenched in his hand, his voice spilling through the screen door and echoing off the patio.

'*Politique*,' he said, 'will get you killed.'

I scuttled through the grass and watched them through the screen door.

Mama turned around, her hands on the sink behind her, her slept-on, bobbed brown hair tucked behind her ears. 'Don't lecture me about politics. *You* are not a true Frenchman.'

Papa's cornflower blue eyes looked black and hard as marbles from where I stood. He ran a light finger over what was left of his ear, a souvenir from the Battle of Gallipoli. It was the first time I'd seen him touch it, preferring to keep it hidden under a tuft of hair that had started to grey.

'I'm the truest of Frenchmen.'

'Then act like it, Albert!' Mama tightened the tie on her silky peignoir, watching him as he paced around the kitchen taking short, quick steps as if he wasn't sure how to handle the anger gurgling inside of him.

'Everything I've done has been for this family. Pétain is the way.' Mama shook her head. 'We will prosper if we follow his lead.'

'The Vichy government is a puppet regime — ruled by German policy, not French,' Mama spouted with her arms lifting in the air. 'Occupied, unoccupied — Pétain got a country of his own, he's happy. Until one day . . . one day when the Reich decides to take it all!'

'You will see. Pétain will not let us down.'

'Pétain?' She sneered. 'He only appeals to the people because he's a hero from the war. Sitting

123

out and waiting for the Germans to conquer Britain is not a plan.'

'Easy for you to say — standing in your kitchen. What do you know about risks?'

Mama's mouth hung open, and her eye twitched. For a moment I thought I saw the fearless nurse she must have been on the fields at Ypres. 'Don't. You — '

Papa pleaded with her to listen to him, stretching his hands out for hers, but she wouldn't take them. 'My way is the way, Pauline. Why can't you see that?'

'*Your* way.' Mama threw a tea towel at the wall, and it hit a framed photo of Charlotte in her wedding dress. 'And what has that gotten us?' The frame dangled helplessly from one corner before falling onto what looked like their supper dishes from the night before.

'Charlotte loves her husband, and she's doing what she can to keep France alive, adhering to Pétain's wishes. You can't blame me for — '

Mama crossed her chest with the sign of the divinity, which stopped Papa from talking.

'And what about Adèle?'

'That,' he said, 'was your doing.'

'No,' Mama said. 'She left because you betrothed her to that . . . that . . . collaborator! A German in French clothing.'

'She left because you gave her the money,' Papa said.

'It's my fault?' Mama's face turned red. 'You came back for a night just so I could throw you out the next morning?' Papa didn't budge. 'Get out!'

124

She saluted Papa the way Nazi soldiers saluted each other, and his mouth pinched. He raised his valise into the air and shook it along with his fist as if he wanted to hit Mama — but he would never.

I threw open the screen door and stepped into the kitchen. Mama jumped. Papa froze, the valise suspended in the air.

'I'm home,' I said, and the door slammed closed behind me.

Seconds passed — neither of them saying a word. Mama's face was indifferent; I couldn't read her at all. Papa slowly lowered his valise, his arms dropping to his sides.

'Glad to see you, Adèle!' I said, since nobody else did.

Mama reached for her cigarettes and a lighter that lay on the counter. 'Your father was just leaving.' She threw her head back to get the hair out of her eyes and sucked on her cigarette as if she mistook the smoke for oxygen. 'Weren't you, Albert?'

A slight smile replaced Papa's scowl. '*Ma chérie.*' He kissed both my cheeks and in that second I knew he really did blame Mama for me leaving. 'You're home! You've reconsidered Gérard's proposal?' A shimmer of cornflower blue pierced the blackness that had marbled in his eyes. 'I'll tell Gérard you've come back. He'll be so pleased.'

My knees nearly buckled. 'You mean . . . he doesn't hate me?' I looked at Mama and then to Papa, disbelieving, but also very relieved.

'Hate you?' Papa almost laughed. 'How could he hate you?'

'Because I left him,' I said, 'suddenly, without a word.'

125

'I'll tell him you're back.' He went for the door as if he were going to do it right then, but I grabbed his shoulder with great certainty.

'No, Papa.' I didn't want Gérard finding out I was home before I was ready. As ready as I could be. 'What I mean is . . . I'll talk to him myself.' I let go of his shoulder after realizing I was squeezing too tightly. 'It's the least I can do.'

Papa took my hands. 'Alliances are very important. And you two got along so well in those weeks leading up to the wedding. He's a war hero, Battle of Sedan.'

I took a deep breath, about to lie straight to my father's face — one of many lies I was sure I'd have to tell. 'I will be grateful if Gérard gives me a second chance.'

He smiled, and I smiled back.

Mama whipped her head away from whatever she had been staring at through the window and shot us both a hard-eyed glare. 'So, you are your father's daughter after all.' Mama shook her head, flicking her cigarette over the sink. 'Unbelievable.'

Papa leaned into my ear and whispered, 'I'm glad you're home, Adèle.' A parting kiss on my cheek, and he made way for the door.

'Where are you going?'

Papa glanced at Mama, who had her hand cocked in the air, her cigarette spewing smoke from between two fingers.

'I don't live here anymore.'

'You don't?'

'Humph!' Mama shifted her legs, taking a drag from her cigarette. 'Tell her why, Albert. Don't leave her to guess.'

126

'I work for the Vichy regime now. I sell the wine they want from an abandoned building next to Charlotte's boutique. I made the office upstairs into a flat.' A hesitant smile followed a short pause. 'It's where I've been living.'

My mouth gaped open, eyes shifting between Mama and Papa.

'Do not worry,' he said. 'Only Charlotte knows the truth. I've told people I live in the city because of the long hours. Our marriage is still very much intact in the public eye.' He looked at Mama and then whispered, 'Sometimes we have to make difficult decisions for the good of the family.'

Papa started for the door but then stopped at the kitchen table and scribbled something on a piece of paper that had once been crumpled into a ball. When he was done, Papa stuck the pencil in the woodblock that usually held Mama's cleaver.

'One last note, Pauline,' Papa said as he left.

Mama tossed her lit cigarette angrily into the sink, but then took a deep, withering breath full of sobs and tears. Together we watched him drive away.

'I knew you'd be back after that old nun came to visit.'

'Gertrude?'

'Was that her name?' Mama's voice was as faint as the cloud of dust funnelling behind Papa's car. Once he was completely out of sight Mama turned around and looked at me, her eyes puffy and red from crying. 'I know what they've asked you to do, and you'll be great at it. You might be his daughter, but you're mine first.'

'The sisters told you?' I swallowed, knowing

127

how she felt about Gérard, and wondering what the conversation with Gertrude must have been like. 'You're not angry?'

'We do what we have to, Adèle. When we have to.' She paused. 'Elizabeth saw the strength in you. I do too.'

'Mama, tell me how you know Mother Superior — Elizabeth — at the convent.' I took the cloisonné lighter from my pocket. 'She has the same lighter.'

'Unused, I imagine. Elizabeth never did smoke.'

'She said it was — '

'Not now, Adèle.' Mama squeezed her eyes shut. 'My head hurts.'

I wondered what mysterious past Mother Superior shared with Mama. Something dangerous perhaps, something meaningful and profound I was sure. I couldn't keep the lighter after knowing how important it was. 'Maybe you can tell me some other time?'

Mama's gaze trailed off.

'I think the lighter belongs with you, Mama.'

She rubbed her head with one hand and grabbed the lighter with the other, slipping it into her pocket. 'If that's what you want.'

I picked up the note Papa had left for her on the table. Below an old message he had crossed out were the words to 'À la Claire Fontaine'. I remembered Mama singing the song when I was a child, walking through Papa's vines with Charlotte and me tagging along on her heels. When I realized what Papa had said with the lyrics, I offered her the note. 'You should read this.'

Mama hit her forehead with the fleshy part of

128

her palm. 'No,' she groaned. 'I haven't the strength for any more words.' She tightened the tie on her crème peignoir and trudged upstairs to her bedroom. 'Get rid of it, Adèle. I don't want to see it when I come back down.'

I read the lines quietly to myself.

'Long have I loved you. Never will I forget you.'

11

I sat at the kitchen table, eating the few pears Mama had left in the fruit bowl and what little bread she had on the table, taking drinks from an opened bottle of Papa's wine.

In the silence of the quiet room and with the equally silent vineyard out the window, the absence of Papa felt very real. Before the war the fields would have been busy with field hands rotating barrels of wine in the barrel cellar before the autumn harvest. And Mama, she'd be singing, hanging up laundry on the line, waving to Papa in the field. Charlotte would be talking about her next art exhibit and the paintings she had completed on the promenade overlooking the Allier River.

Seemed like an eternity ago.

Mama stumbled down the stairs to tell me she was going to bed for the rest of the day and not to expect supper. Her eyes were puffier than they were earlier, and her nose was raw and red as if she had been wiping it with coarse linen rather than a hanky. 'And I don't want to talk about your father. Not today, and not tomorrow either.' She rewrapped her peignoir and went back upstairs to her bedroom. 'You should get some rest, too. You're going to need it.'

I took a second bottle of wine with me down the corridor, heading to my room, drinking as I went. I tried not to think of Gérard, but he was like a hook stuck in my mouth, tugging at the corners of my thoughts, every one of them ending with his hands on my body.

I threw open my bedroom door and stood in the doorway, waiting for my eyes to adjust, gazing upon my room for the first time in so very long.

The silver-plated hairbrush I got the summer before was on my commode. Dried flowers hung from my wall near the window, white ones I had picked from the garden last May. Even the stockings I had soaked and rinsed months ago were still strung up, waiting for me to fold and put away — as if I hadn't left, and as if nothing had changed.

I crawled under my sheets and got into bed, thinking of Mama upstairs by herself and Papa in the city, and me all alone in my room, which brought on an unexpected gush of tears before I finally fell asleep. I woke up to Mama sitting on the edge of my bed, telling me it was morning and I had to get up.

'It's nearly seven o'clock.' Mama threw her silky peignoir over her legs. 'You'll have to take your bicycle since your father took the car.'

All I could do was groan, feeling every drop of wine I had drunk.

'You know what you have to do today. Don't you, Adèle?'

'Gérard Baudoin.' His name felt like sandpaper in my mouth. 'I'll have to take whatever shame he throws my way if I plan on getting a foot in the door of the Hotel du Parc.'

'And Charlotte,' Mama said. 'You need to see her first thing. She'll be expecting it.'

131

'I know.' I sat up to rub a dull pain in my back.

'Not used to sleeping in a real bed, are you?'

'I suppose not.' My eyes closed again, and I felt myself nod off while I was sitting up, only to jerk suddenly awake with Mama watching.

'You have to get up,' she said.

'I know.' I rubbed my ears and was able to throw off the covers.

'Oh, Adèle . . . ' she breathed. 'Much has changed since you've left. The vineyard, our family . . . and Vichy. If it weren't for the French uniforms you couldn't tell the difference between them and a German.'

'The police?'

She nodded. 'Gérard. Even more than before.'

'In what ways?'

'Isa Brochard from the farm behind — he arrested her personally, sent her to the big prison in Drancy. Someone said she was born in Warsaw, but I've never heard a foreign word come out of her mouth.' Mama pulled a cigarette from her case and the cloisonné from her pocket. 'I've been bringing her husband meat pies when I can — when the rabbits are around. My heart pains for their little ones. I don't think they know.'

'What do you mean they don't know?'

Mama struck her lighter several times and then paused to give it a shake. 'He still sets the table for four. I can only imagine what he's told them.' She struck the lighter again, but much harder and a low-burning flame ignited from a spark.

'I thought she grew up in the Dordogne.'

Mama took a long drag from her cigarette. 'Like I said, I never heard a foreign word come out of

132

her mouth. Madame Brochard was, however, of Jewish decent.' She stared at a spot in the wall, and her voice turned faint. 'She left so dignified, too . . . '

She shook her head after a long pause. 'You have a tough job ahead of you, Adèle. Gérard is a very difficult man. I have complete faith in you, but it doesn't mean I won't worry. How are you going to do it? Do you have a plan?'

'I'm going to be myself,' I said. 'He's attracted to the way I am. He'll be suspicious if I'm any different.' I looked at my hands, rolling them around. 'Mama, how did you tell him? Gérard, I mean. How did he find out? The day of the wedding? At the altar?' I didn't put it past Mama to wait until the very last minute.

'That was my intention,' she said. 'Only Gérard sent a note that afternoon asking you to meet him for dinner. I wanted him to wait all night for you, but after I told your father where you'd gone, Charlotte went in your place. I heard he was waiting outside the restaurant, pacing, getting very upset. It's because of her he didn't go out after you. Charlotte never told me what she said, but whatever it was, it was enough to get him to calm down.'

I sighed, relieved, thankful Charlotte was successful. I knew that if Mama had waited for the ceremony I was doomed, and I'd never get a chance to read the numbers on the back of that cigar box.

She got up from my bed and walked to the door. 'He was such a different boy before the war. His family . . . simple spa owners with a service to sell.'

'Do you think so, Mama? Or did the armistice just give people an opportunity to expose their true selves?'

Mama stopped, both hands bracing the door-frame. 'I don't know,' she said, looking over her shoulder. 'I really don't.'

★ ★ ★

After a light breakfast of eggs with jam, I slipped on a clean dress and got ready to go to Papa's wine store near the Gare de Vichy. Two sweeps of rouge across my cheeks and a dab of smooth red on my lips — half the makeup I used to wear, but after being at the convent for so many weeks it felt a little heavy.

Mama gave me a pair of her thickest pumps to hide the blisters I got from walking all night. 'Set your hair,' she said. 'It will make you look more like a woman who went to find herself rather than a child who ran away.'

I agreed and smoothed my hair into barrel curls.

I rode up to Papa's store and found him sweeping RAF leaflets from his pavement with a wiry broom, working his way from Charlotte's store-front to his. Old men with tales from the 1914 war ripe in their heads chatted over dingy bistro tables sipping Papa's wine. Their eyes followed me as I walked up to the front door, then one of them rode off on his bicycle after he saw my face. 'Nun-nery,' I heard in whispers. 'Humiliated.'

Vichy police patrolled the street, looking in shop windows and studying the people in the cafés. I held my head up.

'Adèle!' Papa propped his broom up on the side of the store. *'Bienvenue, ma chérie! Bienvenue!'* He kissed both my cheeks, and the police walked by, pushing us out of their way.

'Come in.' He held his door open, smiling. I was surprised to find Papa's store was actually a wine bar, with tables for people to sit and drink. The space smelled like tangy grapes, not the aged wine he was known to produce at the vineyard, but he seemed happy with it, pointing to the diverse blends of wine he had from the Auvergne region. I couldn't help but notice the empty wine crates from Germany stacked against the wall. Papa watched me as I read the labels stamped on the front.

'To keep certain people content,' he said. 'Customers can sit and have a glass or buy a crate. Mostly the regime and the police, and . . .'

I looked up.

Papa was made from the stain of French grapes — I would have never thought he'd sell German wine over his own. 'Papa,' I said. 'Wine from Germany . . .'

'We do what we have to, Adèle,' he said while moving the crates, turning the stamps toward the wall. 'When we have to.'

'What did you say?' I regretted the cynical tone in my voice.

'We do what we have to . . .'

'You sound like Mama.'

'Sometimes we have to pick our battles. Wine from Germany is no battle of mine.'

I stared at him, wondering where my father had

gone. It was more than just the day suit he was wearing, which months ago would have been field clothes soiled from having his hands in a grape barrel. My father would have called the German wine *vin de merde.* Shit wine, just like Beaujolais made from the Gamay grapes he had warned Charlotte and me to stay away from as children.

Papa took a deep breath. 'I'm glad you're home, *ma chérie.*'

'You don't blame me?'

He scoffed. 'I cannot lie . . . you did delay my plans to secure our family with the government, with Pétain. But like every good Frenchman I have refocused. Do not fear. I knew you couldn't think of something like that on your own.'

I shook my head. 'But I could, Papa. And I did think of it.' As much as I didn't want him to be angry with me for what I had done and where I had gone, I couldn't let Mama take the blame. Though I had a feeling no matter what I said to try and convince him otherwise, he wouldn't believe me.

'What is done is done,' he said. 'You're home now.'

I glanced over his things, the bar, and the bottles and bottles of wine meant to be sold, but why, and who was minding the vineyard?

'Papa,' I said. 'Why are you here? Why aren't you tending the estate?'

He rubbed his forehead, stalling. The vineyard had been in our family for generations, passed down from his father, whose father had passed it to him.

'What's going on?'

Papa placed some cheeses on a board for us to share, motioning for me to take a seat at one of his small tasting tables while adding some walnuts and dried apples from the canisters on the bar. The Fourme d'Ambert looked very blue as he cut into it, offering me a sliver straight from the knife.

'There's no water in the hills,' he said. 'The aquifer . . . it's all dried up.'

'Dig some more, Papa. It's your wine.'

'I wish I could, *ma chérie*,' he said, cutting himself a bit of the Fourme d'Ambert. 'The water is being used for other things.'

'But the vineyard . . . all the field hands are gone,' I said. 'The vines will die.'

'Pétain wouldn't put the vineyards of Creuzier-le-Vieux at risk if he didn't have to — we all have to sacrifice something for peace; this is mine.' He patted my hand when I shook my head. 'Do not worry. I'm making a good profit off what I have bottled. The regime comes only to me for their needs. I have no competition. You will see. Soon enough everything will be back to normal. Pétain has our best interests on his mind.' Papa smiled. 'I'm confident. He's our hero.'

I put the sliver of cheese on the board uneaten. 'But he handed over our soldiers, accepted defeat.'

'Don't believe everything your mother tells you, Adèle.' He swallowed. 'Nothing in war is easy. She tended the wounded, but I lived with them in the trenches, and with the dead buried in the cliffs of Gallipoli. Pétain gave us peace. Now we have to do our part.' He glanced around his wine bar and over the Pétain posters pasted to his walls. 'This is my part.'

'Did you hear about Madame Brochard?'

'The farmer's wife?' Papa grabbed an opened bottle he had under the front counter and poured some wine into the one clean glass he had on hand. He sipped the wine, rolling it in his mouth. When he noticed I was watching him, he turned the label around to show me the bottle was one of his. 'Do you want some?'

'Papa, she was arrested and sent to Drancy.'

'Yes, yes, I heard . . . illegal immigration,' he said, taking another drink of wine.

'No, Papa. She's not a foreigner. They arrested her because she is Jewish.'

'Impossible.' He set down his glass. 'That is not a law. Did you hear this from your mother?'

The door flew open and hit the wall with a clatter, wine bottles clinking and clanging in their racks. Charlotte stood in the doorway, first looking happy to see me, and then not. It was the same look she'd give me when we were young, after she caught me using her paints without asking. 'Back from the nunnery?'

'Charlotte.' I stood up, smiling cautiously, remembering that the last time she saw me I was running away from her.

Papa took his wine glass and headed upstairs to the flat he'd made above his wine bar. 'I'll find you a clean glass.'

She waltzed in, arms crossed, waiting until Papa was out of sight. 'I was so angry with you, Adèle.' She walked closer until she stood a breath away from my face. 'You always do what you want when you want — never think about anyone else. I was tying up your bouquet the morning you left

138

and you said nothing. Your own sister!'

I shook my head. 'I know, and I'm sorry.'

'People are calling you a runaway bride. It's humiliating for all of us! But, I knew you'd be back. You never last more than a few weeks doing any one thing.'

She paused for a reaction. Charlotte wouldn't understand — she was incapable of understanding — I couldn't have told her I wanted to leave.

'And what do you think about this?' Charlotte said, whirling her finger around the room.

'The wine bar?'

'It's because of you.'

I poked my thumb into my chest. 'I'm responsible?'

'You cast a rock into a calm lake and then you turned your back.' Charlotte's brow furrowed, and the light brown curls she usually kept pinned behind her ears sprung from her head. 'Papa left Mama when he realized she helped you, that she planned your escape to the nunnery. She told Papa she was a Gaullist. Now they must lie to everyone, pretend he's only in the city because of the wine bar, when we know they are separated. Our parents, separated!'

'And being a Gaullist is bad?'

She gasped, putting a hand to her chest. 'Whose side are you on, Adèle? Charles de Gaulle is diverting all the progress Pétain has made. We stay the course, like Papa says, follow Pétain, and we will be back to normal sooner than later.'

'Normal?' I was surprised how everyone in my family used the same words to prove their point of view. 'Is it normal for your father to betroth you against your wishes?'

'Papa did you a favour! Couldn't get a proposal on your own — you're the most erratic person I swear — so Papa got a man for you. A good one, too. French police, stable pay, calling the shots.' She looked at a split in her fingernail before folding her arms tightly across her body. That's when I noticed how thin she was, her body back to the shape she always had been. She wasn't pregnant anymore: she must have had her baby.

'Charlotte!' I smiled. 'You've had your baby! Was it a girl like you hoped?' I remembered the pink and blue blankets she needled months ago, wondering which one she ended up keeping. The pink one had lace sewn around the edges, whereas the blue one had ribbon. 'Or a baby boy?' I moved to kiss her, but she pushed me back.

'You would have known had you been here.' Charlotte paused, looking down at the ground before standing very straight. 'The baby was stillborn.'

'Stillborn? As in . . .' I couldn't say the word aloud even if I wanted to. *Dead.* 'My God, Charlotte.' I closed my eyes briefly. 'I'm sorry. I'm so sorry . . .'

Charlotte shrugged, trying to look unaffected by the tragedy, but her eyes swelled with tears, and I could tell she was absolutely devastated. 'A girl.'

'You already buried her?'

She nodded. 'Claudeen's hill.'

Claudeen's hill had been around for a century. It was a mountainous pile of dirt and rock with thick green grass growing at the top. If the grass

140

was hair, then the white fence that bordered it was the crown. Only the rich or the lucky had family tombs at that cemetery.

'I'd like to go,' I said, 'to where she's buried and pay my respects — '

'No,' she said, shaking her head.

'But why?'

Charlotte looked to the ground again, unable to answer. That's when I saw Gérard standing on the corner waiting for a car to pass. I felt woozy and sick from Charlotte's news. Now I felt something else. She went to leave, but I stopped her by the elbow. 'Don't leave just yet . . . ' I said to her, with my eyes set on Gérard as he crossed the street.

Charlotte shook her head. 'No, sister. This is your hole. Not mine.' She kissed my cheek and then whispered in my ear. 'Insufferable as you are, I missed you terribly.'

My knees shook watching Gérard take his last few steps across the street; I was sad then frightened and at a loss for words. All I could do was reach for Charlotte, and we threw our arms around each other, squeezing lovingly and hard. Then she was gone, and I found myself standing alone among the tables, wishing Papa would stop looking for that damn glass and get back downstairs.

Breathe. I counted, thinking of the sun, and the grass like Marguerite had taught me.

Gérard looked through Papa's window, and I stood straight up. He brushed a lock of hair from his eyes, which had turned beady and red as a flare when he spotted me holding on to one of the tables. He pulled open the door, Papa's bell

141

chiming frantically.

'Adèle.' A snarl turned on his lips. 'You're back.'

The old men outside pressed their faces to the window. 'Gérard.'

We stood in silence, Gérard's shoulders puffing along with his chest. Papa banged around upstairs singing a song meant for himself, unaware Gérard was here and standing in front of me.

Breathe, I said to myself, but my heart raced no matter how many numbers I counted in my head, and I wondered what Marguerite would say if she knew I had started to panic. She'd pull me up by the armpits, tell me the Résistance isn't a place for weaklings. I exhaled. *Be yourself. He wants to win.*

I smoothed my skirt against my thighs, holding my head up. 'I want to apologize.'

He laughed. 'What makes you think I'll accept?'

'I got cold feet, Gérard. I was wrong with how I handled it, and I want to make it up to you. Give you — us — a second chance.'

Gérard licked his lips as if he had just finished eating me and had spat out my bones. 'I've moved on.'

'Well if you don't want me then — '

He caught me by the arm. 'Do you realize how much you've embarrassed me, my family?' His fingers dug into the soft part of my underarm. Gérard was all muscle, brutish some would say, with a round nose and face. He was never one for nice words, and I was prepared, albeit mentally, for him to strike me. 'The humiliation of telling Prêtre Champoix you'd run away . . . he's been my family's priest since I was a boy.'

'I'm sure the situation was displeasing — '

'You left me for a nunnery. Lord, Adèle!' His lips quaked. 'Even if I wanted to I couldn't take you back. It's a question of decency.' He threw my arm to the side. 'I can't remember the last time I was that mad. You can thank your sister for — '

Papa bounded down the stairs with a grin glossed red with wine. 'Gérard!' He had his own glass in one hand and a clean glass in the other. 'How lovely.'

Papa handed him the clean glass, which he twirled in his hand, eyes boring into mine. He knew as well as I that Papa had his own interests in linking our families together. Papa talked about the new German wine that had just come in, flipping the crate around as if forgetting he had tried to hide it just a few minutes ago.

A sly smile cocked on Gérard's face. I could see his gums, which was normal since Gérard rarely closed his mouth. 'I was just telling Adèle how the Hotel du Parc needed a maid. Someone to clean the toilets, wash out the bins.'

My faced dropped, and Gérard burst out laughing. 'Kidding, of course. Why don't you bring me lunch tomorrow, Adèle? Let's start there.' He took a cigar from his front pocket and stuck it in the corner of his mouth. 'A second chance.'

Once I saw his cigar all I could think about was the box in his office. 'Thank you, Gérard.'

Papa smiled — Gérard had agreed. He pulled a German bottle of wine from the crate. 'Please, stay for some wine.'

'No time for wine, Albert,' he said, giving Papa the glass back. 'I've got diplomats arriving in half an hour.'

143

'Very well,' Papa said. 'Say hello to your family for me, will you?'

Gérard nodded, looking me over.

'Are you still with the police?' Gérard was dressed in a pressed business suit, the kind I used to see the wealthy wear in the gardens, before the war. 'Because you're dressed rather nice for a day of arresting.'

'Sharp little tongue you've got for someone wanting a second chance,' he said. 'It's good to know you haven't changed too much since you've been gone. Here's a lesson for you.' He ran his fingers down the front of his jacket. 'People who work hard and don't run away from commitment get rewarded. If I ran away from opportunity, well, that would make me a defeatist. Right, Adèle?'

'You're right, Gérard. You can't run away from opportunity.' I smiled, putting my arm around Papa. 'That's why I'm looking forward to bringing you lunch tomorrow.'

Gérard stared at me, sucking on his unlit cigar, while Papa talked about getting me a car. 'I'll make arrangements with our neighbours, the Morissets. He owes me a favour and with enough wine . . . he'll have petrol for the both of you.'

'Thank you, Papa — '

Gérard started for the door, shouting back as he left, 'I'll be waiting!'

'Gérard saved a soldier from the mud during the Battle of Sedan,' Papa said, pouring himself another glass of wine. 'He's just a fine fellow — brave.'

I watched Gérard as he crossed the street, pausing to pick up a lone RAF leaflet that somehow

144

survived morning foot traffic. He crumpled it in his hands and packed it like a snowball before throwing it at a man hunkered against the side of a building, picking stickers from the bottom of his feet.

The man looked up at Gérard with gaunt, sunken eyes.

'Sure is, Papa.'

12

The savoury aroma of Mama's pot-au-feu seeped from the cracks of her kitchen door and hovered in the late afternoon air. Nobody made stew like Mama: root vegetables from the cellar, and most likely the best cuts of meat from a special tin she hid under the mounds of canned ox tails. I dropped my bicycle on the patio, not even bothering with the kickstand. Comfort — that's what I thought, as I smelled the clove and onion in the air, and God knew I needed a little comforting after the day I'd had, and maybe even a scalding hot bath with salts for my feet.

I opened the door and my heart leapt from my chest. Mama wasn't the one at the stove, but a stranger. A man. I must have screamed since he jumped higher than I did. I drew a knife from the counter and waved it in the air. 'Who are you?' I barked.

One hand held his chest as he exhaled; the other held a soup ladle he'd been using to stir Mama's stew. 'You must be Adèle.'

I lowered the knife.

A dark blonde curl fell near his eyes, and he swept it back into a smooth wave. He was too young to be Mama's lover, and by the distinguishing lines near his eyes I knew he was too old to be some boy Mama paid for handy-work.

'Do I know you?'

'No,' he said, 'but we know mutual people.'

'My mother, you mean?'

He glanced back and forth between me and the ladle still in his hand, stirring faster the lower I dropped the knife.

'Who are you?' I said. 'And where's my mother?'

'I'm Luc,' he said. 'Pauline has told me a lot about you.'

'She's told me nothing about you.' I had lowered the knife completely, but still gripped the handle, looking around the room as if Mama was hiding somewhere. 'Where did you say my mother was?'

He smiled slightly as he stirred the pot, and it was hard not to notice his long-lashed bluish-green eyes and the rugged shadow budding along his jawline.

'I didn't,' he said.

My mouth hung open at his gall, and we stared at each other. I wanted to be mad at him, but something gleaming in his eyes and the way his lips looked when he smiled made it impossible for me to feel anything other than an irritating sense of intrigue.

Mama burst through the root cellar door, a jar of pickled onions gripped in her hand. She looked surprised to see Luc and I talking and then oddly complacent.

'You've introduced yourselves,' she said. 'Good.' Mama set the jar on the counter and popped the lid off.

I finally let go of the knife. 'Introduced?' I said. Luc glanced at me, which made me pause. 'I suppose you could call it that.'

Mama asked Luc to pull the bouquet garni out of the pot. He seemed hesitant at first, looking

147

into the pot as if unsure where it was, but then pulled out the soggy twine of herbs she had used for seasoning and set it on the counter.

Luc licked a drop of broth that had gotten on his finger. 'This might be better if it were lamb.'

'You can't get lamb in Creuzier-le-Vieux,' Mama said. 'Pétain shipped it all to Germany.'

Luc took an unmarked bottle of wine and dumped what was left into a tall glass meant for milk. 'At least he hasn't given away all of the wine,' he said, and Mama chuckled, though I could tell she wasn't amused.

The strange scene that had unfolded itself before me took me by surprise as much as making me wonder. Mama didn't share her kitchen with strangers, other than the rabbits and chickens she killed for us to eat. 'What's going on here?' I waved a finger at everything from the boiling pot, to Luc, to Mama. 'And I'm not talking about supper.'

Mama's shoulders stiffened. 'He's not my lover, Adèle. If that's where your mind is.'

'I figured that, Mama.' The sleeves on Luc's collared shirt had been rolled up to his elbows, exposing the fine, ginger-blonde hairs on his forearms. 'From the looks of him, I'm guessing he's half your age.'

Luc smiled. Mama didn't.

Mama pointed at the photo of her and Papa hanging on the wall. It was taken years ago, before I was born. Both posed with their arms wrapped around each other, their lips locked in a kiss. 'Hear that, Albert? Your daughter thinks I'm old.' Mama spoke with ease as if Papa could hear her, as if he wasn't kilometres away in his own flat with nothing but his German wine and Pétain posters to keep him company.

'You haven't answered my question.' I felt Marguerite's stern brow on my face.

Luc looked at Mama while Mama looked at me, the boiling pot of stew spurting broth onto the counter.

'I was meaning to tell you this morning, but you had enough on your mind.' Mama took a cigarette from her case and lit it with the cloisonné lighter she had taken from her apron pocket. 'After you left for Lyon, I found myself in a position where I could help. And with your father gone I thought why the hell not?' Luc had walked over to the window near the door to fix a split in the curtains before Mama blurted, 'He's from the Résistance.'

'The Résistance?' I whispered the words before I shouted them. 'The Résistance!'

Luc put a finger to his lips to shush me, but I had already covered my mouth with my hand.

Mama glared. 'Why don't you shout it from the patio, Adèle?'

Luc moved past me, placing both hands on my shoulders even though there was plenty of room for him to pass. He sat down on a stool opposite me, across the kitchen cart that had now been set to function as our table, and rolled his sleeves up to his biceps before tucking into his bowl of stew, listening to Mama and me talk. He was sculpted in all the right places, and he looked strong, damn strong, as if those arms had muscled the yoke of a plane for many years.

'Are you staying overnight?'

He nodded. 'But you won't see me.' He looked

at Mama, now talking to the both of us. 'It will be like I'm not even here.'

I laughed. 'You're a little hard to miss.'

'What do you mean?'

My stomach did a little flip when he looked at me this time, something I hadn't felt in a long time. I rested an elbow on the cart that separated us, head in my hand, and thought about how his wavy hair complemented his warming smile. 'What I mean is . . . you're here now,' I said. 'And I can see you.'

'Yes,' he said, and then paused. 'And I see you.'

★ ★ ★

After dinner, Luc slipped out the back door and into the barrel cellar while Mama and I cleaned up the dishes. I scrubbed the same bowl over and over again in the sink as I stared out the window.

'I trust you saw Gérard today,' Mama said, and I nodded.

'And?' Mama said.

'I'm bringing him lunch tomorrow at the Hotel du Parc.'

She took a deep breath, nodding. 'I knew you'd be successful.'

My eyes had never left the window, looking for any trace of Luc as he took shelter in the barrel cellar. 'Where's he going to sleep, Mama? In the dirt? Next to the barrels?'

'Why do you care?' she said. 'Or, do I need to ask?' She smiled to herself before taking a drag from her cigarette.

'That's not why I'm asking.'

'Isn't it?' Mama said, studying me. 'Don't forget, Adèle, you have an important job to do. It takes a special woman to use her charms on a tyrant. Best if you keep your mind on your goal. No use in getting distracted. Gérard will sense another man's touch on you,' she said, placing more dirty dishes into the sink. 'And I'm worried about you as it is.'

'I know,' I said.

'Did the Résistance tell you it was going to be easy?' Mama had lit another cigarette and was watching me as my fingers worked their way around the slippery, soapy bowl.

'No, Mama. They did not.'

I thought about Luc's face when I walked into the chateau, and how relaxed he was even after I waved a knife at his face. I winced, thinking how awful I must have looked.

'He sleeps in a hidden room, Adèle,' Mama said.

'What?' I looked at her, mid wash.

'Dug into the ground, right under your father's oak-bending machine,' she said, smiling slyly. 'Albert would kill me if he knew. But *you* should know, in case anyone visits us. Wouldn't want you to stumble upon it.'

'A hidden room,' I repeated.

'What did you expect?' Mama said. 'A bed set up out in the open?' She laughed her dry, smoker's laugh.

'How often does he come inside?' I said, and then wondered if he'd be eating supper with us every night, which made my stomach flip again.

'Not often,' she said. 'The cellar door is shut when he's gone, left open when he's here. The

151

Résistance likes it that way. Luc said it was to throw off suspicious neighbours. If the doors are open, what would we be hiding?'

'What is he hiding, guns?'

'I saw a radio transmitter,' Mama said. 'He said the Germans were driving around Lyon looking for radio pings.'

'Germans?' The bowl slipped from my hands and broke in the bottom of the sink. 'In the Free Zone?'

Mama reached into the sink and fished out the broken bits of bowl. 'It was only a matter of time, Adèle. Only a matter of time.'

* * *

Mama went up to bed, and I wiped down the counters and turned off the lights before taking one of Mama's cigarettes outside with me for a smoke. The night looked darker than it did the other night, with little pricks of light for stars that barely lit up the vineyard. Reminded me of the last time I smoked on the patio.

The night before Charlotte's wedding.

She sat with her back to me as I looked out the door. Mama and Papa had already gone to sleep and I thought she had too, so I was surprised to see her outside all by herself in her blue and poufy sleeping gown. I sat down beside her, accidentally scaring her, and her hand flew to her chest.

'Adèle!' she said, catching her breath, but then smiled.

I offered her a cigarette after lighting my own.

'You know Henri doesn't like cigarettes,' she said.

152

'He'll never know,' I said, pushing it at her. 'It's your last night here.'

She reached for it after a short pause. 'No,' she said, shaking her head, but then took the cigarette. 'All right. One won't hurt.' I struck the lighter and she took a puff with her lips drawn up like a coin purse.

I laughed, watching her struggle.

'Stop that,' she said, coughing, waving the smoke away.

'Just breathe normally. You're trying too hard,' I said, and we smoked together on the step.

'You'll visit, won't you?' I said. 'I don't know what I'll do if I lose my cooking partner.'

'I'll have a house of my own,' she said. 'Henri says he's going to buy us a nice apartment near the square. Brand-new furniture too.'

'Where's he going to get brand-new furniture?' I said, and she shrugged.

'I don't know. That's what he said.'

'Well, you can still visit . . . ' I flicked ash from my cigarette. 'Besides, your paints are here, all your canvases,' I said, and she exhaled. 'You promised me a painting of the vineyard. Remember? Papa's vines in the summer . . . I want to remember it always. The sun and how it shines on the grape skins. Only you can capture — '

'I'll try.' She looked down, sighing.

'Of course, I could try to paint it myself,' I said, and her mouth hung open.

'Don't touch my paints,' she said, but I was only teasing.

'Can I have your bed quilt?' I said.

'Ready for me to leave, are you?' she said. 'Yes, you can have it. But you can't have my bedroom.'

'Why not?' I said. 'You won't be needing it. I think I might like your bedroom. It's bigger.' It was then I thought about what it would be like without Charlotte around, and having her bedroom empty. I didn't even want her bedroom. 'I won't take it. But do paint me something soon.'

She puffed on her cigarette, blowing great big clouds of white into the air, but then she coughed uncontrollably into her arm, laughing.

'What?'

'I can't imagine what a painting of yours would look like.' She slapped the patio with her hand, still laughing.

'Shh!' I looked up to Mama and Papa's bedroom window. 'You want to wake up Mama and Papa?' I said, and she shook her head, her laugh turning into a giggle.

'I can't be that bad,' I said. 'With you as a sister? Maybe I could do it?'

She snubbed out her cigarette. 'Umm. Hmm.'

'I wouldn't even try.' I nudged her.

She adjusted the poufy blue fabric spread out around her and over the step. 'Are you going to wear that tomorrow night with Henri?' I wouldn't put it past Charlotte. She'd probably wet her hair to keep the curls down, and bathe with special salts too.

'I don't know yet,' she said.

'Are you nervous?' I said, and she turned to me. 'About the . . . Well, you know . . . '

She laughed. 'You can say it,' she said. 'The wedding night?'

'All right. The wedding night. Are you nervous?'

Henri was tall and slender with soft features, not the rugged type. It never crossed my mind that he'd be

154

anything other than gentle. Still, I was curious.

Charlotte inhaled deeply, holding her arms to her chest, smiling. 'I can't wait.' She looked at me. 'When you're in love there's no time for nerves. It'll be just me and Henri, and nobody else in the world. Just . . . us.'

Suddenly it felt as if Charlotte didn't have one night left, but had already gone. She felt years away, not my sister, but a woman. A married woman from the city.

'I want a thousand babies!' She lit up. 'All with his brown eyes. Lots and lots of babies. Henri wants a thousand too. All for France. Did I tell you how Henri proposed? It was in the evening, and the sun had just begun to set . . .'

'I know,' I said, taking a drag. 'You've told me a hundred times.'

'Oh, have I?' She laughed. 'I'm just teasing you. I know I have.' She paused, and then put her hand on my knee and sat there for many minutes, staring into the dark vineyard.

'I'm going to miss this, Charlotte,' I said. 'Me and you . . .'

She threw her arms around me. 'I'll always be your sister,' she said. 'Always.'

A rustling on the patio startled me. 'Hallo?' I snubbed out my cigarette and got up, listening in the dark. Peat and sour grapes wafted warmly in the air, and then the fresh burn of sweet tobacco.

'Luc?' I said, and he turned around slowly from the other side of the patio.

'What are you doing out here?' I said, as he smoked his cigarette.

He slid over, patting the empty space next to him for me to sit down. That's when I noticed the kitchen window was ajar and he was just a few feet away from where Mama and me were talking. My stomach dropped, and I felt very embarrassed. And when he looked at me in the dark, cigarette smoking from his lips with his reflecting eyes, I felt exposed and vulnerable.

I sat down, tucking my skirt under my legs. 'Hallo.'

'Hallo,' he said.

'How long have you been out here,' I said, fishing to see exactly what he'd heard.

He blew smoke from the corner of his mouth. 'Not long.'

'Oh?' I said.

'Yes,' he said.

I looked out into the dark vineyard, not sure what to say or how to react, legs pushed into my chest, but then sat up straight. 'Can I have one?' I said, and I motioned to his cigarette.

He smiled, reaching into his back pocket for paper, and then the other pocket for the tobacco.

'What are you doing out here?' I finally asked.

'I could ask you the same thing,' he said, and a surprised little gasp came from my mouth, almost laughing.

'No, you couldn't,' I said, and now he was the one laughing.

'Why not?'

'Because this is my patio,' I said.

'Oh . . . ' he said.

I watched him roll me a cigarette, sprinkling in the tobacco he pulled from his pouch, and then move the paper to his lips to seal it. I hesitated when he offered it to me, both our fingers on the same cigarette, which I was sure he noticed.

156

'Thanks,' I said, pulling away, and he struck his lighter and we smoked together.

'Mama said you're set up in the barrel cellar,' I said, and he nodded. 'Have you been here long?'

'Long enough to know you were in Lyon,' he said, looking at me. 'With the sisters.'

'Mama told you that?' I said. 'What else did she say?'

'What was it like?' he said. 'You're so . . . '

'So what?' I said, back straightening.

'Beautiful,' he said, and I shoved my cigarette into my mouth, puffing nervously, thankful he couldn't see me blushing in the dark. 'Has nobody told you?'

'Not the way you just did,' I said.

I'd heard a fleeting twinge of a British accent, which surprised me. 'Where are you from? Not Vichy, are you?' I said, but I was sure he was from somewhere far away.

'I'm not from Vichy,' he said, pausing, smiling.

'And . . . '

'And that's all.' He laughed. 'I can't tell you where I'm from.'

'Well it's only fair since you know where I'm from,' I said, but he didn't look like he was going to give in. 'How about this . . . What do you miss the most from where you're from?'

'That's a hard one,' he said, but then took a deep breath through his nose, closing his eyes. 'Fresh bread and vanilla oil. Haven't had that in a long time. And sipping wine in the sun, lying in the grass. That's it. All four of them together. Took them for granted before I . . . ' He looked at me. 'Well, you know.'

The last time I had wine in the sun I was with Gérard. 'I've had enough wine in the sun,' I said, and Luc looked at me.

'One day you might find you miss it,' he said, and I realized how difficult his job must be. To not see the sun, to not feel it on your face without fear of someone seeing you and questioning who you are.

'I'm sorry,' I said.

'Sorry for what?' he said.

'I shouldn't have brought it up. I'm sure there's lots of things you miss.'

'I have a feeling you'll know soon enough,' he said. His cigarette was done, and he got up after stubbing it out on the patio, but I still had half mine left.

'Thanks for the cigarette. See you around?' I said, and then winced. That wasn't a phrase I normally used, and I thought he could tell.

He smiled, stepping into the shadowy darkness of the night. 'See you around.' He winked, and my stomach flipped again; then when he was out of sight, I collapsed backward on the patio and smoked my cigarette while staring up into the stars.

'Christ, Adèle,' I said to myself. 'You're such an idiot.'

13

The following morning, I packed a tin with a crust of bread and a jar of peaches from the root cellar. I wasn't going to give Gérard any of our meat until Mama talked me into it. 'He'd know,' she said, 'that you weren't sincere if you didn't hand it over.' As much as I hated to admit it, I knew she was right and stuck a can of the pork in with the rest of it.

Before I could deliver anything to the Hotel du Parc, I had to look for a new dress. Something Gérard hadn't seen before. With the tin hooked on my arm and a gingham towel as a cover, I took the money Marguerite had given me to Le Grand Marché Couvert, a covered market filled with a hundred vendors selling everything they could get their hands on. Nothing lacy, I told myself, but something sophisticated.

Mme Dubois had been selling textiles and exotic foods brought up from Marseilles for donkey's years, as she'd always say. But since the armistice she kept the clothes hidden. Mama once told me she sewed for Coco Chanel twenty years ago, but Madame denied it when I asked.

Mme Dubois' oversized glasses had slipped to the end of her nose and she pushed them back up as she talked. 'I don't want to go out naked, of course. I always stash a little of the fabric away for myself.' She pointed discreetly to the linen-covered bolts of fabric she had under her table.

159

'Madame Dubois, naked?' I laughed softly.

Mme Dubois picked lint from her rose-print skirt before looking over the rim over her glasses. 'It could happen.' She leaned over her vendor table, her striped top grazing the jars of dates and sticky figs she had imported from Africa. 'Not that anyone would want to see me naked.' She laughed, running a hand through her thin brown hair.

A woman selling ground chicory at the table next to hers rolled her eyes as Mme Dubois talked. 'You talk about the strangest things, Dubois.' Madame waved for her to go away, but the woman sprayed rosewater at her from a perfume bottle.

'Ahh, the smell of rose,' Madame said. 'She sprays it to cover up the stink the Vichy police leave behind. They passed by not too long ago, love.' She put her hands together and played unconsciously with her wedding band. 'What can I help you with today?' The spray misted behind her. 'The chicory makes a nice coffee substitute!'

Mama had enough coffee stored in her root cellar to last three more months, but I wouldn't dare tell anyone we had such a treasure.

'I need a dress, Madame. Something fresh.'

Her eyes brightened. 'I have just the thing!' Underneath the bolts of fabric she had under her table were two dresses made from the same cloth as her shirt. 'Pinstripes are always in season, no matter how dreadful the drought is.'

I presumed the drought she was talking about had something to do with clothing rations and the designers in the north. She held the dresses by the sleeves to my shoulders. One was a size too large, but the other was a dead match. She folded it nicely and then set it on the table to be wrapped.

A woman with her arms full of bags reached for the dates, and Madame shooed her away. 'Not for sale,' she told her. 'Not. For. Sale.' The woman tilted her frilly hat before finally deciding to go to another table. Only after the woman was a good distance away did Mme Dubois' smile return.

'You should have a try of these dates before the shipments stop.'

'Do you know something I don't?'

'Only thinking out loud, love.' She lifted her glasses from her face, her eyes large as teacups filled with dark brown tea. 'When Africa is taken by the Allies, all of this will be gone.' She put a finger to her mouth, shushing herself. 'You didn't hear that from me, of course.'

I pointed into a sea of oily bottles. 'Is that vanilla oil?' I said, and she handed it to me.

'Last one,' she said. 'Better buy it before it goes too.'

A yellowy bottle with twine wrapped around the neck and a worn paper label, corked like wine. 'It smells heavenly.' I held the scent seeping from the cork, closing my eyes, thinking of Luc. 'It's perfect. I will take it.' I gave her a few coins.

Two girls about seventeen lingered between both tables; they giggled, talking about how handsome the gendarmes were in the Vichy police. One touched a bag of chicory for sale, and the woman with the rosewater sprayed her with it. 'Her son was given to the Germans also,' Madame said. 'Same camp as my son. But I can't talk about it with Pierre around.'

Her eyes flicked to her husband, who'd been stacking old books on a shelf behind her. A hazy greyness clouded his eyes when he looked up, and Madame cleared her throat. That's when I noticed that behind Pierre was a makeshift changing area made from a hanging curtain and a rod.

'Perhaps I could wear the dress out of here?'

'What a wonderful idea,' she said.

Mme Dubois held the curtain closed while I slipped out of my dress and into the new striped one. I smoothed the soft fabric over my thighs and listened to Madame talk about the crowds and how she could get coffee on the black market. 'You want bread? Forget about it. Unless you were smart enough to hoard some flour . . . '

Mme Dubois didn't have a mirror, but I could feel the fit of the dress against my body, smooth and snug, just enough leg to keep Gérard interested. I opened the curtain and handed Madame my old dress to sell in its place, along with a few francs to make up the difference. She smiled when she saw the Chanel label, but she had never stopped talking.

'Food for everyone Pétain says — what about our sons? Where are our prisoners? Bastard of a man — bargains with the Nazis and gains nothing — ' She groaned and snarled when she said Pétain's name. Then she closed her eyes and took a deep breath. 'Enough talk about the devil. This dress looks divine on you, love.' She glanced at the tin hanging off my arm. 'Need something else? Looks like you have your lunch.'

'No, actually.' I patted the tin. 'This is for Gérard — ' No sooner had his name flown out of

162

my mouth did I wish I could suck it back in and chew it up.

'Gérard Baudoin?' Every wrinkle in Mme Dubois' face flattened. 'Why would you be going to see him, love?' She put a hand on my old dress lying on her table. 'I thought you left him months ago, ran away before the wedding. That's what I heard from your mother, from everyone.'

'I did leave,' I said, standing straight, 'but I'm back now.'

'You're back together?'

I pulled my shoulders back. I was with a collaborator as far as she was concerned. 'He was a hero, you know, at the Battle of Sedan.'

'I don't know anything about the hero, Adèle. But I do know about his reputation as a gendarme with the Vichy police . . . the strings his uncle pulled so that he didn't have to be a prisoner of war.' Mme Dubois looked me over, her eyes skirting over the dress on my body and down the lines of the stripes. 'Like my son.'

A disgusted look pulled at her bottom lip, and I had a feeling she regretted letting me try the dress on. She shoved my old dress into my hands. 'I can't sell this rag. You'll need to pay entirely with francs.'

I handed her enough francs to more than cover the cost of the dress, but still she asked for more, shaking her head saying it just wouldn't do. After I had given her everything I had she motioned to the woman with the rosewater, snatching back my old dress from my hands.

'Spray her.'

163

Thin and measly Armistice Army soldiers guarded the front entrance of the Hotel du Parc between two flapping blue, white, and red Vichy flags. I walked in with my head held high, as if I was used to walking into the Parc with a lunch tin on my arm. The old front desk was now a processing area for visitors, and I made my way toward two men who looked like concierges with French kepi hats and shoulder boards.

'Hallo,' I said. 'I'm — '

'Mademoiselle Ambeh,' one said.

'Yes,' I said, and they both looked at each other, smirking. 'Do you know me?'

'We know of you,' one said, pointing down the corridor. 'Office number sixteen.'

They whispered to each other as I quietly made my way down the stuffy carpeted corridor to Gérard's office. The offices were guestrooms from when it was a spa and the secretaries had small desks in the corridors. I found Gérard's secretary chewing on a pencil and staring out the window. Her hair was done up in tight ringlets — older, maybe early fifties, and probably a wife to someone in the regime. I introduced myself, and she pointed to a chair for me to wait.

She watched me openly, her eyes gazing at my new dress. 'Adèle, you said?' Her cheeks rounded when she talked.

I nodded, smiling. 'Mmm.'

She opened a window to filter out some of the hovering cigarette smoke, and I shifted around in my seat, uncomfortable from the unwavering heat. Sweat beaded between my breasts and on my neck, which made the scent of rose all that more distasteful and stickier on my skin. *Think about the cigar box*, I told myself, shifting again.

I practised what it would be like to open the cigar box and offer him a cigar, choosing one out of many as he looked at me. Smiling — or would he be licking his lips? Then the words I was thinking came tumbling out, 'Want one?'

The secretary glanced up. 'Want what?'

I cleared my throat. 'Nothing.'

She got up from her chair and adjusted her thin dress belt. 'I believe they're almost finished,' she said, putting her ear to the door, listening to the muffled voices inside Gérard's office. She hopped back in her seat and turned toward her desk just as the door swung open.

I straightened up at the sight of Gérard, and my hands instantly trembled. *'He's attracted to the way you are,'* Marguerite had said. I took a deep breath. *Be yourself.*

Gérard's guest was a man with slicked-back hair. I guessed he was a member of the police, but by the style of his suit I started to think he was someone even more important. 'Absolutely, Monsieur Bousquet,' Gérard said, and my heart skipped a beat with this news — René Bousquet, head of the national police.

I closed my eyes briefly, thinking about the grass and the sun, but nothing seemed to help my thumping heart. My palms sweated.

Bousquet stopped in the doorway on his way out of Gérard's office, a cigarette pinched between two fingers. 'We understand each other. Good.'

165

'Fully, sir.'

They laughed, patting each other's backs. His secretary stood, motioning for me to get up. 'Stand,' she said very concerned, and I quickly moved to my feet, but Bousquet walked down the corridor, never even batting an eye in my direction.

Gérard stood in his doorway, his mouth open as if still laughing.

'I see my lunch has arrived.'

I swallowed, feeling my heart thrashing against my ribs. 'Certainly has, Gérard,' I said, placing a hand on the tin.

He glanced at my hands, which were still trembling and I curled them into fists. 'No water from the Source des Célestins?'

The Source des Célestins was a warm spring that flowed from decorated iron taps under the park pavilion. It was common to see people lined up near the Allier River in the morning and early afternoon wanting to get a sip of the sweet, bubbling water. Many believed the water could heal the most vicious of maladies, even reverse the signs of ageing. Others believed it was just water.

'I couldn't get a foot near it. There were people everywhere walking the promenade,' I lied. 'Maybe next time.'

'I drink from it several times a day, Adèle. You could get a foot in, if you wanted.' He motioned for me to come into his office.

'Like I said — ' smiling ' — maybe next time.' Gérard's secretary had sat back down in her chair, but popped back up just before the door closed. 'I did bring you a nice piece of pork, though,' I

166

said, pulling the can of meat out from under the gingham towel.

'What else do you have in there,' he said, looking from a distance. 'I don't like pork, or vanilla oil,' he said, and I turned, tucking the oil into the bottom of the tin. I was willing to give him my body to touch, but by God he wasn't getting the vanilla oil.

'I wasn't sure what to pack.'

Gérard laughed. 'You don't think I asked you here for lunch, do you?' He closed his window drapes and I glanced over the things in his office, searching for that damn cigar box, the light dimming. He took off his jacket and loosened his tie.

This was the Gérard I had come to know. 'I suppose I knew you'd have other plans.' I put the tin on top of the commode and fanned my neck with my hand, finally able to think of the cool grass and lying in the sun.

Be yourself. I smiled. *Thump. Thump. Thump.*

He pulled a silver flask from his desk and unscrewed the top, his eyes dancing over my body. 'You look — '

'Good? After spending time at a convent?'

'I was going to say something else.' A smirk teased his lips as he took a swig from the flask.

'Mmm.'

'I knew you'd be back.' I was ready for him to call me a quitter, say something about how I had never lasted long doing much of anything at all, but instead he twirled his finger around his office and smiled. 'I've been promoted — I'm very important.' He wiped his wetted lips with the fat of his thumb.

167

I leaned back on the commode, both hands bracing the top, checking to see if it lifted like a chest, but it felt very attached. 'Well, you know how I like to change my mind.'

'Like most women.' He took another swig before walking toward me and every muscle in my body tensed.

'Gérard, I — '

He pulled my head back by the hair. 'Yes?' He planted his lips on mine, and I smelled the liquor in his mouth coming from his nose. Even after weeks of being at a convent I couldn't have enjoyed his kiss, but I resisted the urge to pull away, my hands searching the top of the commode as he groped me with his free hand. Then to my relief, I saw a cigar box on a bookcase a few paces away, and closed my eyes, waiting for him to finish.

He panted for breath when he pulled away, and I boldly slipped out from under his compressing arms with his fingers still in my hair.

'Is that how you greet all women? Or just me?'

'Just you.' He wiped his lips with the back of his hand.

I rested my backside against the bookcase and tried to look as relaxed as I could. Gérard had been known to sense fear. I stretched my arms out, my fingers walking up the cigar box.

'Just so we're clear, I'm not marrying anyone right now,' I said.

'Because you'll run away again?'

I paused to think of a reason he'd believe, something only a selfish man like Gérard would understand. 'There's too much going on with the war, truthfully. I could never have the reception I

168

want. Not with the rations getting more restrictive. We'd have to get everything from the black market, and I don't want anything black at my wedding.'

Gérard reached for the box, laying his heavy hand right on top. 'You would only think about yourself.'

I pulled the box out from under his hand and opened it, offering him one of many cigars tucked inside. Gérard slammed the lid down.

'Tell me, why'd it have to be nunnery?'

'The nunnery, as you call it, gave me time to think. When I get married, it will be because I want to get married. Can't go to my father and expect it to be done.'

He held my hand, a light squeeze clenching tighter and tighter. 'Your father will see to it you fulfil our agreement.'

'My father thinks he arranged a marriage to the man you used to be — the one who bought wine for his family's spa, someone who said please and thank you and came from a good family. The one who saved a soldier from dying in the mud.'

Gérard swallowed, his face looking very hard. 'It was the Phoney War, Adèle. We were all in the mud. Not a single battle.'

'The Battle of Sedan wasn't part of the Phoney War, Gérard, and I know it was very bloody. You changed when you came home. You're not the man you were, or the boy I remember from all those years ago.'

He tossed my hand to the side. 'Women know nothing about this war. Phoney or otherwise.'

I looked at him squarely. 'One thing I'd bet my

life on.'

'And what's that?'

'If it weren't for the crafty ways of your uncle, you would've been on a train with the rest of the army headed to a German munitions factory after the armistice.'

He looked surprised. 'Who told you that?'

I wasn't sure if he knew Mme Dubois, but if I mentioned her name I was positive he'd seek her out and punish her. 'Does it matter?'

He touched the lapel of his expensive-looking black suit. 'It's not a secret, Adèle. I take opportunities when I can.'

I shrugged one shoulder. 'Hmm.'

'Hmm,' he said, shrugging his shoulder back.

'If you want me to marry you, you'll have to woo me like any man would.'

He swept my hair back with his hand and then curled a lock of it around his finger, pulling ever so subtly. 'You won't last.'

'You think I'll want to marry you sooner?'

He let go of my hair after a quick jerk. 'With the finer things in life becoming scarcer by the day . . . ' A chauvinistic laugh matched the look on his face. 'Seriously, Adèle, who else can get champagne and black caviar when there are food riots in Clermont-Ferrand?'

He opened his desk drawer to show me the Moët & Chandon bottle he had stashed next to a round tin with Russian writing on it. I reached for them, but he shut the drawer before my fingers had a chance to grace the labels.

'Russian caviar? Where did you get that from?'

'I have friends in the Reich, and the black market.'

170

'Mmm.' I looked at my nails, rubbing them together. 'I told you I didn't want anything black at my reception.'

'The war may drag on for years. Soon enough you'll be begging me to keep your bed warm and your family from scraping the bottom. The old vineyards in the Vichy hills won't be around much longer — there's no water — unless Albert can make water from wine. Everyone knows those hill grapes are inferior to the vineyards in Saint-Pourçain-sur-Sioule.' He laughed. 'But who knows, perhaps by the end of it I'll have my eye on someone else.'

'Is that a bet, Gérard Baudoin?' I folded my arms, holding my tongue — Papa's wine was inferior to no one's. 'I never thought of you as a gambling man.'

He took me by the hair, pulling my head back, and we locked eyes. 'Maybe I should take you right now,' he said, 'right here in my office.'

I swatted at him. 'You know I'm not that kind of woman,' I said, glaring, and he laughed deep from his throat, and it was then I realized that was what he loved the most. The chase.

He smelled me first, nuzzling his face against my neck, kissing me softly, then his knee pried my legs apart, and his hand slid between my legs. I shot up, locking my knees together and books tumbled from the bookcase onto the ground, flopping on top of each other.

The door flew open. 'Did you call me, sir?'

His secretary filled every space of the open door, holding her notepad.

'Get out of here!' Gérard yelled at her, and while

his head was turned, I hooked my finger on the corner of the cigar box and tipped it over. Cigars tumbled out of it and rolled on the floor. I dove to reach the box, but he beat me to it, grabbing my wrist, squeezing tightly, my whole arm shaking. 'Look what you did!'

The head of the police walked back in, and Gérard stood up with a fine jolt. I glanced at the box and read the three numbers off the back before standing up to straighten my dress.

'Emergency meeting, down the corridor,' he said. 'Now.'

Gérard snatched the box off the floor and left with it tucked under his arm. I straightened up, smoothing my dress flat and fixing my hair. 'He's very strong,' I said to his secretary. I reached for the lunch tin and hooked it on my arm.

'As I saw,' she said.

I walked out of the Hotel du Parc with my head high, past the processing desk, and out the front doors with the soldiers standing guard, only to race down the street and stop at the flower cart where Marguerite told me to deliver messages. A woman with grey hair tucked under a tattered head wrap sat on a stool counting coins.

'A single daisy,' I said.

The woman's eyes glowed. 'Just one?'

'Yes, yes . . . One.'

She slipped me a scrap of paper, and I winced, trying to remember the right code to say I was ready to meet, but then thought any code would work — *she'll know to come find me*. I walked away chanting to myself, 'Nineteen. Twenty-five. Thirty -two.'

14

Monsieur Morisset stood in front of his house waiting for me to return the car, tapping his foot, arms folded. He asked how often I was going to borrow it, and when I told him daily, he started counting the bottles of wine Papa had brought over. 'I'll have words with Albert,' he said.

I wanted to remind him about all that our family had done for his over the years, of the field work Papa gave his sons even though we had enough hands to do it ourselves. 'What about the candied grapes? Those dried ones your mama used to put up.'

'I'll bring some tomorrow.'

He nodded, uncorking one of the bottles with an opener he pulled from his pocket. 'Yes,' he said, sniffing the wine. 'Do that.'

I started up the hill to Papa's vineyard on my bicycle, the smell of rosewater in my hair turning my stomach as much as the pasty after-kiss Gérard left on my lips. A sharp rock popped my tyre, and the air hissed like a snake from the hole — nearly knocking me off my seat. I growled many words — words I should've been ashamed to say, but felt better saying.

Mama took one look at me standing in her doorway and bolted from her chair, cigarette burning between two fingers. 'You saw Gérard?' she said, and a violent shiver waved over my body, thinking of Gérard's hands moving up my leg. 'You were successful?'

I nodded, and she exhaled the breath she was holding.

'I was worried, thinking about you all morning,' she said. 'But you did what you had to do, when you had to do it.' She kissed my cheeks. 'I'm proud of you. Now, you need a drink. Something stiff to celebrate.' She snubbed her cigarette out and flicked her chin at the root cellar door.

'Is . . . ' I said, looking around the chateau. 'Is Luc here? I mean . . . ' I closed my eyes briefly. 'Will he be joining us for supper?' I placed my hand on the vanilla oil.

'The doors are closed,' Mama said. 'You remember what I said about the doors?'

'Oh.' I fought hard to hide my disappointment from Mama. I set the vanilla oil on the counter. 'What did you say about a drink?'

'Come on,' Mama said. 'I have just the thing.'

I followed Mama downstairs into the root cellar and toward the back where it smelled like the bottom of one of Papa's wine barrels. The walls were made of dirt and boulder, bugs making their homes in the cracks. Mama lit a fat candlestick and stuck it in between the boulders like a torch. She pointed to a wine rack about knee high and smiled before grabbing one of the wine bottles.

'Your father doesn't know I have these. They're worth a fortune.' She held up the bottle, pointing to its embossed label. 'This bottle alone is worth more francs than I gave you the day you left for the convent.' A smile spread on her face, and her eyes glossed in the dim light. 'His best pinot. Just as well we use it to celebrate your bold move today.

174

If only all the Résistance could celebrate this well.'

'Sounds like you're happier about hiding the wine from Papa.'

'Humph!' Mama took a corkscrew from her apron pocket and opened the bottle. 'Just take a drink, Adèle.' Mama handed me the bottle, and we took turns taking swigs from it. 'What happened today,' she said, glancing up, 'with him?'

I licked the wine from my lips, the faint taste of Gérard still in my mouth. 'I don't want to talk about it.' I snagged a cigarette from her pocket, lighting it using one of the candles in the wall, and filled my mouth with smoke. 'Other than to tell you he's forgiven me. The marriage will wait, however, thank God. He's courting me.'

'That is good news,' she said. 'But be careful. I don't trust him. Not for one minute.'

I rubbed my arms for warmth in the cool cellar. Mama had jars filled with everything from rhubarb to carrots, all stacked nicely on wooden shelves. The canned meat she kept in dirt divots carved into the wall. The secret to surviving war was to prepare for it, she had told me.

'Don't let anyone know about your food cache, Mama. They'd come to steal, I know it.'

'Over my dead body.'

Next to the shelves was a brass-buckled chest. Charlotte's name had been painted on the top in childlike writing. 'What's this?'

Mama waved me off as she drank more wine from the bottle, but I opened it anyway. Inside were hundreds of metal paint tubes, bound by string according to colour — the remnants of Charlotte's premarital dreams of becoming an

175

artist. I ran my hands over them, counting the different shades and hues. 'There's so many tubes. Why are there so many?'

Mama scoffed. 'She's married, remember. She doesn't paint anymore, or do much of anything if it isn't for that husband of hers.'

I stopped counting when I realized I couldn't count them all in one sitting. 'There's enough paint to cover every wall in the city!'

Mama peered into the chest, her lips wet with red wine. 'Waste. All of it.'

Hidden behind the narrow end of the chest, covered in a thick layer of cobwebs, were several canvases that had been slashed right down the middle with a very sharp knife. 'And what about the canvases?'

Mama flipped through them, checking to see if all the canvases had suffered the same dismal fate. 'They're all ruined. Shame. I suddenly had an idea we should paint a portrait of Pétain with one of his prostitutes and hang it at the Hotel du Parc!'

'There's not a canvas big enough for faces that hideous.'

Mama caught herself from gagging. 'I can imagine. Fraud of a man, touting family values while sleeping his way across the country.'

I flipped through the canvases myself. Sure enough, every single one had been ruined. 'Why would Charlotte destroy these?'

'It does seem vicious, doesn't it?'

Charlotte had always taken great care of her painting supplies, guarding them as if they were gold, so it didn't surprise me she had stored the paints in the darkest corner of the root cellar for safekeeping. However, the fate of the canvases had been a shock, destroying them the way she did.

'You remember, after she wed she took all her works off our walls, including that one of the Allier River, the promenade landscape she was so fond of. She says it's hanging in her new apartment, but I have no idea since she never invites me over — have you been there?'

'I haven't seen it either. She's been very private since her marriage.'

'Mmm.' Mama nodded as if she wasn't surprised. 'What she did with the rest of her works I can only guess. By the looks of the canvases, I'm sure they didn't survive.'

The paint's shiny, silver tubes glinted in the soft candlelight. In an odd way I felt as if I was intruding on their resting place, as if the lid was supposed to stay closed forever, and yet there I was, submersed in an intrusive curiosity. I lowered the chest's lid slowly, the hinges creaking.

'It's all very sad.'

'What is?'

I wiped the dust off the letters that made up Charlotte's name. 'Charlotte's dreams. Forgotten as much as this chest, the paints.'

Mama stood silent, looking at the chest with Charlotte's name written below the slashed canvases like an epitaph. A tear welled in one eye, and she sniffed it away. 'I can only guide my children. I can't make you do something you won't — ' She hung her head down. 'Sometimes I feel I can speak for you. But other times, I know I can't.'

I assumed Mama was referring to the cadre of

moments she tried to talk Charlotte out of getting married. Although Charlotte married her husband for love, the timing of her union was suspect, just after the armistice when Papa declared himself a staunch Pétainist, and her husband became a Vichy diplomat. Mama always said the path of Pétain was a dead one, and she had no plans to follow a dead man.

'Is that why you didn't tell me about Charlotte's baby?'

Mama winced hard. I hadn't forgotten she asked me to see Charlotte first thing when I came back to Vichy.

'I'm sorry about that, Adèle. I am. I couldn't bring myself to say the words. It was a private funeral. Just her and her husband is what she told me. I'm still heartbroken about it, too heartbroken to say it out loud.'

'I understand.'

'Did she — has she — taken you there? To the grave?'

'No,' I said. 'I haven't been.'

Mama nodded. 'She hasn't taken anyone as far as I know. I faced many things as a nurse in the 1914 war, but nothing — nothing — has been as hard as watching your family crumble into dust.'

I was stunned to hear Mama mention her time as a nurse; she rarely brought it up. Part of me didn't want to push the subject, but as more quiet seconds passed with her looking at the ground, the courage to broach the subject built inside of me.

'Mama, tell me about the lighter. Your time as a nurse. Elizabeth — Mother Superior.'

Mama sighed heavily, sitting down in a wood chair and slumping forward. 'There were three of us. Different war, but the same enemy — ruthless.' She paused, swallowing dryly, pulling the cloisonné lighter from her pocket and rubbing the inscription on the back before slipping it back in. 'Let's just say I understand why Elizabeth joined the Order after the war.'

Mama downed the rest of the wine. 'That's all I want to say right now.' She gazed at the empty bottle, her grip tightening. 'Damn Germans.' She threw the bottle against the stone wall, and the glass shattered into a handful of sharp chunks, some getting stuck in between the stones, others lying curve side up in the dirt. She took a deep breath, and a reprieving smile lifted her face. 'I should throw bottles more often.'

Mama straightened herself up, tucking her hair behind her ears and smoothing her apron flat against her dress, but then pulled a piece of paper from her other pocket. She looked like she had forgotten it was there with the deep-set creases between her eyes.

'A letter to Papa?'

Mama shrugged, sliding the letter back into her pocket. She walked out of the cellar, touching both walls with delicate fingers to keep herself straight after the wine, leaving me with Charlotte's chest and the light from one fat candlestick that got brighter the longer it burned.

★ ★ ★

The next morning, I woke to find my bicycle standing upright on the back patio with its tyre plump, full of air. Luc. I hesitated, looking back at the thick black strip of air cutting between the cellar's open doors, wondering if he was indeed below Papa's oak bending machine like Mama had said, and what it looked like.

Made of stone and larger than most people's homes, the cellar's vaulted ceiling arched like a cathedral with dark wood beams. It was where Papa aged his wine and kept his work equipment, and it smelled as fruity as the fermented grapes and peaty soil that had been trudged in from his oversized work boots. The door was not built to protect or hide the work of the Résistance, but was in fact very ordinary.

I made up my mind to walk over, and I took the vanilla oil with me.

'Hallo?' I whispered, pushing open the doors. The walls were still lined with Papa's tilling tools; behind them, and ever so faint, were the free-hand scribbles of Charlotte and me written in charcoal from when we were children.

I walked in, shutting the door behind me, and over to the oak-bending machine Papa used to cut wine barrels. I pushed it until it rolled a few feet away, exposing a plank of wood with a hole just big enough for one finger.

I crouched down and knocked on the floor, which felt odd to do. Nobody answered.

I could just turn around; he'd never know I had come. But I'd never seen a real transmitter before, only heard about them arriving by parachute.

I poked my finger through the hole and lifted

180

the board up. A short ladder led into a cave of a room, lit all aglow with a kerosene lantern. 'Luc?' I said, just to be sure. Nothing. I climbed down the ladder and into the room, which was no bigger than a large wash closet with a small table. And his radio. Looked like a metal valise, one a typist would carry, though it was hulky, a massive heap of metal with more knobs and wires than I could have imagined.

My eyes skirted around the small room, and I was thinking I should leave. I set the vanilla oil on his table, but instead of leaving I sat down in his leather chair and picked up the ceramic mug he'd left behind, half-full with diluted tea that smelled of liquorice. 'And headphones . . . ' I traded the mug for the headphones and slipped them on, closing my eyes, and caught a whiff of his cologne, something musky hovering in the air. My mind went straight to Luc. *He's so damn handsome.* I smiled to myself, humming a song I remembered from Charlotte's wedding. The one she and Henri danced to.

We had just toasted them good fortune and Charlotte pulled me aside to gift me her wedding bouquet. 'I know you'll have one of your own someday,' she said, smiling. 'But I want you to have this as a promise. A promise that one day love will find you.'

She kissed my cheeks.

'Charlotte, I . . . '

Henri looked at her from across the garden, under the glowing lantern lights strung across the estate garden. Even from so far away I could see love filling up his eyes. He was everything Charlotte wanted in a man. A commandant in the Colonial Army, turned

181

local diplomat. *Respected. Good family.*

Loving.

The flowers felt incredibly soft. 'Thank you.'We both smelled the same rose, and laughed when our noses touched. 'You're married now,' I said, and she nodded. 'What does love feel like?' I said, and she looked at me, surprised by my question.

'Love,' she breathed, and her eyes glossed with tears. 'There's a fluttering,' she said, cupping her hand near her stomach, 'deep inside, like butterfly wings, where you feel fragile as a hollow egg. But then it pulls, the fluttering, and you feel attached, as if everything in your body is connected ... to someone else.'

Henri called her to him from the dance floor as the band played a slow number. 'I wish this for you someday, sister,' she said just before he swept her away.

'What are you doing in here?' a voice said from behind, and I shot up from the chair, shrieking, only to see it was Luc.

I ripped the headphones from my ears, and he folded his arms. An excruciatingly awkward silence followed, both of us staring into the other's eyes. I set the headphones back on the table next to the microphone. 'Sorry.'

Luc moved the lantern to a hook protruding from one of the oak staves in the wall, rolling his eyes over the table, his radio, and settling on his notepad. 'Your mother ever teach you about manners?'

'Of course,' I said. 'Why?'

'I don't remember inviting you down here.'

He smoothed away a tuft of wavy hair from his furrowing brow, grabbing his notepad. He was angry, though I wasn't sure by the tone in his voice if it was because I was in his room or because I had sat in his chair. But as I stood there watching him shuffle quickly through the pages of his notepad as if I'd had my fingers in them, I thought, maybe it could be both.

'I am *truly* sorry.' I touched his arm, and he stopped moving. 'I wasn't snooping. Just curious. I've never seen a real radio, or headphones . . . '

He picked up the vanilla oil, then looked at me. His entire face had changed.

'I was at the market and I thought — '

'You bought this for me?' he said, and I nodded.

'If you want, you can go through my things,' I said, giving him a smile. 'Though lavender sachets and glass beads are about all you'll find.'

He laughed. 'Maybe in a fortnight, after I know you better.'

'In a fortnight?' I folded my arms, back against the wall. 'Did you fly in with your radio?' A laugh bumped in my throat at the thought of this, making a little joke of his Britishness when he was obviously French, but he didn't laugh back.

'*Pardon?*' he said, and I stood straight, thinking I may have overstepped, but then he looked more confused. 'You don't like my voice?'

'You have a beautiful voice — I mean — your voice sounds fine.' I took a hard gulp, wishing I could trade my tongue in for a new one. 'I thought I heard a British accent. That's all. I'm sorry.'

He laughed, and I thought that was his way of accepting my apology.

'I'll leave you alone,' I said, and I went to leave, but he flipped a switch on his radio and unplugged his earphones, and I heard the scratchy commotion of British radio, people talking, saying words I didn't understand, which entranced me.

He sat down in his chair, turning the radio off.

'Why are you here, Adèle?' He'd looked away, but then his gaze trailed slowly back to me. 'Curious about my radio, or is there something else?'

A bashful longing gleamed in his eyes, as if he hoped there had been more, but what I couldn't tell. His lips could easily tell me lies if I wanted them to. He leaned back in his chair, his shirt stretched against his chest. My knees got weak.

'Well, I wanted to know why you joined the Résistance.'

'That's why you're down here?' he said, smiling, and I nodded.

'What made you join the Free French?' I said.

'I was an operator with the central bureau before the war,' he said. 'After the armistice I couldn't do what they asked of me — work for the Vichy regime. So, I left. Many of us left, snuck out of the country to work with the British only to be dropped back in.'

'Oh,' I said, but then thought up something else to buy some time. 'I also wanted to thank you for fixing my bicycle tyre.'

'You're welcome,' he said, and I turned toward the ladder because I couldn't think of anything else to say, but then he touched me. 'You don't have to go.' His finger flitted down my arm. 'Stay.' He pulled a tobacco pouch from his drawer, and rolled two cigarettes, licking the paper and twisting the end. 'Have a smoke with me.'

I closed my eyes briefly, thinking if I didn't get out of his room quick, I'd melt into the floor like

184

ice cream on a warm day. But when he handed me the rolled cigarette, I gladly sat down, using the ladder rung as my seat.

He leaned in to give me a light from his lighter. 'Thanks.'

'How was Vichy?' he asked.

'You know where I went?' I took a drag of my cigarette, acting casual, but inside I was mortified by his question. He had to have heard my conversation last night with Mama out the window. 'It was all right.'

'Mmm,' he said.

'How was your day?'

His eyes shifted to his notepad. 'It was all right.'

And we smoked together, looking at each other in comfortable silence, not willing to talk about what we'd done.

I motioned to his radio. 'Are you able to tune in foreign radio stations?' I asked. 'And listen to music.'

'Sometimes,' he said.

'How does it work?' I said, and Luc showed me the parts to his radio, the crystals, and even let me listen to some chatter. He seemed to enjoy my interest, and even laughed when my mouth gaped open at hearing British music. He slipped the headphones over my ears, and I closed my eyes, momentarily getting lost in the beautiful bow of strings.

'I've taken too much of your time.' I took off his headphones.

'Wait,' he said. 'Before you leave.' He unpinned an underground newspaper from the wall, handing it to me, but it slipped and fell to the ground.

185

Both of us reached for it, our faces close. Too close. Our lips even closer.

I stood straight up. 'I should go,' I said. 'Sorry for bothering you.'

'Adèle,' he said, but I'd climbed up the ladder.

I opened the barrel cellar doors up wide, and walked straight to the chateau, only then realizing I still had Luc's underground newspaper in my hand, but then laughed to myself. 'I'll have to return it.' I felt a little nervous having it in my hands and stuffed it in my pocket for later.

★ ★ ★

Mama's eggs had been delivered and waited on the patio near the door. I reached for the basket to bring it inside, but noticed a twisted note between two eggs. I set the basket down, unravelling the note carefully, and gasped when I saw Marguerite's coded message. I looked over the vineyard: nobody but the birds, and Mama was inside in her room.

It was a diagram — a rough outline of a map to a field about five kilometres away. *Meet at noon*, Marguerite had written. Or was it one o'clock?

My heart beat faster, and I closed my eyes, counting backward and thinking about lying in the grass in the sun to calm me down, just like Marguerite had taught me, but it was too much with the code. I opened my eyes back up and looked at the message again, heart still beating rapidly.

Noon.

Damn her tests. *Why'd she have to write the time in code?* I thought.

I rode through Papa's shrivelling grape vines to a field at the edge of Creuzier-le-Vieux, where wild French catchfly grew in droves, covering a meadow-sized patch of ground with fluttering pink petals. To the west of it on a dirt road sitting on an old man's bicycle was Marguerite, dressed in a pretty summer dress, which was odd to see. Her hair was done up too, though some of it had been pulled from its twist and lay unkempt near her neck.

I felt myself smiling. I had gotten the numbers she asked for. *I really did it*, I thought, *just like she said I would*. I was excited to tell her I'd succeeded.

I skidded to a stop, because instead of looking pleased to see me, she scowled. 'Do you have to kick up that much dust when you ride? What are the numbers? You have them, don't you? Your message meant nothing, memorize the damn codes . . . ' She talked fast, and sounded more like the old Marguerite, the one I met on the train with her curt, cutting voice. 'Adèle — the numbers.'

The smile on my face slowly faded away.

I got off my bicycle when she got off hers. 'What are they?' She took me by the shoulders and the rest of her hair unravelled down her back. 'I don't have a lot of time.'

At the minimum I thought she'd be glad I read her coded message right. I shook the stunned look from my face to answer her. 'Ah . . . nineteen. Twenty-five. Thirty-two.'

She repeated the numbers. 'Can you get back in if I need you to?'

'Into Gérard's office?' I was sure Gérard would love nothing more. I nodded.

'Keep visiting him. I'll be in touch.' She turned to leave, but I wasn't ready for her to leave. Not yet. I yanked her back by the shoulder.

'Wait.' My mouth hung open. I thought she'd be happy with my progress — appreciative — impressed, but she wasn't. Clearly, she wasn't. 'No thank you?' It was the least I expected after what I went through in Gérard's office, and I needed to hear it; for whatever reason, I needed an acknowledgement, and for her to tell me I'd done well.

She glared at me, first at my touch and then for my voice. 'We don't hand out medals, Adèle.'

'I'm not asking for a medal, Marguerite. Just a damn thank you.' I felt a pinch in my lips even though I was more hurt than angry. 'Do you even know what I had to do to get those numbers? He forced himself on me and I let him — hot breath all over my skin, my lips pasty from his wet tongue — Christ, Marguerite! I don't even want to talk about his heavy hands feeling every curve of my body — but I will if you want me to . . . '

Marguerite's gaze had wandered just over my shoulder, her blank face stretching with fright, which caught me off guard. I whipped my head around and saw a blooming cloud of dust billowing in the air from an approaching car.

I gasped, hand to my mouth, and Marguerite dove to the ground, taking me and both our bicycles with her. 'Over here!'

We dragged them off the road and into the weeds before ducking into the catchfly and burrowing into the ground.

Underneath the flower's velveteen petals grew a

poisonous, prickly stem; its bite a brief, yet penetrating sting to those who dared to disturb it. The venom was meant to catch field bugs, but instead it grazed our faces, leaving strings of poison on our skin as we crawled shoulder to shoulder, the car coming to a sudden, lurching stop. We curled up in the stems, insects buzzing in our ears and sticking to our cheeks. My entire body itched.

I heard German mixed with French and the grave sound of feet walking the edge of the embankment. Marguerite winced when they found our bicycles; then her eyes locked with mine through the catchfly, the whirring cry of locusts warning of someone coming. 'Thank you, Adèle,' she whispered. 'For the numbers . . .' Heavy footsteps came toward us, the crunch of the catchfly under their boots too close to think about, and her eyes got wide, wider than I had ever seen before. My heart hummed.

'I'll never let her go this time,' a gruff voice said.

'Then why'd you let her escape?' another said back. 'She's not here. Those bicycles could be anyone's.' There was a grumble and a growl followed by an argument about not tying knots tight enough. Then a man with the loudest German voice I had ever heard spoke over both of them.

'*Thousand Year Reich!*' Gunfire popped haphazardly all around with tufts of dirt lifting from the ground, and I squeezed my eyes shut.

Please . . . God. Please let me live . . .

A long, hot pause followed the gunfire. Not even the locusts dared to stir. Then the blessed sound of retreating footsteps brought my eyes to open and my lungs filled with air.

They laughed as they opened their car doors, talking about quartering Marguerite when they found her — a message to the Résistance. When their doors shut, Marguerite's body jerked among the catchfly as if each slam was a bullet to her chest.

We sat up once we heard their car speed down the road, dead bugs sticking to our skin and face, bees buzzing above our heads. For a long while we didn't say anything, both of us watching them disappear into the horizon.

'Marguerite,' I said, still shaking. 'I was wrong. You don't have to thank me.'

'You're right,' she said, equally shaking. 'I take it back.'

★ ★ ★

I don't remember the ride home, or the walk from the patio into Mama's kitchen, but I do remember getting a bottle of wine from the root cellar. My hands shook after I popped the cork and started pouring the wine into a glass. A chill bumped over my skin but I was sweating and still sticky from the catchfly's poison. I downed the wine, not wanting to waste another moment sober and awake, small streams of it dribbling from my mouth and down my neck, thinking about how close I had come to being shot. Too close, I thought, *too damn close.*

'Feeling all right, Adèle?'

I jumped, wine spurting from the bottle's neck and onto the floor. *Luc.* He had been sitting at the kitchen table for God knows how long, watching me drink the wine.

'Christ, Luc!' I said, wiping my lips with the back of my hand. 'You're always startling me.'

'I'm sorry,' he said, 'but I was here first.' He smiled.

I took one last mouthful of wine from the bottle, tasting the flavours of the oak barrel Papa had aged it in with a final swallow. My hands stopped shaking, and I combed out my hair with my fingers, pulling bits of chickweed from it.

Luc had gotten up and examined the wine label — a valuable pinot, the bottle as dusty as the spot Mama had stashed it in. 'Long day?'

My whole body soaked in sweat, gritty with dirt, and sticky from bugs on my skin. 'Sure was,' I said, resting my backside against the sink. 'What are you doing out in the daylight?'

He gazed into my eyes, which glinted green rather than a river's blue, and I felt the heat of his body an arm's reach away. 'I know about today.'

'What?' I stood straight.

'I only heard half of the radio transmission, but I put the pieces together. I didn't know until moments before that it was you in the field. With the Germans.'

'Germans and French.'

Luc nodded. 'They're integrating into the Free Zone and into the police.'

I didn't say it out loud, but I assumed that was why Marguerite wanted to know if I could get back into Gérard's office. I dug my hands into my skirt pockets and felt the underground newspaper Luc had given me earlier, which I had completely forgotten about. 'This is yours.' I held it out for him to take but he pushed it back.

191

'I gave it to you to keep,' he said. 'Unless . . . it makes you nervous.'

'Nervous?' The zip of the bullets as they whizzed through the catchfly were still very ripe in my mind. 'It did, honestly, when you gave it to me. But now I can tell you with all certainty, it does not.'

He nodded as if he understood what I meant. Mama had walked outside with a basket full of bed linens to be hung on the clothesline just a few yards from the kitchen window. Luc pointed with his eyes to Mama. 'Pauline doesn't know about today. And she won't unless you tell her yourself.'

We watched Mama as she studied the embroidery on a pillow case hanging from the line, running a flat hand over it before putting it to her cheek — Mama's trousseau, the linens from her marriage to Papa. Sheets of white hanging on the line flapped in the breeze, hiding parts of her body as she pressed the linen to her face.

'I don't think I will. She'll worry, and she's got enough going on with Papa,' I said. 'She doesn't need to know the details.'

We watched Mama out the window, the ginger hairs on his arms grazing mine he stood so close, that same musky scent from his microphone coming from his skin and clothes. He reached into his pocket and pulled out a silver flask, taking a whiff of the alcohol inside after he unscrewed the cap. 'Want a real drink? Not everyone can say they've had their life pass before their eyes.'

'I used the last glass for the wine.'

Luc took a swig and then offered me the flask. 'We can share.'

192

I smiled without meaning to, taking the flask from his hands. The wrought smell of the whisky hovered between us, and I looked at him curiously, wondering where he developed a taste for a drink as stout as most Englishmen. 'Who are you really, Luc?' I took a swig from the flask and let the warm whisky linger on my tongue before swallowing. 'Where did you come from?'

'I came from the barrel cellar,' he said with a little smile. 'Below the oak-bending machine. You saw it just this morning.'

I handed him back his flask. 'You know that's not what I'm talking about.'

He shrugged, and I stared at him, examining the bristly beard budding on his chin and resisting the urge to run a smooth hand over it to feel his face and rugged skin.

'Are you making issue about my voice again, Adèle? Because if you're implying I'm British for a second time, I shall have to ask you to take it up with my mother.'

'Oh, you *shall*?' I said, chuckling.

'Yes!' He took a gulping drink from the flask and then put it back into my hand, wrapping my fingers around it. 'I shall.'

'I should like to meet your mother.' I took a quick sip, wetting my lips. 'It's only fair since you know mine.'

'Someday I will tell you where I'm from.' He leaned in close, and I backed into the counter, knocking over wine bottles Mama had placed there earlier. He reached way behind me, stopping them from rolling. A heavy pause. He smiled, looking deep into my eyes. 'But today isn't the day.'

193

'It isn't?' I asked.

His hand touched the soft part of my arm just under the ruffle of my sleeve, his lips nearing, my eyes closing. All was quiet except the drumming buzz of hawk moths in the arbours as our lips touched, and I felt myself melting, fading, fading, in his long kiss, and then Mama screamed from outside and we jerked away with fright.

She waved her hands at us, and then pointed behind her to a motorcycle driving up our road, dust and rock curling into the air. 'Someone's coming!'

'Oh no,' I said, hands flying to my mouth, looking to Luc and then to the speeding motorcycle. *Gérard!*

15

I clutched my chest, reaching for Luc. 'You have to hide!' Mama threw open the screen door, tossing her linen basket down. Gérard had just parked his motorcycle and was taking off his helmet.

'In the cellar!' Mama said, shooing Luc toward the door, but he hesitated.

'He can't do that!' I said. 'He'll be stuck! Nowhere to go.'

I watched in horror as Gérard walked up the gravel walkway, and into Mama's linen lines, throwing sheets out of the way as they flapped around him.

'We don't have time for anything else!' Mama said.

Luc rushed into the corridor, our hands slipping from each other's, and ran downstairs into the root cellar.

I shut the door behind him. All was quiet. 'Mama?'

'Stay calm,' she said, and I closed my eyes, counting backward from ten, breathing deeply, thinking about the grass and the sun and then to Luc in the root cellar. I whimpered, shaking my hands in the air, breathing through my teeth when it wasn't working. Mama grabbed me by the shoulders. 'Hold it together,' she said, 'if anyone can do this you can.'

My eyes popped open, and I nodded. 'All right,' I said, still breathing hard. 'All right. All right . . .'

Gérard knocked on the door. 'Adèle?' he said, and then peeked through the screen.

'Just a moment!' I said from afar.

'You can do this,' Mama said before letting go of me and moving out of the way. I faced Gérard through the screen door.

'Adèle?' he said.

I smiled. 'Gérard!' I said, and then realized I sounded too excited to see him, more than he'd expect. I slumped forward. 'What are you doing here? This is a surprise.'

He walked in, helmet under his arm, looking at Mama's stern face, as she stood defiantly near the stove, and then around our sitting parlour. 'Is it?' He chuckled.

'What?' I said, and he turned to me.

'Is it a surprise?' he said.

'I didn't expect you,' I said, and I tossed my hair back, that's when he grimaced.

'Lord, Adèle,' he said, 'wrestling pigs, or do you always look this horrible in the middle of the day?'

'Get out!' Mama snapped, but he only laughed.

'Easy now,' he said, laughing that throaty laugh of his. 'Kidding.'

'It's all right, Mama,' I said, and he brushed a smear of gritty dirt from my cheek with his thumb.

'I know you've never liked me, Pauline,' Gérard said, still looking around. 'I'd expect nothing less from you,' he said, and Mama's eyes shifted to mine.

'What brings you here,' Mama demanded, in true Mama style.

Gérard pulled an envelope from his pocket. 'I saw Albert this morning, asked if I'd deliver this money to you — '

Mama snatched it away, and he chuckled. 'Maybe I should have kept it.' She stuffed it into her apron pocket, and he turned his attention back to me, flicking his chin. 'Go clean yourself, Adèle,' he said. 'I have a place I want to take you.'

'Oh?' I said.

He flicked his chin again. 'Go on,' he said, and I looked at Mama who nodded carefully. 'I'll wait.'

He picked through the photos on Mama's sideboard, choosing one of Charlotte on her wedding day to study while I dashed off to my room to change, trying to give him as little time as possible alone with Mama.

I pulled my hair into a bun and took a wet rag to my legs and face, listening to Gérard's voice lifting from the front room, asking Mama questions. I slipped out of my dirty dress and put on a new one, before racing out the door, only to find Gérard standing in the corridor waiting for me, not far from the root cellar.

'What are you doing?' I said, my heart beating fast again.

'What?' he said, and I realized I sounded suspicious.

I cleared my throat. 'It's not proper to wait for a woman so close to her bedroom.'

He folded his arms, and I thought he was thinking about walking away, but then he pointed down the corridor. 'What's down there?'

'Charlotte's old room,' I said.

'Oh,' he said, pausing.

I shut my bedroom door after he caught a glimpse of my bed, but then realized the tease of seeing where I slept was just another thing to

197

keep his treacherous thoughts of me burning in his mind.

'All right,' he said, and he turned on his heel and walked into the parlour but stopped at the cellar door. 'And here?' He pulled on the door-knob.

I laughed to shake off my nerves, trying to act casual and flirty. 'What's gotten into you?' I said, my laugh turning into a giggle. 'Come on,' I said, 'before you give Mama a heart attack. She'll think you came to steal our food. It's the cellar.'

I held my breath walking away, praying he'd follow me, taking wobbly steps down the corridor, when he said, 'All right.'

And I exhaled, closing my eyes briefly. 'Mama,' I said, 'Be back by supper.' I moved in to kiss her cheeks just as Gérard walked past me and out the door.

'Don't be too sure!' he said, as the screen door clacked closed behind him.

'Be brave,' Mama whispered.

I looked down the corridor to the cellar door, hesitating, and Mama patted my shoulder, urging me to leave.

I climbed into Gérard's sidecar, feeling Mama's eyes on my back through the window. 'Where are you taking me?' I said, and I tied a scarf over my hair.

'Do you have to know everything?' he said, and we drove off down the road in a cloud of dust. I looked back, watching Mama's white linens flapping on the laundry line getting smaller and smaller and smaller through the road haze.

Luc.

I thought he might be taking me to the outdoor market, or to the Source des Célestins, give me a scolding and prove the lines were short, but we drove into the shopping district, where light reflected off windows and ladies walked around with frilly hats.

He parked in front of Madame's Dress Shop — the most expensive shop in all of Vichy.

I untied my scarf. 'What are we doing here?'

Gérard laughed. 'You have an image to uphold now.' He looked me up and down after I climbed out of his sidecar. 'Come on.'

A saleswoman opened the door for us and he whispered in my ear. 'See, Adèle,' he said, but his voice had changed and it felt very unsettling. 'I can be nice.'

The saleswoman clasped her hands together, eyes twinkling. 'What's your favourite colour, mademoiselle?' She looked me over, studying my complexion. 'Oh, we're going to have so much fun together this afternoon.'

She whisked me off to one of the dressing rooms where her assistant dressed me in silky Parisian undergarments. 'Where do you get these garments?' I said. 'The clothing rations — '

'I find it's best not to ask,' the assistant said, before looking away.

I saw her face in the mirror as I looked at myself, and I could tell she didn't want to dress me, which made my stomach hurt. 'Excuse me?' I said, when she mumbled.

Gérard's voice drifted down the corridor and

into my dressing room. 'She's my fiancée,' he said to the saleswoman. 'She should look a certain way. Elegant. I am very important, as you know.'

The assistant mumbled some more. 'What are you saying?' I said.

She turned around, big smile. 'Nothing, mademoiselle.' She adjusted the strap on my brassiere, finding a lost pin in the seam. 'Close call,' she said, pulling the pin out only to toss it into a pin pillow like a dagger. 'I'll be right back.'

I collapsed against the wall when she left, listening to her whispering to the other assistants. 'Collaborator,' I heard. 'A Vichy bitch.'

I held my face in my hands, but when the saleswoman walked in carrying a heap of dresses in her arms, I stood straight.

'Now,' she said, 'let's have some fun.'

Only I didn't try on a few dresses. I tried on every dress in the shop close to my size. Nothing satisfied Gérard. Every time I came out and twirled in front of him he'd shake his head. 'Too revealing,' he kept saying, which sent the saleswoman into a state.

She took me back into the dressing room after trying to sell him a satin number. 'I just don't know what else to do,' she said to me, as if it was my fault she hadn't made a sale. She looked me over, my brassiere strap slipping from my shoulder. 'He doesn't like anything on you.' I pulled up the strap.

'I'm sorry,' I said, but she had walked out of the dressing room.

The assistant came in with the last dress in my size. A pink thing with lacy long sleeves and

200

a straight neckline. 'He has to like this one,' she said, looking at the dress, and then looking at me. 'It's the most conservative dress we have.'

She turned me around and tightened my stocking belt, before reaching for the pin pillow. 'What are you going to do with those?' I said, and she tucked one pin between her lips.

'Nothing,' she murmured, pinching the strap that kept falling off my shoulder with one hand, and pulling the pin from her mouth with the other.

'Ouch!' I swatted her. 'You poked me!'

I saw her smile through the mirror. 'Sorry, mademoiselle,' she said, just above a whisper.

'I'm sure you are,' I said.

'What's going on in there?' Gérard shouted from the waiting room.

I sighed. 'Last one,' I said, looking at the assistant. 'You better hope he likes this one.' I stormed out of the room, but then I felt bad and wished I could go back in and tell her I hated every single second of it, and that I hated him too.

I looked at Gérard in front of the big dressing mirrors, swallowing my distaste for the dress, fingering the collar where it suffocated me. I put on a smile. 'Pink,' I said, and he spun his finger in the air for me to twirl.

'That's it,' he said, and the saleswoman all but collapsed on the floor. 'That's the dress.'

★ ★ ★

I climbed back into his sidecar, holding the dress bag in my lap. 'Thank you,' I said, and it was hard to say. 'For the dress.'

201

'I'm doing what you asked, Adèle,' he said.

'I didn't ask for a dress,' I said.

'No,' he said, fitting his helmet, 'but you asked me to court you.'

He straddled his motorcycle and started it up. 'Hungry?' he said, but he wasn't asking.

We drove to a restaurant I'd never been to before, an out-of-the-way place he said he'd heard about at the Hotel du Parc. 'La Table,' I said, reading the sign on the marquee. A fancy woman in a feathered hat walked in with a man in a suit. 'Looks expensive — '

'It is,' he said, and then snapped his fingers at the shopping bag. 'Carry it inside. I want everyone to know where I took you. Only supporters of the Vichy regime eat here.' He looked at me. 'We need to make an impression.'

'Supporters?' I said, 'You mean . . . '

'You know what I mean.' He took a few deep breaths near the door to prepare before we walked inside, and I don't think Gérard was even prepared for the number of eyes that set upon us. He smiled. 'After you,' he said, and the maître d' showed us to our table. 'Hold the bag up,' he whispered from behind.

The waiter handed us menus and poured us some wine. 'Get whatever you'd like, Adèle,' he said, but when the waiter asked me what I wanted to eat, Gérard spoke up.

'She'll have the steak. Medium rare.'

'I don't like steak,' I said, just to see what he'd say, but he kept talking.

'I'll have the steak as well.' He handed our menus to the waiter but looked at me, a strange

202

smile on his face, ordering the rest of his meal. 'And potatoes with as much butter as you can spare.'

'What's that monsieur?' the waiter said, and Gérard looked at him, a little cock in his neck.

'I'm a member of the Vichy police.' He winked.

The waiter wrote something on the order. 'I'll see what I can do.'

'Do that,' Gérard said, but it was more of a threat.

I looked around the restaurant, at the women, eating their medium-rare steaks and the men with their very own butter dish. 'Butter,' I said.

'You want some, don't you?' he said, and I shook my head. 'What's wrong with you? This is where the regime dines,' he said, as if he knew what I was thinking. 'Be glad you have your hands in my pockets tonight. I heard there's a food shortage in Lyon.'

Gérard ate his buttered potatoes in heaping gulps, never offering me a smidge of his butter, which I wouldn't have taken anyway, even if the restaurant was full of miserable people from the regime; the butter, I thought, was worth more than the dress. But the steak — the steak made me salivate. I took a drink of water before gulping some wine.

Marguerite would tell me to eat the steak. Gérard would expect it. He glanced at me once. I picked up my knife and cut into it, bloody and soft.

Gérard gulped down a chunk of steak, pointing across the room with his knife. 'Look there,' he said. 'Isn't that your sister?'

'Charlotte?' I sat up tall. 'What is she doing here?' I said.

'Eating dinner,' he said, but I shook my head.

'That's not what I mean,' I said.

Gérard pointed again, talking with a full mouth. 'That's why.'

Henri had walked out of the restrooms and sat down next to her. A little gasp came from my mouth. Gérard had practically admitted that only collaborators ate at La Table. *Mama was right.* Charlotte never looked up at him, and they ate as if they were seated alone, strangers.

Gérard smeared the last bit of butter he had onto his potatoes. 'That will be us someday, Adèle.' He licked the butter from his spoon with his fat tongue. 'Eating dinner. Husband and wife.'

'I told you I don't want anything black at my wedding, Gérard. Remember? I said. 'Thank you for the dress and dinner, but you know where I stand.'

He laughed, showing his open mouth, chewing up the last of his steak.

I looked at Charlotte from afar, eating her dinner. I hadn't seen Henri since before the convent. He seemed older, with a moustache and a tailored suit and cold eyes. The longer I watched them the more it felt like I was intruding.

Gérard tapped his watch. 'It's getting late,' he said. 'I should take you home.'

'No — ' I said, and then swallowed. 'I mean. Why rush?' I motioned to my plate and the half-eaten steak. 'I'm not finished.'

The last thing I wanted was for Gérard to come back out to the estate, poke around inside, or to see Luc. I had to think of a way to keep him away, but if he thought I didn't want him there, he'd just come by every day.

'You know you almost gave Mama a heart attack,' I said, and he chuckled, sitting back, feeling his belly.

'I did,' he said. 'Didn't I?'

I nodded. 'You really did, Gérard,' I said, and then shook my head.

'What?'

'Oh, nothing,' I said.

He sat forward, elbows on the table. 'Tell me.'

I took a deep breath, thinking of Marguerite and my training; codes weren't going to help me through this one. I took a drink of water. 'It's this, you see . . . Mama has never liked you,' I said. 'Well she did, the boy you used — '

'Enough of that.' He pointed his finger at me, and I shrugged.

'It was no wonder she planted all those thoughts about the nunnery into my head — '

'It was Pauline's idea?'

'I wouldn't be surprised if she mentions it again tonight,' I said, and I let the thought hang in the air, looking into his eyes, hoping to God he'd realize that he needed to stay away from the chateau.

'She's a miserable old woman.' He pressed his lips together. 'When is Albert moving back?'

'The regime keeps him busy all day in the city. It's just easier for him to stay at the wine bar, so maybe not for a while.'

I held my breath. *Please . . . please . . . please . . .*

He nodded, folding up his napkin, taking one last swipe of his mouth. 'I don't want to see your mother again,' he said. 'Not until Albert moves back and knocks some sense into her.'

I smiled. 'Oh?' I said, but I wanted to fall to the floor and thank God he'd agreed. 'But how will I get home?' I waited for him to notice the obvious choice.

He motioned to Charlotte and Henri. 'They can take you.' He looked at his watch again, tapping it. 'I'm working tonight.'

'At this hour?' I said, but when he looked at me, pausing, I realized that meant he was off to arrest someone.

He tossed back the last swig of wine in his glass, but instead of rushing out, he sighed. 'I'm glad you're back, Adèle,' he said, and it was in the same voice he had used earlier at the dress shop, sincere, which sent a chill up my spine.

He stood up and kissed my cheek just as I swallowed a hunk of steak. 'This courting business might be fun after all,' he said, but then whispered. 'Make sure you hold the bag up when you leave.'

He left me at the table eating the rest of my steak alone. Charlotte and Henri had yet to notice I was there, and that was fine with me. The last thing I wanted was for Charlotte to know I'd seen them looking like they didn't know each other.

I slipped out of the restaurant and walked home. After two hours in shoes not meant for walking with old blisters bursting open, and holding that damn dress bag, I finally made it home to the estate. The chateau was dark, and so was the barrel cellar.

'I wouldn't go in there,' Mama said from the patio, and I dropped the bag at my feet.

'Is he gone?' I said, and she shook her head.

'I don't know,' she said, 'but it was enough excitement for one day, don't you think?'

'Did you tell him?' I said, swallowing dryly. 'That it was Gérard?'

'He knows it was a visitor. That's all. The police,' she said, and I understood that she didn't tell him anything more.

I walked into the kitchen, and Mama walked upstairs to her bedroom. 'Now that you're home, I'm going to bed,' she said, but then turned back to kiss both my cheeks.

I sat at the kitchen table where Mama had lit a candle and smoked a few of her cigarettes. I hoped Luc would come inside, but why would he after the fright he'd had? I closed my eyes, only to open them back up, fatigued, and blurry, remembering the Germans, the scare, and Gérard.

I walked to the window, slumped against the sill, and looked at the barrel cellar, wanting so badly to go and see him. But Mama was right. There had been too much excitement for one day. 'Luc,' I breathed, staring into the night, remembering our kiss.

★ ★ ★

The following morning, the door to the barrel cellar was closed. Luc was gone. Mama said he came and went; she never knew when he'd show up. His smell lingered where his body had brushed up against mine and under my sleeve where he touched me. But like a mark that fades over time, Luc's scent got weaker and weaker as the days passed until I couldn't smell him at all on my clothes.

Though, the image of his face — his eyes when they looked into mine like a clear pond — stayed with me.

16

Papa and Gérard walked straight toward me. I had only just walked up to Hotel du Parc with Gérard's lunch hanging from my arm. I pulled the lapels of my wool coat tightly across my chest, eyeing them, a late autumn breeze swirling crinkled leaves around my ankles. The last time I saw Gérard and Papa talking just by themselves was the day I found out about my marriage plans. The sight of them so close together didn't sit right with me, despite the understanding I had with Gérard.

'Hallo,' I said as Papa kissed my cheeks. '*Ça va?*'

Gérard smiled, leaning in to get his kisses after Papa.

'Adèle,' Papa said. 'Would you mind helping Charlotte at her boutique during the week? You won't be able to visit Gérard at lunchtime any longer, but we had a talk and it is all right.'

'What?' I was pleasantly surprised.

'Her husband left for Paris again, business for the government.' Papa smiled. 'And he'll be gone for a few months. As much as it pains me to take you away from Gérard during the lunch hour, I worry about Charlotte working alone in that boutique he bought her.'

'Because of the stillbirth?' I said.

Papa's eyes narrowed. I know I shouldn't have said it out loud and in front of Gérard. A woman's inability to carry a child might run in the family.

209

God forbid if he entertained such thoughts. 'I know I'm next door, but it's not the same — she'd never ask me for help.'

Gérard's teeth bulged from his lips. 'What's the name of the shop?' He chuckled, but I wasn't sure why.

'It's a boutique,' I said, 'for expecting mothers.'

Gérard just smiled.

I turned to Papa. 'Of course, I'll help Charlotte.'

'Thank you, *ma chérie* — '

Gérard elbowed his way between us. 'This actually works for me too, Adèle.'

'It does?' I said.

'As it turns out, I'd like to start seeing you in the evenings. There's a soirée tonight at Antoine's brasserie and I need a date — important people, that sort of thing — maybe spending some real time with the police will rub off on you.'

'An evening date?' I smiled to hide my worry, imagining what it will be like spending a whole evening with him, when it's dark. 'How nice.'

'Wear a formal gown, but not too glitzy — don't want you looking like a prostitute. I'll send a car for you — and don't say anything unless talked to first . . .'

As Gérard rambled on about what I should and shouldn't do at the soirée, I caught a glimpse of what Papa had already noticed: a tired old woman sitting on the kerb in the courtyard across the street from the Hotel du Parc. Behind her was a Morris Column adorned with posters of Pétain's face instead of the nightclub advertisements it had been built for. She sat with her legs open, bent at the knee. Her dirty hands picked at the patches of

210

skin visible through the holes in her woolly stockings — the only garments she had on under her skirt.

Gérard was in the middle of telling me about the jewellery I should wear when he turned around to see what had caught our attention. A loose crowd gathered around her, some clapping, others admiring. I was drawn toward them, stepping into the street, but Gérard pulled me back. 'No, Adèle!' He motioned to the soldiers standing guard at the Hotel du Parc to take care of her, but she wouldn't move, even after one of them kicked her.

The crowd chanted and clapped in her favour, which only upset Gérard more, looking this way and that, down streets and through trees, for somewhere to take her. He snapped his fingers, yelling at the two soldiers. 'There!' he said, pointing toward the cemetery.

I hooked Papa's arm. 'What's going on?' I asked, but his eyes were as fixed as mine on the woman, trying to figure it all out. That's when I reached for Gérard's arm. 'Don't hurt her,' I said, and he glared. 'She's just an old woman.'

'She's a résistant!' Gérard pulled his arm angrily away. 'And if you knew anything, you'd keep your mouth shut.' He ran across the street to help the guards with the woman.

She took a tube of lipstick from her pocket and was able to scribble the word 'women' on her forehead before the soldiers picked her up and carried her away. 'Women of the Nation,' someone cried out, and a whip of wind spun her white hair up in all different directions.

Papa and I stood for a good while stunned, not speaking, watching the crowd slowly break up as the woman disappeared into the cemetery with Gérard and the soldiers. 'Let's go, *ma chérie*,' he finally said, relighting a cigar from his pocket. 'It's cold.'

We walked around the corner and past the flower cart that sold flowers from tins. I took a daisy from the bucket, looking back at the kerb where the woman had sat. Brown leaves tumbled over the cobblestones.

'Just one, *mademoiselle*?' the old woman said.

She asked again when I didn't answer, and I finally pulled my eyes away, blinking, coming to. 'Just one,' I said, but with Papa there I wouldn't dare write a coded message. I handed her a coin. 'For a soirée. Tonight.'

The woman looked a little surprised I'd told her my message instead of writing it down. I nodded once.

Papa and I walked away arm-in-arm to keep warm. Not far from Charlotte's boutique, Papa stopped, eyes closing. '*Ma chérie*,' he breathed, 'why did you have to mention the stillbirth?'

'Sorry,' I said. 'It slipped out.' He looked beaten for having to say the word himself. 'Have you been to the grave?'

'Once,' he said.

'I've asked to go. I want to, but Charlotte won't take me or Mama either.'

Papa took a deep breath. 'I'm sure she'll take you when she's ready. You know how Charlotte is.' He patted my hand. 'Give her some time.'

212

* * *

Charlotte's boutique smelled like flowers, the pungent kind that normally gave me a headache.

'Where did you get lilies?' There was something special about Oriental lilies, something god-awful special, and these, these were the worst I'd smelled yet.

Charlotte positioned her blue vase stuffed full of lilies and what looked like a handful of purple weeds in the centre of an oak commode. She smiled pleasantly at them until she saw me with my nose wrinkled. 'What's wrong with them?'

'Nothing. I didn't say anything. I just asked you where you got them. It's near winter, after all.'

'I saw your nose turn up.' Charlotte's gaze returned to the flowers and she fiddled with the stems. 'If you don't like them just say so.'

My nose tingled, warning a sneeze, but somehow, I was able to hold it in.

'Henri sent them moments after he left for Paris. He loves me. Don't you think? I mean, he bought this boutique for me, and he sends flowers all the time. A man who sends a woman flowers . . . Well, he just has to love me, right?'

Charlotte had dressers set up against the walls, which made the place look like a nursery, an inviting scene for an expectant mother, with lace-bottomed knickers and oversized brassieres folded inside the drawers. Aside from all the clothes, the furniture alone in her shop was worth a fortune; I could only imagine how much her husband paid for it all.

'He loves you. Why would you question such

213

a thing?' I said, but I'd seen them eating at La Table, and suddenly felt very uncomfortable talking about their marriage.

Charlotte's fingers shook arranging the flowers, and I began to understand why Papa wanted me to look after her — she'd become a bag of nerves. I noticed it more so when she looked out the window, as if expecting someone but wasn't, rubbing her shaking hands. After a long while I realized she'd had no customers come in. I wondered out loud how she was going to stay in business, which she didn't like.

'There's a lag in business right now, as you can see. But things will improve soon.'

'Because our men are in a German munitions factory.' I smoothed a pair of silk stockings out on the table, flattening them with my hand. 'Prison, if we can be honest with ourselves. A woman can't be having babies with no men around.'

'Not all the men, Adèle,' she said, folding the stockings I had touched. 'As you know with Gérard, the Vichy police is chock-full of desirable men. You're very lucky he's giving you a second chance. I know a lot of women who would love to be in your shoes.'

I raised my eyebrows at the stockings, nudging her to talk about the clothes rather than Gérard, and she switched to the things in her boutique, where she stored the extras and how to display the lacy items on the counter, fanning them just right to showcase the intricate details in the patterns. She asked me to fold something, and I did it her way with a pair of lacy, knee-length pantaloons, but I couldn't keep the ends from dangling off the edge so I crisscrossed them to make them fit.

Charlotte shooed me away. 'You are doing it all wrong — it's a wonder you're even my sister — really, Adèle, the way you handle such delicate things.' She placed the garment on the counter, running her fingers over the ruffles until the fabric looked fluffy, but in the end the pantaloons didn't look any better than the way I had them. 'The display alone is a work of art. There has to be thought put into it, and done just right.'

I snatched them out from under her hands, smiling, holding them in the air just out of her reach. Charlotte had an irritated little smile on her face that gave way to laughter. 'Give me those.' She was grinning now, getting ready to chase me around the table for them.

'Come and get them,' I said, dangling them in the air.

She darted one way, and then the other, circling around the table until she caught the pantaloons and me, tickling me in the ribs. Her face got very close to the flowers, and she caught a good whiff, grimacing from the stench I knew was emanating from them.

'Smell something?' I said, hands on my hips. *She can't deny it now*, I thought.

'God, I know they stink,' she finally admitted, closing her eyes briefly, 'I know they do — like an old woman's cologne. But my husband gave them to me. He couldn't have known how bad they smell. Could he have? It's the thought that counts,' she said, rubbing her shaking hands. 'Right?'

'Of course — he didn't know.' I sneezed into my sleeve, and we both laughed, Charlotte a little

215

louder than me. 'Is it all right if I move them near the door? You don't think I'm offending my husband if I do?'

'God, no! Please move them.'

Papa had left his store to help Charlotte replace her rickety office door with a new one, lifting the dreadful thing off its hinges and carrying it away for scrap. He stood against the wall, the door in his hands, smiling at us. 'Just hearing my girls, seeing you together . . . Feels good.'

I looked at Charlotte, and she looked at me. We both knew the separation was hard on them both. Though, I wasn't going to mention Mama, thinking it would be too upsetting for Papa if our conversation turned into a political spat. I turned away, but Charlotte piped up.

'Mama knows where you are if she wants to apologize.'

I gasped. 'Apologize?' I said. 'Charlotte, for what?'

'Isn't it obvious?' Charlotte said.

'Girls . . . girls,' Papa pleaded. 'What's happened between your mother and I shouldn't burden you two. Don't worry yourself with our problems.'

Charlotte glared at me and I at her for bringing the whole thing up. 'Sorry, Papa,' Charlotte said. 'We'll stop.'

'What has gotten into you?' I said behind Papa's back. 'Bringing Mama up to Papa like that?'

Charlotte shushed me. 'We're not talking about it, remember?'

'There's something else,' I said, and she looked at me, surprised I'd kept talking. 'I want to pay my

216

respects to your —'

She grabbed my wrist, squeezing forcefully. 'Not. Now.'

'Ow,' I said, pulling away.

The door flew open and we all looked. There in the doorway, with a furry fox muff wrapped around her big head, was Blanche Delacroix, hard inflection on the "croix". The last time I saw her we were washing hair together at Salon Fleur.

She waved a limp-wristed greeting from the front of the boutique.

'A customer,' Charlotte said, latching on to my arm. 'Blanche!'

Blanche was a real know-it-all, and we'd been known to bump heads in the past. Her penchant for rumours was unprecedented, even in the hair business. She took the muff off her head and ruffled her pressed hair back to life before touching the maternity brassieres in one of the dressers.

Charlotte tugged on my elbow, and I followed her reluctantly to the front of the shop while Papa snuck out the back, lugging the old door with him. 'Be nice,' she said, under her breath.

I rolled my eyes. 'She's the one who should be nice.'

She tugged again. 'Be. Nice.'

'I will,' I said, pulling my arm away. Charlotte knew the power of Blanche's words and her ability to twist things. Appearing confident was the best way to approach her, Charlotte always maintained. But I was never one to care what Blanche thought.

'Wait,' she said. 'You've got an eyelash...'
Charlotte removed the eyelash gently from my

cheek. 'There. Now remember . . .'

'I know. Be nice.'

We faced Blanche together.

'*Bonjour!*' Charlotte said, kissing her cheeks. 'Can I help you find something in particular?' Charlotte leaned forward to see the exact size and style of brassieres Blanche had been thumbing through.

Blanche slipped off her coat and draped it over her arm, her eyes still on the brassieres. 'I'm not sure what size I need.'

To my surprise, Blanche was half the size she had been the last time I saw her. People used to call her a horse because of the size of her thighs and the sound of her feet thudding against the ground when she walked. Her skin looked loose, as if the sudden weight loss wasn't a planned decision but a forced one.

'Blanche!' I said. 'You've lost weight.'

Charlotte glared through her big smile. Pointing out Blanche's weight loss was different from saying she looked great, which I damn well knew.

Blanche pulled her hand from the drawer to wave her fingers in front of my face, showing off her Art Deco wedding ring. 'That's not the only change.'

'Congratulations,' I said for Charlotte's benefit.

'You look wonderful, Blanche.' Charlotte grinned. 'And congratulations on your marriage. Someone local?'

'Oh no,' Blanche said with a little gasp. 'Nobody from here — certainly. I had to go to Paris to find him, and find him I did! Just in time, too. In Paris, *on vit mal*.' She chuckled. 'Everyone goes hungry.

218

I was wasting away under the strict rations those Parisians live under in the Occupied Zone when I found him. I'll plump up in no time. He's German, so now I get things others can't.' She laughed, and her teeth bucked out from her mouth.

'You don't say — '

Charlotte jabbed me in the ribs with her elbow. 'Just in time for gaining weight for the pregnancy,' she said. 'That's why you're here shopping at *Mamans et les Bébés*, isn't it? You have a baby on the way?' Charlotte smiled with the word baby.

Blanche rubbed her belly's sagging skin as if she were several months along. But in truth it was hard to tell how far along she was under all that flab.

'And what news of you, Adèle? Last time I heard about you . . . let's see . . . you were off to become a nun? Rumour has it you were frightened about the wedding night.' She smiled. 'Gérard is a big man . . . '

I turned slowly to Charlotte, eyes wide. 'Is that what you told him?'

She shrugged, and Blanche had a giggle, enjoying my reaction.

'Charlotte!'

'You didn't see how angry he was,' she said, eyes glancing once to Blanche, lowering her voice.

I took a deep breath — the last thing we should be doing is having this conversation in front of Blanche Delacroix.

I turned to Blanche. 'Truth is I had cold feet,' I said. 'I'm back now.'

'Yes, you certainly are.' Blanche plucked a lacy brassiere from the drawer and inspected the cup

219

size as if she gave a damn. 'I heard you've been trying to make up with him, bringing Gérard his lunches at the Parc.' She glanced up from the drawer, and I could see a thousand questions floating behind the irises of her eyes.

'Sure have been.'

Blanche grinned, coy-like, and it irritated me a great deal. It was the same smile she used to give me at the salon. I knew, just like before, that no matter what I said, all of Vichy would know about our conversation the moment she left.

'Adèle is doing her best,' Charlotte blurted. 'And we are proud of her for having a change of heart and coming back to us.'

'The runaway bride had a change of heart.' Blanche tucked the brassiere back into the drawer after holding it to her chest and realizing it was made for a woman even smaller. 'Interesting.'

'Now she's here helping me.' Charlotte put her arm around me. 'I'm not sure what I did without her.'

'I suppose I shouldn't be surprised.'

'I like to try new things, is all. I'm very choosey.' I felt my dimples pop. 'Spending my life setting hair sounds like a dreadful existence. Life is worth experiencing, is it not? Gérard invited me to an important soirée, and honestly, I don't want to wake up many years from now, old and weary and thinking back on my life and wondering . . . what if.'

Blanche squinted her giant brown eyes until they looked normal size — I squinted back. There was no more talk about Gérard.

'Speaking of old women,' Blanche said, 'did

you hear about the résistant outside the Hotel du Parc today?'

'You mean the old woman they dragged to the cemetery? I saw it myself. She never said a word.'

'It's the silent ones you need to look out for,' Blanche said.

'That makes sense to me, Blanche.' Charlotte subtly rearranged the items Blanche had disturbed in the drawer. 'Those silent ones.'

'The woman wasn't doing anything, Charlotte, and the more she sat doing nothing the more guards she attracted.'

'Don't you know what's going on in Paris?' Blanche chuckled through her big teeth, putting her coat back on. 'That woman was making a statement. Her shabby dress, sitting with her legs propped up, her woman parts exposed and pointed at our nation's seat — it's a metaphor. She's blaming Pétain for her misery, her sons and husband most likely working in a munitions factory instead of at home. *Les Femmes de la Nation* — that's what they're calling themselves.'

'Women of the Nation?' I gasped as soon as I understood what Blanche was saying. I noticed the woman only had knee-high stockings on under her skirt.

'What's the metaphor?' Charlotte said, mouth drawn open. I could tell she wouldn't allow her own mind to take her to a place that could potentially disrupt her beautiful day.

'Charlotte,' I said, touching her shoulder. 'She was portraying herself as having been raped — *Les Femmes de la Nation* — by the regime. For her suffering. The armistice. The loss of France. She was

221

dressed head to toe in rags but her bottom half was exposed under her skirt, and aimed at the Hotel du Parc.'

A deafening silence swept through the boutique. The word 'rape' did not belong in a boutique that catered to expectant mothers, and I could tell by the way Charlotte's curls seemed to tighten around her face that she felt very uncomfortable with the topic of our conversation.

'Are you all right?' I said.

'I don't want to think of such abhorrent things.' She took a deep, withering breath, rubbing her hands to keep them from shaking. 'People are incapable of seeing the good, the beautiful — Pétain's legacy.'

'The beautiful?'

'Like a great painting, outshined by a glop of paint brought in from some indigent, unworthy of having his canvas placed alongside real artists. The old woman, she's the . . . the . . . '

Her voice rose with each new word, and I knew she wasn't only referring to Pétain's legacy, but something very personal. Before the war, Charlotte's paintings were on exhibit in Paris. The critics panned everything except the ugly ones painted by men, which she said was because of their bold statements and gall. According to Mama, Charlotte was inconsolable by the end of the exhibition. She never talked about it after, and when someone did ask her how her art worked out in Paris, she'd say she never went.

Blanche snuck out of the boutique while Charlotte and me were talking, and without buying anything. It was the only time I was glad to see

Blanche's backside.

'Ach!' Charlotte said, putting the back of her hand to her forehead. 'I'm exhausted from this conversation. I had some news I wanted to share, but now I have a bad taste in my mouth, and I don't want to share it anymore.'

'News?' Papa had just finished hauling away Charlotte's old door and was walking in from the back room, rubbing his tired eyes with both hands. 'What news, *ma chérie*? Some good news would be nice.'

He rubbed his eyes again after blinking, and I began to wonder why Charlotte would tease him with an announcement if she had no intention of sharing it in the first place. She was shaking and pacing, and I was handling it fine by myself but involving Papa? 'Charlotte, just tell Papa your news.'

Charlotte picked up a gingham dress fit for a woman having twins and refolded it. Her hands settled into a light tremble. 'Well, I was going to wait. Then I decided to say something, then . . . well . . . ' Her smile broadened and she held her breath before blurting: 'I'm having a baby.'

Papa's face perked with life. '*Ma chérie*! That is good news!'

'Thanks, Papa,' Charlotte said, beaming as he hugged her. 'I knew you'd be excited.'

She looked to me, waiting for me to say something, but what was she thinking getting pregnant so soon after a stillbirth? I wanted to ask her, but by the look on her face I knew now was not the time for such a question. I forced a smile, reaching out to kiss both her cheeks. 'When are you due?'

She caressed the flat area of her stomach just below the belt of her dress. 'I'm a few weeks pregnant. I told Henri before he left for Paris.' Tears welled over her bulging cheeks. 'By the time he gets home I should be as big as this building.'

She laughed and it was good to hear her laugh. I kissed her again. 'Before you know it you'll be nice and round.'

Papa raised a finger in the air. 'I'll write a letter to Pauline!' He stepped into Charlotte's office and began rummaging around her desk looking for a blank piece of paper to write on.

'No, Papa,' Charlotte said. 'I'll tell Mama myself. I'll follow Adèle home.'

'You're coming out to the estate?' I knew Mama wouldn't be pleased to hear Charlotte was pregnant again so soon after a stillbirth. If Charlotte sensed her disappointment, only God knew how she'd react. I had to get to Mama first.

'Is that a problem?' she said.

'No, of course not. But it will be late soon. Why don't you tell Mama when she comes into the city? Then you don't have to bother with taking a drive. You really should be resting.' I held my breath, waiting to hear her answer.

Papa offered Charlotte a chair. 'Adèle is right, *ma chérie*, you should rest.'

Charlotte sat down, and I brought her legs up, putting her feet on a cushion. 'If you think so,' she said.

'I do,' I said, and I reached for my pocketbook to leave.

'You promise, Adèle?' Charlotte said. 'You promise you'll let me tell her?'

'I promise,' I said.

17

That night I asked Mama to brush my hair out in her bedroom. I waited for the right time to tell her, but there was no easy way around it, no matter how many times I practised in my head.

'She's what?' Mama glared at me through the mirror in her vanity. 'Pregnant!'

'I thought you should be warned, Mama. Charlotte's changed — she's as frazzled as a caged bird with her husband gone all the time. I had to be the one to tell you. She couldn't take the reaction you're giving me now.'

Mama threw the brush onto the vanity, cracking her oval mirror. 'Warned is the right word.' Her cheeks plumped to ripened tomatoes, and I started to regret saying anything at all.

'I promised her, Mama. We told her we wouldn't say a word.'

Her eyes widened. 'Your father knows?'

'Yes. Papa knows. She told both of us at the same time.'

She pressed her lips together before letting out a shrill little scream.

I suddenly felt warm and sweaty in the dress I had put on for Gérard's soirée, and fanned myself with opened fingers while Mama walked around in circles.

'I cautioned her about getting pregnant too soon,' she spouted, arms flapping. I wasn't sure by the look in Mama's eyes if she was going to charge out the door for Charlotte's or sit down and smoke a cigarette. 'Her body hasn't even had time to heal! Ugh, that girl! I didn't want her to get married. I swear she spends her time trying to punish me, whether it's by supporting Pétain or getting pregnant to prove me wrong. And that no-good husband of hers, conspirator, collaborator — God will deal with him.'

I never told Mama I saw Charlotte and Henri dining at La Table with all the collaborators. It would have been too much for her to take on top of everything, knowing that's where they dined, even if she'd already made her mind up about Henri.

'Did you know Charlotte's husband asked her to stop painting? He said it wasn't the Pétain way.'

'Henri said that?' I said, surprised since Charlotte never mentioned it. 'Maybe she'll paint again after she has a child.'

Mama stopped pacing and lit a cigarette. The red in her cheeks had turned to pink, which I thought was a good sign. 'Perhaps.' She sat on the corner of her bed and gazed at her own reflection in the cracked mirror, blowing smoke from her mouth. 'Enough about him. I'm talking about Charlotte. She's not ready. In her head.'

'I think she is, Mama. She runs a boutique that specializes in clothes for expectant mothers.'

'No, Adèle. That's not what I mean.' Mama took several long breathy drags from her cigarette before stubbing it out in a crystal ashtray on her nightstand. The fury I saw in Mama's eyes had dulled almost completely — I had softened the blow, for them both.

'Tell her not to drink the water drawn from the Source des Célestins.' She grabbed a hold of my arm. 'I may be the only person in France who doesn't trust it — the whole city drinking from the same tap. She won't take my advice — make up a story the Résistance poisoned it — she'll stay away if she thinks it is poisoned.' She let go of my arm after squeezing it tightly. 'The walks along the promenade next to it would be good for her, though. Make sure she walks . . . '

I nodded, taking the brush Mama had thrown earlier and running it through my hair, switching my thoughts from Charlotte to Gérard. It was the first time all day I had allowed myself to think about the soirée and his feeling hands.

Showing up would be the easy part; spending an evening with him in the dark would be another matter. 'I need to think about tonight.'

Mama handed me her cigarettes as if she knew I needed a smoke. I burned through two before she spoke up and asked me where I was going.

'Hotel du Parc, Antoine's restaurant. The Vichy police love it there.' I had my hands in my hair when I spoke, the last of my cigarette bobbing with my lips. 'I was lucky enough to find Charlotte's gala gown in the closet, buried behind so many things. Leopard chiffon — I'm sure it was very costly.'

'It was,' Mama said. 'She threw it out after the Paris exhibition — doesn't know I saved it from the rubbish bin. Are you going with Gérard?'

'Don't say his name,' I said, wincing. 'We know who he is — don't have to say it out loud. And who else would I be going there with?' I brushed

227

my hair out, trying to get it into a style, but nothing seemed to work. I stubbed out my cigarette and groaned, looking at my face in the mirror and thinking about Gérard, his soft, wet lips on mine. I shivered from head to toe.

Mama had been watching me with a discerning eye. 'Your forehead's creasing.' She tapped her cheeks. 'And your dimples are popping. What are you thinking about?'

'It's nothing.' I looked up, my hair in a frizz, and Mama stared at me through her cracked vanity mirror.

'Are you leaving me to go live with your father?'

'No!' I said. 'I wouldn't leave you, Mama. That's not it.'

Mama looked relieved, taking her brush and whipping my hair into a twist. 'Then what?'

'My mind's on Gérard, Mama.' I shivered again. 'Feels so degrading. I wish there was something else I could do for the Résistance. Surely, a woman has other talents. But what else could I do? Tonight it will be me in a small room, looking beautiful and surrounded by fifty police. And one Gérard.'

'Are you worried?' She clipped a jewel-encrusted pin into my hair twist, and we looked at each other through the mirror.

'I'm always worried,' I said.

'Will you see your father?' She pulled a letter from her pocket and played with it in her hands.

Only God knew how many letters Papa also had written and never sent. 'Not tonight, but I see him every day. Is there something you want me to give him?' I watched her stare at the letter.

'No.' She turned away.

I stood to leave, taking a moment to look at myself in the leopard dress. It was long and flowing, the epitome of elegance. I used to beg Charlotte to let me try it on — she never would allow it. Mama watched me from the bed with her cigarette in hand as I smoothed the dress against my skin. 'I can't believe I'm finally wearing this — and it was in the closet this whole time.'

'Mmm,' Mama said, through her cigarette. She reached for her perfume bottle and sprayed me from behind with rosewater. 'To cover the scent of that cold sweat you have on you,' she said.

I waved it away, coughing and gagging from the smell of it, and the feel of the mist falling on my arms. 'Use the Chanel, Mama.'

I went to leave and stepped through a creaking floorboard — a secret compartment hidden right in Mama's floor. 'What's this?' I said, very surprised. I brought the board up by its corner. Underneath was a small grey gun lying inside an opened black box. 'Mama, you have a gun?'

Mama stood over me. 'A woman needs to protect herself.'

'Can I pick it up?'

Mama flicked her chin at it, and I reached in. 'Easy, Adèle. There's a bullet in it.'

I looked it over from side to side, checking the gun for markings, but the sides were smooth. 'Where did you get this?'

'The Résistance gave it to me when Luc showed up. It's from America — the Liberator, they call it.'

'Have you shot it?'

'God, no,' she said. 'But there's directions.'

I pulled a sheet of paper from the box that had twelve numbered pictures on it, each demonstrating how to hold the gun properly and fire it.

I held the gun, aiming at the wall. 'Luc must know how to use it,' I said.

'Throw the directions out and ask him how to shoot it if you want,' Mama said. 'But I wouldn't want you to do anything *too* unpleasant.'

'Luc's arms wrapped around my body, showing me how to aim does sound very unpleasant indeed.'

'Indeed,' Mama repeated.

'Have you seen him lately?' I said.

'The last time I saw Luc he was in my kitchen kissing you.'

The mere mention of the last time I saw Luc got me warm and flushed. 'What do the instructions say?'

Mama glanced at the instructions, flipping the page over where it was blank. 'You have to reload after you shoot it, and the target has to be close up.'

Gooseflesh bumped over my arms. 'I hope we never have to use it.'

'I forgot I had it, to tell you the truth, Adèle. You know as well as I that if the Germans come this damn thing isn't going to help us. I never believed in Satan until I met my first German. I'm sure Elizabeth would agree.'

I held my tongue, waiting to see if she'd say anything else about her and Mother Superior unprompted, but she looked rather breathless and weak from having just mentioned her name.

230

'As dangerous as the Résistance is, you know what would happen to us if someone knew we had a gun? Put it away, makes me nervous,' she said, and I put the gun back in the floor. Headlamps shone through the window and Mama looked alarmed. 'Jesus Christ, is that — '

'He sent a car,' I said, and she heaved a sigh of relief.

'I don't want him in my home. I know you said he wasn't going to show up again uninvited, but I don't trust him. Not one bit.'

I straightened myself after having been on the floor, tucking in loose hair strands and checking my makeup. 'How do I look?' I said.

'Adèle,' Mama said. 'Be careful. Don't anger him.' She kissed my cheeks, and the driver knocked on the door. 'Do you understand?'

'I understand,' I said.

★ ★ ★

I felt the stuffiness of the room even before I opened the door to Antoine's brasserie. There must have been at least twenty police, all similarly dressed in evening suits, standing around tall bistro tables without any stools. Beautiful women gathered around them, taking sips from fancy cocktails in crystal glasses.

I stood in the doorway after taking my coat off and looked for Gérard, through the haze of cigarettes and cigars, trying to remember all his *rules*. 'Don't look like a prostitute,' he'd said, and a flit of warmness came between me and the chiffon dress, which suddenly felt like an invitation.

231

'Adèle!' Gérard barked from the bar, and I waved.

He commanded the waiter to fetch me a drink with a snap of his fingers, but I had grabbed a glass of gin off the bar myself.

'*Bonsoir*, Adèle.' He kissed both my cheeks, the stink of a cold cigar souring on his breath.

'*Bonsoir*.'

He smiled, smoothing his jacket against his chest. 'Aren't you going to say anything about my suit?'

I drank heartily, the jewelled pin in my hair blinding one eye. The maître d' answered for me in passing while I sucked the gin down. 'Extraordinary.'

I should have known Gérard would say nothing about how I looked, and instead seek out compliments for himself. He cosied up next to me at the bar, sticking a cigar in his mouth. 'It's a good night for us, Adèle.'

I pulled the glass from my lips. 'For us?'

He chuckled as if I should have known better. 'The police.' He lit his cigar and let the smoke balloon from his mouth in clouds. 'A very good night.'

I downed the rest of my gin and then asked the waiter for another. 'Whatever do you mean, Gérard Baudoin?'

He leaned into my ear. 'Résistants,' he said as the waiter handed me a fresh glass of gin. 'We got some. Important ones.'

'Résistants?' I tried to act more afraid than concerned, jolting to a stiff stand, spilling a drop of gin from my glass as the waiter poured a generous amount of lavender syrup over the ice. 'Here?'

'Not here! Lord, Adèle. A résistant wouldn't survive a minute in this place with all these police — we're trained to sense a traitor's blood.' He laughed, and I saw clear into the back of his throat.

'Then where? You're scaring me, Gérard — all this ado about the Résistance.'

He swung his arm around the back of my neck, pointing at the crowd of police before us. 'You're in the safest place in Vichy. No need to worry.'

A woman slunk past wearing a floor-length satin dress. She had an eye for Gérard and she let him know it, smoothing her dress against her thighs as she walked. His arm slipped off the back of my neck from the distraction, but when I moved, he pulled it back up.

'What do you mean you *have* some résistants? As in tied up, prisoners?' I tapped my foot on the floor as if checking for a loose board. 'In the basement?'

'Ahh, you are intrigued?' Gérard smiled, his eyes gleaming.

'Maybe,' I said. 'Maybe not.'

Gérard held me close, his warm hand above my dress, sliding down my back to my waist. 'We paid a man,' he whispered. '*Le mouchard* — the informer. Turns out he'd tell us anything we wanted to know for a little money and two tickets to Cannes.' He nuzzled my neck, lips skimming over my skin with small kisses. 'The Résistance won't know what happened when my men drive into Laudemarière tomorrow, take them by surprise.'

233

My heart raced. *A raid?* I moaned, pretending to enjoy his kisses, but inside I was spinning. 'Laudemarière?' I said, and he pulled away. 'What could possibly be there but some gnarled grape vines and abandoned spas?' My hands shook a little from learning so much information in just a few minutes.

'I can't say any more — it's fragile still, the operation.'

The waiter asked him if he wanted another drink, and I counted backward from ten in my mind, thinking about lying in the grass in the sun just like Marguerite had taught me, breathing slowly. My hands stopped shaking. I touched my chest, feeling the thrash of my nervous heart and my warming skin, and thought some more about the grass, sipping my gin slowly. *Don't push, I thought, be nonchalant.*

Gérard took a bottle of champagne from the bar meant for someone else and mixed his own drink with gin and lime before tossing it down his throat in one gulp.

I helped him make another — hoping then he'd tell me more about *le mouchard.*

Two men, one in a suit, the other in a guard's uniform, walked up to Gérard, drinks in hand. They looked me up and down, one of them settling his eyes on my breasts as if he could see through the chiffon.

'So, this is the nun, huh Gérard?' one of them said, laughing.

Gérard shrugged, looking away, setting his elbows onto the bar. He was either incapable of defending me, or unwilling.

I held my head up high, waiting for them to finishing eyeing me in Charlotte's gala gown. 'Do I look like a nun?'

One of them noticed Gérard's reddening cheeks. Nothing could clear a room faster than Gérard's temper. The man tugged on his friend's sleeve and they moved away from us both.

'Why do you have to do that, Adèle?' He talked into his glass as he drank, shaking the ice that was left at the bottom.

'Do what?'

'Look so damn irresistible. Make men notice you.'

I choked down a laugh. 'Irresistible is a strong word.'

Gérard's eyes rolled over my body, a slight scowl brewing on his face. 'You're a tease, and you know it. Why didn't you wear the pink dress I bought you?'

'It's a day dress,' I said.

He gulped the last of his drink, the ice clinking against his teeth. He was angrier than I thought. I knew not to move until he had calmed down. 'Gérard, I — '

He slammed his empty glass down, and everyone at the bar jumped. 'Don't move,' he gritted, and then took the hand of the woman who'd slunk by earlier and pulled her into the middle of the room where cheers and glasses chinked together.

'Kill the traitors!' they shouted.

Elbows nudged me to join, but I drank quietly at the bar.

Gérard smiled as the woman placed her hands on his chest, her dark brown hair looking very

235

black against the grey smoke hovering in the air and her lips a deep scarlet red — a distraction that cooled his temper. I retreated to the street-side windows near the door and lit a cigarette the bartender gave me, watching passers-by outside, some trying to catch a peek of the excitement inside the brasserie.

I leaned into the folds of the velvet curtains, repeating Gérard's words to myself about the raid as I smoked, wondering what kind of person would be so selfish to give up the Résistance's where-abouts for two train tickets. Down the street, just behind a patch of fog misting over the roadway was the square where I'd seen Les Femmes de la Nation. The chanting booming behind me was an eerie contrast to what I'd seen, and a reminder of what the regime had done to us.

'Adèle!' Gérard grabbed my hand and I instinctively pulled away, but his nose turned up and, remembering where and whom I was with, I apologized. 'Don't scare me like that, Gérard. I'm having a cigarette. You want to kill me like you do your résistants?'

'I wouldn't kill you,' he said. 'Not yet, anyway. I've invested too much time.' He moved in for a kiss, but noticed a black car drive up outside. 'René Bousquet,' he said, letting go.

The head of the police. I perked up.

Bousquet walked briskly from the car and into the Hotel du Parc, motioning for Gérard on the other side of the window with a wave of his hand. '*Le mouchard,*' Gérard said, eyes wide. 'He's here!'

I put my hand to the glass, catching first glimpse of the informant Gérard had been waiting for, and I was surprised to see it wasn't one person, but two. A man and a woman. They got out of the back of Bousquet's car, walking together, holding hands. I inched closer to the glass, watching in earnest, thinking I saw something familiar in the way they looked, their walk, the way they held their heads.

The man lifted his hat.

'Mother of Christ,' I breathed, and I collapsed into the curtains, grasping at the folds to stay upright.

18

The bald man and his wife. They looked the same as they did all those months ago, greedy, and angry as the day they buried Marguerite's fiancé. The pair stopped on the pavement while the wife adjusted her wool coat, sliding a thick roll of francs into her cleavage. *Marguerite, the raid.* They must have told the police all about her, and the Alliance. I could barely breathe.

'Be here when I get back,' Gérard said, pointing at me as I hung on to the curtains, and he rushed out of the brassiere. People on the dance floor stopped and stared, first from the commotion of Gérard leaving and then from me and my desperate bid to stay upright. I swallowed, hand to my chest.

The waiter came by with his tray. 'Another drink, mademoiselle?' He looked at me strangely as I struggled to compose myself. I snapped my fingers. 'My coat!'

I ran down the street and around the corner, breathless in the cold air. That's when I saw what I already knew: the flower cart was bare; the old woman had long since gone home. I raced back to the brasserie and hopped into the car I arrived in, waking up the driver who'd fallen asleep with a newspaper over his face. '*La maison! La maison!*' I said, closing the door. 'I'm not well!' The driver crumpled up his newspaper and started up the engine. '*Now!*' I laid my hand against my forehead

238

and moaned, thinking about Marguerite and the ambush the police had planned.

The driver sped away, shooting sharp glances at me through the rear-view mirror. 'Don't vomit in the car!' He tossed a paper bag into the back seat as we squealed around a corner. My heart raced thinking about Luc — he was the only other contact I had — and I prayed like hell he'd be in his radio room when I got home.

The driver nearly kicked me out of his car thinking I'd throw up. I waited until he was completely out of sight before running over to the barrel cellar in search of Luc. The room was dark, even after I left the doors wide open. I pounded on the trapdoor. Nothing. 'Luc,' I yelled, futilely.

Mama ran barefoot into the barrel room dressed in her peignoir. 'Adèle!' She shouted at first but then whispered, 'What are you doing?'

'There's a spy in the Résistance,' I said. 'I have to inform Luc.'

The trapdoor flung open. Mama jumped back while I peered down the ladder and into the room. A dimly lit lantern shined on two faces: a man I'd never seen before, small, with thin brown hair, and a woman with piercing eyes, the kind that could look right through a person, see their guts and tell you what was inside.

'What do you know?' the woman said.

I stared at them, unsure who they were and if I should talk. She climbed up the ladder, the man right behind her, the scratch of Luc's radio a nervy cadence deep below.

She held the lantern up to my face. 'What did you say about a spy?'

239

I looked at Mama and then to her, still not answering.

She shook me by the shoulder. 'Adèle, I know who you are and where you have been. Tell me, what did you hear?'

Her eyes burrowed into mine, and it was then I recognized who she was. Dressed in the same tan trousers and white shirt she wore in the crypt all those months ago, she was the one they called Hedgehog, the leader of the Alliance. *Résistance*.

'You remember me, no?'

Her hair was darker than before and she was skinnier, but there was no mistaking that look of hers and the paralyzing feeling I felt in my knees when she locked eyes with me. I nodded.

'Then tell me what you know,' she said.

'There's a raid planned for tomorrow. In Laude-marière.'

'I must hurry,' she said to the man beside her. He pulled a gun from each pocket, and she hid them on her person, one in a holster around her calf, the other down the front of her shirt. 'Stay here and man the radio,' she said to him. 'If I'm not back by sunrise, then something went wrong.'

Her eyes flicked to mine. 'I hope I'm not too late.'

I paced inside Mama's dark kitchen, trying to find a way to calm the pulse in my veins that had been thumping since I left the brasserie. Changing into a comfortable housedress didn't help. Mama did nothing but watch me from the woodblock, her backside flush against the counter.

'What's wrong with you, Adèle? You did well tonight. Now be at rest with it.'

240

I laughed in jest. 'I feel like a revved car lurching and stopping, lurching and stopping, all the way down the road. I'm either on full alert or left to wait, and wondering what the hell to do.'

Mama lit a lantern with her lighter. 'Follow me,' she said, walking toward the cellar.

'I need more than a drink, Mama.'

'Just follow me, Adèle.' The hem of Mama's crème peignoir brushed the dirt floor and got dirtier and dirtier as she moved toward the back of the cellar, her feet black from being outside without shoes. Bottles of wine had been pulled from the racks and sat upright against the wall, showing Papa's dwindling supply. Mama waved a hand at the wine. 'Not this,' she said. 'That is not why I asked you down here.'

'Then why?' I said. 'If we're not going to drink . . . '

Mama opened Charlotte's chest of paints. 'Why don't you paint?' Mama said, taking a tube of paint into her hands.

I laughed. 'Paint?'

'Painting always relaxed Charlotte. It's why she got started.'

I glanced at the paint in the chest, the metal tubes shining from the lantern's light. 'I don't know how to paint, Mama.'

'Have you ever tried?'

'Yes,' I said, 'actually I have. Besides, Charlotte wouldn't want me using her paints.'

'Charlotte isn't here, now is she?' Mama pulled Charlotte's old painting palette from the chest and stuck it under her arm as she dug through the paints. 'Someone might as well use these.'

241

Painting at the convent felt like a task. I didn't see how it could be relaxing. 'I don't think — '

'You have someplace else to go?' Mama said.

'But what about the slashed canvases? Should I paint the walls?' I joked.

'Yes,' Mama said, looking up from the chest. 'Paint the wall. Nobody will ever see it down here.'

'You're serious?' I watched Mama pick through the tubes; she was intent on me painting, no matter what I said. I sighed, studying the stones and feeling them with both of my hands. The cracks and grooves between the rocks were rough, not smooth like a real canvas, but I wasn't painting a masterpiece — it didn't have to be perfect. And like Mama said, nobody would see it. 'And you think it will help?'

'I really do, Adèle.'

I held my hand out. 'Give me the paint.' I squeezed paint from several different tubes onto Charlotte's paint-stained palette, choosing from an array of brushes tucked inside her cotton organizer. I picked the fattest brush, as Mama suggested, and twirled it in a blob of red paint, slapping it onto the wall. The bristles glided over the stones, sticky, slippery, swirling.

'The colour's bright.' Even in the dimly lit cellar, the red jumped from the wall like a flame. 'Unusually bright.'

Mama lit a cigarette and talked as she puffed it to life. 'That's because of the cadmium in the oils — expensive little suckers. Charlotte had to have the best paint.'

'Of course, she did,' I said.

Mama tightened her peignoir before taking a

seat on a dusty old chair wedged in the corner. 'Charlotte always said inspiration came from within.' Mama tapped the middle of her forehead with one finger. 'Said it was always in her mind.'

'In my mind . . . ' I stood in front of the stone wall. 'Should I take a deep breath?' I kicked off my shoes and got comfortable in my housedress, thinking I should count backward and think about the grass and the sun to find inspiration.

Mama shrugged. 'Do what feels right to you.' She nestled her back into the crook of the chair, brushing her bobbed brown hair from her face, her lit cigarette burning between two fingers, waiting for me to paint.

I closed my eyes, and took two or three deep breaths before I noticed the darkness in my mind had turned into a swirl of colours, some bright as the sun, others a mix of blue and grey. *What do I paint?* Thoughts of the police, the urgency of what I'd heard at Antoine's ebbed like a slow pulse through my veins. And the woman I saw at the Morris Column . . .

My eyes popped open, and I painted what was in my heart. A naked woman, beautiful, raw, and bold.

'Christ, Adèle. You can paint.' Mama held the lantern up to her eyes, leaning closer to the wall. 'What is that you wrote underneath? *Les Femmes de la Nation?* It's very good — this painting. Almost better than — '

'Don't say that, Mama. It's not better than Charlotte's.'

She shrugged. 'Say what you will.' She flicked her cigarette. 'A Picasso if I didn't know better,' she said, and I laughed.

'No, Mama,' I said. 'It is not.'

I dabbed the brush into the red paint to touch up the last letter before standing back to admire my work. I had to admit it was better than the painting I did at the convent. With this one, I almost thought it was worth a winter's rationing of coal.

'Did you hear about the woman in the square?'

'I heard.' Mama snubbed her cigarette out in the dirt wall, exhaling after a long inhalation. 'This painting of yours would cause just as much panic for the regime.'

'You think so?'

'Think of how much commotion that woman caused in the square.' Mama's eyes brightened next to the lantern. 'Adèle, you could paint this!' she said, pointing at the wall. Her voice was full of excitement, something I hadn't heard from her in a long time. 'There are thousands of walls in Vichy that could serve as your canvas. You said it before, there's enough paint to cover every wall in this city!'

'I said that?'

'You did,' Mama said. 'The last time we were down here together.'

Using Charlotte's paints somehow seemed wrong, knowing how strongly she felt about painting. The leopard dress was one thing; she had thrown it out, didn't even know Mama had saved it from the rubbish bin. 'I don't know . . .'

'Does this have something to do with Charlotte?'

'You know how she is, Mama. If she ever found out . . .'

'She doesn't visit. Even if she did, she wouldn't come down here.' Mama walked away holding the wall with one hand for balance, talking as she went. 'Won't even let me know where my granddaughter is buried . . . ' She yelped a little cry, and I chased after her.

'Mama, wait!' I said, and I caught up to her near the kitchen.

'If Charlotte throws a fit that her paints are gone, so be it,' she said. 'I'll have a talk with her. I bought the paints.' She patted my shoulder. 'All right?'

She left me to go upstairs to her bedroom, and I stood in the dark. The vineyard was quiet, and so was the chateau, and I sat down at the table, waiting for morning.

I woke up to the sun rudely shining through the kitchen window, with my head slumped over on the table. I shuffled out to the patio, heavy and dog-tired, with a crick in my neck from sleeping slumped over on the table. The doors to the barrel cellar were closed, and there was a settled quietness.

'She made it to Laudemarière,' I said, yawning. 'She must have.'

I rubbed my ears, yawning again, when the barrel cellar door burst open, and I jumped from the crack of wood on wood. The man from last night paced in circles. He looked to the vineyard and then the field making sharp turns. I rushed over.

'It's sunrise — she's not back.' He unravelled a crumpled piece of paper in his shaking hands, his lit cigarette glowing brighter with his breath, but then pounded his forehead with his fist. 'I don't know where this is,' he said to himself.

'She's not back?' I took the paper.

'Would I be standing here now if she were?' The cigarette slipped from his mouth onto the ground. 'I'll have to go in her place,' he said, taking a frantic breath. 'She was probably arrested. But I know nothing about the spas in the Auvergne.'

Arrested? The paper had been crumpled over and over from having been in his hands for hours; the writing now just faded scratches, but still I recognized the retreat listed. Papa used to sell his wine there, before they closed after the armistice. 'The Sleeping Lady Retreat.'

He grabbed my shoulders. 'You know where this is?'

I nodded, knowing what he was going to ask next, but I wasn't sure if I could do it, with Gérard probably on his way there. I told myself Hedgehog had managed to tip them off, that she wasn't back because of some other reason. Lies, all lies. I'd have to go. I'd have to.

'I need you to go,' he said, though I couldn't take the car, I'd have to take my bicycle, but it wasn't a far ride. He gave me a shake. 'Many people are staying there. Lieutenants, agents from the Alliance — résistants, some of the bravest.' His voice lowered, and his eyes squinted into tiny slits. 'Someone you know.'

'Luc?'

He nodded slowly, and I felt my lips pinch, but not because I was mad. I felt something different bubbling inside of me — I wasn't sure what to call it — as I faced an entirely different situation. *Luc.*

'Are you going or not?' His brow furrowed, his

breath blowing a cloud of white into the cold.

I wadded up the paper and threw it at his chest, running for my bicycle.

19

I rode faster than I'd ever ridden in my life, only to slow down once I made it to the retreat. I pedalled up the long gravel road, looking around cautiously. I hadn't been up that way for many years, and I was surprised to see how similar it looked to Papa's vineyard. Overgrown bushes in need of a trim crowded the roadway from many months of vacancy. Plaster crumbled from the nineteenth-century chateau, and half the gardens looked dead.

I got off my bicycle in the main courtyard, listening for a sound, any sound, other than the whirl of the river not that far away. Shutters hung from corners, and a dead cat lay flattened near the front steps, which made the place even more unsettling. My hands shook a little, thinking the police could show up any minute. I walked up to the front, trying to get a peek through the window, but then the door opened suddenly and I was yanked inside.

'Marguerite!'

'Adèle!' Her face dropped. 'What are you doing here?' She looked out the only window without boards nailed to it.

'You must leave!' Words shot from my mouth. 'A raid! Hurry — '

She moved quickly, slinging guns that had been resting against the wall over her shoulder, yelling for others to get up and move. Men and women of all ages flooded down the stairs and out of every room. The parquet floor shook as they plodded through the corridors, grabbing crates and carrying them down to the basement. People folded up maps and threw papers into the fire. I called out for Luc, but my voice was one of many shouting for someone. Then everything got very quiet and still. Incredibly still.

'In the basement there's a passageway that leads into the hills. Someone has to close it from the outside.' Marguerite touched my arm and her voice turned soft. 'You understand, Adèle. Don't you?'

I swallowed. 'I can't go with you.'

'If the police are waiting outside then . . . '

'Go, Marguerite . . . Go!' I said.

I followed her down a long but wide marble staircase that led into a room that smelled of salt and looked like it had once been a place for the baths. A round mosaic of nymphs set in the wall was actually a door. Marguerite was the last one to go through it.

'It's heavy. Push it until it clicks.'

I got ready to push when Marguerite reached for my hand. She opened her mouth, about to say something.

'You're welcome,' I said. 'But next time you're pushing the door.' Her hand slid from mine, and I gave the door a good shove, but then panicked because the door was much heavier than I thought, and by now everyone had fled into the dark tunnel. I was all alone, pushing and grunting and sweating, feet slipping, trying to get the door to shut. 'Ack — ' I screamed, face beet red, eyes bulging, and then it closed.

I tore out of there panting, racing up the stairs and out the front door. I grabbed my bicycle and ducked behind the chateau, riding through a field of thicket and overgrown brush crawling with mice in a frantic rush to get as far away as possible.

The sound of rapid gunfire kicked me off my bicycle into the thorns. '*BRAAAP! BRAAAP!*'

Shouts from the police waved through the brush. I heard pounding, then the frightening sound of one loud boom. The chateau's chimney peeking over the trees lit up with fire blazing out its stack, shooting sparks into the late morning sky. I scrambled to my feet, ditching my bicycle in the brush, hurrying away, until I reached a dirt road I hoped would lead to the river. A plume of thick dust from an approaching car billowed behind me down the road. I ran before I had a chance to even think about running, glancing over my shoulder, my heart bursting from my chest, watching the plume of dust expand like a balloon behind the speeding car.

The road vanished ahead of me — a cliff. Feeling every inch of the road in my legs and muscles, I pushed harder and harder to outrun the car, but even a leopard's lungs could only carry it so far. I jumped, the skirt of my housedress parachuting around me as I hurled myself into the air, only to land knees first in a sandy hole, every bone in my body smacking against the other like fists to a palm.

Rocks tumbled down the slope and caved in around me. Everything got dark and grey, and I felt life slipping away with each struggling breath.

250

Then suddenly I saw Gérard standing over me, his foot pressing on my chest, laughing with his mouth hanging wide open. But soon enough the laugh gave way to a woman's voice telling me to hold on, and the vision of Gérard disappeared in pieces with every new and wonderful thought I had about making it out alive. 'Help,' I gasped through the grit and the dust. 'Help!'

I poked my hand through a pocket of air, searching, and a warm hand grabbed mine. Then I saw the most relieving sight of all, a familiar face to match the voice.

Marguerite.

She lifted the rocks away one by one, giving me a second chance at life. I looked up and out of the hole, the crisp blue sky above me with the sun on my face, and I knew — I'd use those paints after all, and cover every wall in Vichy if I had to.

She grabbed on to me, and we hugged tightly. 'Are you all right?' She pulled away to look at me. 'Any broken bones?'

'It's you . . . ' I said, hugging her again. 'I'm so glad it's you. How did you know where I was?'

'That was my car you were running from,' she said. 'I thought you might head toward the river for cover.' She pulled debris from my hair. 'Is this paint?'

'Yes,' I said, dusting myself off. 'And don't ask.'

She dropped my hair as fast as she had picked it up. 'I like your housedress. What's left of it at least.'

'You do?' I ripped the dangling hem off. She cracked a smile, and so did I. We hugged again.

'I missed you,' I said.

251

'I missed you too,' she said. 'Now, let's get out of here. The police aren't that far away.'

We walked down a rocky embankment to the river where she had parked the car. A man and a boy wearing a tattered youth legion uniform guarded the vehicle with guns pointed in all directions. I stopped before I got in. 'Where are we going?'

'Into the hills,' she said. 'There's been a big development in the war. The Reich has disbanded the armistice to fight off our shores in the south, the Allies invaded North Africa. Now the Germans are storming the Free Zone looking for résistants.'

'So, it is over,' I said. 'The armistice — the Free Zone.'

'We knew it was only a matter of time,' she said, motioning with her head to get into the vehicle.

I nodded, though I'd hoped against hope what I knew for so many months would never come to pass. I got into the vehicle. The Germans were coming.

We drove for a good while, through villages Marguerite said were sympathetic, and into the volcanic Puy-de-Dôme area of the Auvergne just south of Vichy. 'We'll be safe with the Maquis,' Marguerite said, holding her hair back from the front seat. 'They live in the hills; it's where they hide. A brutal group of French Résistance, but also the most accommodating. You can rest before going back to Vichy. The camp is near a hot spring.'

Papa and Mama used to take Charlotte and me into the volcanic hills when we were little for day picnics and rest. There were lakes, but I wasn't sure where — the basalt cliffs were just as towering as I remembered, shooting up from the ground in columns.

We headed up switchbacks into a forest with many kinds of trees, finally coming to a stop at the end, marked by a boulder of granite. 'The Free French come here for the transfer,' she said, slinging a rifle over her shoulder. 'What the Alliance hoards, and then gives to the Maquisards.' She pulled a hunk of crusty bread from her pocket and handed it to me as we walked down a long footpath that cut in between some trees.

'Transfer?' I shoved the bread into my mouth, my stomach growling, chewing as she talked.

'The guns in the crypt,' she said. 'We give them the intelligence we've collected and the guns. Weapons to fight with . . . the ones we steal from the Germans.' She stopped and touched my shoulder. 'The codes you got from Gérard's office unlocked the largest load we've had in a single collection.'

I gasped, smiling, and she patted my back.

A camp came out of nowhere at the end of the path; fabric draped from tree limbs and sparking fires cooked meat on a spit. The women, some old as grandmothers, others younger than the delinquents at the convent, smoked and passed guns to men wearing berets in vehicles who had their sleeves rolled up to their biceps, which bulged under the tattered fabric of their old French uniforms. Unshaved faces and the grittiness of an underground war thick on their skin was their patch.

'Remember, they call me Chameleon here,'

she said.

'What's my name?' I joked, but then started to wonder if I did have a code name.

'I've been calling you Catchfly,' she said. 'When we hid in those bug-infested weeds, wanting to itch but couldn't for the sake of our lives . . . It's not an animal name, but I'm sure the Alliance can make an exception.'

'It's perfect.'

Marguerite walked me over to a small group where she introduced me by my new name. One was a man who looked dirtier than dirt with bloodshot eyes. 'This is Gill,' Marguerite said, pointing with her head.

'Like a fish?' I asked.

He popped an unlit cigarette into his mouth and pulled back his shirt, exposing what looked like healed bullet holes above his collarbone.

'He's been known to breathe underwater,' she said.

Gill laughed, which turned into a hacking cough when he lit his cigarette. Marguerite adjusted her collar, pulling it from her neck, and I wondered if she had scars. She caught me looking, and dropped her hand.

'We heard you knew about Hedgehog, that she was arrested late last night. Coming in her place was very brave,' Marguerite said.

'Not any braver than you,' I said. 'Saving me from the dirt.'

There were no more words about bravery.

'There's a man I'm looking for,' I said, 'someone in the Résistance who . . .' Two men emerged from the tree line, carrying cases and wearing

254

headphones around their necks. I lit up, heart fluttering. *Luc.*

He glanced up, catching sight of me, ripping the headphones from his neck, and I ran into his arms. He squeezed me tightly before pulling away, looking dreamily into my eyes. 'Why'd you do it? You could have been arrested, or worse!'

'Did I have a choice?' I smiled. 'You still haven't told me where you're from.'

He pulled me in for a kiss, a quick peck. 'Come on,' he said.

'I'll be right back,' I said to Marguerite, but we'd walked away from camp and into a secluded part of the woods where we could have some privacy. Our feet dangled over the edge of a basalt cliff, catching the last tailings of sunlight as the sun dipped into the hills.

'I thought about you every day since we drank whisky in your mother's kitchen,' he said.

'But you left,' I said. 'Not even a goodbye.'

'That night I watched you sit in your mother's kitchen from the field. I smoked all my cigarettes in the dark, wondering what you were thinking, and how the hell I was going to stay away from you.'

'You watched me?' I breathed, and the rest of the world seemed so far away.

He held me in his arms.

'Does this mean you'll tell me where you're from?' I said.

Luc laughed. 'I'm from Nancy. I was born there.' I rested my head on his shoulder.

'And your voice?' I said, and he laughed again. 'Where's the accent come from?'

'As for my voice, well, that's what happens when you spend time in Britain, talk to them on the radio. They rub off on you — those Brits — like shoe polish. But we need them, and they need us. You and me, and what we do — the Résistance.'

I sat quietly, thinking of what I'd done for the Résistance, and then sat up. He asked me if I was all right.

'Do you know . . . ' I looked in his eyes, gulping. 'Do you know what I've done for the Résistance?' The flutter I felt deep inside turned into a hot ball of nerves when he looked away, into the distance. 'Luc?'

'Well, do you know what I've done?' he said, and there was a pause. 'What I mean is, we do what we have to.'

When we have to.

'Understand?' he said, and I don't think I've ever felt closer to one person in my life.

'Yes,' I said, and I took his hand. 'But I realized something this morning I hadn't before. Maybe it was the rocks caving in around me like a tomb, or maybe it was the light of day on my face that made me wake up. One thing I know for certain. The work has to be my own.' I looked up from our hands. 'It's time for me to carve my own path in the Résistance.'

We kissed again, only this time long and slow, the sun sinking very low into the hills, turning all the leaves in the trees fire-orange, and the moment felt right. I tugged on his hand. 'Come on,' I said, and I led him to the bubbling hot spring steaming behind us where I slipped off my dress.

He pulled his shirt up over his head and

unbuckled his pants. I shivered from a forest chill, and he embraced me in the night, hands sliding down my bare back, thinking I'd trembled. 'Are you nervous?'

His question caught me off guard, then I remembered what Charlotte had said to me. And she was right, when you're in love there's no time for nerves.

'No,' I breathed. 'I'm not.' We eased into the pool, and he held me close, kissing me lovingly as leaves fluttered off long branches and tumbled like pinwheels over the forest floor in the quiet black, black night.

★ ★ ★

We fell asleep next to a crackling fire, cuddled in blankets Luc had stashed in a nearby vehicle. Résistants who had rendezvoused with their lovers shared similar makeshift beds in the forest and around the camp. I woke at the break of dawn to his arms wrapped around me. I felt his biceps, thinking he was still asleep, but he was very awake.

'It's from the parachutes,' he said.

I raised my head up. 'I was teasing when I asked if you had flown in with your radio.' I felt him again, wondering if we'd ever be able to lie in the sun out in the open one day. I wished it, closing my eyes and imagining it, but everything had changed now with the Germans.

'Hear that?' Luc said, and my eyes popped open. He shifted under the covers, listening. Others sat up. The drone of a faraway aeroplane turned into a roaring squadron of German fighters flying over the treetops. 'They can't see us,' he said, but I was shaking as they flew over us lying in the trees.

They'd come out of nowhere, furious, and we watched them disappear, flying south. I swallowed. 'What's going to happen to us now?' I said.

'The Wehrmacht will drive south to fight the Allies in North Africa,' he said. 'And try to take the French fleet.'

I gasped. 'There really won't be anything left of France, will there? But, what about here, Luc?' I said. 'How will life change in Vichy?' I searched the sky, wondering how our lives would change even more than they already had.

'Expect more restrictions. When the fleet falls into German hands, Pétain won't have any leverage, and the government will have to do what the Reich says. We've heard whisperings about a French-style Gestapo.' He looked at me. 'How many guns do you have?'

'I don't have one,' I said, and I think he was surprised. 'Mama has one hidden in her floor, but . . .'

'I think you need one of your own.' Luc reached into his pack and pulled out a gun, not a big one, but not as dainty as Mama's either. 'Here, let me show you how to shoot it.'

I slipped on my ratty housedress and we moved into some trees. Luc stood behind me — his presence comforting — his arms and hands lifting mine into an aim. 'See that tree?' he said. 'Aim at the knot in the middle.'

I raised the gun out in front of me with both hands, aiming. 'There's two barrels when I do,' I said, repositioning my feet. 'And seems too far away to hit.'

'Now,' he said. 'Close one eye.' He held me tighter, the smell of his skin almost as distracting as his strong, warm touch. 'And look down the barrel, you should see one target.'

I closed one eye, and the distant target was now much closer, more manageable to hit. 'I see it now.' I lowered the gun, his hands slipping from mine.

'Keep the gun on you,' he said. 'Even if you think you don't need it.'

I had to wonder where I was supposed to put it. Dresses didn't have pockets big enough to hide something so bulky. 'Where?'

Luc touched my inner thigh. 'Here. Around your leg,' he said, kissing me.

I resisted the urge to throw my head back and let him take me once more, but with the gun in my hand and the busyness of the Maquis moving arms and trucks down the road away from camp, I knew our time together on the cliff was nearing its end.

He shouted to someone running equipment between sputtering vehicles for a leg holster. I fastened it to my thigh myself, pulling the leather strap tightly around my leg.

'When will I see you again?' I said.

'I'm not sure,' he said. 'I'll miss you every day.'

Gill motioned for Luc to hurry up and get in his running truck. 'We're leaving!' he yelled to Luc.

Luc looked back and forth between me and the truck.

We kissed, holding each other's hands, drawing out our last few moments together, but then Gill

259

yelled again, and our hands slid excruciatingly away from each other.

★ ★ ★

Marguerite drove me to Vichy in an unassuming black car after she changed into a clean postulant's skirt and shirt. We stopped a kilometre or so away from Papa's vineyard, the door to Mama's kitchen a hazy outline in the distance.

'Be careful, Adèle. Know the costs of love in the Résistance.' She turned toward me as she sat behind the wheel of the running car, and I caught a glimpse of the locket under her smock. 'You'd be wise not to tell anyone. Not even your mother. Gérard will kill him if he finds out what you're doing.'

'I know.'

She rubbed the locket in her fingers, and we sat without a word between us, the midmorning sun shining onto the Vichy hills and over Creuzier-le-Vieux, over Papa's craggy vines.

'Marguerite,' I said, and she looked at me. 'There's something else I'm going to do for the Résistance. I thought you should know.'

She didn't look surprised but rather turned my forearm over to get a better look at what little paint the spring hadn't washed off. 'In the Occupied Zone some are scrawling the letter V in places for *Victoire*. Timing is everything,' she said. 'Résistants get caught when they're careless. Remember that.'

Timing. 'I will.'

'One more thing,' she said. 'There will be a lot

of police activity after the foiled raid, and a lot of distrust. They will be looking for leaks, spies. You'll need to find a way to distance yourself from the Hotel du Parc and Gérard during this time. For a little while anyway, until things die down.'

I was surprised, to say the least. Pleasantly surprised.

'It will be a delicate walk,' she said. 'Be careful. Make it seem natural, be conveniently busy. He will be busy himself.'

'All right.'

We took each other's hands. 'If you would have told me months ago I'd be holding your hands, I would have called you a liar,' Marguerite said.

'Actually, *I* would have called you a liar, and then you would have swatted me with a switch.'

'Hanger.' She smiled. 'I think I'd prefer the hanger.'

'Indeed,' I said, laughing.

'We were awful to each other on the train, weren't we?' I said.

'Saving my life makes me like you a lot more, Adèle.'

'I feel the same.'

We kissed each other's cheeks before I opened the door, the wrought smell of old vines and soured grapes coming from Papa's crusted, broken-down vineyard reminding me I was home.

'Adèle?' Marguerite stopped me with her voice. 'I always wanted to know,' she said, leaning over the seat, catching my gaze as I stood outside holding the door open, 'in Lyon you said one of the reasons why you didn't marry Gérard was because he was a collaborator.'

261

'Yes,' I said. 'That's true.'

'What's the other reason?' she asked. 'I heard he was different before the war.'

'He was different,' I said. 'But even if he went back to the boy he was before and grew into an honourable man, there'd still be one thing missing.' I shut the door.

'What's that?'

'My fluttering heart,' I said.

I walked down the hill to the chateau where Mama sat in an old chair she'd dragged out to the patio. A half-drank cup of chamomile tea sat on the armrest. She had a notebook in her lap and a pencil in her hand. She looked up as I neared, almost surprised. 'Did he give you anything for me?'

The warmth of Luc's touch was still on my mind, and I found it difficult to concentrate on her words. The scent of the hot spring moistened on my skin didn't help. 'Who?'

Her eyes crossed. 'Albert, of course.'

'Papa?' My mind scrambled.

'Isn't that where you've been? With your father?' She wrote on the paper even though her eyes were on me. 'You said you weren't going to leave me.'

'No . . .' I said.

'No, you weren't with him?' Her brow protruded from her forehead. 'Or, *no* he didn't give you anything?'

I hesitated. 'Both.'

'Humph!' She went back to writing, a long letter by the looks of it, waving for me to leave.

I took a wet rag from the counter and cleaned myself up. Looking out the window, it was hard not to think about where Luc was, where he had gone after he drove away. Our trees had gone bare from the cooler weather, and leaves rustled in piles under Mama's clothesline. Winter would be here soon.

On the other side of the field I saw a thin ribbon of smoke rising over the hill. The longer I studied it, the more I could smell the faint acridity of the burn lingering in the air, which didn't smell like kindling. A fighter plane buzzed overhead, then another and another, flying south. I leaned over the counter, straining to see out the window. Vichy planes never sounded that menacing. *Germans.*

Mama shuffled in as the windows rattled, ripping the page she had written on from her notebook. 'There'll be more rabbits for us this winter. Won't be making pies for the neighbours.'

'Why is that, Mama?' I said, watching the planes fly by.

'Because the Brochards are dead.'

I whipped my head away from the window. 'What?'

Mama nodded. 'There was no sound. Only the smoke is left. Killed himself and the little ones — figured out his wife wasn't coming back. Things will be different now since the invasion. He knew it. We all know it. Didn't want the Germans to do what he could do himself with dignity.'

I turned back around. The planes had flown off, but the smoke from the Brochards' farm clouded into a fresh haze. 'The children?'

'They were Jews.' Mama sat down at the table and relit a cold cigarette. 'Doesn't matter if they were French. If the Germans want them, Vichy

263

will hand them over.' She patted her apron pocket, pressing it against her thigh to make the lump of paper thinner, flatter, which made me wonder how many letters to Papa she had stashed in there. 'When will you see your father?'

I watched her as she sucked on her dying cigarette, bringing it back to life, the crackle of its ember the only sound in the room as she sat in a chair. I had come close to dying more times than I ever thought I would in one lifetime, but seeing that smoke hovering over our vineyard lit another fire, this one deep within my soul.

'Does it matter?'

Mama's eyes bounced, but she said nothing. Then she glanced over my hair where it was flat from the spring, as if she just now realized that not only had I been gone all night, but I had been somewhere far away.

I pointed to her pocket. 'How many letters did you write that you'll never send?' My voice peaked and her eyes bugged from her head. 'Stubbornness is not a virtue, Mama.'

She gasped. 'Adèle!'

'What good are unread letters if you're dead?' I bent down in front of her, my eyes level with hers. 'Living is not a luxury meant for us all.'

Mama sat in silence, taking a shaking puff from her cigarette. 'Your father chose the regime over me, Adèle.'

I shook my head. 'Did it ever occur to you he thinks choosing the regime is choosing you? Do what we have to, when we have to. Right?'

The blood drained from her face, leaving her very pale.

I motioned for her to hand me the letters. 'You can't change yesterday. But today is what you make it.'

Mama stared at my open hand a good while before I finally left her to think, walking down the corridor into my bedroom and taking a few heavy breaths against the wall. I'd never talked to Mama that way, but felt better saying what was on my mind.

After I changed into a clean dress and fixed my hair, I came back into the kitchen only to find her still sitting at the table with her cigarettes. I stood next to her, fastening my earrings, getting ready to head out to Charlotte's boutique.

'I've listened to Albert explain himself until I've turned blue, and gotten so mad I thought I might burst open my blood pumped so hard. And Charlotte, she's just taken his side.' Mama reached into her pocket and pulled out a wad of letters, tossing them on the table in a messy pile. 'But you're right. If I'm dead none of it matters, now does it?'

My mouth gaped open at the sight of so many letters. 'Mama . . .'

'Give this to Charlotte.' Mama handed me a knitted hat for the baby. 'She'll be mad the whole day that you told me. There's nothing I can do about that.' Her eyes welled with tears at the mere mention of Charlotte's baby. 'And please tell her I've been saying prayers for the granddaughter she won't let me pay my respects to.' She cried two heaving breaths, her face bunching up, and I put my hand on her shoulder, my heart breaking from hearing her cry.

'And the letters?' I said.

'All of them go to your father.' She put a finger on one she had folded tightly into a triangle and slid it toward me. 'But tell him to open this one last.'

1943

1943

20

A new threat flooded the city almost overnight one day in January, this time dressed in double-breasted blue uniforms and a deceivingly French blue beret. The Milice. Created by our government to hunt and destroy the French Résistance, this new French militia was designed to work side-by-side with the Gestapo — our own countrymen turned against us.

Milice flags unravelled and flew from poles, blue, white, red, and black. People watched from the cobblestone streets in front of the Gare de Vichy, clutching that morning's meagre rations from the butcher, as the miliciens walked down the street in formation, hands on their rifles, ready to shoot, with their shined black boots and thick, waist-high black belts.

Clomp, clomp, clomp . . .

'So, it's been done,' I said, gazing at the marching miliciens. 'Word swept through the street last night, but I didn't believe it.'

Papa shoved an old cigarette in his mouth and lit what was left of it in the face of a bitter wind, puffing hard until the crumpled end finally caught fire. 'Word?' He closed his coat by crossing his arms, watching them assemble under the Gare de Vichy's stone archway.

'The Milice, Papa. Gestapo, by another name.'

A lorry pulled up next, and a gendarme in the Vichy police led a handful of men as dirty as a mud hole out of the back with their hands on top of their heads. The Milice barked at the prisoners to stand against the stone wall in front of the train station; one had a clipboard and seemed to be checking names off, while a Gestapo officer in a warm wool coat and matching gloves stood menacingly over his shoulder, monitoring.

'*Le Résistance*,' Papa said, squinting, trying to get a better look at the men as they lined up, backs flat against the wall in their shredded clothes, torn and ripped. Women wept openly for their husbands and sons, kneeling on the cold cobblestones, begging for the Milice to keep them in France — not send them to Germany, but they only pushed their rifles at them, shooing them away like vermin.

Papa mashed his cigarette on the ground before walking into his wine bar, and I followed him inside. He moved crates of wine away from the wall. '*Vin de merde*,' I swear I heard him say.

'What's that, Papa?'

'Nothing, nothing,' he said, taking a loose cigarette from his pocket. 'I wish I had a cigar. That's what I said.'

The women's cries outside seeped through the door like a spill and Papa struggled to light another crumpled cigarette pinched in his lips. A delivery of flowers arrived shortly after, six of the fullest, most luxurious red roses I'd ever seen, almost unheard of these days, and very expensive. The deliveryman handed me the card, and I swallowed, knowing roses like this could have only come from one person.

I closed my eyes briefly. *Gérard.*

After the raid, he'd been busy with the police,

270

travelling to Lyon and Paris, and when he was in Vichy, I used Mama as an excuse to get out of his dates, saying she needed me at the estate — a natural absence, like Marguerite had suggested. What I didn't expect was for the distance to fuel his infatuation for me.

I opened the card.

'I'm the cat and you're the mouse. One day I will catch you. Enjoy the roses.'

My stomach turned.

'Why aren't you at Charlotte's shop?' Papa said, and I looked up, tucking the card back into the envelope.

'Because I'm here with you, at your wine bar.' I could feel the tension behind me and between us, the weight of the miliciens' presence and the existence of Germans in Vichy and now Gérard's flowers in my arms. Papa kept his head down as he continued to pull crates of wine away from the wall, oblivious to me and the scene unfolding outside.

Suddenly Charlotte walked around the corner and reached for Papa's door. I panicked, wondering where I should stash the flowers but there was no time. She nearly ran into the deliveryman as he left, stomping inside. I hid the card behind my back, but those damn flowers were still in my arms.

'Adèle!' Upon seeing Papa, she pulled me to the side to talk. 'What's going on between you and Gérard?' she whispered.

'What do you mean?' I played with the card behind my back. 'I ran into him yesterday and he said you've been busy helping Mama, but we all

271

know that isn't true. What possible things could she need help with? She's perfectly well.'

I wondered what Charlotte was doing near the Hotel du Parc to *run* into Gérard. Part of me wanted to tell her exactly where my mind was concerning Gérard, and that I had no intention of marrying him, but I knew that was too much for her to hear. 'He's been very busy with the police. He is just as much to blame.'

'You make time to see him. He can't be busy every second of the day. The more he doesn't see you, the greater the chance he finds someone else. Adèle, think about what you're doing . . .' Charlotte suddenly looked very sad, the way her eyes drew downward and her shoulders too, but then she spotted the flowers and her mouth slowly gaped open. She reached for one of the roses, her finger very close to touching the velvety petals, before shooting her pointed glare back at me. 'You're insufferable.'

'Me?' I pulled her in close, squishing the flowers between us in my arm and crackling the paper. 'Well,' I said all breathy, 'since we're confronting each other . . .' A little voice inside told me not to talk about it, not to bring it up, but I'd had enough of her brushing me off, and brushing Mama off and making her cry. 'When are you going to take Mama to your child's grave? You haven't let her pay her respects. It's been months and I'm starting to believe you're keeping her away on purpose. Me too. I asked to go and you said no.'

The door flew open and four miliciens walked into Papa's wine bar, startling both Charlotte and me with the clang of bells. Charlotte yanked her arm away, glancing up at the miliciens who were now closer to us both. 'You're bringing this up now?'

'When else am I supposed to bring it up?'

'Certainly not right now,' she said, lowering her voice as they chatted next to her.

'If you don't want me to go, fine. But Mama — '

'Leave it alone,' she said through her teeth.

I turned my back on her after realizing I was getting nowhere. The miliciens helped themselves to the wine Papa had out on the bar, as if they were used to helping themselves to whatever they wanted, and then looked out the window and made comments about the prisoners. Papa still wouldn't look up.

Charlotte struck up a conversation with the one she recognized, and they traded stories about their days together in school. 'How's your husband?' he asked, alternating his gaze between Charlotte and the prisoners on the other side of the window.

'Very well,' she said. 'He's in Paris, though he should be back next month.' Charlotte looked over his uniform and commented on the brass buttons pinned to his lapel. 'I believe these uniforms are the best I've seen.' She ran her hand down the arm of his coat, but then pulled it away when he looked at her.

'Do you recognize that one?' he said, pointing at one of the prisoners.

Charlotte squinted at the men lined up against the wall. 'Should I?' She laughed a sort of girly giggle. 'I think all criminals must look like each other.'

'I suppose.' He sipped the wine he'd poured.

'It's Jean Paul. From school.'

'Mmm,' she said. 'I don't . . .' Charlotte shook her head slowly then her eyes lit up. 'Wait, I do remember him! He sat next to me once. Has a sister with curly hair — like mine — who bit her fingernails.' The light in Charlotte's face faded the longer she stared across the street at the man, the grim reality of his fate settling into his face as the Milice ordered them into the station where the Gestapo waited, eyes shifting, monitoring.

'We arrested him this morning,' the man said. 'Our mothers used to put us in the same pram as children.' He took another sip of Papa's wine. 'That one, right there.' He pointed to a woman kneeling on the ground just outside Papa's wine bar as she wept for her son, the sound of her wail seeping through the door crack should have been enough to make Charlotte cry out and ask "what are we doing?" but she only looked at the woman with a slight bit of confusion resting in her thinking eyes.

Charlotte turned around. 'I have to go. But we'll talk about this — ' she pointed at the flowers ' — later.'

I exhaled, glad she was gone, but the miliciens were still inside drinking wine, waiting for their turn across the street. 'What's Albert got to eat back there?' He snapped his fingers at me, motioning to the bar.

I begrudgingly served them the walnuts Papa had out, and was about to walk away, but then they sat down and talked about a meeting that was to take place that night.

'What time is the meeting?' one said.

'Nine o'clock. Hotel du Parc. Arrive early, police and all the Milice. Supposed to take all night with Germans coming in from Paris.'

An all-night meeting?

I couldn't believe my ears. Timing was everything, Marguerite had said. My palms turned sweaty, thinking the opportunity to use Charlotte's paints had finally come. With the Milice and police occupied, nobody would be around to patrol the streets, or the train station.

One of them noticed me staring out the window into the sky, and he stood up, looking at me suspiciously.

'Are you all right?' he said.

I clutched the flowers in my arms. 'Yes,' I said. 'Of course. Can I get you anything else?' I smiled, glancing briefly at Papa, who was still plenty busy with his wine crates, but they got up to leave. Throwing down their glasses in a hurry, and following the last of the résistants into the station, leaving the stone wall as plain as it was before the prisoners got there. I looked at my hands, feeling the perspiration on my skin.

'Adèle?' Papa said from the back. 'Shouldn't you be getting over to Charlotte's next door? I can handle things here.'

'Yes, Papa,' I said, and I rubbed the sweat from my hands.

★ ★ ★

Charlotte had me switch out the silky peignoirs in her display window with the cheaper terry cloth robes from the back closet — still, few could

275

afford the prices she charged. Some offered to trade ration cards for garments, but Charlotte wouldn't consider something so illegal.

She spent most her day sitting in the back in her chair, giving me the silent treatment, which was fine by me. I found it incredibly hard to concentrate on anything other than the wall, just catching peeks of it while working made my heart bubble like a hot bath. I felt the paint tube Mama helped me hide in the lining of my coat when I went home for lunch, and then the gun in its holster under my dress. 'Wait until everyone is asleep,' Mama had told me. '*And by God, be careful!*'

'Adèle,' Charlotte called, and I broke away from the window. 'Can we talk about what happened this morning? I'm exhausted and I don't want to fight.' The glow had drained from her face and she did look tired, more tired than I'd seen her. She hung her head down.

'Charlotte,' I said, setting down a pile of clothes. 'I wanted to talk to you about that,' I said, and she looked up. 'I should have never brought up the . . . You know.'

She took a shuddering breath, and I thought she might cry. I held her hands.

'I want to apologize too,' she said. 'I only want what's best for you, sister.' She paused, swallowing. 'Best for all of us.'

I'd seen disappointment before, but never had I seen it hang so heavy as it did in Charlotte's eyes.

'Gérard,' she breathed. 'He's — '

'Let's not talk about it,' I said, and she took another breath.

'I want us to be like we used to,' I said, and

276

she nodded. 'Remember when we'd drink wine together and cook in Mama's kitchen. Mama would show off her herbs in the garden, and Papa with his grapes . . .'

'And you'd burn the leeks,' she said, a little smile lifting her mouth.

'I never burned anything,' I said, though she was telling the truth. 'Well, there was that one time, but it's probably because of all the wine you'd poured me.'

She laughed. 'You loved it.'

'Yes,' I said. 'So did you.' I smiled.

'I remember those times,' she said, 'like they were yesterday.'

'Now, there will be a baby around, and maybe one day our children will run through the vineyard like we used to, feet black and giggling in the vines . . .'

'It's getting late.' She looked down at her feet, exhaling.

'Oh, ah . . . all right,' I said, and she put her hand out for help from off the chair, but when she stood up, she unexpectedly wrapped her arms around me. No words. Just an embrace.

'It's hard being pregnant and alone,' she finally said.

I pulled away to look at her. It was strange hearing her be so forthright.

'My husband was expected home weeks ago.' Her hands slid from mine and she shuffled away slowly.

'Let me walk you home,' I said. 'I'm worried about you.' I looked at her belly as if its size was an indication of her health. 'And the baby . . . Do

277

you feel all right?'

'I'm fine,' she said. 'And it's a short walk. I can go alone. I'm going to finish the yellow quilt I've been needling for my nursery and then go to bed.'

'Mama's been needling more hats for the baby too,' I said, but she kept her back turned. 'Charlotte? I said Mama —'

'Well, I'm off,' she said, slipping on her coat. 'I'll see you in the morning.' She buttoned it the best she could over her growing stomach before kissing both my cheeks. 'Would you mind dusting the shelves before you go? They're too high for me to reach in this condition.'

'Of course,' I said, and I watched her walk away across the square, toward her apartment.

I spent some time thinking about her after she left. She would have let me walk her home if something was wrong with the baby, I thought. It was her husband, I decided. She said it herself. She was lonely.

I dusted Charlotte's shelves slowly, stretching out my time in her shop until close to midnight. With her gone, and the square dark and shadowy, all I thought about was getting caught. They'd send me to prison like the rest of the résistants who stood against the wall. Maybe even to a work camp like our French soldiers. I felt my throat constrict. *Who am I kidding?* Prison would be the least of my worries — the French loved a clean white neck.

I scolded myself for thinking such thoughts and pulled on my lapels, closing my eyes. If I only thought about getting caught then all those résistants in Laudemarière would have died at the

278

hands of Gérard's men, I reminded myself. *I can do this. Romancing a collaborator is more dangerous.* 'Christ, it's just a little paint,' I said out loud, but then looked at my shaking hands.

I locked up Charlotte's boutique and snuck outside into the cold dark, the tube of paint clenched in my hand. A dog barked somewhere behind me, and I wondered if someone could see me. *Papa!* I whipped around, looking at his pitch-black window as I clipped across the square to the wall.

I unscrewed the cap, and it fell through my fingers along with a few drops of paint. I gasped, looking around in the dark, and one more time up at Papa's window, my warm breath like smoke from my mouth in the cold. Another dog bark, this time louder, closer, and more agitated, and I hastily squirted paint onto the brush, my heart pounding — *thump, thump, thump.*

I slapped the brush onto the wall, smearing paint this way and that, and then signed it like a real artist would, like I'd seen Charlotte do hundreds of times.

Catchfly.

I stepped backward, trying to get a look at my work, but then a hand gripped my wrist in the dark, and I threw myself against the side of the building. *Luc.* I smelled him first, and then I felt his warmth. 'It's you,' I said, and we kissed. 'I can't believe it.' We kissed again. 'It's been so long . . .'

He glanced back at the wall. 'That's certainly going to cause some concern tomorrow.'

Glass bottles crashed nearby, followed by clopping footsteps down the street. 'Someone's there,' I said.

279

Luc put a finger to his mouth to be quiet, and we snuck away, the collar of his coat popped up against his face. 'Where's the car you've been using?'

'It's parked near the promenade, to save petrol.'

We hugged the darkest spaces of the street until we made it to the promenade that ran along the Allier River where the tree branches cracked and creaked from the cold. A RAF balloon flew over our heads, dropping leaflets all around, into the icy river lapping against the bank and over the pavement, where Luc stopped and twirled me in the dark among hundreds of falling white papers.

We hopped into the car, giggling, full of excitement, driving right past Monsieur Morisset's and up the hill to Papa's vineyard and rushing into the barrel cellar. I yanked on the lapels of his coat, pulling him in for a kiss as I kicked the door shut, smelling the salty sea on his skin from a distant land. 'I want you so much,' I said, and then was overcome by my own insatiable urges, pulling him into his secret radio room, tugging on his trousers and unfastening his belt, where we devoured each other in a fury of heated kisses and fast-moving hands.

* * *

I barely slept, waking several times throughout the night, thinking of the mural, and Luc, even as he held me. 'Is it morning?' I asked when I felt him stir. I breathed in an excited breath, and he rolled over to kiss me. 'I can't wait to see what the wall looks like.'

'Wait,' he said, 'before you leave. I have something for you.' He reached into the pocket of his trousers that lay crumpled in a pile on the floor. 'Don't look.'

'What,' I said, closing my eyes. 'What is it?' The kerosene lantern hanging on the hook warmed my face, and I pretended we were in the sun. I could almost smell Papa's post-war grapes bursting from the vines. 'The war is over and Hitler's dead.'

He chuckled. 'Not quite.'

Something dangled above my face, tickling my nose, which made me giggle.

'All right. Open your eyes,' he said, and I gasped, smiling. A heart pendant the size of a pea hung from a delicate gold chain. He clasped the necklace around my neck, centring it just below my collarbone. 'A deserving gift after your success last night.'

I kissed him. 'Thank you,' I said. 'It's beautiful, and I shall never take it off.'

'Shall?' He smiled. 'Now who is sounding British?'

He kissed me passionately, but I knew I had to leave. 'I must go,' I said. 'I have a painting to see about.' I slipped on my clothes, barely able to hide my excitement.

'I'll see you after,' he said, and I kissed him one last time before hurrying off.

Mama was already up and in the kitchen. 'Don't move,' I said, rushing past her for my bedroom. 'I have a lot to tell you!' I slipped on a new dress only to rush back into the kitchen to scrub off the paint in the sink and tell her all about last night.

281

'It was dark,' I said, 'but I think it's actually good. I'm off to see it now, helping Charlotte.' I stopped short of telling her I'd spent the night with Luc, and she didn't ask.

'Were you scared?' she asked.

'Yes,' I said, and my stomach fluttered, thinking of the image, and how bold I'd been to paint out in the open. 'Still am a bit. Nervous — an excited nervousness.'

'I was scared,' Mama said. 'Oh, Adèle . . .' I looked over my shoulder to her sitting at the kitchen table, surprised by her tone. 'I was so worried. More worried than I've ever been when you've gone off with Gérard.'

'What?' I dried off my hands. 'Mama . . .'

She put her hand up. 'Never mind me,' she said. 'I shouldn't have said anything. It's natural for a mother to be worried. Between you and Charlotte I don't know who worries me the most.' She lit a cigarette and smoked at the table. 'I'll be better after a smoke. How is she?' she asked. 'Charlotte. The baby.'

'Come into the city with me, Mama,' I said, and she shook her head. 'And risk seeing your father? No. She can come here. She knows I want her to visit. Will you remind her? That I want to see her.'

I nodded. I'd remind her.

I turned the tap back on after noticing I'd left a streak of paint on my skin. I scrubbed a little harder this time. Luc's smell lingered on me and in my hair. I closed my eyes, getting lost in his scent, while Mama smoked her cigarette.

'I think you've got it all, Adèle,' Mama said, and I looked at her. 'Wouldn't want to wash off anything other than the paint.'

I turned the tap off. 'You're right, Mama.' I smiled, but then remembered I still had Monsieur Morisset's car. 'Damn!' I looked out the window. 'I forgot to bring back the car.'

'You'll need to take care of him. Monsieur Morisset is as salty as they come, and greedy, which is to our benefit. Pay him off with some of the money I have bundled in the drawer under the woodblock. Tell him it's so you don't have to return it every night. I'm sure he won't object.'

'Why not?'

'Because they eat more eggs than a family of two should. Both their boys were sent to the munitions factory, but you tell me why they still eat enough to feed them all? Food on the black market is expensive. He'll need the money.'

'Do you think he's one of us? A résistant?'

'I don't know. My guess is someone in that house is — someone other than the two of them.'

'I'll go there now.' I slipped my wool coat over my shoulders, tucking the money into my pocket. 'I'll see you tonight, Mama.' I kissed both her cheeks while she exhaled, the heart pendant dangling from my neck.

'You *are* very excited about it,' she said. 'Aren't you?'

'Well why wouldn't I be?' I said.

'Don't look too excited,' she said. 'People will think it's suspicious.'

I kissed her again. 'Bye, Mama.'

283

21

I arrived at the boutique earlier than normal, heart thumping the more I thought about the mural. Two old men stood on the corner gazing at the wall, but I wouldn't dare look just yet for fear they'd know it was me. I unlocked the bolt on Charlotte's door, and slipped inside.

I did busywork until Charlotte came in through the back door. She threw her coat over a chair and sat down immediately. By this time, people had gathered in front of the wall and in the street. I folded pantaloons, pretending not to notice, mixing the cotton knits with the lacy garments. Normally, this would have bothered Charlotte a great deal, but she made no mention of it or of me from her chair in the back.

'How's Mama, Adèle?' Charlotte said unexpectedly.

'Mama?'

Charlotte rubbed her belly in a swirly pattern, nodding from her chair. 'I never thought I'd have to go through a pregnancy without my mother. She never leaves the estate. She never visits me here. What you said last night about her needling hats brought it all back up.'

'Why don't you visit her?' I said.

'And leave Papa in the city?' she said. 'He'll think I've chosen a side.'

'But he doesn't think that of me,' I said.

Her hands stopped mid swirl on her stomach.

284

'I know how she feels about my husband, Adèle. And this pregnancy so soon after the — '

I looked at her.

'You think I don't know?' she said, trying to get out of her chair. 'She's never supported my marriage.'

'She supports *you*, Charlotte,' I said.

I moved to help her up, and once standing she finally noticed the commotion outside, looking around her boutique as if she heard music; something she couldn't put her finger on. When I saw her take a deliberate glance out the window, I brought it up.

'What's going on over there?' I said, and my heart jumped just mentioning it.

Charlotte walked to the front. 'What's the fuss about this time? Another arrest? God — people need to stop caring about such things. Arrests happen all the time.' She tried catching glimpses out the window of what they were looking at, but the crowd was too thick. 'More RAF leaflets telling us lies about Pétain and our alliances?' She turned to me. 'We should burn them in the streets.'

'It must be something important,' I said. 'Some fresh air would be good anyway. Let's take a peek.'

She hesitated, and I held my breath.

'All right,' she said, and I exhaled heavily, trying to hide all traces of anticipation.

We walked outside, only she was moving too slow, so I took her elbow and walked her through the crowd. 'Not so fast,' she said, trying to pull back. 'Adèle . . .'

My pulse quickened once we made it across the street, remembering the excited moments it took

285

for me to paint it, moving closer and closer, until the next thing I knew we were feet from the wall. I let go of her arm as much as she pulled away. My own painting had taken my breath away. I was speechless and proud — yet I dare not even smile about it.

Charlotte stood quietly staring at the image before reaching out to touch the wall where some of the paint was still wet. She looked confused and distraught feeling the paint between her fingers. Some others stood stupefied as if in a dream, before backing up to the kerb, not wanting to be too close to it. Whispers of 'Catchfly' fluttered over the crowd.

'Catchfly? Is that what they're saying?' She never looked at me but asked those around us, tapping shoulders. 'Catchfly the weed?'

An ageing man with his wife by his side leaned in. 'It's signed Catchfly,' he said. 'That must be who painted it.' The pair smiled to themselves and then put their arms around each other as if they were looking at a piece of art hanging in a museum. 'It's very bold,' he said. 'Brave.' He elbowed Charlotte, but she grimaced as if his touch hurt her like a poking finger.

'This is not art.' She wiped the paint from her fingers with a hanky she pulled from her pocket, and then folded her arms over the top of her tiny baby bump. 'This is a disgrace.' Her chin quivered. 'Disgusting as the words painted above it.'

Men took off their hats while women prayed openly for the members of the Résistance. Charlotte grew increasingly upset by the second, and pale, her skin looking pasty and white. A truck sped up to the station and lurched to a stop, spraying bits of rubble into the crowd. A handful of Milice jumped from the back, aiming their rifles at the wall as if it were alive. They looked over the crowd, yelling into people's faces to back up.

People scattered like flies when they aimed their guns into the crowd. I reached for Charlotte's coat sleeve, but she'd waddled off ahead of me, holding her belly up from the bottom. 'Wait!' A stream of watery blood coursed down her leg, and I slipped in a small puddle of it left on the ground where she had stood. I gasped, taking only a quick moment to look at it before chasing after her. 'Charlotte!'

She ran into her boutique and flipped the closed sign over in the window. I turned the knob over and over again, bumping my shoulder into the door asking her to open it, but she had locked it up good.

Papa flew out of his wine bar when he realized something was wrong, looking somewhat upset. 'What's the matter?' he said as my painting unveiled itself from the fleeing crowd. 'Is it the picture?' Papa tried turning the knob himself, mumbling under his breath, 'Damn Résistance — upsetting everyone.'

'Papa — ' A little boy hopped through Charlotte's blood trail, stamping his feet on the cobblestones, giggling, as his mother shielded his eyes from the painting. 'It's not the Résistance,' I said.

'No?' Papa let go of the knob and then smiled to himself after scratching his head. 'Women! Reminds me of your mother when she was expecting.' Papa motioned for me to follow him into his

287

wine bar. 'Come now, *ma chérie*. You know if Charlotte doesn't want to open up, she won't. You'll have to wait.'

I shook my head, looking at Charlotte's door, and then to Papa's as he'd led me inside. Unsure what else to do, I sat down at a small table next to the window, waiting for Charlotte to come out of her boutique next door, my stomach twisting into a knot.

Papa reached for two glasses and a bottle of wine. 'Papa,' I said, swallowing. 'It's morning.'

'Wine comes from the heavens,' he said. 'Morning, evening. Doesn't matter. It always comes.' He turned the bottle around so I could see the label. Mama had at least three of the same bottles in the root cellar, his best year. 'Last one I have of these. Let's savour it together.' A sweet smile rested on his lips as he sat down and handed me a glass, but I felt dizzy and sick.

I should have realized something serious was wrong with her — she was so different yesterday, but I wasn't paying attention, not like I should have. I closed my eyes, wishing I could rewind time.

'Adèle?' he said, and I turned to him.

'Yes?'

Papa reached into his pocket and pulled out what was left of the letters Mama had me give him. 'I've been thinking about your mother,' he said. 'Tell her I haven't gotten to this one yet.' He held up the letter that had been folded into a tight triangle; the one Mama wanted him to read last.

My mouth hung open. 'Papa!'

'What?' He looked shocked that I had yelled,

which was unlike me — I knew it was — but with Charlotte, and now Papa wanting to talk about Mama, it was too much.

'It's been weeks since I gave you her letters.' I felt my face scrunch. 'Haven't you two wasted enough time playing games?'

A slight gasp followed a long pause. 'Games?' he said, pushing his wine glass away. 'She kicked me out as much as I left.'

'Ugh!' I put my hand to my forehead with his scowl. All I could do was think about Charlotte and what she was doing, what was happening to her baby on the other side of the wall. I got up to put my hands on the bricks. 'Charlotte!' I shouted into the air. 'Are you all right? Charlotte!'

Papa walked past me to his back office, stuffing the letter into his pocket as he closed the door behind him. I rested my head against the wall. 'Open up,' I whispered.

An hour or more passed before Charlotte finally burst out her front door, her hair wild and curly and loose. I bolted outside, chasing her through the streets. A bottom-heavy bag hung from her clenched fist that looked plump and purple and seemed wet as laundry. Just when I thought I'd caught up to her, I lost her in a thin crowd near a park where a little old woman knitted socks next to a broken wagon.

'You look lost, child,' she said, looking up at me. Time had made its mark on her face in the form of a hundred wrinkles and creases. Her nose, the biggest thing on her body, was pitted from just as many years in the sun and in the cold.

'My sister. I was following her, but now she's

gone.' I looked out over the park; it was bare except for a lone goose picking at some brown winter grass. 'Her name is —'

'Charlotte?' Her voice had perked, and she seemed surprised I was looking for her, setting her knitting needles and yarn into her lap. 'I can tell you're related by your deep-set eyes. The dimples threw me, but the eyes. The eyes say it all.'

'You know my sister?'

She smiled. 'Yes, of course. I see her every Sunday.'

'What for?'

She flicked a wrinkled finger at me, asking me to follow her. 'This way.'

The old woman took a walking stick from the wagon, and I followed her around the corner to Claudeen's hill, and the cemetery, perched on top of a mound of rock and dirt that shot straight up out of the flat ground, its all too memorable white picket fence bordering the top like a crown. Charlotte's husband's family tomb.

'The cemetery?'

The old woman nodded, hacking and coughing, motioning with her hand for me to keep following her. We stopped in the dirt at the base of the hill. 'Sometimes she takes the path. But other times she goes this way.' She pointed up the hill.

'To do what?'

I followed her straight up the hill through the dirt and rock — surprised by her spryness — I was more out of breath than she was when we got to the top. 'She hires me for flowers,' she said. 'Every week I decorate their graves. Hydrangeas in the spring. Hearty ones in the winter months.

Though not much coming up from the south any-more.'

'Whose graves?'

She turned me around by the arm. 'There, dear,' she said, pointing. In between the many raised tombstones was a flat area with a simple grave marker that had several cup-sized holes dug around it, a tiny mound of dirt on top of each one.

'She buries her miscarriages,' the old woman said.

I stumbled backward, my body aching a sick little space for each hole I counted. 'Five,' I said, 'graves . . . these are graves?

All of them?' My lips curled with a mix of disgust and horror.

'*Limbus infantium*,' she said. 'Flowers for her babies in limbo.'

I pressed my hand to my mouth, closing my eyes briefly. 'But . . . there are so many.' The old lady held out her hand, and I took it, withering to the ground like a violet under the weight of a heavy boot. A tear snuck down my cheek, now I realized why Charlotte had kept Mama and me away.

'Oh, Charlotte.'

* * *

I hadn't been to Charlotte's new apartment, the one her husband bought her while I was at the convent, and I had to guess which corner of Rue Charasse it was on. I tried the doorknob, and to my surprise it was unlocked. Charlotte sat in her kitchen, the winter sun shining coldly through the

291

window and onto her face, a half-empty bottle of gin in her hand as she sat back in her chair, a dazed, glassy look in her eyes.

I shut the door behind me and Charlotte looked up, nearly spilling her gin.

'How'd you get in here?' she seethed.

I looked around, walking closer. 'Your door was unlocked.' Jars and jars of baby food had been opened and left to spoil in the sun, hearty greens and sweet and sickly ham. I had to wonder where she got that much food to preserve. Each one had a different colour of ribbon tied around the neck. Yellow for fruit, green for vegetables and brown, I assumed, was the meat.

She hiccupped. 'Well, now you know,' she said, hiccupping again. 'Now you know . . . ' She swung the bottle around the room, gin spilling over her legs and onto the table. 'And my husband is gone. Barely comes here anymore. Probably because I can't keep his babies.'

'Charlotte, that isn't true,' I said, bending to one knee. 'He loves you.'

'Love!' she spurted out.

'Yes,' I said.

She poured gin into a tall glass until it overflowed onto her tablecloth. 'What do you know about love?'

'I know he bought you the boutique, and he's provided for you,' I said. 'Look at your new apartment.' It felt odd not having been in her apartment sooner, not knowing exactly where she lived, looking upon her things for the first time, a stranger in my own sister's home.

'Look at your things.' She had a light blue divan

with hand-stitched pillows near a window with cushions too firm to have ever been sat on, and two cut-crystal vases stuffed with wax flowers I recognized from her wedding. Porcelain figurines from Limoges were displayed in a curio cabinet with glass shelves. Her very own painting of the promenade in an ornately carved wood frame hung on the wall — the only piece of artwork that had survived since her marriage. 'Henri bought you all of this during your marriage.'

'Marriage!' she scoffed, kicking back the gin, glugging it like water. 'You had a marriage all planned out — a brilliant union.' She slammed her empty glass down on the table. 'You threw it away with no regard to others. Now you're doing it again, but this time right in front of our faces.'

'Gérard?'

'Oh, you remember his name? That's amusing.' She caught a glimpse of the necklace Luc gave me, squinting her watering eyes to get a better look. 'What is that?' She got up from her chair and stumbled into the table trying to grab for it in the air.

I threw a hand to my chest, blocking her. 'Gérard is not a man, Charlotte. He's a tyrant.'

'Gérard has importance, you ungrateful . . . *imbécile!*' She held on to the table, creeping toward me. 'All he wanted to do was love you, and you pushed him away.' She looked directly into my eyes, her voice bitter as a salt lick. 'You ran away.'

'You're drunk.'

'Oh, the dimples . . . there they are!' She threw the empty bottle of gin to the wall and it shattered

293

everywhere. 'Adèle and her dimples! Gérard is always talking about them. Too bad he can't see you now. Look at you.' She flicked her finger at me, mouth pruning. 'Look at you!'

Her words pricked like needles over my skin — I was angry about the way she spoke to me and who she had become. I wanted to lash out at her, but the miscarriages and her fragile state kept me from it.

I threw open the door. 'Pull yourself together,' I said. 'Then we'll talk.'

'Go ahead,' she said as the door slammed shut between us, 'run away again!'

★ ★ ★

The next morning Papa stopped me outside Charlotte's boutique. 'You can help me in the mornings full time. If you want. Charlotte isn't herself and needs some time alone.' Papa's bottom lip quivered as if he knew as much as I did about her babies.

I felt Charlotte's eyes on me, peeping through her lace curtains. I thought for sure she'd have regrets after she sobered up. I was wrong. I looked at Papa. 'I see.'

Papa put his arm around me, leading me into his wine bar. Across the way, I could see the Milice had wasted no time covering my painting with black paint and Milice propaganda posters. Two Vichy police patrolled it as if I had the nerve to come back. Passengers on their way out of the city paused to look at the black blotches, talking among themselves as if remembering the scene

294

from yesterday.

The little old woman who sold daisies from tin buckets rolled her cart up to Papa's wine bar. She flashed an intriguing smile as she peered through the window, adjusting her gloves at the wrists.

'Sure has caused a commotion,' Papa said, sitting down with a glass of dark red wine. 'That painting. People talking about the Catchfly all day yesterday in my store . . . in the street. In the toilets at the brasserie.'

'You don't say?'

I watched the old woman walk around her cart and rearrange the simple mix of flowers she had for sale, petals drooping from the cold. She glanced up at me through the glass every so often while Papa breathed in the aroma of his wine, swirling it in his glass before taking a short sip and rolling it on his tongue.

'Yes . . . quite the stir.'

'Maybe there are others,' I said as the old woman plucked a single daisy from her bundle and offered it to me from the other side of the glass. 'Somewhere else in the city.'

Papa glanced at the ceiling as if pondering the idea. 'Haven't heard.'

I got up and went outside while Papa drank his wine.

'For you, *mademoiselle*,' she said, handing me the flower. I smiled, wondering why she'd give me a flower when I was the one who had always sought her out. 'Your friend says — ' glancing at the wall where I had painted ' — well done.'

'My friend.' I smiled. *Marguerite*. I took the flower, twirling it under my nose, taking a whiff.

'Merci.'

She moved her cart down the road while I walked back into the wine bar. Papa didn't even know I'd left, only giving a fleeting glance to the flower in my hand. We watched the miliciens point their guns at the painted stones, laughing, acting as though they were shooting at people.

'Catchfly,' Papa said between sips. 'It's a damn weed.'

'Drink your wine, Papa.' I tapped the table near his glass.

Papa looked at me as he drank. 'Gérard came in yesterday asking for you.'

I set the flower on the table. 'Oh?'

'He left for Paris. Emergency assignment. Might be gone till the spring. He was very distraught at having missed you, but his train was leaving. He asked me to buy you flowers in his name.' Papa pointed to a wilted bouquet of flowers on the far shelf.

'He left?' My mouth hung open for a second. 'Not back until the spring?' I didn't expect this.

Papa raised his eyebrows for his answer. Months had gone by keeping Papa in the dark about Gérard. I felt a push in my gut. Maybe it was the black paint on the wall across the street, or maybe I was just tired of living a lie. Either way, I felt compelled to be brutally frank, honest with him in a way I hadn't been since I came home.

'Papa, I'm sorry if this hurts, but Gérard's not the man you think you betrothed me to all those months ago.'

Papa seemed surprised by my statement, the cornflower blue in his eyes sparkling like icicles.

296

'He's a fine man. He's a soldier — saved troops with his own hands — Battle of Sedan!'

I shook my head. 'First you said Gérard had saved a man, now whole troops? Papa, that French soldier you're talking about died long ago.'

'He's prestigious. Secure.'

'Now he's just a man who's doing bad things.' My back got very straight and the words I had always wanted to say flew out of my mouth. 'Collaborator! That's what he is, Papa — arresting people left and right. He'll beat a man for a promotion! How many children has he made orphans?' I dug my palms into my eyes before pulling them away. 'I'm glad he's gone.'

Papa looked up, pausing, mouth pinched. 'He'll be back.'

We stared at each other across the table, his face similar to the way he looked at Mama just before they'd get into a fight, creased around the eyes.

Angry shouts came from the street, and I broke away to look outside. 'Jews,' I heard someone say as I stood slowly from my chair. 'Undesirables.' Armoured lorries drove up to the train station, rattling the windows and shaking the trees, infecting the square with the roar of humming engines. Milice jumped out the back, guns drawn, surveying the roads.

'What's . . . ' I looked at Papa, only to turn back to the window. 'What's going on?'

The lorry engines turned off, and I heard marching not that far away, getting closer, watching in horror as men and women walked trance-like past Papa's window and into the train station under the drawn guns of the Milice, handing them over

297

to the police who collected identification papers. Children clung to their parents, bundled in wool coats and scarves for a long journey. The men pleaded with the miliciens to let their families go, calling themselves Frenchman — an ominous word to go with the shuffling of their feet.

Gestapo filed stiffly out of the train station, monitoring.

'Papa,' I said. 'When are you going to believe?' Sad, desperate faces pleaded for help from the other side. 'The police,' I said, looking at him over my shoulder, 'anyone who works for the regime takes orders from the Reich. Always has, Papa.'

He'd kept his head down. I threw my fists on his table and he jerked, wiping his eyes with a hanky from his pocket. 'Don't you hear that sound? Papa!'

He scooted from his chair, and walked out of the room and into his office, softly closing the door behind him, leaving me to boil by myself.

I looked at my pocketbook, and then my keys, grabbing them as I flew out the door.

22

I drove home in a fury, bursting through the front door, crying and sniffling at what I'd seen. Mama turned away from the sink. She stared at me for a second or two standing in the entryway, and then went back to her dish. 'Mama,' I said, and she snapped from her fog.

'Yes?' she said, and then wiped her hands on her apron, rushing over. 'What is it? What happened?'

'Something awful.'

I told her about the Jews I saw walking past Papa's wine bar. She didn't seem surprised, nodding. I stopped short of telling her about Charlotte's miscarriages, knowing Mama wouldn't be able to handle such news.

'Are you angry, or just sad?' she asked. 'I find I'm both most days.'

I put my hands on the sink and looked out Mama's kitchen window to the barrel cellar, which appeared to be locked up tight; no sign of Luc, and I needed him. 'Right now, I'm angry.' I let out a shrill little scream that scared the sparrows living in the eaves. 'I don't know who anybody is anymore.'

I went downstairs into the root cellar and came back up with a tube of paint and a nice-sized brush. 'What are you going to do with those?'

'What do you think?'

'Where will you go?' Mama suddenly looked worried. 'I don't want you painting in open squares. There're informants lurking around all over the city, now with the Milice handling things. The police are too dumb to think you'll strike again so soon, but the informants . . .'

'I need a better way to get the paint onto the brush,' I said, remembering how careless I had been the other night dripping paint. 'I need a palette.'

'A palette?' she almost laughed. 'You can't do that . . .'

I eyed Mama's apron sheers, and used them to snip the top off, making it one deep dish. 'There,' I said, tucking it into my inner jacket pocket. 'Nobody can see.'

'Where are you going?' Mama said.

I thought for a moment. 'The shopping district. I don't want to be predictable, and you're right about the open squares.'

'Promise me you'll tell me where you go every time you paint. I'm worried about you. Gérard, he's a tyrant, but he's also stupid. As strange as it sounds, I think the painting is more dangerous.' She kissed my cheeks. 'You're all I have left.'

'Mama,' I started to say, ready to tell her about Gérard leaving for Paris, but she'd gone back to washing her dish in a fog. 'I'll be careful,' I said.

★ ★ ★

The shopping district looked dark and forgotten in the dead of night, shaded windows facing each other from across the street. Metal doorknobs glinted, tucked and hidden in even darker doorways. I tightened the scarf over my hair. Watching,

300

waiting, listening, pulling my coat tightly across my chest.

I pulled the brush from the tube of paint.

I thought about Charlotte's scrunching face when she yelled at me — she'd never last in the Résistance, living with dirt on the hem of her dress, lying to keep her stories straight, taking pins in the shoulder and sprays of rosewater. Marking buildings in the night. Even if she did believe in our cause, the inconsistency of where and when to strike would throw her into a childlike fit; she was incapable of being spontaneous. I was my parents' only daughter who could handle such a task.

A swift breeze howled through the buildings, cracking through the trees, and I walked, scooting delicately down the pavement, another shadow in the night, holding the wet brush from a closed fist near my thigh. 'For the Jews,' I said, heart racing as I methodically, and ever so deliberately, flicked the brush over every one of the door's handles, coating them in Charlotte's red paint. 'And for France.'

A door burst open from down the way. 'Who did this?' A man yelled, and I ducked down, writing excitedly, heart bubbling, 'Vichy Catchfly' in cursive on the pavement before disappearing into the dark and motoring home.

I arrived back at the chateau very late, headlamps rolling over the dead vineyard and Papa's craggy vines, only to see Mama pulling her old bicycle up to the patio. She had her peignoir on as if she'd already been to bed and climbed back out of it.

'What are you doing?' I said, and she squinted

into the headlamps.

'Turn those off,' she said, and I cut the engine, then the lights.

'Mama,' I said, walking up to her. 'What are you doing out here? It's late.' She shivered, holding her peignoir closed in a cold breeze. 'Where's your coat?'

Mama rested her bicycle on its kickstand and handed me the tyre pump. 'You shouldn't take the car as much,' she said. 'I didn't think about it until after I went to bed. You can use my bicycle. Or, walk. If someone recognizes Monsieur Morisset's car . . .'

I didn't want to use her bicycle, but if it made her feel better, I would. I took the pump and fixed the flat tyre while she swiped at some cobwebs. 'I won't use the car as much,' I said. 'If it makes you feel better. Don't worry. Ah, Mama, you should have seen it.' My heart still bubbled, and I threw my hands up, looking into the stars.

'It does make me feel better.' She held her hair back and kissed my forehead. 'And you can tell me all about it tomorrow,' she said, and she walked through the screen door, leaving me to celebrate by myself on the patio.

Luc would have loved it. I smiled.

Mama slept in the next morning, and I left for Papa's wine bar, buttoning up my coat for a long ride. I missed the car right away, and then even more so when I pedalled into a crowd waiting for a Milice parade to start, getting stuck behind two women. They chatted about jewellery, or so I thought with their talk of rubies and diamonds. I rang my bell, but they did not move. I rang it again, but now I was at a standstill and got off my bicycle.

'Just like the Avenue des Champs-Élysées,' one said to the other. 'Rubies for the red tail lights and diamonds for the headlights. Oh, how I miss shopping in Paris!'

'I will have to see it myself,' the other said. 'I bet it is striking.'

Only after I heard them talk about the brightness of cadmium paint did I interrupt. 'Hallo?' I said. 'Hallo, I don't mean to eavesdrop, but what are you talking about?' I straddled my bicycle in the crowd, waiting for them to tell me. One looked at me coldly.

'The Catchfly,' she said. 'He's struck again. This time taking a cue from Paris and the avenue of rubies and diamonds.'

'He can't be a man,' the other woman said, sounding somewhat surprised her friend would think such a thing. '*Les Femmes de la Nation* is a woman's cause.'

'Only a man would be out at night roaming the streets,' she said. 'Besides, a shop owner saw him racing away in a car. A nice one.'

'A car?' I said, and I was very glad to have taken Mama's bicycle that morning.

They turned to each other, almost forgetting I was there and continued debating whether the Catchfly was a man or not.

'What about the rubies and diamonds?' I said.

'There's marks in the shopping district. He —' her eyes shifted to her friend just briefly, who glared in return ' — painted the doorknobs red. The whole road looks like the Avenue des

303

Champs-Élysées with the knobs glinting red on one side and silver on the other.'

'What?' I was surprised the police hadn't scraped it off yet with the noon hour approaching. 'The police haven't taken care of it?'

She scoffed. 'They're private buildings, *mademoiselle*. The owners have to give their consent, and I'm sure they'll take their time.' Her face got very stiff before she whispered into the other lady's ear about whose side she thought I was on. 'Man, woman, does it matter?'

The parade started. Shouts of standing at attention and walking with pride rolled down the street. And the Milice marched, holding their new flags side-by-side with the Vichy flag, rifles, and wearing berets. People looked on, stunned, quiet.

'I think she's a friend of the regime,' the other said before they both fell away into the crowd, and I closed my eyes briefly, with the sun on my face, thinking of other days.

The year the French Army left for the Maginot Line the entire city turned out to see them off, blowing kisses. Republic flags rolled out of windows and flapped delicately over our heads. Veterans from the 1914 war, dressed in their military best, stood at attention.

I opened my eyes to see a Milice flag unfolding out a window above me, and the Milice marched on, and the crowd stayed quiet. A small contingent of German Wehrmacht trailed up the rear, stiffer than the Milice, watching, monitoring.

★ ★ ★

Days turned into weeks and soon enough spring had come, warming up the pavements and turning the trees green. I stood outside Papa's wine bar, a grape-stained apron wrapped around my waist, listening to a fight break out in the street, two men arguing, followed by fists on flesh, one punching the other, calling his brother a traitor.

Flower carts had rolled in, and people roused from their homes into the squares. A girl rushed past, yelling for her sister to hurry up before the flowers were gone, and the two men got off each other, each feeling their jaws where they'd been punched.

I stepped away from the wall, watching a little closer. People grabbed flowers from baskets, wrapping them quickly in brown paper, something to conceal.

I stopped the same girl on her way back from a flower cart, a bundle in her arms. 'What's going on?'

'The Catchfly,' she said. 'Everyone's doing it.' She peeled back the brown paper — French catchfly — an armful of the flowering weeds, bursting with red and pink petals. 'It started a few hours ago; everyone's throwing catchfly at the walls that have been painted. This morning's *Le Combat* calls for it — every mark the Catchfly has made throughout the city.'

My hand flew to my mouth, gaping with a smile, shuffling into the street, not caring a lick if anyone saw me, watching people throw catchfly at the wall, on the Morris Column where I'd written RAF days ago, and to every swipe of paint I'd left, remembering.

305

The Vichy police ran out of the train station, sweeping the catchfly into piles, yelling at us all to get away, get back! But the square had already swelled with people, and the flower carts were as bare as any food cart in the city.

Charlotte walked out of her boutique with a cling of her bell, and watched me in the street, her curly hair tucked behind her ears. A woman tried to sell her a single stem she'd pulled from her bushel. Charlotte glanced at her once before folding her arms and looking at me, her stare turning into a glare.

We'd made a practice of avoiding each other since our fight, and I was surprised to see her outside, looking at me like she had something to say. I walked up to her, only to be stopped by the postmaster.

'Adèle Ambeh!' He flapped a letter in my face, barking my name. He set his heavy bag of parcels on the ground. 'That's you, no?' He pushed the letter at me, postmarked from Paris. 'Every week a letter comes. I've got enough mail to deliver without walking all the way to the train station for weekly special deliveries.' He stormed off, heaving his bag up over his shoulder.

I gasped, trying to hide my concern in front of Charlotte. *Gérard's writing.* I ignored the nervous little tick in my stomach, and then got a bit sick looking at the heart-shaped doodle next to my name. *Every week a letter?* Charlotte leaned her backside against her building. She probably had the rest of the letters in her office, having read them while drinking her gin.

I pulled my shoulders back, looking up at her.

'It's not like you want them,' she said. 'So, stop looking at me that way.' Her voice was higher than I remembered, sharper.

I ripped the envelope right in half, tossing it into the gutter.

She sucked air in through her teeth, but then laughed. 'Watch out, Adèle. For when he comes back.'

Her words hung in the air between us.

'What do you mean?' I said.

'You know what I mean.' She pulled a cigarette from her dress pocket, which she lit with short puffs, creating a thick white cloud above her head as she exhaled.

'Since when do you smoke?' I said.

Her dagger gaze slid over my shoulder down the street. 'Great,' she said, puffing some more. 'First you, and now Pauline . . .'

Mama had just come out of the Catholic church and stood on the street corner, talking to Prêtre Champoix, nodding, before noticing Charlotte and me. I was surprised. Mama didn't ride with me, and I wondered how she got into the city without a car. She glanced back and forth between us and the priest as they finished their conversation before walking up to Charlotte, her hands clutched around her pocketbook. 'Why didn't you tell me?'

Charlotte turned her head, blowing smoke from her mouth.

'I had to hear about your loss from gossiping clergy? Didn't have the decency to tell your own mother?' She reached for Charlotte's dress where her baby bump should have been proudly showing and pinched the fabric to gauge the size of her body. 'When did it happen?'

Charlotte glared at her, swiftly taking Mama's hand off her dress. 'What were you doing with the Catholics? Prêtre Champoix can sense an imposter.'

'Don't change the subject, Charlotte.'

'Why don't you ask your darling?' Charlotte said, stomping her cigarette out. 'I can't believe she didn't tell you — honestly, Mother.'

Mama squinted. 'You knew?'

'It wasn't my place, Mama.' I put my hands up, but the look in Mama's eyes nearly crushed me.

'Humph!' Charlotte puffed. 'You mean you kept your nose out of my business? That's a new one.'

We matched each other's cold stare, while Mama gazed at both of us, alternating her glances between both her daughters. 'How could my girls turn out so different from one another? You used to be best friends. Inseparable. When you were children, I couldn't tell which was which, both of you covered in dirt from running around the vineyard all day.'

'That was many years ago,' I said. 'We're women now, Mama.'

'Indeed,' Charlotte said.

A single catchfly fell from a woman's bundle big in her arms as she ran past. I picked it up and handed it to Charlotte. 'Here,' I said. 'Join us. It's still not too late for you. Pétain's path isn't the way. The Reich has rolled right over him. You must realize that now.'

She snatched the catchfly from my hand only

to throw it on the ground next to her smashed cigarette. Mama's eyebrows rose from the rub. 'I raised you to behave better than that.'

'Oh, did you, Pauline?' Charlotte turned her cheek.

Mama took a short breath when Charlotte called her by her given name, and then looked sad. And we stood there, all three of us, waiting for the other to do something, the din of the crowd rising from the square.

'I miss you,' Mama said, reaching for Charlotte, but she turned away.

A Milice paddy wagon lurched to a stop just in front of the train station; miliciens poured out like army ants from the back doors, their rifles drawn on the people, outnumbering the police still sweeping catchfly into piles. People scattered, the bulk of them moving across the street onto the pavement.

'Come on, Mama,' I said. 'Let's go for a walk.'

Charlotte walked into her boutique, slamming the door, shuddering her windows. Mama reluctantly moved her hand back, looking at Charlotte's closed sign before gazing through Papa's window next door; a dim light glowed in the rear. Mama leaned to one side, looking a tad woozy as she put her hand on the doorknob and gave it a squeeze.

'Do you feel all right? I said.

Mama tightened her grip around the knob but still she wouldn't turn it. 'I'm fine,' she said. 'I'm fine. I haven't seen him since . . . Since that fight in our kitchen.'

'Go in, Mama.'

Papa bent over some crates, shelving his wine,

having no idea his wife was watching him, missing him. She whimpered, a sickness crying out from her eyes for the man she loved, but who had left her. 'I wasn't supposed to be in the city today — '

'Does it matter, Mama? He's all alone. Talk to him.'

Her hand gripped the knob tighter before she let go of it completely, putting her fingers to her lips. 'I can't.' She turned away. 'Not now. Not after — '

She clutched her chest, glancing at Charlotte's boutique.

Damn my sister. 'Let's get you home.'

I moved to walk away and a spray of rose-water hit me like a pie in the face, the mist falling onto my arms and hands. 'Collaborator,' I heard in a breathy whisper. A woman in a striped shirt walked the opposite way.

'Mme Dubois.' The smell of the rose against my skin, and the faint taste of it in my mouth was as vile as a shot of sour milk.

'Shake it off, Adèle,' Mama said. 'Shake it off.'

I watched Mme Dubois walk away, her floral skirt ruffling against her little legs. 'I don't think I'll ever take a liking to rosewater.'

'I understand why,' she said.

Mama handed me a hanky from her pocketbook, and I wiped the mist from my face.

'Mama,' I said. 'What were you doing at church? Since when are you Catholic?'

'I'm Catholic,' she said. 'When I want to be.'

I gave her back the hanky, and she picked up the catchfly Charlotte had thrown on the ground. 'Now,' she said, wrapping the hanky around the catchfly's sticky stem. 'Let's show this weed some respect.' She threw her head back, smiling, and for a moment I saw a glimpse of the youthful woman she had been before the armistice, before Papa had left, when she looked more like Coco Chanel than a widow with grey streaking through her hair.

'Yes,' I said. 'Respect.'

We walked down the street, the catchfly in Mama's hands. 'Mama, how'd you get here? I have Monsieur Morisset's car.'

She looked at me, her eyes shifting slyly. 'You're not the only one with friends in Vichy.'

★ ★ ★

That night, Luc and I lay in the field behind the chateau on a blanket, wild grass growing up around us as we gazed into the speckled night sky. Catchfly had grown in patches, trying to take over the field as much as it had the hill. 'You should have seen her eyes,' I said, rolling over on my side to face him. 'Like Pétain, in one of his posters . . .'

Luc let me go on about the face-to-face I had with Charlotte in the square, how even for Charlotte her attitude was very sharp toward Mama and me. The war had changed us all in some way, but Charlotte looked haggard, older than she should. Alone.

'Makes me sad,' I said. 'Thinking of my sister. What she's become.' I took a deep breath. I didn't want to spend what precious time I had with Luc talking about sad things, and switched the subject. 'And then there was the call for catchflies from

311

Le Combat.'

'What?' he said, and I told him the story. 'That's incredible! The paper could have called for anyone, résistants who mark cities with the Cross of Lorraine . . . or the V for *Victoire*. You, the Catchfly, caught their attention.'

Attention. I smiled slightly with this word, before telling him about Mme Dubois and the rosewater.

He brushed a lock of hair from my eyes. 'She doesn't know the truth about you.'

'I know. Doesn't make it any easier, people thinking I'm a collaborator.'

'And what about Pauline?' he said. 'How is she?'

I played with the heart pendant he'd given me as I thought about Mama's disposition — which had no doubt changed since I left for the convent. 'I think the state of her and Papa's relationship — Charlotte's too — is taking a toll on her. I can see it in her eyes when she looks at me; sometimes her mind seems very far away and foggy. I could be Hitler himself and she wouldn't know it.'

'What about you?' I said. 'How are you?'

'What do you mean?'

'Every few days you sleep somewhere else. God knows what kind of near misses you've had, especially with the Milice working with the Gestapo. You must feel drained.'

Luc fell to his back and expelled all the air from his lungs. 'You never hear of it,' he said, 'the exhaustion. But it's there. Inside all of us.' He patted my leg. 'In you, too.'

We lay for many minutes thinking quiet thoughts, the stars sparkling, with the light buzz of field bugs moving about in the grass. We shared

312

swigs of whisky from his flask, our bare feet tickling each other's.

'Tell me about your family,' I said as he played with the heart pendant around my neck. 'Do you see them? Your mother?'

'I haven't been back in two years, since the Occupation. But one day I'll go back to Nancy,' he said, taking a swig, 'and you'll go with me.'

'I will?' I perked up, taking the flask from his hands and a long savoury drink from the spout. 'Tell me about it — Nancy. What's it like?' I lay back listening to him with one hand under my head.

'There's a fountain in Stanislas Square, in the city centre, made of gold and wrought iron, and the railings — there's a reason why Nancy is called the city of the gilded gates, and it's simply magnificent when you see it in person — Neptune and Amphitrite surrounded by spraying water.'

I breathed in his words, the images of Nancy. At times it felt like he was describing a distant land untouched by war, the armistice, and the Germans.

'At night the fountain is lit all aglow, golden arches sparkling from the reflection of the water. You might think of Saint Peter when you see it for the first time, Catchfly.'

'Sounds beautiful,' I said, though I wasn't just talking about the fountains. I loved it when he called me Catchfly.

'Yes, it is beautiful. But that's not the most intriguing part.'

'It isn't?'

'It's the Neptune babies. It's where you make

313

your wish. Everyone in Nancy does it sooner or later — can't call yourself a local if you don't.'

'Make a wish?'

'Ah, it's the source of a powerful legend. If you make the same wish for three days straight it will come true. But there's a catch,' he said. 'You only get one wish in your lifetime.'

'Only one?' I could practically see the Neptune babes myself and the pool of coins, each one representing someone else's dreams, with my skin feeling very cool from being so close to falling water. 'Have you made yours?'

'Yes,' he said, 'I have.'

'What did you wish?' My eyes grew wide, wondering what Luc had wished for.

He rubbed his chin. 'Well, I'd tell you, but I can't for the life of me remember what it was!'

'Oh, you!' I said, and we laughed and then lay back on the blanket, our legs curled up together and our bodies close. The images of Nancy were so grand in my head, lovely, like a sunny day that smelled of fresh baguette and blooming lilacs. I sighed, enjoying the thoughts, feeling them as I felt the warmth of Luc's body next to mine.

'A spring wedding,' he said. 'That's what my mother would like. If it's all right with you.'

I sat up, blinking like a deer into his eyes. 'Is that a proposal?'

'Well, if you want me to take it back I can.' He smiled.

For the first time in my life the thought of being married didn't make me shiver with dread, but instead filled me with so much joy I could feel it bulging in my dimpled cheeks.

Luc kissed me warmly, the way a woman ought to be kissed after being proposed to, a bit of our breath blowing softly on each other, a piece of our souls touching with our lips.

'Well?' he said, after pulling away.

'Well, what?'

'Are you going to accept?'

'That's why I kissed you back!'

He exhaled, hand on his chest, taking the last swig of whisky from his flask. 'You like to make a man sweat, do you?'

'Only you, *monsieur*.' I used my thumb to wipe whisky from his bottom lip. 'Only you.'

I can't say why I thought of Marguerite at that very moment, as Luc wrapped his arms around me in a warm embrace. But I remembered what she said about falling in love in the Résistance — her warning tugging at the very arms that held me. I couldn't tell anyone, not even Mama or Charlotte. My head suddenly felt very heavy.

'I love you, Adèle.'

His words brought with it a strange tingling deep inside, which left me feeling as fragile as a hollow egg. This must be what love feels like, I thought. Charlotte said it would happen one day, but she never said anything about the crushing weight of it where the hollowness felt so vulnerable.

I squeezed him a little tighter. 'And I love you.'

23

The outdoor cafés opened after a rash of summer thunderstorms ripped through the hills. Metal chairs had been wiped down, and waiters bobbed around pouring chicory coffee from silver pots, touting it as the best faux coffee this side of Paris. I sat at a table for two near the kerb across from Papa's wine bar, tallying every swipe of paint I had made in Vichy on a tiny piece of paper I kept hidden in the silky lining of my pocketbook.

I sat back quietly and drank my faux coffee — for a price — the cost of everyday items such as chicory had risen since the Free Zone disappeared. I tucked the paper into my pocketbook, glancing around, trying not to act suspicious, when a forceful hand gripped my wrist.

Gérard.

My stomach sank, and so did my face.

'Caught you,' he said, and he sat down across from me. 'Finally.'

I gulped, moving my pocketbook into my lap. 'You're back,' I said, trying to collect myself, but my heart raced. 'From Paris.' I counted backward in my mind.

His mouth hung open for a moment, studying me, his jacket tightening around his chest from not having unbuttoned it. 'You've been avoiding me.'

'You've been in Paris, Gérard,' I said, and he slicked back his hair. Silver stubble budded on his

316

chin, odd for a man not yet thirty, but even more than that, he seemed older than the last time I'd seen him, which was months ago, and angrier, the creases in between his brows more like valleys. 'What did you want me to do, visit?'

'Would it have hurt?' he said. 'I wrote you countless letters to visit.'

I blinked several times as if I wasn't sure what he was talking about, but I remembered his letters — the one I ripped up in front of Charlotte and tossed in the gutter.

'I sent them to Charlotte's shop,' he said. 'I didn't trust your mother.'

'Oh, I did get some . . . Charlotte and I aren't getting along,' I said. 'It's between sisters, you know women. But I did write you once,' I lied, 'surely you received it. It was so sweet of you to write to me too.'

He shook his head. 'I received no such letter.'

'Hmm,' I said as if I too had wondered where my letter was. 'Pity.'

'Charlotte thinks you have someone else.'

I sat up straight. 'You talked to Charlotte? About me? How long have you been back?'

'I talk to lots of people,' he said.

I stared at him, not sure where he was going with his interrogation, when he reached over the table and flicked the heart pendant around my neck.

'So, is there someone else? Tell me.'

'A man?' I asked.

'No, a dog — of course a man — Lord, Adèle.' He tapped his fingers on the bistro table so hard my empty cup rattled in its saucer. 'Tell me if it's

317

true. You have a new guy.'

'No,' I said, taking a slow deep breath, remembering to count and thinking of Luc. 'No *guy* as you call it.'

He leaned over the table. 'I hear you have a car to drive — and Albert didn't buy it for you, so who did?'

'Monsieur Morisset's car?' I laughed. 'I paid him an advance to use his car. I don't use it all the time. Charlotte knows. It's the car I was driving before you left.'

'Oh, right. I remember now.' He looked relieved, finally unbuttoning his jacket and sitting back in his chair. Then he smiled, his lips looking very slick. 'I need you at a dinner. I might be promoted to Milice headquarters. Tonight. Wear a nice dress.' He reached into his pocket and pulled out a piping-hot strawberry croissant wrapped in wax paper, his name written on the outside in women's writing.

'Opportunity seems to find you often, Gérard.'

Gérard smiled, laughing with a pulsating throat. 'Yes,' he said. 'Opportunity finds me. Doesn't it?' He squeezed his croissant and my mouth watered when a bit of the filling oozed onto the wax paper. I hadn't eaten anything sweet in months; nobody had, unless you were German or a collaborator. He'd kept laughing to himself, but when he noticed my blank look, he stopped abruptly and cleared his throat. 'As you said . . . it does find me.'

The waiter handed Gérard that morning's newspaper. 'What have you heard about the Catchfly?' he said, and I sat bolt upright in my chair.

'What do you mean?' I said, and I wondered if

318

he could hear my heart beating. It was strange to hear him say Catchfly. I didn't like him saying it.

He slid the paper to me on the table, showing me the headline. *Milice Hunt For The Vichy Catchfly. Vows Vigilance.*

'What could I possibly know?' I said, playing dumb, but he looked like he knew quite a lot. 'What do you know?'

He smiled, a mouth of gums. 'You never could resist a good story, could you, Adèle?' He took three chomping bites of his croissant, licking his fingers and gulping it down. 'We know he's driven an expensive car at least once. We have investigators looking into many things. Vichy wants him squashed. And they will. Squash him. The head of the Milice carries rank with the Reich. He'll want to save his face.'

'It's just some paint,' I said. 'Is it really more harmful than blowing up cars, trains or stealing guns like I've heard of résistants doing?'

'At first it wasn't, but look around.' Gérard pointed to the patrons of the café, many talking into each other's ears so as not to be heard by others. 'What do you think they are talking about?'

'The Catchfly?' I laughed, followed by a gulp. 'Certainly people have other things to talk about.'

Gérard swallowed the lump of croissant he had in his cheek. 'How can we be sure? Every mark of paint is mud in the eyes of the Milice, and Vichy. People know it, and they've become empowered because of him.' His eyes wandered off and he gritted his teeth. 'There's more résistants than ever, now.'

My hands shook on the table, and I moved

319

them to my lap.

A motorcade of three German vehicles rumbled past us, stopping a few yards away at a document-processing office. Roaring engines turned off one by one. They sat in their parked cars, eyes shifting, studying everyone, before getting out and filing into a building adorned with flapping Nazi flags. 'They're checking for illegals,' Gérard said. 'Anyone with an expired visa or not of this country will be sought out and punished. The Résistance has a lot of Jews; most will be gone in the coming months. Arrested, dead.'

'Is that a new form of lawlessness?'

'What?'

'Being a French Jew?'

Gérard sat up, catching his tongue. 'This is war, Adèle, and we're allies with the Germans.'

Pétain and his regime hadn't declared French Jews as undesirable. That was the Reich's position, but I saw it myself in front of Papa's wine bar and nobody could tell me I had imagined it.

Gérard motioned to the waiter. 'I heard a bag of real coffee made its way to this café not that long ago. Something just for the Milice, and police?'

The waiter nodded. 'Several bags were seized from a derelict restaurant now under German control.'

'Excellent!' Gérard smiled. '*Deux cafés.*'

'No,' I said, and the table rattled from my jerk.

Patrons looked over, one by one, whispering. No matter how badly I wanted a drink, if I took his offer of real coffee — which I hadn't tasted for so long — I'd get something worse than rosewater thrown in my face.

'What I mean is, waiter, I've had plenty to drink. Nothing more for me.'

'Your loss, Adèle. I don't even have to pay anymore. You should enjoy the benefits of having your hands in my pockets.' He laughed, waving the waiter away.

A dingy white poodle with patches of fur missing from its coat sniffed Gérard's pant leg before licking something off the toe of his shoe — something a deep crimson red that looked too dark to be from his croissant. She wagged her tail despite the end of it being burnt to a crisp from a fire. I went to pick her up just as Gérard kicked the poor thing in the ribs. 'No!' The dog cowered behind a rubbish bin, yelping.

The waiter brought Gérard's café to the table, setting down a stiff white napkin and a silver spoon for stirring. The aroma wafting from his cup smelled heavenly, conjuring up one of many lost memories of what used to be. I called the dog as Gérard stirred sugar and cream into his cup, but she wouldn't come.

'That dog will be someone's dinner soon,' he said, blowing into his coffee before taking a sip. 'Don't feel sorry for it.'

'You're awful, Gérard.' Fresh meat was hard to come by. Warnings had been issued by the regime on the dangers of eating pets, but that didn't stop the gypsies. The few who hadn't been arrested by the French police were kept in resident camps and were known to venture out at night in search of strays — God only knew what the Reich was telling the French to give them to eat.

'Perhaps the regime should open up the reserves,

give the people something to eat.' I smirked as if I were joking, but inside I was as serious as I could be.

Gérard crumpled up what was left of his croissant in the wax paper, and then pushed it into my hand as he chewed and swallowed. 'I'll have a car pick you up.'

'For what?'

'The dinner. Eight o'clock.'

'I can't,' I blurted. 'I have work to do at Papa's, and then Mama needs me.'

'Yes, you can.' He smiled. 'It's my first night back in so long. Albert will be all right with it, maybe even your mother if she's suffering like so many others under the rationing. You will be there, and you might just enjoy it. The last time I invited you to a formal dinner you left for the nunnery, missed my police promotion. You won't miss this one.' He winked. 'I know it.'

I gulped. 'Gérard, I —'

'It's good to see you again, Adèle.' Gérard took a deep breath, slumping back in his chair instead of leaving as I expected him to. 'You're prettier than I remembered. The way your hair brushes up against your shoulder — it is like a woman but also very innocent.'

He sounded like a real man — not the sly collaborator I knew him to be, and I sat, dumbstruck by his sincerity. Then an odd sensation roiled in my gut — nervousness, which I hadn't felt for a very long time

'I'm back now,' he said, 'for good. We can stop with the cat and mouse game. Can't we?' He tugged on my hand, pulling me in for a kiss across the table. 'Remember, eight o'clock.'

I went to leave, slinging my pocketbook over my shoulder. 'I told you I can't.'

'Meet me there if it's easier,' he said. 'Dinner's at Antoine's.'

I walked away in a hurry, ducking into an alley to collect myself. *He's back.* I closed my eyes. Charlotte had warned me, Papa had warned me. I peeked around the corner to see if he had watched me leave, catching a glimpse of him still sitting at our table, unfolding the newspaper and sipping his coffee.

The cowering dog had followed me and was now at my feet, her little brown eyes looking up at me, licking her lips, a wagging tail between her legs. I unfolded the wax paper and gave her the last of Gérard's croissant, kneeling to pet her as she ate. She took gulping bites, looking up at me every so often while licking the paper.

'Gérard,' I breathed. I still couldn't believe it. I peeked once more, but he'd moved away from the table and was now talking to one of the Germans, monitoring, pointing down the street and to businesses, and then to his newspaper and the headline about the Catchfly.

I gasped.

'Come on,' I said, picking the dog up and tucking her under my arm. 'You're nobody's dinner.'

* * *

Mama took one look at the dog and then mumbled about having another mouth to feed. She counted the number of fruit jars she had left in the root cellar. 'We've eaten too much of the meat, and the pickles are gone.'

'I couldn't leave her behind the rubbish bin. A scrap to be eaten.'

The dog hid under Mama's skirt and licked her calves as she sat at the kitchen table, tearing a two-day-old crust of bread in half. 'Not much flour left either. This war has taken everything. Now it's taken my food too.'

I hadn't wanted to admit it before, but the flour really had started to go, most of it crawling with weevils.

'I didn't think it would come to this,' Mama said. 'We're damn near the bottom now.'

I felt guilty for bringing the poodle home, but what else could I do? 'If the dog becomes a problem, I'll take care of it. Not sure how, but I will.'

Mama glanced up. 'Don't name it. If you do it'll be that much harder to get rid of, if the time comes.'

'All right.'

I picked the poodle up from the floor and sat down with her on my lap. Drool oozed from her jaws as she watched Mama pick at her bread, taking small bites to make it last longer.

'There's something else,' I said, and she looked up. 'Gérard's back.'

Mama gulped. 'What?' She closed her eyes. 'Is he . . . '

'He thinks we're still together.'

'Jesus Christ, Adèle,' she said.

'I know, Mama. I know. He thinks he's getting a promotion tonight. There's a big dinner.'

'A promotion?'

I bit my lip, pausing. 'But that's not the worst of it.' I reached into my pocketbook and pulled out the front page of the newspaper. I hesitated with it in my hand and her eyes grew wide.

'What is it?' Mama said as I slid it to her, and her hand clamped over her mouth.

'Don't worry, Mama,' I said. 'They don't know I'm the Catchfly. They think he's a man with an expensive car.' Gérard's voice was still in my head, and my stomach turned from the unsettling tone of his sincerity, a stark contrast to the newspaper and how he talked about the Catchfly. 'All right?'

Mama had her head down, shaggy hair hanging over her eyes.

'Mama?' I said, and she pulled back the clump.

'What are you going to do?' she said, and I shook my head. 'What does Luc say?'

'Luc?' I said, surprised she'd brought him up.

'Don't give me that song and dance, like you don't know who I'm talking about. I know that pendant is from him. But I don't expect you to admit it.'

I put my hand to my chest, feeling the heart necklace under my dress, wondering what Mama would say if she knew we had plans to marry. The words were on the tip of my tongue, but I dare not even hint of it. 'You know Luc, Mama. He comes and goes. It's the Résistance — there are no set schedules.'

'He'd tell you to take heed if he were here, not paint for a while,' she said. 'Promise me you won't paint for a while. Wait for it to die down.'

I nodded. 'I won't paint,' I said. 'I promise.'

She seemed relieved, taking a breath and sitting

back. 'And Gérard?' she said. 'The timing of that man. I'm surprised he didn't demand you accompany him to the dinner. Very surprised, especially if he thinks you're still his fiancée.'

I sat quiet and still, petting the dog's head. If I told her he invited me, she might tell me to go to keep his temper in check, but I just couldn't. Everything was different now, with Luc and our engagement.

Mama brushed breadcrumbs from the table linen and gave them to the dog. 'Anything from your father?' she said as the dog licked from her palm.

'Last time I talked to Papa about your letter he had tucked it in his pocket. That was months ago.'

'Mmm.' Mama reached for her cigarettes, but all that was left in her metal case were a few shreds of tobacco. She shook the case close to her eyes as if one might be hiding in the rusty hinge. Then she scooted her chair away from the table and walked to the kitchen counter, catching herself from running into the cupboard.

'Are you all right?' The dog jumped from my lap when I stood.

'Yes,' she said, putting a hand to her head. 'I have a headache because I don't have any more cigarettes. The Germans took all the cigarettes. Just like they took France. My husband and my daughter, and my grandchildren. I invited her to visit today so we could talk. I got up early from my nap and waited, but Charlotte never showed.'

She gripped the sink's edge, looking out the kitchen window. Spring blossoms had fallen from the trees outside and speckled the ground with

326

spots of pink, the branches swaying as much as Mama's linens used to, when she had the soap to clean them. In the distance, and completely unobstructed, was the all too painful reminder of Papa's forgotten vineyard, which had turned into a mass of tangled brown knots.

'Albert, goddamn you.' Her voice quivered as she spoke and then she hung her head down, sniffling, waving at me to leave the room, but I put my hands on her shoulders instead.

'It's not your fault, Mama.' She looked as haggard as Charlotte and appeared more broken than ever without Papa. I started to wonder how much longer she could last. It was possible, I thought, that even Mama had a breaking point. 'It's the war.'

She kissed my hand and put it to her cheek. 'The war,' she breathed.

Mama went back to bed. The chamomile I had been drying in the windowsill wasn't ready, but I used it anyway, warming up a kettle of water to have a cup of tea. The dog watched me, probably thinking I had food, as I dunked the tea strainer into the steaming water, trying to get it to turn.

The garden was green with weeds, but when I looked out the window and off into the horizon, I couldn't tell they were weeds. I thought about Mama waking up from her nap, waiting for Charlotte to come for a visit and then the disappointment she must have felt when she didn't. My eyes trailed off to the garden once more, and then back to the tea strainer, dunking it in and out of the water, watching loose bits of chamomile swirling around in my cup, only to whip my head back at the garden and to a set of tyre grooves I was sure weren't mine.

My stomach sank.

I leaned out the window, and saw what Mama and I couldn't have seen from the kitchen table: Charlotte's car parked around the side. I waited for her to walk in, quickly wondering how many seconds it would take to walk that distance from the car, but I knew she wasn't outside — I knew she couldn't be outside. I had been at the window for a while; I would have seen her drive up.

It was then that I noticed her driving gloves lying on the bookcase near the door. Bright blue, just like her divan. She had come to visit and was in the chateau, somewhere, and she'd heard us talking — the Résistance, Luc and Gérard.

Catchfly.

I whipped around, hands grasping the sink, eyes wide. 'Charlotte,' I called out, shakily, but there was no answer. I raced down the corridor, opening doors as if she were hiding in one of the bedrooms, but she was nowhere in sight.

The cellar door was last. 'Christ,' I said into my hand. 'She knows.'

I breathed heavily against the wall, staring at the door. Mama said she'd handle Charlotte when the time came, but this was more than just the paints, and she'd become fragile in her own way and as delicate as a snowflake on glass.

I put my hand on the door, closing my eyes. 'God, let this be quick,' I said to myself, and I walked down the creaking old wood stairs into the dark cellar.

'Charlotte?' A lit lantern flickered next to the

wall, lighting up the mural I'd painted down there months ago, the blazing red paint still shiny and wet-looking from the cadmium in the oil. 'Charlotte,' I said, again. 'I know you're down here.' I swallowed. 'We need to talk.'

The dog trotted up from behind only to back up and growl like a dog ten times her size, rabidly gritting her teeth at something set in the wall. 'Come out.'

From an obscure cleft beside the chest of paint, Charlotte emerged into the flickering light. Her lips snarled and her hair was as ratty and stringy as I'd ever seen it, wild as the snakes on Medusa's head. I took a step back when I saw a tube of paint in her hand.

She slapped the tube into her palm, over and over again.

Slap! Slap! Slap!

The dog growled at her from between my legs as Charlotte stopped in front of the mural, her face looking pasty white and her eyes silver-grey, gazing at the painted wall.

'Let me explain — '

'I want no explaining — ' she ran the tube over the painted stones, an evil eye shifting toward me ' — from you.'

I collapsed to the ground, the chill from her icy eyes numbing my legs — never had I seen her look this way. Nothing could have prepared me for such a sight. She started mumbling about the Paris exhibition and comparing my art to hers, studying the lines of the letters, tracing the bends with her fingertip, the dog nipping at her heels. 'I couldn't tell you — I knew you wouldn't understand,'

I said as she walked up the stairs. 'Come back, sister, come back and talk to me.'

The kitchen door cracked from having been slammed shut. The dog ran in circles, barking and squealing. Tomorrow, I thought. *Tomorrow I'll talk to her.* Maybe then I'd miss the worst of her breakdown, and she'd listen to what I had to say.

★ ★ ★

I stood outside Charlotte's boutique that morning, waiting for her to arrive. After a while, I started to wonder if letting her leave Mama's was a bad idea. *What if she's at the cemetery, delirious? What if she drank herself to death?* As delicate as Charlotte was, how could I have left her alone? My hands shook when I realized it was well past ten o'clock and she wasn't coming. *I should have followed her.* Flower carts wheeled past and people rushed by, chatting, some laughing, a morning noise that built and built. I rubbed my shaking hands together, beginning to pace. I'd have to go to her apartment. *Yes, that's it,* I thought. *I'll find her in her apartment.*

There was a commotion down the way; women took their children's hands, moving into the street, making a path.

Someone yelled that the Milice were coming; then I heard my name. 'Adèle!' Gérard charged through the parting crowd, sweaty and beet red, dressed in a navy blue Milice uniform and steaming straight toward me. 'You stood me up!'

'What?' I stepped backward into Charlotte's closed door.

'The dinner!'

'I said I couldn't go!'

He got a few inches from me, calling me a tease and a bitch in the same breath. 'Stop it!' I cried. 'Stop it!' Spit spurted from his mouth onto my face as he berated me.

'Once wasn't enough! You *had* to do it again and on the night of my promotion!' He threw his hand back and Papa flew out of his wine bar, demanding that Gérard stop cursing at me.

'Leave her alone!' Papa yelled. 'Leave her be!'

Gérard growled, abandoning me for Papa, pointing a finger at him. 'Your family will pay for this, Albert!' He stepped closer and closer to him, but then froze at the sight of Prêtre Champoix rising up behind Papa.

'Gérard!' he said, voice booming. The longer he stared at him, the smaller Gérard seemed to become under the priest's black cassock and the white eye of his clerical collar. 'This woman is not yours to torment.' He put a hand on Papa's shoulder. 'She's broken no laws.'

There was a long, cold pause where nobody spoke.

'You're not welcome here anymore, Gérard,' Papa said.

Prêtre Champoix pointed down the street with his Bible for Gérard to leave, but he looked at me first, flattened against Charlotte's building, snarling, before adjusting his new Milice uniform jacket and stiffly walking away.

Papa took me in his arms. 'Forgive me, *ma chérie*,' he said, tearfully. 'I believe you. I believe you.'

331

Papa and I sat across from each other at his usual wine-stained wood table. For a long time we sat in silence. I kept wondering when the next handful of Milice would come through the door, sit down and pour their own wine on Papa's tab, but he had locked the door, and the shade was pulled down. He could barely look at me without tearing up. 'I'm sorry,' he said, reaching for my hands. 'I'm sorry for everything.'

I nodded, wiping a gush of tears away. I wanted to be mad at him for taking so long, but I felt more sad than anything. 'What's done is done, Papa. We have to move on.' I reached for an unopened bottle of wine with a label I didn't recognize, something German, though I couldn't be sure.

'No, Adèle,' he said, touching my hand. 'No wine today. Not from this place, not anymore. I should have never left the estate, or your mother.'

My eyes got wide, praying I heard him right. 'Does this mean what I think you're saying? You're coming home?'

'I heard Creuzier-le-Vieux isn't what it used to be — that it smells of dust and rotted grapes — that the old Vichy vineyards are all but gone.' He slumped forward, pulling Mama's last letter from his pocket. 'But that's not what I think about when I think of Creuzier-le-Vieux.'

'What do you think about?'

'My family — how it used to be before the war. You and Charlotte cooking in the kitchen, laughing, being sisters, me and Pauline walking in her garden, being husband and wife.' I touched his arm, and a spill of tears slid down both our cheeks as he fumbled with the letter. 'What if it's too late? What if she doesn't want me back?'

For the first time in a long time I understood Papa, realizing why he hadn't read Mama's last letter. 'You thought Mama wrote to say it's over? No — it isn't like that. She's stubborn, yes, but the separation between you two is killing her. I see it in her eyes, the way she walks.' I swallowed dryly, compelled to guess what she had written. 'I think it's an apology.'

'I hadn't thought of that.' He unfolded the letter, adjusting it for light, reading it carefully. My stomach sank when I saw his eyes fade the further — the deeper — he got into her letter.

'What is it, Papa?' I tugged on his arm. 'What does it say?'

He slammed his hand onto the table, cursing to himself. 'Your mother's sick.'

'What?' I reached for the letter, but Papa pulled it away.

'It's her sight,' he said. 'She says there are days when she can't see, and she's afraid she won't remember what I look like.' He put his fist to his forehead, clenching his eyes painfully shut.

I thought about all the times Mama had a headache, the way she walked — a little slanted at times — and her wavering moods. I couldn't help feel a little responsible — I should have seen the signs.

'Does it say anything else?'

Papa looked up, his eyes watering and blue, sliding the note across the table. There, scribbled in her best handwriting were the words to 'À la

Claire Fontaine'.

'Our song, *ma chérie*. Long have I loved you . . .'
He couldn't finish the words without breaking
down. I put my hand on his.

'Go,' he said. 'Tell her I'm coming home.'

24

I lurched to a stop near the patio and ran inside, only to realize something felt terribly off. The chateau was dead quiet — and in the middle of the day. The laundry was half-hung on the line outside, some of it dangling in loose dirt. The dog whimpered from behind the rubbish bin, her burnt little tail wagging cautiously between her legs, afraid to come any closer. That's when I noticed what looked like two drops of blood spatter on the floor.

I gulped — Germans.

I ran upstairs to Mama's bedroom. Two more drops led to three, then four — a trail — leading into her room, each one getting fatter, redder and less watery than the last. 'Mama — ' I threw open the door and my hand flew to my mouth.

She sat in a chair bound with ropes tied to her wrists and ankles, a rag wadded in her mouth to keep her from screaming. 'Mama!' Her head hung off to the side, the mark of someone's knuckles pressed into her left cheek. A shallow slash across her chest oozed blood onto her apron, metallic-smelling, warming with the midday sun coming in through the window.

I ran to her, taking the rag from her mouth and working to loosen the ropes. The one eye that hadn't been bashed in, opening a hair. 'Who did this?'

She mumbled, her head lifting.

'What are you saying?' I untied a knot from her wrist. 'Who did this — '

'He knows,' she moaned. 'I don't know how, but he knows.'

'Who? Knows what?'

The kitchen door slammed shut down below, the dog suddenly barking like a crazed animal. Four stomps of heavy feet — the dog yelped — and then there was pure silence. I raced to shut Mama's door, locking it with a heavy bolt as the footsteps started up the stairs, one after the other. *Thud. Thud. Thud* . . .

I worked frantically on Mama's wrists. 'Germans? Is it a German — ' A kick to the lock and the door burst open behind me, cracking against the wall, and Mama straightened with a jolt, her eye large and wide looking over my shoulder, her whole body shaking.

'Gérard.'

I flew to my feet and he grabbed my throat, pulling me to him, his wild eyes meeting mine before he threw me to the floor. 'Not mine to torment,' he growled, taking the little bit of rope I had managed to untie from Mama's wrists and reaching for my hands. 'A priest can't tell the Milice what to do.'

'Gérard. Don't,' I cried, one arm frantically searching for the gun Luc gave me, my fingers gracing the holster under my dress as he pinned my body down. 'You don't have . . . to do this.'

He wound the rope around my wrists, tying one to the foot of Mama's bed and the other to the leg of her vanity as I screamed.

'Shut up!' he shouted through clenched teeth,

punching my face with a closed fist — a piercing blow of pain that left the grit of broken teeth loose in my mouth.

He stood over me once I was tied down, first carefully hanging his blue Milice jacket on the back of a nearby chair and then unbuckling his belt buckle, ranting about the Catchfly and how I was a whore. He reached under my skirt and snatched the gun Luc had given me from its holster and stuck it behind his back. 'I found your lover's radio,' he added, as Mama wept under the rag he had stuffed back into her mouth.

Gérard hooked his finger on the top button of my dress and began to pull, popping every button from its hole. He flipped back both sides like a coat to get a good look at me. 'Just a necklace?' He rubbed my heart pendant in between his roughened fingers, a glaring eye examining every curve before yanking it off and throwing it across the room. 'Or a gift from your lover?'

He pulled a sharp knife slicked with Mama's blood from a sheath tucked under his belt. Slowly, he cut my brassiere and panties from my body, pressing the tip of the knife into my skin, dragging it downward from my navel. 'That's for after,' he said, sticking the knife back into its sheath. 'First there's this.'

Gérard pulled a heap of white fabric out from under Mama's bed and threw it at me. 'Remember this?' he said. Yards of Mechlin lace lumped around my neck — the weight of the heavy fabric on top of me an all too familiar feel from the last time I had it on.

My wedding dress.

Mama shook her crying head for having saved it after I thought she'd thrown it out.

Gérard pulled Luc's flask from his pocket and drank what alcohol was left inside, his brow furrowing from the taste of the English whisky. He mumbled in between gulps about the torturous things he was going to do to Luc when he found him. 'Hang from a tree,' he said. 'Drain like a deer.' I lay helplessly on the floor staring up at him, my eyes fluttering, on the verge of blacking out.

Gérard threw the flask against the wall once he had emptied it. A swipe of his thick hand across his mouth wiped the gloss of whisky from his lips. '*Merde*! This is shit!' he said with utter disgust. 'Where's Albert's wine?' he asked, though he didn't expect us to answer. He stomped downstairs, slamming the door shut behind him so as not to hear us crying as he guzzled Papa's wine in the kitchen. I could hear his heavy plodding from one wall to the next, smashing wine bottles.

Mama spit out the rag. 'My gun,' she said. 'Adèle, my gun!'

'Gun?' The word roused me like a splash of water to the face — I'd forgotten about the gun Mama had in the floorboard. The thought of escaping gave me enough strength to pull my hand from one of the knots and feel around for the loose board — frantically, frantically, and then I found it. I lifted the board up by my fingertip, unseeing, and grabbed the gun from the secret compartment. 'I have it,' I whispered, and Mama breathed heavily. I hid my whole arm under the dress, finger on the trigger. 'Weep for Christ's sake, Mama. Weep!'

She went back to wailing while I waited, palms sweating, remembering what Luc had told me about aiming. *Look down the barrel, close one eye and use the other to aim.*

I counted backward from ten in my mind, eyes closed, thinking of the grass and the sun and calming my nervous heart, breathing deeply, too deeply for my pounding heart. Then Gérard started up the stairs and my eyes popped open, listening to the thumps. The door flew open, slamming against the wall — only one shot. Mama hopped in her seat, her cry more like a squeal.

'Enough!' he yelled as he threw a full wine bottle at the wall. *Crash!* Wine splattered behind Mama like blood from a bullet to her head, her squeal turning into an outright scream as the shattered glass rained down on her skin.

Gérard stood in the doorway unlooping the belt from his waist, his eyes pointed as daggers looking into mine. He paused when he noticed my arm wasn't tethered to the vanity. Where's — '

I pulled my hand out from under the dress, Gérard's face a mix of fear and anger as I aimed my one shot. *Pop!* My eye lay fixed down the barrel, frozen, as his body fell like a tree on top of me, onto the wedding dress.

Mama's wailing was now a search for air as I moved my body out from under Gérard's, untying the rest of my limbs from the constraints he had tried to rape me in, the dress soaking up his blood.

I felt a mix of sadness and loathing as I stared at Gérard lying motionless on Mama's floor — Gérard, the good soldier I kept hearing about, really *had* died years ago, crushed by his own ambition and greed.

'My God, Adèle,' Mama said after I untied her, both of us moving to the floor, kneeling and gazing at his body. 'My God!'

'Better him than us.'

'I know!' Her voice was shrill. 'Jesus Christ!' Mama put both hands to her head, worry as much as fright keeping her swollen eyes open. 'Let me think!' she shrieked. 'Let me think of what to do —'

Gérard moaned and we both screamed. 'He's alive!'

We scrambled to get clear of him, but his meaty hand latched on to my ankle. 'I'm going to kill you.' He spat blood from his mouth. 'You and your mother!' Mama went for his hands but he got her throat, the wedding dress pillowing underneath their knees as they both tried to gain a footing.

'Reload,' Mama rasped.

I frantically tried to reload the gun with the extra bullets from the box. I had no time to read the directions, aiming straight for his heart and firing the gun.

This time I was a perfect shot.

'He's dead,' I cried out, using every bit of strength I had left. 'He's dead . . .'

Papa flew into the room, bracing both sides of the doors with his hands, his eyes stretched in a million directions, first looking at Gérard's body slumped on the floor and then at the gun still smoking in my hands. When he saw Mama pulling at her throat with blood streaking down her chest, I thought he might die right on top of Gérard.

340

'*Ma chérie!*' he cried, wanting to touch Mama but unsure where.

Mama sobbed his name, the sound coming from deep within her body: 'Albert.'

Papa wept into Mama's shoulder, saying her name over and over again as if an apology, wiping the tears from his eyes with the back of his hand. 'I'm here,' he kept saying. 'I'm here.'

Mama swallowed relentlessly trying to feel her throat again. Thin red veins had bloodshot her eyes. 'Adèle, you must run,' she said with coarse breath. 'Run far away.' She put a hand to her mouth as if she couldn't believe she'd even say such a thing. 'It's the only way.'

Papa's eyes swelled pink. 'Yes,' he said. 'Run away. Into the hills if you have to.'

I scooted back, my body shaking, thinking about the consequences of what I had done. Regardless of what Gérard had planned for me, I had shot a member of the Milice.

Mama grabbed my shoulders. 'You'd be lucky to get a quick death if they give you to the Gestapo. Germans — they're ruthless. My time as a nurse — ' Mama caught herself, a brief glance to Papa to collect her words; then the truth of what bound her and Mother Superior spilled from her mouth. 'They killed my friend because they thought she was a spy. The way they killed her, pulling her organs out while she was alive, making me and Elizabeth watch . . .'

I shrieked from her words and Papa wailed along with Mama.

'Albert!' Mama said, wiping tears from her face. 'We'll bury him in the field.'

They talked in hurried whispers over Gérard's body, deciding where in the field was the best spot while I ran down stairs, my heart racing, thinking about what I should pack, my feet skidding across shards of broken glass strewn across Mama's parquet floor, the ringing of the gunshot still piercing my ears, and I stopped — right in the middle of the kitchen — my eyes clenched and my fists just as tight, until the sound of the gunshot faded and I could hear myself think: if I did run I'd only be known as the girl who ran away. Forever.

Mama had started crying again upstairs, telling Papa who I really was. 'The Catchfly,' I heard. 'Résistance, both of us.'

The Catchfly.

My hands stopped shaking; the glint of a paint tube lying on the kitchen counter amidst the rubble of glass caught my eye, and I knew what to do. A fleeting glance upstairs and a kiss meant for them both.

'We do what we have to, Mama.' I swung open the kitchen door, the paint gripped tightly in my hand. 'When we have to.'

The door swung back and slammed shut behind me.

★ ★ ★

I stood in the middle of the road, the train station at the end of it, cars swerving out of the way, honking for me to move. My dress looked like a mere shred of a rag stained with Gérard's blood, held closed by one blood-stained hand.

There was no time for a breath. People started

342

to gather on the pavement, staring, wondering what I was doing and if I had gone mad. A shrug of my shoulder and my dress slipped off, falling into a lumpy, soiled pile at my feet — gasps, men pointing, women hiding their children's eyes as I stood naked, a fire in my soul lighting up my eyes as I squeezed paint onto my fingertips, writing across my chest and breasts, the word in red bleeding from my skin: Catchfly.

A stillness swept over the gathering crowd. Cars engines turned off. Women dropped their hands from their children's eyes to place them over their hearts while men took off their hats. And I walked, straight toward two Milice standing under the large clock that hung above the station's stone archway.

There would be no running. Not today.

Charlotte sat on the bench outside her boutique, shaking her head in her hands. She bolted to a stand when she saw me, her eyes like lemons and puffy from crying. She shrieked before dropping to her knees, begging for me to turn around. When she realized I wasn't stopping, and that the Milice were seconds away from noticing me, she tried covering me with a lacy robe she took from her display window. 'I'm sorry.' Her face drooped like a melting candle. 'I was delirious when I told him.'

I gasped — *Gérard*. I thought an informant must have told him. Never once did I think Charlotte had something to do with it. '*You* told him?'

She barely nodded — but it was there, a slight jitter of an admission. I shoved her from me, and she folded to the ground weeping. I turned toward

343

the Milice, who stood dumbfounded as much as some others, the smell of last night's champagne and black caviar wafting from their wool jackets.

A shout, '*Vive le Catchfly*!' rang out from the crowd. People clapped, low at first, but then it turned into an outright roar. The miliciens grabbed on to me, their hands like meat hooks, and dragged me to the nearest Morris Column, tying me to it with ropes they had looped near their waists like cowboys. They circled like vultures, blood in their eyes. They'd want me to scream. I pressed my lips together and hoped I could hold it in.

'Say something,' one said. 'Ask for mercy — see if you get it.' He pointed the barrel of his gun between my eyes, Charlotte's horrific scream the only thing that stopped him from shooting as she crawled to her knees just a few feet away.

'This is how we treat résistants,' the other one shouted at the crowd, taking his thick leather belt from his trousers and holding it between his hands in the air, Charlotte's body quaking at the sight of it.

He swung his hand back, and in that split-second with his hand suspended in the air, my body seized up.

Wpssh! My eyes bugged from my head when the leather struck my ribs, the pain like a million bee stings. *Wpssh! Wpssh!* 'Forgive me, sister,' Charlotte cried through heaving wails, and my mind travelled to a faded memory of Charlotte and I running barefoot through Papa's vineyards, the cool-black volcanic soil heavy between our toes, a lofty giggle from us both, the sight of her dress ruffling against her calves as I chased her in the sun and through the grass — clear as my skin ripping under each lash. 'Forgive me . . .'

Everything got still, the smell of the leather against my wet-with-blood skin curdling under my nose. And then I heard what they had heard — a rumbling in the distance, people marching, an army if I ever heard one. Under the swell of a bruising face I saw the Milice step back, dropping the whip.

'Riot!' someone shouted, and people scattered. The miliciens ran to their truck as people with sticks poured out of the alley and rushed into the square, throwing what little food merchants had in their markets out into the street and tossing bottles into the air that crashed like bombs against the cobblestones.

'Open the food reserves,' they shouted. 'Bastards!'

A thin layer of smoke rose in the street, Prêtre Champoix appearing like an apparition, moving toward me from within the haze. He crossed his arms and stood like a wall with his back to me as two nuns untied the ropes from the Morris Column. I fell into their arms, and we slipped away into a building not far away, my whole body hidden in the thick folds of their black habits.

The nuns held me up by the arms against the wall in a brick room — the only parts of my body that didn't ache — as people I couldn't see talked about what to do with me next.

A woman with oversized, black-rimmed glasses sitting on the tip of her nose, looked me over. 'First, she needs some clothes.' She slipped a thin floral dress over my head and then pulled it down from the hem, fitting it to my body as she talked. 'No rosewater for you this time, Adèle.' She wrapped a striped shawl around my shoulders, and then whispered near my ear even though she didn't have to. 'Now that I know who you are, love.' She pushed her glasses up the bridge of her nose and smiled.

'Mme Dubois?' I could barely push the words from my mouth.

She nodded, putting a hand to my swelling face. 'No need to talk. You're sorely beaten. Rest.' She helped me onto a beige divan set against the wall. 'Sit here while we figure out how to get you out safely.'

The nuns assembled an ice pack consisting of a lump of ice wrapped in a scrap of striped fabric and held it to my cheek. The initial sting of the cold, wet press made me scowl. 'Christ!' They moved it away from the welt, shock lifting their eyes wide open from hearing me swear. 'Sorry,' I said, motioning for them to try again. 'It's very cold.'

A woman with her hair pinned back, thin as a rail, paced around, talking about the nearest safe house. 'The best option is to get her out of Vichy,' she said to Mme Dubois, exchanging something wrapped in brown paper. 'Pack her with the shipment. I'll radio for transport. You know where. Wait until sundown. I'll need a few hours.'

Mme Dubois nodded, glancing back at me. 'She walked right up to them as if she wanted to die. Defiant, that one.' After pondering her own thoughts she turned toward me. 'What was in your head, love?'

346

'I don't know,' I said, not wanting to elaborate.

The woman placed a hand on my shoulder. There was something about her touch, and in the long pause that followed, that made me think she knew what had been in my head, and she understood. 'I wasn't supposed to be in Vichy today.' She leaned into the light coming from a lantern Mme Dubois had lit and placed on the ground. 'After what you did for us at the Sleeping Lady, I couldn't leave you tied to that column.'

I moved the ice pack from my face, squinting, getting a good enough look at her face. 'Hedgehog?'

She winked. Then she turned around and left, disappearing into a corridor.

Mme Dubois draped a blue scarf over my head. 'You must mean a great deal for the leader of the Alliance to personally save your bottom,' she said, tucking my hair underneath the fabric, tying a loose knot under my chin. She helped me off the divan and walked with me outside. She pointed to a car parked against the kerb with its back seat pushed forward.

'Where am I going?' I got in the car without waiting for an answer.

Mme Dubois shifted her eyes suspiciously toward the square where the riot was still plenty rife, not at all concerned with my question. 'Through the seat. Crawl back as far as you can.'

I hunkered down in the boot from behind the back seat, piled to the brim with bolts of fabric, sewing machines and bags of scrap tossed haphazardly all around; a hard squeeze even for someone who could move without pain.

'No matter what happens . . .' Mme Dubois used both hands to push the seat back into place and everything turned pitch-black. Her voice was muffled and barely audible from the other side of the seat. 'Don't move.'

The engine flared and we sped away. The smell of petrol and burning rubber from the squeal of her tyres permeated the air. I buried my nose into a soft pad I figured was fabric. Bumpy roads were made worse by speeding turns, stopping and starting, until I heard the engine shift into a high gear and felt a smooth street under the tyres.

Just when I started to feel safe and out of the city, the car stopped abruptly. The engine cut off, and everything got very quiet. A German voice spoke up. Then Mme Dubois got out of the car and started talking in a high-pitched, very girly voice. 'Seamstress on a job,' she said. 'Late for delivery.'

I lay still, and then even stiller when I heard a tap near the back bumper.

'*Öffnen!*' I heard, followed by more tapping. 'Open it!'

Mme Dubois mumbled as she fit the key into the lock, making much more noise than she had to — a warning not to move. I felt a push of cool air penetrate the scarf wrapped around my head when the boot opened. My heart raced as I realized I'd die from another beating. I barely had the strength to breathe, much less move. *If I get caught this time*, I thought, *it won't be from my doing.*

'Fabric, bags . . .' I heard him say, mixing French with German. He poked a few bags with the tip of his long gun, rustling things around.

348

'Sew machine,' he said, tapping the machine's hard case. 'Needle case . . . ' He hit the top of my head and paused, as if he was considering the difference in sound my skull had made compared to the sewing machine.

'I'm very late.' Her voice turned exaggeratingly high. 'You want me to sew something up for you? Or can I be on my way?'

He poked the bags once more, slow and deep, the barrel of his gun dangerously close to my body. Then he pulled his gun back and questioned Mme Dubois about her documents. I wanted to breathe deeply and quickly, feeling very much out of breath, but couldn't for fear of moving, my heart beating rapidly in my chest.

The boot closed with the squeal of a rusty hinge, and a radiating pain where his gun had hit me spread over my head. Then I passed out or fell asleep, because I didn't remember the car starting up again. All I felt was a sudden lurch and a waft of air from when Mme Dubois pulled open the back seat. 'We're here, Adèle.'

I opened my crusty eyes, swollen with a bruised face. We had stopped on a dirt road somewhere in the middle of a field. Another car's headlamps shone on us from a near distance, its engine running. Mme Dubois helped me out of the car with one hand, the dress she gave me sticking to the wounds on my skin.

'God bless you, love.' Mme Dubois hopped back into the car and then waited for me to move, raising her eyebrows as I stood slumped over, holding my stomach. 'Your transfer has all been arranged.'

'Transfer?'

'You're in hiding now. Just be glad you're not dead.' She reached through her open window and patted my arm. 'Go along.'

I started toward the car, shuffling through the dirt, the headlamps lighting up the flowers on my floral dress. The engines were a duet of burning petrol and sputters. I pulled the blue scarf from my head, my sight ebbing in the colour black from the whiteness of the light. Feet from the car, still I saw no one. Then, out from the darkness, a figure draped in something heavy and long stepped into the light. A nun. I stopped, and she pulled her veil back.

A cool smile spread on my face. 'Marguerite.'

She reached into a hidden pocket and pulled out a man's lighter and my old cigarette case — the thing was full of Gitanes. 'Looks like you could use these.' I held in a laugh simply because it hurt too much, but then started to cry. I had forgotten about that damn case — the one I had thrown across the room after Marguerite asked me to go back to Vichy.

'What about the smoke?'

'I'll be fine,' she said, helping me into the car.

A driver — a girl — I didn't know, sped off just as I closed the door, turning her headlamps off, using moonlight to drive. I slunk down into the cracked leather seat and smoked, the cigarette hanging off my lips in between puffs because I was too weak to lift my arm. A rash bumped over Marguerite's cheek, but she never said a word. Not long after, she threw the skirt of her habit over my legs as a blanket.

After a dry, hard gulp I told Marguerite about Gérard, and how Mama and Papa were covering up the murder. 'My sister turned me in.' I could barely say her name it hurt so much. 'Charlotte.' Marguerite put her hand on mine and I closed my eyes, the sound of the leather belt slapping against my skin and Charlotte's pleading voice replaying over and over in my mind like a sad, haunting song. I leaned into her shoulder, shivering, though I wasn't cold, and she petted my head.

We pulled up to a cottage nestled between two hills on the outskirts of Lyon just before sunrise, the horizon a mix of sunny-pink and orange blossom bursting through the clouds. There was a long pause as we sat next to each other in the back seat of the car, looking out the window.

'This is where I've been sleeping most the time,' she said. 'We call it the hill cottage. It's a safe house for many résistants.' Marguerite took her headpiece off and gave it to the girl driver who meticulously folded it along with the wimple Marguerite pulled from her neck. 'Lyon is different now from when it was part of the Free Zone; Vichy has the Milice, but here we have more Gestapo than anything. It's just safer to stay out here,' she said, taking rests between her words, 'than at the convent.'

I could tell she was tired by the sound of her dragging voice, but when the light caught her face I noticed the bags under her eyes and realized she was more tired than I thought.

'You can help me with the guns in the crypt. Mavis — you'll remember — she's very helpful. She found her voice with us in the Résistance and doesn't squeak like a mouse anymore. The work is different from before — tenuous at best with the sweeps . . . and the Germans. Mother Superior stays at the convent, doesn't come out into the open. Or Sister Mary-Francis.' She handed me a *Carte d'identité* — a forged set of documents with a grainy photo of a woman who looked like me if you were drunk enough to imagine a resemblance. I also got a new name: Jeanne Calvet. 'It was the best I could do on such short notice.' Her eyes sagged when she looked at me.

I nodded. 'It's fine — Jeanne.' I flipped open the book and read the typed print inside. 'From Lyon.'

'Adèle, you can't tell anyone where you are. Not your family and definitely not your lover. They'd unknowingly lead the Milice straight to us if the Gestapo doesn't make it first.'

'What if Luc comes looking for me?'

'He's a résistant, Adèle. He won't jeopardize your cover or his. You know that.'

I remembered the last time I saw Luc. The feel of his hands on my skin; the comforting warmth I felt deep inside when I took him into my body, his lovely, syrupy voice when he'd call my name. *Catchfly*. A name that belonged to the past, its memory as thin as the perspiration my body left behind on the Morris Column.

'I'm sorry, Adèle,' she said, carefully. 'This is the way it has to be.'

I closed my eyes when I felt the tears welling. The sound of Charlotte's sobs — the painful wounds on my body were nothing compared to the memory of Charlotte's regretful cry. And

Mama and Papa — what would become of them now?

'Don't be sorry.' Tears rolled down my face when I opened my eyes. 'This was my doing.'

1944

25

The sisters' crypt smelled of old bones and rotting flesh despite the cologne I rubbed under my nose. 'To keep the Gestapo away,' Marguerite said. 'Germans are afraid of germs so the sisters lay the dead in catacombs, uncovered.' Dug into the ground under the old convent in the centre of Lyon, the crypt had hundreds of tombs set head to toe, linked like dominoes through winding corridors of dirt and stone.

Marguerite looked on from behind as I wedged my body in between two beams searching for a gun that had been stashed in a hole two days prior, her face very close to the low-burning lantern she held in her hand. 'Reach all the way back.'

I peered into the crude dirt dug-out set into the wall and then reluctantly stuck my hand in. Spiders, biting ones, and scorpions, I thought, as I felt blindly around, breathing in the putrid, thick air wafting from the tombs. 'Why did you stick it so far back?' I reached further into the dark hole, feeling for the barrel of the gun amidst cobwebs and crumbling sod, suffocating me as much as the smell.

'It wasn't me. Get the gun, all right?' Marguerite was irritated; I could tell by the sharpness in her voice and the jerky movements she made with her head, as if her headpiece wasn't fitting right, which made me glad I didn't have to wear a habit like she did.

I pulled the gun from the hole like a snake. Long and thin, a German MG 42. 'There,' I said, tossing the gun into a crate with some others. 'The last one.'

Marguerite took inventory of the arms we had smuggled while I dusted dirt from my postulant's veil. 'Now we have to wait for the transport truck. The Maquis will collect the arms at the hill cottage.' As she closed the crate's oblong lid, I saw its metal handles and instantly felt a pull in my palm from the last time I had carried it — Marguerite's travel crate, the one I helped her lug to the convent on our first day. We both picked up an end and carried it upstairs into the sewing area of the old convent.

Just as I was locking up the crypt door, Mavis came scampering through the front doors. She had a smile on her face that bordered on panic, waving a note in her hand as she closed the doors behind her. 'Adèle,' she said all breathy. 'It's for you — news from Vichy. One of our agents.'

I hadn't allowed myself to think about my family, not knowing where they were and if they were safe for fear of shrivelling up like one of Papa's gnarled grape vines.

I held my breath, looking at the note, my eyes wide.

'Go on,' Marguerite said. 'Have a look.'

I ripped open the envelope — so many thoughts flying through my head — the gold heart pendant Luc had given me slid out from a heavy crease, and I nearly fell to the floor with it in my hand. Marguerite helped me into a chair next to one of the sewing machines, bolts of fabric stacked high

358

like a wall. I held the heart in my hand, rubbing it in between my fingers, reading the letter written by someone I didn't know but who had talked to at least one of my parents by the sound of it.

'They're at the chateau together,' I said. 'The Milice blame me for Gérard's disappearance and have been at the chateau regularly searching for signs I've been back. Luc hasn't been seen since I left and is in hiding.' I sighed heavily, sad about Luc but glad my parents hadn't been arrested — they must have hidden Gérard's body well. At the end of the note was a scribble in Charlotte's handwriting. Forgive me.

I pulled my eyes from the note. 'Forgive *her*?'

'What about the news of your parents?' Marguerite said. 'That's something, isn't it? They haven't found Gérard's body, and they don't know where you are. Both those things are keeping your family safe, and alive. The Milice must think you're close by.'

Mama probably knew I was here, as cunning as she was, but she'd never breathe a word. 'Yes,' I said. 'It's something. But Charlotte . . . I've given up on her as a sister. She knew telling Gérard my secret would bring violence upon me.'

'The war makes people do things,' Marguerite said, 'sometimes awful things they wouldn't normally do — '

I put my hand up, stopping her. The conversation about Charlotte was finished.

Marguerite helped me clasp the necklace around my neck. I pressed it against my chest, the coolness of the metal a refreshing feel on warm skin. And for the first time in a long time, hope had lifted my thoughts like a rising bubble — fragile, breakable, yet there. 'I know you said Luc wouldn't come looking for me, but I have to believe . . .'

Marguerite put her hand gently on my shoulder. 'Then believe it.'

We pushed the gun crate against the wall, used a linen tablecloth to cover it, and then put a stitching machine on top, which Marguerite broke open like a valise to expose its mechanical guts. Thread had been pulled from it and working tools lay off to the side. 'Has to look as if the machine is broken and placed on the crate haphazardly . . . in case.' Marguerite took a deep, exhausted breath. 'In case there's a raid before the truck comes.'

I motioned to Marguerite for more cologne. We passed the vial to one another while standing in a loose circle, dabbing the cologne under our noses, talking about the elegant scent of Chanel compared to the fragrance Marguerite had made from mixing several bottles of unknown perfumes.

'Shh — ' Mavis reached out, touching my hand. 'Did you hear that?' Her eyes shifted from side to side, and then I heard it too: a light noise that could easily be dismissed as a bird rustling around in the eaves. 'Sounds like a bird,' she whispered, 'but not . . .'

Mavis's gaze locked on to the far window set high in the stone wall, her eyes widening, her throat gulping as the noise grew into a continuous scratch, something that could only be made by a person, a finger scraping dirt from the glass. A shiver waved up the back of my neck, then Marguerite shivered and we all held our breaths.

'We're being watched,' Marguerite said, smiling. 'Everyone breathe.' Her voice was steady, but her tone was unlike anything I'd heard, which added to the nervy feeling of eyes on my back. 'Pass,' she said, motioning for the vial. 'Think about lying in the grass in the sun, feel the warmth, steady yourself, your nerves . . . Just like I taught you.'

We continued passing the vial around, the sound of fingers pulling at the window ledge outside very clear and present, not even trying to be discreet, as we breathed and thought about lying in the grass. Then came an odd tap against the outer wall that moved from the window to the front of the building. Two quick raps on the front door followed.

Mavis gasped as if she had come up out of the water. I closed my eyes briefly. One last breath.

'We're here to clean up sewing scraps,' Marguerite said, face straining. 'If we're asked.'

I entertained the thought that perhaps it was someone who'd lost his or her way, needed directions, an old man with a cane perhaps? But whoever had looked through that window had made an effort, climbed up on something, as I had all those months ago when I saw the Résistance hiding guns in the crypt. No — I knew — whoever was on the other side of the door was searching for something, someone, maybe even me. Crumpling the note in my hand, I stuffed it down the front of my dress.

Marguerite took a deep breath near the door, shaking out her hands and shoulders. She cracked it open. 'Hallo?' she said, and Mavis reached for my hand, only to drop it when she heard a man's

361

voice behind the opened door — a German voice.

The conversation seemed innocent enough at first, listening to Marguerite talk about the weather and the cafés in Lyon. Then the conversation changed — he was asking about the convent, the crypt and how long the Sisters had been in Lyon. My heart sank when I heard her say, 'Come in.'

I recognized his Gestapo uniform immediately as he walked in with his pointed hat and his dark, knee-high boots. His eyes skirted over all of us but at the same time skimmed the walls, ceiling, and sewing machines.

Marguerite pushed the door closed. 'What brings — '

'Not yet,' the officer said, motioning at Marguerite. '*Mach auf*! Open up!' He walked around the room with his hands clasped behind his back as Marguerite held the door open for another officer, followed by another, the door pushing closed between each one only to be stopped by another hand until there were four officers in all.

They moved about the machines, eyes interested in everything, chatting in German, chuckling occasionally. The darkness of their uniforms, saying words I didn't know as they circled about, made me feel queasy.

One officer stood in front of the crate we had stuffed with guns, his black baton dangling from his belt loop scraping against it as he moved. When he spoke, he looked directly at Marguerite even though he addressed us all.

'What's been keeping you busy this morning, Sister . . . and?' Another officer looked Mavis and me over, saying something in German.

'And postulants,' Marguerite said.

'Of course.' He put a hand to his chest and bowed cynically. 'Officer Baader. Lyon Gestapo.' His thin smile spoke more than his words as he took off his hat, and tucked it under his arm. A chiselled face to go along with his strong, bony hands. 'This congregation has many sisters. Doesn't it?' He put two fingers to his head as if recalling some prior knowledge. 'Are there twenty-three?'

Marguerite looked at me before answering. 'Twenty at present. Recently three went to the Lord.'

He smiled. 'We have something in common; there are about that many Gestapo at Hotel Terminus. Our headquarters here in Lyon.'

Marguerite flashed him a quick smile. 'Yes — Hotel Terminus. I know where it is.'

'Oh, you do? That is good.' He put a hand to his chin and tapped his lips just below his thin moustache. 'That is good you know where it is.'

There was a long, hot pause where he and Marguerite looked at each other and nobody talked. Perhaps it was his critical smile, or perhaps it was the way he stood back, relaxed near the crate of guns, watching his men circulate around the room rummaging through scraps of cloth near the sewing machines, but I felt he knew the answers to his questions before he asked them.

'What's this?' He bolted toward the crypt door, and we followed. 'Something valuable I can tell.' He held the lock that dangled from the door handle in his hands, pressing his thumb into the key hole. 'Impressive lock.'

'Absolutely,' Marguerite said.

His eyebrows lifted into his forehead, and his whole head rippled. He whistled with a flick of his finger, and another officer joined him at the crypt door.

'This is our crypt,' Marguerite said. 'The bodies of the sisters.'

Baader's face relaxed. 'Ja,' he said. 'I can smell it now. *Das Stinkt!*' He turned to his men while pulling on the lock. '*Tote Nonnen.*'

His men laughed when he said the one German word I understood, 'dead'.

'I can open it up if you like,' Marguerite said.

Marguerite held out her hand for the key, and I gave it to her. Mavis licked her shaking palm to smooth her hair against her head while Marguerite opened the door. The officers peered into the dark space, instantly covering their noses, the smell of death as thick as their wool uniforms.

'Ach!' Baader reached for the hanky tucked in his breast pocket and held it over his nose.

'Do you want to go inside?' Marguerite stood back and gave them more than enough room to charge down into the crypt if they wanted, but not one of them moved.

'That's quite all right,' he said. 'I think we've seen enough.'

Marguerite closed the crypt back up, and they walked toward the door as if they were done looking the place over, the ruffle of her black habit and our quick feet hurrying them out.

Officer Baader stopped a foot from the gun crate and turned toward Marguerite, his baton scraping against the wood, lifting the linen that covered it up just a hair. He squinted, turning slowly toward

364

Marguerite. 'Now, you — ' he snapped his fingers at her and then pointed them like a gun ' — aren't Mother Superior.' Marguerite smiled and a bead of sweat snuck out from under her wimple and dripped past her eye. 'You're someone else.'

'Mother Superior is at the convent on the hill. I'm Sister Marguerite.'

'I had a sister named Marguerite,' he said, eyes shining, 'once.'

'Something else we have in common.' Marguerite's bottom lip quivered. 'Officer Baader.' It was the first time in a long time I saw the mark of worry streaking in her eyes and face. We had talked about the possibility of a raid, prepared for one, but nothing can *really* prepare you.

He smiled then turned toward the door as if he were about to leave for good this time, but stopped before setting a foot outside. 'I've seen you before,' he said, pointing a finger at Mavis. 'But you.' His finger moved to me. 'I don't think we've met.'

I opened my mouth to speak, but Marguerite stopped me with a firm hand on my arm. 'She's one of our very own delinquents,' she said. 'Only recently decided to become a postulant.'

'Mmm,' he said. 'What did you say your name was?'

I smiled, my mind going white-blank, forgetting the name on my documents, watching Mavis out the corner of my eye smoothing her hair against her forehead, over and over again until it was slicked flat.

'Jeanne,' Marguerite said.

'Jeanne,' I repeated.

He smiled, and then finally stepped out the door.

I clutched my chest, suddenly feeling myself breathe. Marguerite pressed her back against the wall after she closed the door, looking at the ceiling and grasping for my hand, which she squeezed firmly. Mavis paced around the sewing machines with her arms folded.

'He's seen me before?' I said.

'He's fishing,' Marguerite said. 'That's what they do. They want us to misstep, get caught mixing up our own stories. It's how they work.'

I rested my head against the wall, exhausted. 'The Milice just tell you what they know. Gestapo . . . they . . . '

'The Gestapo want you to prove what they already know,' Marguerite said.

Mavis stopped pacing, her cheeks puffing nervously as if she was looking for the right words.

'*Merde!*' I said to Mavis. 'I'm sure God won't mind if you say it. It's all shit!'

Mavis leaned against the wall, her eyes welling with tears. 'I'm . . . I'm worried.'

Marguerite put both hands on Mavis's shoulders, was about to say something, but then looked away.

* * *

In the late afternoon a rumbling lorry pulled up to the old convent. Two gruff men with grease-smeared jumpsuits hopped out of the side doors. They talked loudly in the street to Marguerite about what sewing machines needed to be repaired before all three of them ducked into the building and got busy loading the guns. Marguerite and I got in with the cargo, closing the doors behind us, settling into the stuffy hatch space that was full with bulging canvas bags and crates.

She pulled her wimple from her head and then wadded up her habit. I crouched down in the corner, slipping the veil off my head as the lorry started up and then barrelled down the road. Out the back window I caught a glimpse of Mavis locking up the old convent's front doors. I felt woozy watching her, my head light from being shut up with the dead sisters for so long and now being crammed into the back of a moving truck.

A man appeared from around the corner and walked straight toward her with a determined, hand-pumping gait while her back was turned. I gasped. When he grabbed her by the arm, I shot up.

'Mavis — ' Marguerite whipped her head away from whatever she had been looking at, but the hustle and bustle of the day's busy foot traffic swallowed up the road behind us. A blink and Mavis had disappeared. I stuttered, not sure if I had actually seen what I thought I had. 'She ... she ...' A flit of cool air whistled through a crack in the hatch. We were long gone from the crypt now. I crouched further into the corner of the hatch and convinced myself I saw nothing.

Marguerite closed her eyes.

* * *

We waited at the hill cottage for the Maquis to claim the cache of guns. Marguerite sat stiffly in a broken chair sipping cold lavender tea, her cup rattling in its saucer when it wasn't held to her lips. Hours passed; Marguerite was now unable to keep still as a surge of rain splattered against the windows outside, her bottom lifting from her seat, shifting here and there every few seconds.

'They're just late,' I said.

The clock chimed and Marguerite bolted from her seat. 'I saw it too,' she said, pacing around the room. 'Mavis — when we left.'

'What? You did?' I sat down, having not allowed myself to get frightened until she admitted she was scared too. 'Why didn't you say anything?' Mavis, her veil and devotion to Christ, wouldn't be enough to save her from the Gestapo. 'Mavis, tiny little Mavis — '

'What could we do? We were driving away with a crate of guns.'

Two other résistants, a husband and wife the Alliance called the Dove Birds because of their matching blonde hair and soft voices, sat on the ground poring over maps, glancing up at us in intervals. I threw my hands up, not knowing what to do about any of it — Mavis, and now the Maquis being late. 'Do you think the Gestapo know about us, at this cottage?'

Marguerite looked through a split in the curtains and into the dark night. 'I don't know.'

The door flew open and a woman dressed in cut-off men's trousers with a rolled-up shirt walked in. She adjusted the gun slung over her shoulder, shivering from being out in the rain. 'The Maquis

368

aren't coming,' she said. 'Gestapo. They're everywhere.'

Marguerite hurriedly shut the door behind her.
'Where?' Her eyes were closed tight when she
spoke, asking the question we needed to know.

The woman used a candle from the mantel to
light a loose cigarette she pulled from her pocket.
'In the fields. Gunshots. A line of them.' She took
a nervous, deep breath. 'Last time I heard a line
of shots, twelve résistants fell backward into a
trench.' The Dove Birds sat up, looking at one
another and then to the woman. 'There was a
raid, and not just one group but many. Maquis,
Alliance . . . I had just left to come here when I
heard the shots.' She smoked through her cigarette and lit another, moving about the room,
her feet clicking and clacking against the wood
floor from wearing men's dress shoes — a souvenir from someone she had killed. 'An entire radio
command centre not far from here burned to the
ground. Took the men with them into the wilder-
ness.'

I sprung from my chair. 'Radio operators?'

She snarled. 'Bastard Germans got 'em all and
our notes — valuable ones if you know what I
mean.' She shook her head, peeking through the
curtains. 'Never heard them coming.' I pulled the
curtain closed, and she looked at me, shocked at
first.

'Was there an operator named Luc — medium-
sized man, strong arms — '

'I don't know,' she said, turning away. 'Maybe.'

'It's Luc.' I started for the door, but Marguerite
stopped me by the arm.

369

'In the morning, maybe there will be more news.'

I paced the room, feeling very jittery, emotional, rubbing my hands together. The thought of never seeing Luc again alive suddenly felt like a reality. *I can't wait here till morning.* I thought about the long months I'd been hiding out at the hill cottage. Not one moment went by without wondering where Luc was. His voice: I barely remembered what it sounded like. His face: vaguely familiar after an incredibly long absence; but the feel of his hands, his breath on my cheek when he kissed me, and the flutter in my stomach when he said my name — Catchfly — was as real as my heart beating in my chest.

I thought I was going to burst from my skin if I didn't get outside. I played with the heart pendant Luc gave me, glancing fleetingly at Marguerite, catching her playing with the silver locket her fiancé had given her. *Philip.* My stomach sank, remembering how he died. I took my coat from the hook and reached for the door. 'I'm leaving.'

Marguerite blocked me. 'What do you expect to do? Wander around until you find someone, or someone finds you?' The Dove Birds got off the floor and refolded their maps, wanting to get far away from our rising voices.

'You can't stop me.'

An odd look strained in her eyes. I'd seen this face of hers before when we were at the convent together, and I remembered it very well. 'I watched the man I loved die right in front of me and then be buried in that . . . that most brutal way. And what good came of it?'

I shoved my hands into my coat pockets, staring at her. She wasn't going to stop me, but it was up to her if she wanted to join me. 'If you were me, would you stay here?' The woman with the cigarette looked at me admiringly, while the Dove Birds got close, holding each other. I reached behind Marguerite and opened the door. Rain spat into the cottage as I waited for her to answer.

'You're impossible!' Marguerite thrust a pair of Wehrmacht binoculars into my hands before throwing on her coat. 'After you.'

I tucked the binoculars into my pocket and we walked into the dark, rain-splattered night.

26

We trudged through a field of thicket until we got to an area Marguerite called the cradle, where the British dropped supplies in the middle of the night to résistants. Usually the valley bustled with activity, but on this night the only sound was the wind rustling through the tree limbs and the splat of raindrops blowing off leaves. Marguerite bent down to inspect the dirt road, which was muddy with puddles of rain filling in the tyre grooves. She pulled a lighter from her pocket.

'There was a scuffle,' she said, holding the flame to the ground. 'Right here.' She pointed to a swampy area with waterlogged footprints.

People shouted from somewhere, and I latched on to Marguerite when she bolted to a stand. 'This way!' she said, and we climbed up the mushy hillside, using our hands, holding on to the grass to keep from slipping until we reached the summit. Dropping to our bellies, we peeked over the top.

A line of men and women stood with their hands on their heads as the Gestapo pinned red paper to their chests for aiming. Their faces turned toward a barrage of headlamps shining from sputtering cars. 'No! It can't be — ' I pulled the binoculars from my pocket, scrambling to get a closer look.

'Look at them all,' Marguerite said. 'There's so many.'

Faces of white, beards that needed to be shaved, mud on their skin and in their hair. Women with their dresses half-torn off, bare breasts and bruised faces — but no Luc.

'He's not there,' I said, heaving with relief. 'He's not there.' But then my heart broke anyway, gazing upon the résistants' white-lit faces, thinking about their families, and whom they left behind. Some would never know what happened to their loved one, others would know and would be punished for being related to them.

'Is that Mavis?' Marguerite snatched the binoculars right from my hands, peering down the hill. 'I can't tell . . . I can't tell!' She fumbled with them, trying to get a clear view. Then the Gestapo raised their guns. My stomach dropped, a sinking feeling from knowing lives were about to end. Marguerite let go of the binoculars and laid her head on the wet ground. 'What use is it now?'

Headlamps flashed brighter; one German voice shouted over another; guns aimed straight. 'The red paper . . . it's meant to show where their hearts are.' Marguerite squeezed my hand, bracing for the inevitable. 'But their hearts are with France.'

Pop, Pop, Pop —

We flinched, and their bodies fell backward into the mud.

Everything got quiet, like a hush after a thunderclap; smoke steamed from the barrels, bare legs lay crisscrossed on the ground, some jerking, fighting to live.

As quickly as the shooting happened the Gestapo piled into their cars and started driving out of the cradle. 'What do we do?' I said to Marguerite, realizing they would see us if we didn't hide. The roar of a sweeping, rolling rain suddenly poured from the dark sky, soaking our coats, the purr from their car engines getting closer, louder, and their lights brighter.

'Hurry!' Marguerite took me by the sleeve, and we slid down the muddy hill on our thighs. We clung to a tree trunk at the bottom, digging our fingertips into its knotty bark. Beams of light from oncoming headlamps shone through the hills. Marguerite turned to me, rain streaming down her face, her voice fraught. 'In the bushes!'

We ducked into a bushy area surrounded by rocks just as the cars cast a wide light over the narrow road cutting through the hills. We worked frantically to create a hollow to hide in, popping up every few seconds as the lights approached, moving rocks out of the way, water gushing through the cracks like a creek, only to move them back once we wedged ourselves inside. Our mud-scraped legs tangled with each other's, and we listened.

One car rumbled past followed by another, the ground shaking, worms wiggling from the wet soil onto our shoulders. I closed my eyes tightly, wondering when it would end, when they'd be gone, but then the heart-dropping sound of a cut engine shook me to the core. Every muscle in my body tightened. I searched for Marguerite's hand, the rain calming into a sprinkle, dripping softly from exposed bush roots and onto the rocks.

'*Sieh*!' A German voice shouted, and my eyes popped open in the dark.

Car doors slammed. The sound of people walking around through the slush at the base of the hill followed, very close to where Marguerite and I were hiding. French mingled with German words — nothing audible enough for me to know what they were saying.

'Adèle,' she said. 'No matter what happens. Never say a word.'

'Shh,' I said. 'They're close.'

'Promise me, Adèle.' She tugged on my hand, her breath but a wisp on my face in the pitch-black hole. 'Tell me you understand. It's what will keep us — your family — alive. If they catch us — '

The hole started to cave in slightly on one side — the weight of someone standing above us — and my whole body shook, the sound of one German talking casually to another feet from where we hid. A flicked cigarette butt fell between the rocks.

My teeth chattered, and I bit down hard to make them stop, squeezing Marguerite's hand. A long pause followed, long enough for me to wonder if they were still walking around looking for us before I heard the rev of an engine and their car speed away.

We waited in the hole for what seemed like many minutes before slowly, and very gently, crawling out of it on our hands and knees. Marguerite wiped dirt from her face and snot from her nose with the back of her hand. 'I shouldn't have let you go,' she said. 'I knew it wasn't safe.'

'I thought Luc was going to die. I wasn't going to stand by and — '

'You're not invincible.'

'Oh, I'm not?' I wrung the rain from my hair. 'I'm here, aren't I?'

'I'm the one who came for you,' she said. 'Let's

375

not forget that detail. It was very risky for me to travel that kind of distance, save you from the mess you got yourself into.'

I felt a snarl on my lips. I remembered people throwing catchfly in the streets, men taking their hats off, women putting their hands over their hearts paying homage while I was tethered to the Morris Column, when I went by the name Catchfly.

'I didn't ask to be saved,' I hissed.

Marguerite's arms dropped long at her sides, and she stared at me as I crossed my arms. 'What do you mean . . . you didn't want to be saved?'

I knew I sounded like a spoiled little girl who just wanted to be remembered, and I couldn't help it. Germans had taken over the whole of France; the only things we French people could cling to were our remembrances of bravery. Our families were torn apart. People had died. Our memories were the only thing left.

'I was somebody. Once. Now, nobody knows who I am. I might as well have run away. At least then I could have saved myself the agony of seeing my sister's guilty face.'

Marguerite reached out for me. 'No — '

A car's headlamps lit us up followed by the cock of a gun. We jumped, nothing to be seen other than clear black space and the glare of two bright lights. One Gestapo officer walked forward with his gun drawn.

'*Hallo,*' he said. '*Mademoiselles.*'

Marguerite took a strained look into my eyes. Her face smeared with mud and dirt, more visible than before in the white light.

'Out for a walk?' he said in muddled French. Marguerite swayed back and forth on her feet as if she was entertaining the idea of running. He pointed his gun at Marguerite and then at me. 'What are your names? *Carte d'identité!*'

I reached into my coat pocket and pulled out my identification. He glanced at it with a discerning eye. 'Jeanne Calvet,' he said, 'and from Lyon.'

'Where's yours?' he said to Marguerite, but she did nothing but stare. The rain-heavy tree branches creaked, and their leaves fluttered like a thousand butterflies from a gust of wind that blew right through us. He lowered his gun and picked at his teeth with his fingernail as two other Gestapo appeared from behind him. Marguerite stopped swaying. 'We know what you saw.'

He pointed to the muddy hill, the streaks from our bodies sliding down it looked like tyre grooves even in the dead of night. 'Now, speak up, or I'll give you something to speak up about.' He paused, one nail in between his teeth, the buzz of the light drawn upon us as piercing as a mosquito in my ear. Marguerite shook her head very subtly as if to remind me not to say anything.

'Well, *mademoiselles*,' he said with a bit of a laugh. 'If that is what you are. Looks like we're going to have to make you talk.' He motioned at the other Gestapo. 'Take them to interrogation. Hotel Terminus.'

'Jeanne,' Marguerite said, reaching out for me as I reached for her, our hands grasping for each other's while he stepped in between us and pulled us apart. 'Jeanne — '

Be strong.

The architects of the grand Hotel Terminus would have been appalled at what the Gestapo had done to their building since they took it over as their headquarters. Blood-red carpet runners covered the marble floors, and Nazi flags lined the corridors. Hitler's portrait hung from every available hook and nail. The guest rooms, which were known for their exquisite furnishings and luxurious linens — even more of a tragedy — had been stripped down to splintered wood floors and plasterboard.

I sat for hours, moaning from not having eaten and enduring a painful, burning sensation to urinate when a woman guard dressed in a mouse-grey uniform opened my door. Her belly was as big as the barrel she held in her hands, which she placed in the middle of the room.

'Where's my friend? I demand to see her.'

She laughed before stepping back, and taking a good look at me. 'Take your clothes off,' she said in a very thick German accent. 'All of them.'

'I will not,' I said.

She put a hand on her holstered gun. 'You will.'

I felt my lips pinch, and took my coat off and then begrudgingly unbuttoned my dress.

'Slower,' she said, 'there is no rush.' A smile slithered across her face as I peeled my wet dress from my shoulders and let it fall to the floor around my feet. She grabbed at my undergarments, flicking her tongue over her bottom lip as she unfastened my brassiere.

Gooseflesh bumped over my arms from standing

naked in a bare, cold room. 'What's this little gem?' She snapped my heart pendant from my neck with one quick pull. I shuddered and quaked, feeling as if she had reached into my chest and ripped out my heart for real. She eyed the heart closely in her hand before stuffing it into her pocket. 'Now, tell me who you are.'

'Jeanne.'

She laughed. 'We know your documents were forged.' She took a few steps back. 'Get in the barrel.'

I didn't move.

'Get in!' she yelled, her face flattening like a frying pan. 'Now!'

I stepped carefully into the empty barrel, shivering, as she brought in five metal pails that had been filled with water. She dunked her hand in one and then flicked some water on my back, laughing about how cold it was.

'I've been in water before —'

She dumped the whole pail over the top of my head. I gasped from the shock of the freezing cold water waving over my skin and then shook violently, searching for the right word. 'Christ!'

'This is how an angel dies,' she boasted.

Clumps of sopping-wet hair hung over my eyes, my jaw clattering. 'Angel?'

'Isn't that what you are?' She took one finger and dug it into her cheek with a twist. 'Your dimples. Makes you look like a little angel.' She peered into the bucket to see how much water had filled up inside. 'Now, tell me who you are.'

I looked straight at the stone wall like Marguerite had taught me all those months ago. *Be strong*.

This was the real test.

The guard sighed, smiling. 'Very well.'

Another pail, this time laced with shards of ice that scraped and pierced my skin. I felt numb to my bones with a shiver I was sure had turned my lips blue, but she pressed on, pouring another and then another, the barrel filling with water, first over my ankles and then halfway up my calves.

'I'll stop when you tell me who you are,' she said.

'Let me see my friend.'

'No!' she barked, and my gaze drifted to the wall, which made her huff and puff.

'I need to urinate,' I said.

She laughed. 'If you pee in that bucket, you'll get ten more pails on you.'

Instantly I started peeing — the cold water made it impossible to hold.

Her eyes got wide and her mouth snarled. She lifted another pail, but she bobbled it and a wave of water splashed onto her face.

I laughed, soft at first, bordering a giggle, taunting her with my only weapon.

Her face scrunched up like an old prune listening to me laugh, and she dumped what was left in the pail over my back and then threw the pail at the wall. 'Amusing, is it?' She opened the door — someone was screaming not far away as she called out to another guard. 'More pails!'

Soon enough more metal pails were brought in and laid out in a line. The guard gave me a strange look as he left, probably wondering how I was able to handle more, and it was that look that lit a fire inside my cold bones. My laugh turned into a screeching shrill, which startled even me, getting louder and more pronounced the more pails she poured over me. 'Stop that laughing!' she yelled, which only made me laugh more. 'Get out!' she finally said, lips puckering, pointing to the door with a stiff finger.

I stepped out of the barrel, my feet unfeeling against the cold stone floor, my laugh more like a metal pitchfork scraping against slate. 'Ah ha, ah ha, ah ha . . . ' I screeched, following her down a long corridor and into a room with floral paper peeling from its walls and a hole in the floor for a toilet.

I flung my arms out, laughing in the face of the guard, ignoring the little voice in my head telling me to shut up and put my arms down, but all I could think about was Marguerite and that maybe she'd hear me . . . know it was me. The guard threw a plain beige smock at my face and then slammed the door, locking it up tight. I succumbed to a wave of tears and sobs when I realized she'd left, then everything got very hazy, and I wobbled. I heard a slap — my face hitting the ground — and I plunged into a dark, cold dream.

★ ★ ★

After weeks of cold-water treatments without talking, and no signs of Marguerite, the Gestapo moved me to Lyon's infamous Montluc prison for what the guard called, 'formal interrogations.' Three times a day a guard brought me a hunk of stale bread and a cup of rust-coloured water, which was pushed through a slit in the door. If I was lucky, I got a rotted apple or a bowl of mouldy mush. These were the easy days, when I'd sit on the floor and stare out the caged window in my room. But when I heard footsteps marching down the corridor and the clinking and clanging of keys near my door, my heart began to race, and I had to remind myself who I was, and who I wasn't.

I sat up, listening to the key as it slid into the lock, wondering how much cold water I'd have to stand in, or how much yelling I'd have to endure, lips to my face.

The door opened, and a Gestapo officer I'd never seen before stood in the doorway. '*Hallo*, Jeanne.' He laughed. 'Or whatever your real name is. I'm Klaus Barbie.'

I scooted away from the door. I had heard of Klaus Barbie every day since I arrived at Montluc. The guards had warned me this day would come, the day when the head of the prison would visit.

'You've heard of me, no?' He ran his fingers down the lapels of his woolly Gestapo uniform. His face, stern with sharp lines, was typical for a German.

'I've heard.'

'They call me the Butcher of Lyon. But look,' he said, holding his hands out, 'I have no knives.'

He poked his finger into my ribs, where my bones protruded from under thin skin. 'But if I did, not much to butcher here.'

'You don't find me attractive?' I brushed a swatch of matted hair from my eyes.

'You have a sense of humour.' He smiled. 'After spending weeks at Montluc? Interesting . . .'

'Mmm.'

'Let's take a walk.'

I stared at him as he waited for me to move, wondering what kind of interrogation the Butcher of Lyon had in mind for me, and if I'd be able to withstand it.

'It's not a question, *fräulein*,' he said, but then shouted, 'Get up!'

We walked to the end of the prison corridor, past a dozen wooden cell doors and into an office adorned with fine furnishings. He pointed to a table with a stiff white linen set for two with china and silver chargers, sparking crystal wine glasses and water goblets filled to the edge with clear drinking water. A bread basket with rolls wrapped in a blue tea towel had been placed next to an antique soup tureen. Barbie poured wine from a decanter and then offered me one of the wine glasses.

'Please,' he said, smiling. 'Drink.'

I took the glass he offered, wondering if it were poisoned or not. 'Trust me,' he said. 'If we wanted to kill you, we would have done it already.' Barbie poured himself a glass from the same decanter and took a drink. 'Please,' he said again. 'Have a drink.'

I took one sip only to spit it out like I'd been taught, wine spraying from my mouth. '*Vin du merde*!' The disgusting, gritty taste of Gamay grapes saturated my mouth — shit wine, as Papa had always called it.

Barbie glared — I had not only spit the wine out but had gotten some on him. 'You don't like it?' he snarled.

383

I wiped the wine from my mouth with the back of my hand, laughing — a guttural chortle that spread a wide smile on my face. 'Germans know nothing about wine.'

Barbie sat down in one of two high-back chairs, his dark hair perfectly slicked back with pomade. 'Tell me more. Please, have a seat,' he said, pointing to the chair opposite him.

I sat down as he lifted the lid off the soup tureen. 'Creamed leeks,' he said, and my mouth watered. 'I believe you call it . . .

Vichyssoise.' He ladled a full helping into a wide brimmed bowl. 'Tell me who you are, and you can have some.'

My eyes absorbed every bit of the soup as if it were in my mouth. Breathing, breathing, thinking about the sun, the grass . . .

'How about you tell me who your friend is,' he said, and I glanced up. A slow smile curled on his lips. 'Your friend interests you, no? She interests me.'

Barbie put his nose to the bowl and breathed in the creamy, salty vichyssoise. 'Reminds me of a dish back home.' He lifted the silver spoon from his napkin and dipped it into his bowl, licking his lips before slurping from the spoon. I swallowed along with him as he rubbed his lips together.

'All you have to do is talk. That is it.' Barbie reached over the table and ladled a bowl of soup he meant for me to eat, filling it to the very edge. 'And this can all be yours.'

I watched him eat, staring at the creamy yellow, telling myself it had been made from pureed maggots just to keep my tongue from lapping it up.

He scraped his bowl clean, padding his lips with a napkin. '*Ahh . . . ist gut*? Is good, no?' An unusually long pause followed. He set his napkin down, growling, gritting his teeth. 'Is good — ' He leapt over the table like a tiger, shoving the spoon in my hand, trying to force me to taste it. Soup sloshed over the sides of the bowl as we battled with each other over control. 'Eat it!' he said, the spoon clinking against my teeth as he pried my lips open, pulling back my head, soup spilling onto my chin and face.

Unsuccessful, he stood back, his teeth baring and breath panting. 'You leave me no choice.'

Barbie opened a set of curtains that ran along the wall behind him, exposing yet another room with two chairs side.by-side with two pieces of rope wound up on the ground. He grabbed me by the collarbone and dragged me toward one of the chairs.

'You like rope?' He tied my ankles up, and then my wrists tightly to the armrests.

'No.'

He laughed.

Another Gestapo officer walked in pulling a woman by the arm. Her head hung low, and her hair had been pulled out in patches.

'Oh, good! Your friend,' he said, and I thought my heart had split in two.

Marguerite.

He pulled her head up by a patch of stringy hair, and I gasped, looking swiftly away, but I'd already seen her, and tears flooded my eyes.

'Didn't they teach you not to look in your . . . *training*?' Barbie laughed, and then

385

forced us to look at each other, moving her chair directly in front of mine where he tied her up just the same, only there was no resistance from her; she had no strength. Her bones were larger than mine with flesh in between, a walking corpse if I had ever seen one. She opened her mouth, her jaw gaping open, but no words came out, only breathy moans, and tears spilled over my cheeks.

'Now,' the other officer said as he walked around the two of us tied in the chairs. 'Officer Barbie seems to think he can get you two to talk.' He laughed. 'I can't imagine how he expects to do that, but he does have his ways . . .'

'*Ja*,' Barbie said. 'I do have my ways.'

The officer laughed as he left the room. Barbie laughed too, his eyes narrowing as he gazed upon us. I was imagining what he was going to do to us when a very attractive woman about my age wearing a delicate pink dress walked into the room.

'I know how women like to talk to other women,' Barbie said, 'so I've invited my friend to our little date. Perhaps you might find her appealing.'

She lit a thick brown cigarette and waved it around in the air as she talked. 'I do love a good chit-chat.' She was undeniably French, dressed in the silkiest and most expensive clothes I had seen in a long time, pearl buttons and shiny jewellery around her neck and wrists. She was from Paris, I had decided, with her thick makeup and tightly curled hair — no woman from the Auvergne would look like that in the middle of the day.

'But where am I to sit, honeybear?' she said, looking around the room. 'Wait — ' she put both hands on Barbie's chest, resting her hands on the breast of his uniform ' — how do I say honeybear in German?'

'*Honigbär*,' Barbie said before he kissed her.

She giggled and played with the bracelets on her wrist as he got her a chair. Then she sat back and smoked her cigarette, smiling at us as if we were friends.

'What should we do, Claudette?' he said.

'Burn their nipples, *honigbär*.' She leaned in, her eyes beady. 'Burn them right off!'

Barbie ripped open Marguerite's smock and exposed her breasts, which were covered in pocky, round scars. 'Looks like you have been through this before.' He smiled. 'You interest me more every minute.'

He curled his fingers around the neckline of my smock as if he were about to rip it from my body, but then slowly started to tear it, lower and lower it went until my breasts popped out. He felt me with the back of his hand before cupping each one of my breasts in his palm. Claudette shifted uncomfortably in her chair. 'But this one hasn't.' He put his lips to my ear, playing with my nipple until it got hard. 'I heard you have the skin of an angel.'

He snapped his fingers at Claudette, and she took several short puffs from her cigarette until the ember burned bright red.

'Tell us who you are,' he said to Marguerite, but she turned her head to stare at the wall. I knew our silence was what was keeping us alive — our information had value. She would never answer him. A sinister smile spread the width of his face. 'As you wish.'

Claudette laughed hysterically, puffing on her cigarettes as Barbie lifted my breast, exposing the plump underside. He snapped for her to give him her lit cigarette, and my feet scraped the floor.

'No . . .' I said, praying for the strength I had when I faced the Milice, but I hadn't a shred of it left. 'No — 'The ember glowed, and I screamed a moment before he pressed it to my skin.

'Tell us who you are!' he yelled to Marguerite over my screams, 'and I'll stop!' Marguerite wept openly as Claudette lit more cigarettes to replace the ones he'd broken while burning me — three in all — until finally I heard her say something that gave me hope.

'I've run out.'

There was a devilish look in his eye and in his mouth as he searched the room for something else to torture me with, shouting into the air in German. He kicked my chair, tipping me over, the back of it pressing my head against the floor. He leaned onto the chair, crushing me.

'This is your fault,' he said, pointing to Marguerite as my skull cracked.

Barbie stood up with a jolt and straightened his uniform jacket, which had gotten ruffled while trying to kill me. A dull moan came from my mouth, words, but not really.

'You did good. Lasted a very long time under such . . . *pressure*.' Barbie tipped me back over. He padded his brow with a hanky from his pocket and looked at me as I sat upright. The room spun, and my ears rung. Then I felt something wet dribble off my earlobe, moments later blood dripped onto my shoulder.

'And you . . . ' he said, looking Marguerite over. 'What is that?' He pointed to the bright, pink rash puffing over Marguerite's chest and up her neck, a confusing look creasing in his face.

'Ahh, yes,' he said, smiling. 'I remember you now, the allergic one. Colmar, about two years ago.' Marguerite never said a word. 'Tomorrow,' he said. 'I'll have to work on you tomorrow.'

'Humph!' Claudette turned in her chair, crossing her legs at the ankles. 'Why finish up tomorrow when we have today?'

'Patience, *honigbär*,' he said. 'These things must be handled — ' he caressed my cheek with a delicate hand ' — with finesse.'

Barbie knocked on the door, and a guard walked in. 'Put them in the same room,' Barbie said. 'Let's have them remember each other.'

The guard untied the both of us and then brought us to a jerking stand.

'My cigarettes are gone,' Claudette huffed. 'Can we get Gitanes in Germany?'

'Of course.' Barbie took Claudette by the hand and kissed her passionately on the lips, tipping her back, letting her hair dangle with her jewellery, before moving his lips to her supple white neck. 'Tomorrow, ladies,' he said as she nibbled his ear. 'Be ready.'

The guard hauled us out into the corridor and then threw us into my room together, closing the door and locking it behind him. Marguerite lay on the ground where he had thrown her, too weak to move. She moaned, and I held her hand.

'Adèle?' she rasped.

'Shh,' I said. 'Don't speak.'

389

'I'm sorry,' she said, swallowing. 'For the burns.'

'No,' I said, knowing all too well it was because of me we had gotten caught in the first place. 'It's my fault. All of it.'

'We're in this together.' She took a long pause in between her words, closing her eyes. 'Not your fault.'

'Shh,' I said again. 'Save your energy.'

We sat in the warm room, our thoughts as thick and stifling as the air. Every now and then we'd hear the clink of doors locking, but we'd had our day's interrogation and had no reason to fear the noises, not now anyway, not until morning.

'Tell me a story, Adèle. Something that will take my mind off the aches in my stomach and in my bones.'

I rested her head in my lap and petted her. 'I could tell you about the time I used another woman's seat on the train as a footrest, made her stand in the aisle, but you already know that one.'

'Yes.' She smiled. 'That one I know.'

I thought for a moment, unsure what she wanted to hear.

'Tell me about your father's vineyard. Tell me how beautiful it was before the war.'

I ran my hand over her head, wondering if I could do it — the memory of what was — with the sting of the burns on my chest and the iron-like smell of death lurking in our room.

'Give it a try,' she said. 'For me.'

I closed my eyes and grasped at the far reaches of my memories. 'The vineyard.' I sighed. 'I remember the grapes hanging off the greenest of vines in rows that went on for kilometres, and the smell, earthy yet sweet as jam. The good years, Papa said, were when the grapes hung the lowest to the ground. And when I was young they always hung low to the ground. The Creuzier-le-Vieux was as beautiful as it smelled, with rolling hills and breezes that carried with it the scent of herbs and citrus fruit.'

The more I talked the faster the memories flowed, and I saw myself as a young girl standing barefoot in the dirt, rows of vines on each side, playing a game of chase with Charlotte. 'Mama would yell from the chateau when it was time for supper, but we knew when it was getting late by looking at the grape skins, which turned pink from the setting sun. There was a hill next to the vineyard that was always covered in catchfly. I'd run through them, the skirt of my dress riding a gentle breeze capped with free-falling giggles and bees bumbling up from the grass. But Charlotte never would — not through the catchfly.'

'Catchfly,' she said, 'very fitting.'

'It is, now that I think of it — catchfly — but that was a very long time ago. A different life.'

'You miss her, don't you?'

'There's a lot to miss.'

'War changes people, Adèle. I've said it before. Don't give up on her. She's your sister.'

I cried from Marguerite's words, sniffling the more quiet seconds that passed with my thoughts on Charlotte. Her babies graves, the pain she must have felt, must still feel — it would make any woman delirious.

I did miss her, and once I admitted that to myself the ache in my gut, the longing for what

391

once was, felt more like a gaping, empty hole. And for the first time since being captured I thought about dying, sobbing over Marguerite's body as I petted her head, thinking I'd never see my sister or my family again.

Marguerite got very still. I thought she'd fallen asleep, her skin settling over her bones like a thin blanket, but then she spoke up.

'Adèle,' she said, taking a long pause. 'I don't know if I can survive more torture. I wanted to fight the war with all my bones. Now my bones are all I have left. Barbie will come back tomorrow — he said he would — and I can barely stand.'

'The war will end, and we will have France back,' I said. 'The way it was.'

'You don't know that.' Tears seeped from the corners of her closed eyes, making wet tracks down her face.

'I know because my friend, Marguerite, told me so. She's a résistant, you see, and she saved my life.' Tears dripped from my chin as I caught my breath. 'Once from a spy's knife and again from a tomb of fallen rocks, so I feel like I can trust her.'

'If only I could go back to the beginning.' She put a hand to her face to mask the quivering. 'I want to go back and remember — feel — the reasons why I joined the French Résistance in the first place.'

'Feel,' I repeated as I sat numb on the floor.

'I miss my mother, my father. I miss Philip,' she cried. 'Everything has been taken from me. Everything. And it's been so many years.' She moved her hand so I could see her eyes. 'Do you remember the days before the war?'

392

'I remember Mama and Papa kissing in the garden. My sister and I cooking together in the kitchen, drinking wine.' I paused, trying to remember how many years ago that was. 'So many years have passed . . . '

'That's what I mean, Adèle. How much longer is it going to be?' She looked angry now, trying to sit up, but her strength wouldn't allow it. 'Are the Germans winning? The British? We don't know — been locked up here for months. It's hard to stay hopeful without word of victories.'

I thought back to the day I peeked through the dirty window of the old convent and saw the Alliance hiding arms in the crypt, the spirit that burned in my chest for the Résistance. Now the only thing that burned were the sores from Claudette's cigarettes. 'I think of these things too, Marguerite.'

'Perhaps I was naïve,' she said, collapsing back onto my lap, 'thinking I could be so bold as to be remembered — that many years from now people would look back on this time, and say, remember the French Résistance — the guns the women moved?'

'I'll remember.' I looked at her. 'I'll remember you.'

She kissed my hand.

The sun set below my caged window and the room got very grey and dark, the walls closing in, reminding us that soon we would experience another day. Marguerite fell asleep on the floor where she lay, twitching and shivering.

27

That night I was woken by the most unusual thing: sound. Lights rolled over the ground and I heard the shuffle of weary feet marching along the shadowed edge of the building — prisoners. The Gestapo ordered them into hatched trucks, a hundred of them from what I counted. The rest of the Gestapo and guards alike rushed around, throwing boxes they had hauled out of the prison into the back of cars before speeding away, their headlamps shining over the humps of barbed wire that ran along the prison's perimeter.

Marguerite lay on the floor, shivering under a soiled blanket despite the warmth of the summer night. 'What's going on?'

'I don't know,' I whispered. 'Movement. A lot of it.'

The wounds on my chest had started to form pus and stuck to the fabric of my smock when I moved. Each blister held the memory of Barbie's laugh, the way his teeth gritted when he burned me, and Claudette's very French voice buoying the German cuss words coming from his mouth.

After the last car sped away a cool breeze blew through the window, and I felt a burst of fresh air on my face. I took it in, holding the air in my lungs, trying to remember what France smelled like — not the smell of diesel, and prisoners' sweat and blood, iron and metal, but the drifts of lilac and jasmine coming from the flower carts and the yeasty warm smell of baguettes baking in ovens. I sank down onto the floor with Marguerite.

That morning I waited for the clink of keys at my door, the dread of the guard's footsteps coming down the corridor, but the whole prison was silent. Hours passed; I sat with my back against the wall, an anxious feeling brewing in my gut, telling me that what I had seen and heard last night wasn't just a prisoner transfer, but something else entirely. I put the back of my hand to the wall, made a fist, and thought about knocking.

Marguerite stared at me from the ground, her eyes a glassy brown. 'Do it,' she said, as if she knew what I was thinking.

We shared our walls with many prisoners, but nobody ever made a noise. If you did, they'd shoot you in the courtyard. I'd seen it from my window many times. Women who had shouted out the windows to their children below on the street, begging for signs of life that their résistant-mother was still alive, and men who had whispered secret messages about the guards, planning sabotages even though they only had their hands to fight with — gone in a matter of bullets.

'Go on, Catchfly,' she said, her cheek against the floor. 'Do it.' We both knew I had nothing to lose, not now, not since Barbie took an interest in us. I held my breath and then knocked two times. The sound echoed like metal ricocheting off metal.

My heart banged in my chest from having broken the cardinal rule of Montluc. A moment passed, maybe even a few seconds of complete silence, before I heard the most amazing, breath-drawing noise in the world: a knock back.

Another knock followed another, low and slow growing into a steady, banging beat. Marguerite lifted her head, her arms quaking as she tried to move her body from the floor, listening to the sounds — knocking, followed by people shouting their names and where they were from.

I wept uncontrollably from the sound of their voices. 'The guards left — the Germans — '

Something even more extraordinary happened, so extraordinary had I not seen it with my own eyes I wouldn't have believed it. Out my barred window off in the distance, among the pure white clouds and baby blue morning sky, a plane flew straight for us. The walls shook like an earthquake from the ground and from the ceiling as it passed directly over the prison, the rumbling pulsating the marrow in my bones. A blasting cheer erupted from the prisoners at the sight of an American star painted on its flank.

Marguerite smiled, settling back onto the ground, exhausted by lifting her own weight. 'Marguerite,' I said, holding her hand. 'We made it.'

More planes rumbled overhead, and I swear the walls were going to crumble to the ground. Prisoners stuck their arms out the windows, waving at a rush of armed résistants storming Montluc's gates, dressed in black with guns slung over their shoulders, fists in the air, shouting words of a victory.

Doors unlocked, people ran down the corridors, searching for their loved ones in other cells. I stumbled out of my room, people running this way and that, my vision very blurry and grey from having stood so quickly. I heard my name, but many women were named Adèle. Then I heard 'Catchfly' yelled in the same breath, and I started to cry.

'I'm here!' I screamed with all my might, holding on to the stones in the wall as my sight returned, creeping down the corridor. 'Luc!'

I felt his arms around me before I saw his face. 'I thought I'd never find you.' He held my face, wiping tears away as prisoners ran through the corridor shouting about freedom.

'We have France back?' I felt as if I were in a dream, hearing what I wanted to hear and seeing Luc again. 'Is this real? Are you real?'

His eyes shined. 'The Résistance has taken control of the city. We stormed the prison as soon as we could.' We hugged again, my legs buckling, surrendering to his embrace, before going back for Marguerite.

I staggered into the cell. With all the noise, the sweet racket of victory rattling the walls, our barred little cell seemed as quiet as a closed box, stifling, reeking of exhaustion and sadness but also glory. Everything we had fought for, everything we wanted had come. I bent down to where her body lay, and her eyes fluttered, the slightest bit of life fading along with her breath.

'Don't wait for me.' Marguerite swallowed, her lips dry and cracking white. 'I can't come.'

I looked at her questionably, but then fell breathlessly next to her when I realized what she meant. She sounded so sure of herself, unafraid, and matter-of-fact, but I wasn't ready for her to go. I wasn't ready. I caressed her face, not knowing what to do to stop her from dying, looking over her body as if I could, and then muttering a tearful request I knew she couldn't honour, 'Don't leave me.' She got still, more still than she had ever been, and then limp. Undeniably limp, her body sinking heavily onto the floor.

'No — ' My hands shook, her name coming from my mouth in unrecognizable guttural groans when I realized she was gone — truly gone — taking her hand and pressing it to my cheek. The day we met on the train, the look on her face when I hit my own hand with the brass hanger, the light in her eyes when she pulled me from the rocky tomb — all I had left of her now. In many ways I felt as though half of me lay on the ground dead with her — a part of my life that didn't exist anymore. My only comfort was knowing she had heard the chants of victory before she died.

'Be with your patriot,' I said, closing her eyelids, 'be with your Philip.'

* * *

We buried Marguerite next to her lover. She would have wanted it that way. Then we made the slow journey to Vichy in a borrowed car. Advancing armies, tanks and military trucks moving east through France were a welcome sight, leaving in their wake a sense of hope and renewed spirit among us all as we crept through the congested roads.

For a moment I thought I smelled chamomile in the air, then as we approached what was left of the vineyards in Creuzier-le-Vieux, I realized it

398

was the rotten tinge of shrunken grapes still clinging to crumbling vines. But when we stopped at
the top of the hill behind Mama's chateau, all I
could smell was the catchfly, which was in full
bloom rolling down the hill next to Papa's estate.
We stood at a distance as Mama and Papa walked
out onto the patio to see who we were, Papa holding on to Mama as if she might fall. He talked to
her, pointing toward Luc and me, and she put a
hand to her chest.

Luc reached for my hand just as Charlotte
walked out of the kitchen and onto the patio. She
had an apron on as if she had been cooking, and
her hair was pulled back with a loose ribbon, that
dingy poodle I had saved so long ago now fluffy
and white and right on her heels.

Charlotte put a hand to her forehead. 'Adèle!'
She ran toward me only to stop at the base of the
hill, nothing but the pink flowing petals of the
catchfly between us.

A warm breeze swept through Papa's vines,
carrying with it the memories of what our lives
were like before the war; the sound of our voices
laughing in the vineyard, our feet bare and cool
from the black soil. 'War changes people,' I heard.
'Don't give up on her.'

Tears spilled over my cheeks, her name but a
breath on my lips. 'Charlotte.'

And she ran through the French catchfly, up
the hill and into my open arms.

Author's Note

This story and its characters were inspired by two women who fought their country's enemies with courage, creativity and relentless perseverance. The first was Élise Rivet, Mother Superior of Notre Dame de la Compassion in Lyon, who hid weapons and ammunition in her convent's crypt for the French Résistance. The other was Marie-Madeleine Fourcade, who had amassed 3,000 agents across France and created the Alliance, one of the largest and most effective organized spy networks in all of history. Élise Rivet was arrested for her crimes and died at Ravensbrück just weeks before the war ended. Marie-Madeleine Fourcade, after evading capture multiple times, survived the war.

I decided to write this book after finding Marie-Madeleine Fourcade's out-of-print memoir in a used bookstore in 2013. I was amazed by her story, the Alliance, and the role of women in the French Resistance. As far as setting, I have always been intrigued by the political divisiveness inside the Free Zone, where politics not only divided the people as much as the country, but also entire families. Marshal Philippe Pétain, the leader of the Vichy regime, was France's WWI hero and many people looked up to him, if not trusted him completely. Knowing this, while drafting the outline for this story, there were a few questions I had that drove the narrative: Once the collaborationist policies of the Vichy regime became clear, how hard was it for those who supported Philippe Pétain to admit they were wrong? More so, what would it take to bring a family back together? Would the wronged be willing to forgive?

The Girl from Vichy was my way of exploring the complexities of Vichy, with the Milice and with the French police, and giving readers a story that highlighted a different aspect of the war.

At the end of the book, Marguerite says, 'I wanted to fight the war with all my bones. Now my bones are all I have left.'

This statement is a testament to the incredible courage and relentless spirit that burned inside every member of the French Résistance, and inside so many women. Incredible to think about — to literally fight to the bone for what you believe in. And so many of them did.

Thank you for reading my book! I hope you enjoyed it.

Acknowledgements

I'm incredibly thankful to my talented editor, Hannah Smith. She's a manuscript doctor, and one of the nicest people I've ever worked with. Thank you to the incredibly talented team at Aria Fiction for the behind-the-scenes work they did to bring my novel out into the world. Thank you to my agent, Kate Nash, and her fabulous team at the Kate Nash Literary Agency for their constant support and guidance. I owe a lot to my critique partner, Paula Butterfield, who read various drafts of this novel many years ago and provided the best feedback. During my debut year, I discovered the most amazing writers' group called the Renegades; I would be lost without your writing advice, support, and laughs! Thank you to my parents and sister who raved about this book long before it was acquired. Thank you to my husband, Matt, for being the most supportive human being alive, and to my two awesome kids, Zane and Drew, for listening to me talk about this book for more than half their lives.

We do hope that you have enjoyed reading this large print book.

Did you know that all of our titles are available for purchase?

We publish a wide range of high quality large print books including:
Romances, Mysteries, Classics
General Fiction
Non Fiction and Westerns

Special interest titles available in large print are:
The Little Oxford Dictionary
Music Book, Song Book
Hymn Book, Service Book

Also available from us courtesy of Oxford University Press:
Young Readers' Dictionary
(large print edition)
Young Readers' Thesaurus
(large print edition)

For further information or a free brochure, please contact us at:
Ulverscroft Large Print Books Ltd.,
The Green, Bradgate Road, Anstey,
Leicester, LE7 7FU, England.
Tel: (00 44) 0116 236 4325
Fax: (00 44) 0116 234 0205

Other titles published by Ulverscroft:

THE GIRL I LEFT BEHIND

Andie Newton

When her childhood best friend shows Ella that you can't always believe what you see, Ella finds herself thrown into the world of the German Resistance. On a dark night in 1941, Claudia is taken by the Gestapo, likely never to be seen again, unless Ella can save her. With the help of the man she loves, Ella must undertake her most dangerous mission yet and infiltrate the Nazi Party. Selling secrets isn't an easy job. In order to find Claudia, Ella must risk not only her life, but the lives of those she cares about. Will Ella be able to leave behind the girl of her youth and step into the shoes of another?